The Years In Between

Praise for UNEARTHING CHRISTMAS

"A heartfelt story with writing reminiscent of J.K. Rowling." Kathryn Canavan, Author of *Lincoln's Final Hours* and *True Crime Philadelphia*

"Great story that I didn't want to put down. I had to find out the answer to the mystery! This book will make you laugh and make you ponder the depths of the human heart. Highly recommended." Rose Folsom, Author of *Virtue Connections*

"A genuinely unique holiday story. It comes at you in a melding of past and present, in a dwelling designed to preserve life, and where the lives of two teenage girls from different eras are mingled so mysteriously. Through insightful writing and characterization, Piscarik makes it all work in a timeless and entertaining tale." Dennis D. Skirvin, Author of *Jubal's Christmas Gift* and *The Treasure of Nonsense Woods*

". . . very inspirational and brought back memories of my childhood in the 50's. It was excellent, and I look forward to this author's next book." Goodreads posting

"A clever and well written book that offers a sweet and soulful study of the challenges of growing up no matter what era. An excellent read for the times we live in!" Amazon posting

"Unearthing Christmas is a visit to the past and a gift to the imagination." Amazon posting

"Rich characterization and a compelling journey make this book a delightful read . . . that will touch the hearts of everyone who enters into this life-changing story." Amazon posting

". . . an easy and thought provoking read. I definitely recommend this book not only for teen girls but for all age groups." Amazon posting

THE Years IN Between

The Miriam Chronicles
Book Two

ANTHEA T. PISCARIK

Published by Saint Martin Productions, LLC

Library of Congress Control Number has been applied for by the publisher.

Cover and interior layout by Blue Pen

ISBN: 979-8-9856300-2-2 (hardcover)
ISBN: 979-8-9856300-0-8 (paperback)
ISBN: 979-8-9856300-3-9 (case laminate)
ISBN: 979-8-9856300-1-5 (ebook)

To my brother, Terry, and all veterans of foreign wars

". . . the LORD, your God, carried you, as one carries his own child,
all along your journey . . ."

–Deuteronomy 1:31

Contents

Part I

In the Beginning

(1956)

Chapter 1
Hall Pass

Lori Hopkins heard the news from her grandmother. Her best friend, Joy, was found lifeless from a deadly tornado. The same one that killed Lori's mom and dad.

"Why'd you wait to tell me?" Lori asked, her voice strained. "Why?" She pictured Joy with her corkscrew curls and apple cheeks bounding up the steps of the fallout shelter decorated for Christmas.

Lottie Mitchell's hands rested on the steering wheel. She stared ahead for a minute and caught glimpses of students filing through Lubbock High's multi-arched walkway. The majestic bell tower and red tile roof gave the impression of a church complex instead of school grounds. Slowly, Lottie turned toward her fourteen-year-old granddaughter. Strawberry blond hair, thick and wavy, framed a heart-shaped, lightly freckled face. Her refined features, upturned nose, hazel-colored eyes, all reminders of loss, the loss of her own daughter, Miriam Hopkins—Lori's mom.

"You were in shock. The doctor said not to mention Joy's death right away. Wait a few days." Three weeks had passed since Lottie had arrived at the scene that devastated five ranch homes. In a heart-stopping moment, Lottie had believed she'd lost all of her family—her daughter, Miriam, her son-in-law, Tom, and Lori. Until she'd remembered Lori's treasured hideaway and had raced down the stairs to find her asleep.

"But she said goodbye and went home," Lori pleaded. From the car window, she stared down at a widened crack in the school's cement sidewalk. Her thoughts turned back to that fateful day. December 18, 1955. Joy's words echoed through her mind. *"It looks fab, Lori, really fab. Don't stay down here too long . . ."*

Every day since, Lori had relived the carnage she'd witnessed when she'd emerged from the shelter. And there had been no word of Joy's death. Until three days later.

Lottie lifted her hands from the steering wheel and crossed her arms. She repeated the story she'd retold in the last few weeks. "And your mom invited her to stay for dinner. I'm sorry, sweetheart."

"You should've told me right away! You're a coward!" Lori slammed the car door and made quick strides to the school's front entrance, ignoring the stares and waves from the other students. *Joy is dead, Joy is dead. Joy is dead.* The silent words repeated and wrapped like tentacles, squeezing, suffocating her heart and soul. Even so, tears were beyond her, a lifetime of them spilled in the last three weeks.

The school counselor, Gladys Whitcomb, released Lori from a perfunctory meeting and a vital signs check from Annie, the school nurse.

"I can escort you to your homeroom, Lori," Mrs. Whitcomb said.

"I'm okay," Lori insisted.

"Well then, let me give you a hall pass."

"Why do I need a pass? The bell didn't ring." Lori hugged her books. Her shield.

"It's a special pass. You can use it to leave any of your classes today, this week. No one will question you." Her voice quivered. "We're here for you, Lori. If you feel an urge to leave, go and see Miss Annie."

"Can I leave now? I'll be late." She left the counselor's office, flooded with memories of Joy. The flash of a pink woolen skirt on the shelter stairs. The Star of David and chain against a white angora sweater. And the kindest eyes in all of Texas.

Lori clutched her textbooks stuffed with term papers and old homework assignments. The empty hallway widened until the walls disappeared. She felt faint, ready to collapse. Blood-pulsing sounds filled her eardrums, competing with distant, muffled voices from classrooms.

The final morning bell rang, sharp, loud, alarming. Lori's books tumbled onto the floor. With no one in sight, she scrambled for her belongings and considered rushing out the nearest exit. Instead, she lumbered to her homeroom. Nothing seemed real, until she knocked on her homeroom door.

Mr. Dugan, her secret crush teacher, looked timeworn, less dreamy. He filled the threshold like a gatekeeper and tilted his head of receding blond hair. "Lori, did you get our card?"

She vaguely remembered the card filled with thirty signatures and well wishes of her classmates. "Yes, Mr. Dugan. Thank you." The heat of embarrassment rose in her neck and cheeks.

He moved aside, and she entered the classroom. A white paper banner with brush-stroked blue letters, *Welcome Back Lori!* blocked double windows. A chorus of rising students echoed the sentiment. And the tears didn't stream, though they hotly scorched her insides.

Mr. Dugan gestured to an empty desk in the middle of the room.

Lori's eyes darted about as she avoided the direct stares of familiar faces. Her mouth trembled with attempts at a smile. She slid into the desk chair and folded her hands in her lap.

Jane Patterson, a tiny slip of a person with eyes like blue pools, sat behind Lori. She placed a hand on Lori's shoulder and whispered in her ear. "Hi, kiddo. Glad you're back."

Lori soldiered her sorrow, pasted a fake smile, and turned to Jane. "Thanks."

Mr. Dugan began his lesson. "In the years following World War II, Italy and the rest of Europe rebuilt its economy."

Lori cracked open a notebook and copied words from the chalkboard. *Peace Treaty of 1947. End of Fascism.* Each minute of lecturing seemed like an hour. She wanted to scream and rush out the door. Lori glanced halfway across the room at Joy's desk, now occupied by Gerald Wilkins. He slouched. Lori watched him, and he saluted her, as if recognizing a wounded warrior. *He understands.* Now fatherless, motherless, at least she wouldn't be friendless.

She copied more words and dates. All meaningless. A note made its way down a line of surreptitious hands. The last student, Abigail Jenkins, tossed it into the fold of Lori's notebook. No one turned to acknowledge the team effort. Lori stared at the creased paper and mustered up courage to open it. *Everything happens for a reason. You'll know why some day. Be strong. Gerald.*

Lori was incensed, wounded by Gerald's words. *I thought he understood! Is he making me the butt of a cruel joke?* Her parents dead. Her best friend dead. *For a reason?* Lori, dazed and humiliated, felt more alone in that moment than she had in the days following the storm.

The hall pass! She raised her hand.

Mr. Dugan was in mid-sentence. "Yes, Lori?"

"I'd like to be excused."

"Of course. Would you like someone to go with you?" Mr. Dugan's concern made Lori anxious.

"No, that's okay." She kept her tone light, but her cheeks burned with resentment from the note she clutched.

Lori gathered her books and quietly shut the door behind her. The hallway that had widened earlier closed in, the walls so narrow, she sensed herself pushing between them. *What is happening to me?* She rushed down the corridor and banged on the nurse's door.

The school nurse's round face glowed with a saintly quality. "Come sit, dear. Stay as long as you need." She motioned Lori to the sick bed that nearly filled the room.

"I'm worried, Miss Annie. I think I need to cry, but I can't. I don't know what I'm feeling."

"Don't hold back, Lori. You're trying to keep it together. This is your first day. It'll get easier, I promise." Annie took her pulse.

Then the dam broke. Lori dropped her head into the sick bed and cried as she never cried before. She muffled her sobs into the linen pillowcase, punching it with her fists.

"Do you want me to call your grandmother?" Annie asked.

Lori ended her waterworks and without lifting her head lay in the bed for a few minutes more. "I'm going back."

"Why don't you wait out a few classes? You can rest here as long as you like," Annie said.

"I'll go now." Lori read the note's last words, *Be Strong*, then crumbled the paper and tossed it into a nearby trash can. She rearranged her skirt, smoothed out a few wrinkles, and peered into the locker-sized mirror hanging on the wall. Swollen eyelids. The banner of tears.

The hallway overflowed with students—faces and bodies pressing forward shoulder to shoulder. It was second period, health class. The bell clanged. Miss Higgins closed the door on the first bell. Lori reached for the doorknob, but a hand was already there. Gerald Wilkins opened the door.

Their eyes met. Lori dismissed him with an angry glare. Nothing could undo the note, even if he believed every word of it.

Chapter 2
Salutations

With searching eyes, Gerald cruised through the cafeteria food line. Students congregated into familiar camps along rows of blanched white tables. Lori sat at an end section with Jane and Abigail from homeroom and a new student, Tally, relocated from Manhattan's Lower East Side.

Gerald approached their table. "May I join you?"

Jane nodded and bit into a tuna fish sandwich. "It's a free country." She spun to Lori. "Okay with you?"

Lori, stone-faced, looked up from her grilled sandwich. The melted cheese, in orange strips, stuck to the plate's bottom. "Sure." She forced herself to remain calm and emotionless.

Gerald's sable brown hair, side-parted and combed, gave a startling contrast to gray eyes so pale they looked colorless in the harsh cafeteria light. His white oxford shirt and engraved tie clip implied wealth. Lori knew little about him, only that he saluted her earlier, and she assumed it was a secret code of understanding. His note was callous and insensitive, and she felt singed, maybe scorned.

"I want to apologize if I hurt your feelings. I thought it would help." Gerald sat a few feet away at the end of the table and buried his spoon into a bowl of tepid chili.

"I accept your apology." Lori hadn't disclosed the note to anyone. In a strange twist, she clung to his words—*Be Strong*—but the initial hurt lingered.

With his apology accepted, Gerald smiled, saluted, and stood up to leave.

"Wait a minute. Why'd you do that? Why are you saluting like that?"

"I guess I kind of know what you're going through. I live with my uncle. That's all." He walked away, a slight sadness shadowing his features.

"What gives?" Jane asked.

"Nothing, really." Lori scraped rubbery cheese off her plate. "Food's as good as ever." She felt the trace of a smile on her lips. "So catch me up on things."

Abigail, the auburn-haired pixie, brightened up at the cue to spin out tales of secret romances and such from Christmas break. Lori politely feigned interest in the latest gossip. Her thoughts returned to Gerald's injured look as he left their table. He mentioned living with an uncle. She wondered about his parents and, for a brief moment, let go of her own grief.

Late that afternoon, Lottie waited at the school's curbside pickup lane. She checked her watch—quarter to three, no phone calls or frantic messages. Clusters of chatting students scattered. She caught sight of Lori's bouncy red-gold locks shimmering in the glow of the sun.

Lori grabbed the handle of the 1954 Chevy Bel Air, flung open the passenger door, threw her books by her feet, and settled in. Lottie started up the motor and allowed it to purr a few seconds. "How was your day?"

Lori stared straight ahead and shrugged.

"I thought maybe we'd go out to eat," Lottie said. "My treat."

"No, I'd rather go home."

"Okay, it's going to be whatever we can scrounge up."

Lori gazed out at the dry, flat land. The drive to Lottie's house in Abernathy, the Gateway to Lubbock, was nineteen minutes—fifteen with no traffic.

"Gran, do you believe everything happens for a reason?" Lori eyed a black-tailed jackrabbit hopping through a cotton field.

"Yes, I do. The big things, yes." Lottie's voice was hesitant yet filled with conviction.

"Then I'll never understand my life, I guess. I'll never understand why they died while I slept. Safe. Underground."

"Well, sweetheart, only God knows the day and hour."

"I'll never understand. My faith isn't that strong." The word echoed. Strong. Be Strong. Oh, how she resented Gerald's scrawled note a few hours ago. And now she pondered it. *Did he know his words would get me through this day? Any day?*

Lottie pulled into the loose gravel driveway.

They sat in silence, a generation apart. The space of a lost mother and daughter kept them separate yet clinging to each other all at once.

"Gran, remember what you said this morning?"

"About?" Lottie was slightly distracted by her mailbox. The flag was up, meaning the mailman hadn't stopped by yet.

"Boston. You said we could visit Dad's family in the summer."

"Yes, and I crossed my heart." Lottie smiled and broke the spell of sadness that had overcome them. "Well? What do you think?"

"About what?"

"Dinner."

"I'm not hungry." Lori shook her head. "No, actually, I'm very hungry. I'll make dinner."

"Really?" Lottie barely concealed her surprise.

"I'm going to make us the best grilled cheese sandwiches ever!"

Lottie was certain she saw a glint of joy in her granddaughter's eyes. A spark. A start.

Chapter 3

Boston Bred

In the summer, Lori and Lottie headed to Boston for a visit with the Hopkins family. Lori was met with warm greetings and her first taste of certain Boston fare, namely brown bread. Although her mom had prepared baked beans countless times, Texas-style with chile peppers, the brown bread was as foreign to Lori as Beantown itself. The sliced rounds—dense, deep brown, and raisin-studded—were cooked in soup cans by Bernadette, the cheery family baker. She tendered slices on a cream-colored ceramic platter as a gesture of welcome. Lori studied the earth-colored discs, dark and drab against delicate pink hand-painted roses on the dinnerware's edge.

"Go ahead, try it," Bernadette said. "Wait, try these too." She spooned out a clump of beans in a thick sauce the color of burnt sienna. Baked beans and Boston brown bread. The die was cast.

Lori gripped the fork, cut into the bread, dipped it into the beans, and shoved the concoction in her mouth. *It's like I'm in a tree house club!* she thought. *Eat mud or you can't be a member.* As if on a dare, Lori chewed the pulpy beans and rough-textured bread and swallowed hard. She centered a rose-colored napkin atop the remaining brown bread on her discarded dinner plate. Bernadette noticed the act of dismissal, maybe defiance.

"Dessert anyone?" Penelope Hopkins, Lori's paternal grandmother, came to the rescue. Known as Grandma Penny to everyone who knew and loved her, she was nothing if not sensitive to family dynamics.

On a side table, Lori spotted a Boston cream pie topped with a thin, glossy layer of chocolate icing and filled with two thick slabs of creamy custard sandwiched between vanilla sponge cakes. The confection conjured thoughts of her mom, who'd whipped up the best silky-smooth filling imaginable. Oh, how memories stirred emotions, like rekindling a dying ember.

Lori observed Grandma Lottie and the Hopkins family circled around the lace-covered mahogany table. A massive hutch and china closet dominated the dining room. Noisy chatter, clinking of silverware against plates, and an occasional burst of laughter kept Lori alert even with mental exhaustion driven by the burden of putting up a good front.

"You make the best custard filling, Penny. What's your secret?" Lottie asked.

"My secret is Bernadette. She's our baker," Penny chirped.

In the present moment, Lori and Lottie savored slices of Boston cream pie. Spoonfuls of sweetness met the bitter taste of sadness and loss.

Lottie noticed how pleased Penny looked with family gathered around her. As young mothers, she and Penny had become fast friends in a tight circle of doctors' wives. Now, years later, Lottie still marveled at how Penny ran a tight ship and recalled one instance nearly thirty years ago . . .

• • •

Lottie paid a visit with clothing that her daughter Miriam outgrew. Penny stood stoutly blowing a bosun's navy whistle in the middle of her parlor room. The children, running pell-mell over couches and chairs, froze in their tracks. The family's Boston terrier, Pugsy, knew the drill and sat as if awaiting a treat.

Lottie saluted Penny. "Aye, aye, Captain."

"It works!" said an unabashed Penny, twirling the whistle.

Who knew Penny's sweet boy, Thomas, tantalizing Pugsy with a sugar cookie, would court and marry her daughter, Miriam, a stunning beauty by anyone's standards. One week after college graduation, he proposed marriage to Miriam in the same sandbox they had played in as children.

• • •

Lori's father, Tom, had seven siblings—four older brothers and three younger sisters. The eldest, Joel, died in a plane crash. He and his crew were lost when their B-24 bomber went down over Italy in 1944.

Bernadette, the baby of the clan, kept a cheerful undertone to any somber occasion. At twenty-eight, she possessed the same kind countenance, dark brown eyes, square jaw, and ready smile as Lori's father, Tom. Lori was immediately drawn to her warmth. Upon arrival in Boston, she had insisted Lori call her Bernie and forego Aunt Bernadette. Much too formal.

Lottie and Penny possessed a shorthand of signals and a particular way of reading each other after so many years.

"It's been a long haul, right, Lottie?" Penny asked and moved aside her half-eaten plate of dinner.

"We're a bit tired, Penny. We'll head up to our rooms and see you in the morning."

Ben Hopkins, the oldest sibling, checked his watch. He was the only Hopkins who had ventured to Texas when his younger brother Tom transferred to Lubbock over a decade earlier. He had stayed two weeks and never returned, claiming the heat and dust were unbearable for his Bostonian constitution.

Lori glanced in one sweeping head turn. Blood relatives, but strangers really, trying to give comfort, even if cold comfort, to her aching heart. Awkward, vapid expressions hovered above lace, linen, and fine china rimmed with pink roses.

"Need a little breathing space?" Ben winked at Lori. Tom's brother looked nothing like him. He was a head shorter, sported a ginger-colored mop, and resembled an elf who kept secrets behind a perpetual grin. He asked questions, lots of questions, lined up in rapid-fire succession.

Yes, breathing space! Lori thought, nodding politely. *I'm suffocating in this room stuffed with dining chairs and talk that's meaningless to me right now.*

"Thanks, Ben. We'll call it a day," Lottie said.

Ben always showed appreciation for Lottie's courage, refinement, and willingness to relocate to Texas from her life in Boston. He'd rise when Lottie entered or exited a room, as if royalty were in his midst. But he had been skeptical of Miriam, Lottie's daughter, a fragile creature, weak-minded and anxious, yet stubborn and willful, even if she was a bona fide Bostonian.

Tom had assured his older brother that Miriam, or Mir, was a treasure of a gal. He was intent on marrying her from their first childhood encounter. Tom was a torch holder in Ben's judgment, and the flame was inextinguishable. Oh, Miriam was pretty enough—actually, a knockout. But there was an uneasiness that made Ben uneasy, as if she closeted a skeleton or two. And then the news Ben received a week before last Christmas . . .

• • •

Tom, the favored little brother, and his wife had been found broken, bruised, and lifeless under piles of rubble. The Hopkins family had decreed Lori shouldn't witness her parents' corpses dressed for their burial. Lottie had deferred to their decision, still haunted by the carnage laid bare in a wide path of destruction and her frantic search for Lori directly following the storm. On a Sunday evening, Lori's light had gone out, and a candle of hope extinguished.

No viewing had preceded the funeral. No open caskets or corpses with rosary beads entwined in stiffened hands. It wasn't the Irish way, or any way to mourn a loved one.

The mass was held in the Infant of Prague side chapel of a Texas outpost church. Tom's colleagues and Miriam's ladies' church club had attended the closed-casket funeral. For Lori, the sadness was palpable. She had eyed her Uncle Ben Hopkins, his head lowered, gripping the back of the pew as if holding on to a storm-tossed boat. Penny Hopkins had stood next to him with waves of emotion rippling across her face. Lori had wondered how

Grandma Penny didn't crumble under sorrow's weight. A second son gone, as was her husband, Lori's Grandfather Bill, who had died three years ago from a cardiac arrest in his sleep.

Framed photos, mainly of the Hopkins family and Tom's and Miriam's high school and college yearbook portraits, were displayed on a mahogany table draped in a white linen runner, along with a few personal possessions—Miriam's marquee-shaped diamond engagement ring and a pair of monogrammed cufflinks and Tom's Rolex watch, both gifts from Miriam.

None of Ben's brothers, sisters, nor their children had filled the pews in a sad chapter of their family history. A memorial mass had been planned for a later date in Boston. Lori, the sweet, sanguine girl, was now a cheerless adolescent with drooping shoulders and head bent in utter defeat. In the Texas chapel, Lori had raised her eyes to stare, as if boring holes in the Infant statue cloaked in a gold, silken cape and holding up an orb.

• • •

Now in Boston, months later, Lori seemed more at ease. Her lips, no longer pursed, gave way to a smile more readily.

"We're happy to see you here, Lori," Ben said.

Lori fixed her gaze on his wrist. "Uncle Ben, why are you wearing my dad's watch?"

Twenty-odd frozen faces and pairs of eyes were on Ben. He absentmindedly covered the watch face and assumed the posture of a courtroom defendant awaiting the jury's verdict. "Well, Lori, it reminds me of your dad, and you're welcome to it."

Lori's eyes scanned her aunts' fingers before directing attention back to her Uncle Ben. "My mom's ring—do you have that too?"

"No, dear, I have your mother's ring. I let your Uncle Ben have the watch and the cufflinks," Lottie said.

With a passive expression, Lori studied the length of family circling the dining room. They seemed so eager to please . . . maybe too eager.

"I'll clear the dishes." Bernadette reached for Lori's covered plate first.

Penny and Lottie traded nods.

"I can show you to your room, Lori, dear," said Grandma Penny.

"That's okay, Penny. You sit and relax," Lottie said.

Minutes later, Lori stared at a stark white ceiling and molding of robin's egg blue matching a paisley wallpaper pattern. A dark, mahogany bed frame with large, imposing posts and coordinating bureau and mirror took up the majority of floor space. The room was small and tall, such a contrast to the sprawling Texas rancher that had been her home with its sleek, teakwood furniture, spacious living areas, and modern amenities. All gone, all dust, rubble, sticks of wood, broken dishes, scattered clothes. *Stop it!* an inner voice cried out.

Alone, Lori lapsed into sorting out puzzlers, like the engagement ring found in rubble following the storm. She reckoned her mom had removed it to sculpt a pie crust. But the watch confounded her. Why would her dad take off his watch? He routinely checked the time, unless he was showering or going to bed at night. *Maybe he was in the shower,* she pondered.

Yes, he was showering, and Mom was making a pecan pie. All was copacetic in the early dusk, the quiet time before supper. And then it happened. The fierce, whirling tunnel and force of nature consuming everything in its path. Everything but Lori, sound asleep while deep in the ground, the fallout shelter, her hideaway as a protest against a fake Christmas tree. The reason she was still here, still wondering why things happen in life with its fleeting quality and vulnerability to sudden, irreversible change.

Seven months ago, she lay in her own room cradling Raggedy Ann and conniving a plot against her mom's choice of an aluminum Christmas tree, so garish and unnatural. She was spared, unharmed, but at what price? The cost was too costly. Lori wished memories could melt away like snow drifts.

Lori sighed heavily in the Boston guest room bed. A knock on the door startled her. "Come in." She sat up. A stream of light entered from a hallway chandelier.

Lottie sat at the foot of the bed. She held a black velvet box. "Lori, I want you to have the ring."

"I'll take it, but I don't want to see it. Not now." She put the box under her pillow, as if to imprint her mother's essence into her head and heart. Lottie, a trained nurse who'd seen her share of shell shock on the French battlegrounds, brushed the red-blonde strands off her granddaughter's forehead.

"They care about you, Lori. You're family. Let them into your life." Lottie's angelic voice, soft and low, could comfort a bawling infant, a blood-soaked soldier, or in this case, an injured soul.

"I'd like the cufflinks too. Uncle Ben can keep the watch." Lori, eyes closed, buried half her face into the two pillows she embraced.

"I brought those too." Lottie set down the cufflinks on a nightstand. "Anything else?"

Lori faced her grandmother, her life support system. Lottie's words echoed. *Let them in.*

"The bread. I'll try the bread again."

Chapter 4

Tea Mates

On the visit's first evening, Lori returned to the kitchen with its turquoise-colored walls—a cool, modern color, so discordant with the antiquated, embossed wallpaper in rooms adjoining it. Bernadette poured Ceylon tea from a white ceramic pot into a matching bone china cup, opaque and delicate, like her fingers. Lori noted a white cuckoo clock framed in carved wooden leaves with gold highlights. She didn't remember the clock from her few visits to Boston as a small child. The cuckoo bird swung out from behind hinged doors and tweeted, "Eight o'clock."

Lori observed the fleeting ceremony.

"Your Uncle Ben bought the clock in Germany ten years ago, after the war." Bernadette decanted brewed tea into her cup. "He likes timepieces."

Lori examined her third slice of brown bread. "I could've guessed that."

"Leave it to the Germans." She noticed Lori's questioning gaze. "Precision." She set the teapot on the counter. "Pendulum clocks have been around for three hundred years. The pendulum always swings exactly the same. It keeps accurate time by weights that move the gears."

From the kitchen window, the sun, a half peach rimmed in scarlet, disappeared into a bed of cottony clouds. Lori gulped the steamy amber liquid. Her darting eyes took note of objects around her—a red-and-white checkered dish towel hanging from the oven door, an oval multicolored rag rug near the sink—anything and everything in the present to take her mind off of the past. Lori took inventory of it all, then her attention went back to the cuckoo clock.

Bernadette spoke up. "He'd give you the watch, Lori."

Lori's random thoughts were reinforced by the intimate kitchen and its tall mid-wall-to-ceiling chalk-white cabinets. Tall and small. Unaccustomed to the traditional townhouse floor plan, she soaked in the tall and small. Bits of conversation sifted through the kitchen walls from the dining area.

Bernadette exhaled. "Did you keep anything? I mean anything that you have now?"

Lori blurted out, "No, I kept nothing." Images flowed through her mind—a fleecy, blue afghan lovingly crocheted by Grandma Lottie, a heart-shaped clear glass ornament with *Lori* etched in red sparkles, her beloved Raggedy Ann, and the Infant statue. Time to bury the memories, again. "What's he do? Uncle Ben?"

Bernadette poured the remaining tea in her empty cup. "He's a news photographer for the *Boston Globe* and a few magazines."

"What magazines?" Lori was intrigued.

"Hmm. *Life, Vanity Fair, Esquire* . . ."

"*National Geographic?*"

Bernadette shrugged. "Maybe. You could ask him."

Lori reclined, feeling more relaxed. "Can you help me?" She pressed on the folds of her daffodil-colored sundress, a near replica of one modeled by Audrey Hepburn, her favorite actress, in *Vogue* magazine's April issue. She had discovered the breezy frock in a dress shop three days prior to boarding the plane to Beantown. Grandma Lottie, a Hepburn fan, had nodded in approval.

Bernadette lit a front burner under her brass kettle. "Sure, with what?" She offered more leftover brown bread. Lori politely waved it away.

"The names. I can't remember all of them." She hugged her arms at her waist.

Bernadette picked apart a slice of bread. "We're a big family. There were eight of us. The oldest, Joel, died in the war."

"I knew that much."

"I'll give you the rundown. Your dad's in the middle. Three before and three after." Bernadette's tea kettle whistled. "You know bop?"

"The music?" Lori perked up. She was a nascent fan of bebop. Her Christmas gift list included the latest LP from Clifford Brown, her favorite emerging bop artist.

Bernadette transferred boiling hot water into the ceramic pot and dropped in a silver tea ball filled with aromatic dried leaves. "Okay. Bop. B for Bernadette, O for Olivia, and P for Portia. Then, your dad, Tom, is the T for transition." Bernadette had mentioned Tom repeatedly during dinner, the link in the sibling chain, the transition from the girls to the boys.

"Portia?"

"That's Rose," Bernadette said.

"Why is Aunt Portia called Rose?"

"Her third grade teacher told the class that Portia meant 'pig' in Latin. She came home, slammed her books on the kitchen table, and said she'd be Rose, her middle name. She signs as P. Rose Henry, her married name."

Hands clasped, elbows on the table, Lori concentrated. "B-O-P. Bernadette, Olivia, and Portia. But it should be B-O-R."

"Stick to bop. Now for the uncles. Eat franks and beans. Edward, Farley, and Ben." Bernadette pressed a few moist crumbs to her fingertips.

"What?" Lori's eyebrows furrowed.

"Edward, Farley, and Ben. Eat franks and beans." Bernadette sipped freshly brewed tea. "I know it sounds silly . . ."

"Franks and beans?"

"Every Saturday night. You're in Yankee territory."

"Do you miss my dad?" Lori uttered the words before thinking too hard on them.

"He's my favorite. Always will be, Lori. He made me feel special."

"But you didn't see him very much."

"No, but he wrote letters. He wrote to all of us. I have a box of his letters."

"Letters?"

Penny Hopkin's snow-white ponytail popped through the threshold. "What are you girls gabbing about?"

The cuckoo bird burst out at the half-hour mark at 8:30 p.m. Lori studied Grandma Penny's wide-open, unblinking eyes. *Oh, she's like the bird*, Lori thought with a giggle thinly disguised as a cough.

"Did I say something funny?" Penny cleared her throat. "Well, may I interrupt?" She entered, hands clasped, and smiled. "Lori, you have a visitor. From Texas."

Chapter 5

Tally Forth

*P*enny's smile met Lori's frown. Boston was a refuge, an escape from Texas. No ghosts, no shadows, not now. Even memories of Joy, like a comforting mantle, were left behind. A twin heart, lost in the devastation of December 18, 1955. *Why did you turn back? Why? WHY?*

"Who is it?"

"Talia. She's here with her mother."

"Talia?" Lori tilted her head. "Tally?"

"Why don't I have her join you in here? We can entertain her mom," Penny added.

Bernadette's hands slid down the side of her skirt. "I can leave you two . . ."

"No, don't! Uh, I'd like you to meet her. I mean, I barely know her." Lori addressed Penny. "Did she say why she's here?" Lori, usually eager to strike up a conversation, felt drained of her usual buoyancy and energy.

"Maybe she can tell you." Penny tapped her white moccasin.

Lori weighed the situation, stalling at playing hostess to her school-mate. *Not Texas,* she chanted to herself. *Not now.*

"Okay," Lori said. It's all she could muster.

Talia insisted on being called Tally. Her signature greeting was, "Hi, I'm Talia, but call me Tally." She was tall—Lori guessed five feet, eight inches—and big-boned. "I'm sorry we're visiting so late." Her presence filled the room. "My mom wanted to find your house. We're staying with my aunt who lives a few blocks away."

Talia crossed the threshold. Bernadette poured tea into a third cup. Lori forced a smile and greeted Talia, a.k.a. Tally, who was wearing a short-sleeved faded blue oxford shirt with a ruffle bib and a white, pleated skirt. Standing in the middle of the kitchen, she appeared nervous in the limelight while fingering the blouse's ruffle.

"Who's your aunt?" Penny asked with renewed interest.

"Veronica McFadden." She took a deep breath. "Uh, sorry to barge in . . ."

Penny side-hugged Tally, giving a modicum of comfort to the reticent teen. "How nice of you to stop by. How long are you here?"

Lori wanted all chitchat to cease. The whole idea of Boston was to leave behind Texas like a bad dream. Now it lingered and reemerged with Tally, even though she wasn't native to the Lone Star state.

Tally sensed Lori's disinterest. "Uh, I'm not sure. We arrived yesterday."

"Hi, I'm Bernie." The energetic Bernadette could turn any discomforting occasion into a pep rally. She gestured to a seat, set down the teacup, and poured some tea. With Tally settled in, the awkward moment was diffused. "I have copy to edit by tomorrow. I'm sure you two will catch up." She slid her palms down her narrow hips, her sign of a fait accompli. In a flash, she was gone, leaving Lori behind as hostess.

"I know it's late." Tally sipped her tea. "I'll stay a few minutes."

Then why did you bother? Lori mused, adding a silent reproach to the intrusion.

"Nonsense," Penny replied. "Any friend of your Aunt Veronica's is a friend of mine."

Lori quickly patched together a plot. Was this staged? She would confront Grandma Lottie with mounting evidence of a prearranged visit. But the "why" instantly troubled her.

"Well, then. I'll go visit with your mom. You girls catch up," Penny said.

Catch up? On what? Lori was suddenly desperate to make a quick end to the evening. The Texas teens sat alone and listened to the ticking clock.

"My aunt has a cuckoo clock too. It's brown and has two dancers. No bird like yours." Tally gulped her tea with jittery fingers and placed the cup in its saucer. "So how long are you here?"

"A few weeks. And you?"

"Uh, like I said, I don't know. Maybe a month." Tally rapped her nails on the table. "I saw Gerry before I left. He was asking for you."

"What?" Lori fired back. "Wait a minute. Did you know you were visiting me?"

"Uh, I guess no one told you?"

"No, not at all." The heat of indignation rose from deep inside, flushing her cheeks.

"I'm sorry. I thought you might know, but maybe they thought you'd be upset. Maybe they didn't want to . . ."

"I'm not upset," Lori retorted. "I'm furious!"

"I can leave." Tally, singed by the outburst, drew away from the table. "It's getting late anyway."

Lori's flare-up subsided. "I'm sorry, Tally. It's not your fault. None of it. I'm a little confused right now. My gran is keeping things from me. She treats me like a child. And my Aunt Bernie just told me she has letters from my dad. I don't know what to believe or where to turn sometimes."

"It's okay, Lori. You didn't know. I'm not sure how I'd feel either." Tally drained the teacup. "Maybe I should go. Like I said . . ."

"No, no, your mom might want a few more minutes." Lori feebly attempted playing hostess in a foreign territory. "Have you tried any of this brown bread?"

"Brown bread? I've never heard of it." Tally fiddled with her black curls.

Lori offered the plate of raisin-dotted rounds neatly sliced.

"Ah, no thanks," Tally said. "I don't care for raisins. But if you handed me a Coney Island hot dog, well, that's another story."

A wave of compassion and gratitude washed over Lori, and she warmed up to the Texas newcomer. "You miss New York, huh?"

"Yeah." Tally twirled a curly lock. "Well, I guess I better get going."

"You just got here," Lori blurted, to her own amazement. She couldn't figure out her emotions, motives, or responses. She was like a babe learning to crawl over or under the confusion.

The cuckoo bird thrust itself on the scene. Lori shook her head. "I don't think I could live with that bird!"

Tally nodded. "Yeah, it's annoying at my aunt's house too. Every fifteen minutes!"

Their eyes met. Lori angled as if sizing up abstract art. "Can you believe we're sitting here in Boston talking about cuckoo clocks?"

Tally took in the ambience, the turquoise walls, white cabinets, minimal floor space, miles apart from her newfound ranch life in Texas. The Boston milieu and its melding of cultures reminded her of New York and formative years in Brooklyn.

Lori brightened up. "Would you like to explore Boston with me? I'm here for a while."

"Sure! Me too."

"My guess is that was the plan." Lori shifted like the wind to a somber tone. She waited. "So, anyway, what did Gerry say?"

"What? Not much. Just to say hi, that's all." Tally grew fidgety. Her mission fulfilled, she became more uncomfortable with the contrived plot so clumsily revealed.

"Oh, that's all?" Lori wondered why she wanted further news. He meant to comfort her with his note. *Everything happens for a reason . . . Be strong.*

Lottie strolled into the room. "How are you two—"

"You arranged this meeting without telling me." The accusation stung like a suddenly thrown dart. Lottie was lost for words. Lori gripped her sides.

Tally shrunk in her seat. "I think I'll go now." She inadvertently scraped the chrome-plated chair across the tile floor. "Thanks, Mrs. Mitchell, for inviting us." The truth like spilled milk.

"You're welcome, Tally." Lottie put her arm across the girl's rounded shoulders. "We'll see you tomorrow, then?" She directed piercing eyes at her granddaughter. Her smile was strained, tinged with equal measures of joy and sorrow. "We're going on an excursion tomorrow."

Lori bit back the bitterness of a harsh reply. One word found its voice, the one she'd been uttering a lot lately. "Why?"

Chapter 6

Silent Letters

The gathering to greet Lori and Lottie lingered through the evening and finally broke up with aunts, uncles, and cousins embracing and promising to return for a weekend brunch. By midnight, the house was still—Penny, Bernadette, and Whiskers the cat were tucked in their upstairs quarters. Ben decided on a spare room he frequented when his wife, Kathy, was on a golf tour.

Lori's angry stare conflicted with the oddly cheerful kitchen. She paced in a circle, imprisoned between the chalk-colored cabinetry, linoleum floor, and breakfast table. Her recourse was a line of questioning in her self-ascribed courtroom with the accused. Lori took a seat and crossed her arms and legs, a posture resembling a tightened fist. She cut into Grandma Lottie with words like shards of glass. "Why are you hiding things from me?"

"What do you mean?" replied Lottie evasively.

"I feel like I'm always being set up." Like a fueled rocket, she shot up from the kitchen chair yet managed to keep her tone to a heated whisper. "Stop trying to protect me!" Tears stained her cheeks. Tears that had been building up since she arrived the day before. Last December, she desperately wanted to abandon Texas. Boston seemed like the best choice with familial ties, if not familiar ground.

Now she was the hurting child in a strange kitchen, its turquoise walls so opposite from the earth tones of her Texas rancher. The cuckoo bird stuck out its head and squawked. Lori took off her straw-weaved sandal and threw it at the clock as the carving retreated behind its doors.

Lottie said nothing. Many times, it was her greatest strength. Penetrating silence. She picked up the shoe and handed it to Lori. Her actions said everything. *I understand. You're still hurting.*

Lori took the shoe as if nothing happened. She rubbed away a few last tears. Her lips quaked like a two-year-old following an explosive, out-of-nowhere tantrum. With folded arms and a calm demeanor, she resumed her questioning. "What about the letters?"

"Letters?"

"You know, the letters my dad wrote." *Letters.* She mulled over the word, wondering if she'd even recognize her father's handwriting. Even while entertaining Tally, she was distracted by thoughts of letters and secrets. Too many secrets. But the letters. What would they reveal?

"Well, Lori, I'm sure he's written many letters to his family."

"Aunt Bernie has letters from my dad, and I'd like to see them."

"Then why don't you ask her?"

"She might say no." Bone-tired, Lori resisted returning to her room.

Lottie stifled a yawn, trying to keep up with her granddaughter's random and, at times, puerile thoughts. "Ask her. The worst she can do is say no."

"Do you think she'll let me?" Lori was persistent.

Lottie massaged Lori's hunched shoulders. "Yes, I think she will. Now, let's go to bed. We have an early day."

"Have you read any of the letters?"

"No," Lottie replied. "I've written a few of my own to your dad."

"About me?"

Lottie twisted Lori's shimmery red-gold mane into a single French braid. "Of course." Lottie finished. "Pictures too."

"Gran, fix it like Mom's." Lori's voice was raspy. She hadn't uttered the name "Mom" since December 18.

Lottie unraveled her handiwork. Lori had foregone her girlish bangs, headband, and above-the-shoulder coiffure in the last six months. Her hair had grown nearly two inches, and her former bangs were sidepieces, hanging loosely by her ears in soft waves, reminiscent of an early Grace Kelly. The reigning Princess of Monaco came in as a close second to Lori's favorite movie icon, the gamine-like Audrey Hepburn. Lori and Grandma Lottie had watched the fairy-tale wedding in April as the former Philadelphia socialite and member of the Hollywood elite stepped into the role of Royal Highness. They had fallen in love with Princess Grace's dress and its exquisite lace bodice that complemented her stunning natural beauty. Lori fancied notions of becoming a fashion designer with a specialty in gowns and evening wear.

"You didn't say where we're going tomorrow." Lori bent her head, and Lottie worked at the nape of her neck, creating a chignon to match the one Miriam had worn for the last year or so.

"Why tell you now and spoil the surprise? We're hours away, and we both need rest."

Lori patted her hair. The cuckoo bird sprung from its hiding. Lori jumped. "I'll never get used to it," she said a little self-conscious of her overreaction.

They watched the bird carry out its routine. A bleary-eyed Lottie stood back and admired her work.

With a restrained head turn, Lori spoke soberly. "Okay, you can undo it now."

A fleeting thought crossed Lottie's mind that Lori punished her by conjuring up Miriam. She dismissed the notion, much too upsetting to ponder.

"No more secrets, Gran, okay?" Lori rose from the kitchen chair and stretched her arms to the ceiling.

"Let's go before our friend cheeps again," Lottie said. "But I have a question. Why did you ask me to fix your hair?"

"Like Mom's?" Lori wore a sad smile. "To know what it felt like."

They stood like marble statues, the Greco-Roman ones from antiquity displayed in museum hallways. Chiseled figures with blank eyes, missing limbs, expressionless. They were broken yet strangely whole in spirit. Survivors. Lottie reached for the light switch.

"So how should I dress for tomorrow?" Lori, the indefatigable inquirer, asked.

Lottie's face shone bright and cheery as a full moon as she gingerly climbed the stairs. "Anything you like, but wear a camisole. And bring your raincoat."

Chapter 7

Sewing Deeds

At the break of dawn, a starling's trill woke Lori out of her short-lived slumber. She stretched up alabaster arms and luxuriated in the down pillow and light throw wrapped around her. The feathered friend atop the windowsill stared into her room and pecked at its reflection. *Silly bird,* thought Lori. She wished the moment would linger long enough for her to savor the absence of familiar people, places, and things. No schedule, no school, no plans, no classmates, other than Tally. She reached for the travel alarm clock purchased the day before leaving Texas. *Oh no!* Twenty minutes to get ready!

Lori raced down the stairs. Tally sat in the parlor.

"Okay, I'm ready. I'll just eat something along the way. Where are we going?"

"Your grandma said we can walk. It's only a few blocks away."

Lottie orchestrated the surprise outing with nary a hint of their destination.

Filene's Basement was a mecca for bargain hunters willing to sort through heaps of clothing and housewares. Shoppers lined up outside like racehorses at the starting gate but disregarded rules, regulations, or etiquette once the doors opened. Holiday times were especially frenetic, with hostile customers fighting over sale items strewn across tables or wedged into clothing racks. The best of the rest were the wedding gowns, a tradition for starry-eyed brides seeking out a perfect eye-popping stunner for their ceremonial walk.

Strolling down aisles, Lori and Tally were entranced by rows of designer dresses, coats, blouses, skirts, and lingerie. A ruby-red cocktail dress shimmered and beckoned between a black chiffon skirt and pearl-white A-line shift. Lori separated hangers and gazed at the striking design.

"That's a Claudia Young design of ruby silk and a tulip skirt. It's my favorite," said a salesclerk, rhythmically straightening up blouses piled in a bin. Her bored expression turned to one of delight with the diversion. "Why don't you try it on?"

Lori stroked the silky texture. "It's a little old for me."

"The tulip design works for any age. I'm guessing you're fifteen?"

"In September."

"Perfect. There's homecoming, Christmas dances. You'll be a standout."

"You'd look fab in that one, Lori," Tally said.

"I think it's too sophisticated."

"Let's see, Lori. Hold it in front of you," Grandma Lottie said.

"It's for cocktail parties." Lori wanted the dress but also reassurance. The skirt's folds, like the petals of a flower, would fall gently against her slim hips. The scooped neckline was modest, and the sleeveless style would complement a pair of gloves and simple wrap.

"The color is perfect for you, dear." Lottie hoped the dress would be a welcomed distraction. *Good medicine*, she thought, *at the proper time and place.*

"Try it on. I think you'll like what you see," the clerk said.

"Where are the dressing rooms?" Lori craned her neck above the tables piled high with folded sweaters and accessories.

"We only have changing areas for men." Hours earlier, the clerk had sipped coffee and confided to a co-worker. "If I had a dollar for every time an out-of-towner asked me for a dressing room, I'd be planning a cruise."

"We'll form a circle." Lottie held out the lightweight raincoat Lori left behind on the arm of a parlor chair as she rushed out the door.

Shoppers milled about. Lori's entourage formed a makeshift dressing room. Lottie draped the slicker across Lori's shoulders. She unzipped her A-line shift and let it fall to her ankles. The salesclerk swooped up Lori's dress as she stepped out of it. The threesome encircled her, lending support and encouragement, like Cinderella stitched into her ball gown by mice friends. A sudden burst of warmth and love entered Lori's stony heart.

The dress slipped into place like a glove.

Tally cheered her on. "You look like the model, Suzy Parker!"

Lori smirked. "Yeah. Red hair, freckles, and half her height."

Lottie waved her hand like a magic wand. "We'll take it."

The clerk nodded. "Yes, ma'am, but before you dress, let's have some fun! We have exquisite ball gowns. Are you familiar with the designer, Charles James?" Lori, ready to decline the offer, noticed Tally's brows lift and eyes light up.

"The Tree gown. Oh, Lori, let's try one." Tally practically jumped out of her brown flats.

"And our wedding dresses. Girls love peeking down those aisles. I'll be right back with a couple delicious creations." The salesclerk hastened, her flaxen curls bouncing with each step, a departure from mindlessly sorting clothes.

"Delicious?" Lori remained shrouded in the green slicker. "I'm already hungry."

"We'll take the subway over to the North End neighborhood," Lottie said. "Bernadette is joining us."

"How late will we be?" Tally focused on the floor. "I have dinner at five with my mom and aunt."

"We'll have you back in plenty of time." Lottie draped a protective arm around Tally's sloped shoulders. "Don't want to wear out you two on the first day."

The pint-size salesclerk nearly disappeared under the long, weighty frocks folded across her short arms. It was all she could do to prevent stepping on a flouncy hem.

"That's a lot of dress." Lottie preferred the sleek designs of Coco Chanel, made famous by her timeless little black dress.

"Mr. James was impressed with the bustle skirts, so he updated his collection. The gowns are full below the knee. They're quite flattering." The salesclerk handed a gown to Lori. The bluish-green hue matched the kitchen walls in the Hopkins townhouse.

"I'll try the gold one," Lori said.

"Okay," replied the clerk. "I thought turquoise would complement your gorgeous red hair."

"I like turquoise," Tally said. "I'll try it. Lori, can I borrow the raincoat?"

"Uh, in my skivvies, here."

"Skivvies?" Lottie asked.

"My dad called underwear skivvies."

The salesclerk interrupted. "Mr. James was a fan of curves. The corsetry emphasizes the feminine shape."

Lori stepped into the designer frock and felt the pinch of rigid boning in the bodice. She glanced down at the voluminous folds of shimmering gold satin. "I feel like a cabaret singer. Rosemary Clooney." She tossed the raincoat to Tally.

"Hey Lori, would you hold up the coat?"

Lori stretched her arms, barely reaching Tally's armpits as she worked herself into the second-skin gown. Tally's height and broad shoulders were ideal for balancing the voluminous folds flaring below her knees.

"A star is born!" Lori admired Tally's stately presence. "You're ready for the red carpet."

Tally sashayed, making the most of the expansive skirt. Out of the corner of her eye, Lori caught sight of a slender, redheaded figure coasting by an adjoining aisle. The woman held up a dress of yellow-orange like a Georgia peach. Lori, unblinking, noticed the uncanny resemblance, at once vexing and comforting.

Her attentive salesclerk observed. "Oh, you like the bubble hem? It was fashionable two years ago."

Lori half whispered. "I know. My mom had that dress. Same color, same dress." And with that, her mind retraced the worst shambles of a day . . .

• • •

Lori wrote the last paragraph of a composition on Of Mice and Men *by John Steinbeck. Her father drained the coffee pot and tucked a hardcover book under his free arm. "This is the best Civil War account I've ever read."*

Miriam polished flatware and hummed "Autumn Leaves," a perennial hit made popular again by pianist Roger Williams. "What's that, dear?"

"Andersonville. The prison used by the South."

"Oh dear, Tom, can't you read something more uplifting? Christmas is one week away." Miriam resumed her humming.

Lori was annoyed by her mother humming a song heralding gentle breezes and the annual fall release of red and gold leaves, so natural and picturesque, that signified the dying away season. Such a contrast to the aluminum Christmas tree and its spindly, unnatural branches jutting out from a metal pole now framed by the dining room window. She quickly penned the last two sentences of her report and stuffed the loose-leaf pages in her folder.

"Finished. I think I'll head to my room before Joy gets here."

Her parents knew she meant the underground shelter.

• • •

"Lori?" Tally's voice dragged Lori back to Filene's Basement crammed with saleable items and a sprinkling of shoppers. "May I have the raincoat?"

Lottie recognized Lori's faraway gaze reliving the past before blinking away memories, and it triggered her own. The fresh pain of loss.

Last night, as she had drifted off to sleep, Lottie had called to mind the final outing with her daughter and granddaughter. Once a month, the trio would treat themselves to lunch and a movie, each selecting four movies within a year. November of 1955, Lottie chose *Gentlemen Marry Brunettes*, a musical starring Jane Russell and Jeanne Crain as New York show girls seeking fame and fortune in Paris. The film studio had hoped to repeat the success of the smash hit *Gentlemen Prefer Blondes* years earlier with Marilyn Monroe nearing the apex of her meteoric rise to fame. But the movie billed as "big, buxom, beautiful" had received a lukewarm reception from critics and audiences. Lottie's interest was predicated on the film's locale, France—the meeting ground nearly forty years before between her, a freshly minted nurse, and John Mitchell, a dashing surgeon.

In the stillness of the previous night, Lottie had thought about *Gentlemen Marry Brunettes* and actress Jeanne Crain singing "My Funny Valentine," a show tune by Richard Rodgers and Lorenz Hart, to love interest Alan Young amidst larger-than-life sculptures in a darkened museum. The song's quirky lyrics, "My funny valentine / Sweet comic valentine / You make me smile with my heart . . ." had tugged at her heartstrings. John would whisper the lyrics into her ear as they slow danced no matter what song was playing. It was their secret song, and she'd chuckle before resting her cheek on his broad chest . . .

"Gran?"

With a jolt, Lottie returned to Filene's Basement. The salesclerk pressed further on showing off the bridal gowns. They trotted down rows of white in all shades, fabrics, and fashions—satin, silk, lace, velvet, and so many pearl buttons. Buttons, bows, and lace, like wedding cake toppers on hangers.

At half past noon, they reached Boston's North End neighborhood. They met up with Bernadette, a jolly greeter even though mired in deadlines. As editor of a regional literary magazine, she rarely dined out for lunch. But at this juncture, she enjoyed her role as city guide extraordinaire. "Welcome to the North End, Boston's oldest neighborhood and home of the Great Molasses Flood."

"I'm getting hungry, but not for molasses." A tired Lori dreaded further sticky details.

"The disaster occurred on January 15, 1919."

"I was in Boston," Lottie said. "John and I were married. He was on the surgical team at Boston Medical Center. The flood happened just past noon. There was no escape for those trapped." Lottie slowed to a halt.

They walked along the cityscape and stopped at the corner of Hanover and Prince Street. Bernadette continued, "Paul Revere's house is to the left."

"What happened with the molasses?" Tally reveled in gory details. Her Uncle Tony had often retold mafia stories and underhanded dealings to her as a wide-eyed, breathless child.

As they approached the waterfront, Bernadette explained, "A large storage tank burst, and molasses gushed into the streets traveling thirty-five miles per hour. Twenty-one were killed and a hundred and fifty were injured. People say you can still smell the molasses on hot summer days."

"Any happier stories?" Lori asked.

"How much was in the tank?" Tally conjured up her own version of *Godzilla*, her favorite movie, and the mutant monster dripping globs of molasses.

"Well, the tank was fifty feet tall and contained over two million gallons," Bernadette said. "Rescuers were knee-deep in molasses."

Lori gave Tally a tug on her sleeve and what Uncle Tony called "hard eyes," as if to say, "Drop it!"

"We're here girls." Lottie's buoyancy was welcome relief.

The streets lining the wharf section were alive—boys playing stickball, girls playing hopscotch, and war vets playing cards and soaking up the sun's warmth with old, tired bones.

"Anyone for the best pizza in Boston?" Bernadette's cheerfulness was irresistible if not contagious.

"Swell!" Lori spoke on behalf of the weary shoppers. She loved her aunt's spark and from that moment, claimed a first pick from her dad's family tree.

Bernadette pushed on heavy wooden doors with leaded stained glass panes and wrought iron handles. The aroma of fresh oregano, fragrant spicy tomatoes, and hot bread greeted them. "What? No molasses?"

Lori sniffed and wrapped an arm round a very surprised Tally. Another bond formed.

Lottie held court at Slice of Italy's red-leathered booth edged in brass studs. Grandma Lottie—the good guardian, the grieving mother, a.k.a. Charlotte—the conscientious, spirited nurse who'd tended wounded, sometimes limbless, soldiers so many decades ago. She stroked a smooth rock in her pocket that she'd sorted out from the rubble of an obliterated Texas rancher on a Sunday six months earlier. It was a stone etched with a cross by Miriam at the age of nine. An Easter gift, carefully chiseled, one for herself and the other for Lottie.

Miriam's girlish voice echoed in Lottie's mind. "Sister Joan said we're one body in Christ, Mommy. I don't know what it means, but I made these so we'd both have a piece of Jesus."

Lottie safeguarded her rock in a black velvet pouch in a nightstand drawer in Texas. The miracle find of Miriam's rock accompanied her, a reminder of the unexplainable, the extraordinary, and the mystery of God's presence in her life.

Chapter 8
A to Z

Before dawn, at the darkest hour, Lori dreamt of wedding dresses in a basement warehouse. Row upon row of white confections, sparkly, billowing, lacy, frilly, every style imaginable, peeped out in a line from gleaming steel hangers. She floated down the aisle, touching each silky creation. One gown caught her eye, and she was drawn to it, leaping and landing in front of its full skirt. She freed the lace bodice from the jumble of dresses. Pearl buttons trimmed the dainty neckline. And then the nightmare. One by one, the buttons dropped and rolled on the cement floor. When one button fell off, another replaced it, only to fall away, replaced by a button, which fell away too, endlessly. Lori tossed and turned and piled two pillows over her head. But the dream continued. The dress was covered in buttons that spilled to the floor like a hailstorm in a basement. Yes, the basement! Her basement. The bomb shelter. And the hidden buttons.

Lori stared into the dark. Loud snoring made its way down the hall. Most likely it was Uncle Ben, who frequented a spare room when his wife was on a golf tour. He made the sound Lori's dad referred to as "sawing logs," ordinary and earthy, unlike the haunting image of buttons. The button box took shape in her foggy, half-asleep mind. Yes, tucked under a tree in the bomb shelter. In Texas. Buttons belonging to her mom, Miriam. Buttons Lori hid. Buttons that fell away from clothes. All shapes, all sizes, from sweaters, gloves, jackets. Miriam had a nervous habit of twirling and loosening buttons before she could reinforce them with needle and thread. Lori had stolen the buttons, a spiteful act that left her unsettled and anxious.

The bomb shelter, built with conviction by her father, was her sanctuary. She had forged a Christmas cave in protest of her mother's purchase of a garish aluminum tree sitting tinsel-like in the dining room picture window. It all seemed senseless now.

She had planned to give the buttons back as a Christmas gift, a peace offering with a handwritten note. *Merry Christmas, Mom. I'm sorry it's taken me three years to return your lost buttons. I hope you enjoy them once again, and please forgive me for not returning them sooner. Love, Lori.* The Christmas of 1955. The Christmas that didn't happen. Not really.

A light knock and her pulse quickened. A voice whispered. "Lori, are you awake? Can I come in?"

Lori held the snowy white chenille cover. The fog of sleep disappeared. "Aunt Bernie?"

"Yes, it's me. Sorry if I woke you," she said in a louder whisper.

"From a bad dream. Come in." Lori propped up against the heavy mahogany headboard.

Bernadette glided in. She wore a thin flannel robe of pale pink, nearly the shade of her fair complexion, her contrasting dark hair barely visible in the wash of moonlight. "I hope you come back in the spring. It's my favorite season." Bernadette dug her hands into deep pockets. "I like to watch the birds carry bits of grass, string, twigs, anything to build their nests."

"It's their instinct, I mean, to build nests."

"It fills me with hope. Everything starts again for the first time." She sat on the bed's corner. "Maybe Boston's your home, Lori. Your springtime."

Lori remained edgy. "Gran says it's too cold in the winter. She never got used to it."

"I don't mean both of you. Consider moving here after high school. You have a home here. Family."

A prolonged pause. Lori couldn't conceive of life without Gran. Suddenly, a notion came to her. "You have the letters."

"I do. Letters your dad wrote, two from last year, one in June and one right before the tornado hit."

"Why now? It's three o'clock in the morning." Lori yawned.

"I have an early deadline." Bernadette's careworn, troubled profile alarmed Lori.

"What's the matter?"

"Clifford Brown. He died in an auto accident yesterday on the Pennsylvania Turnpike."

"The jazz musician?" Lori wiped the sleep from her eyes.

"He was twenty-five." Bernadette's tone belied her sadness.

"I'm sorry. That's so young." Lori wished she had feigned sleep and ignored the intrusion before the break of dawn and avoided hearing of a sudden death. Her consolation was proof of the letters.

In the gray shadows, Bernadette handed over the bundle, and Lori shared a privacy with an aunt she barely knew in a house too far from home.

In solitude, Lori skimmed the most recent letter first. Maybe it was an urgency to see her father's latest written words. Maybe it was the postmarked date, so close to the day her life changed forever. Whatever the reason, the first letter revealed truths she was unwilling to accept. Truths about her family life and, most importantly, herself.

The penmanship was similar to her large, loopy letters, which indicate fear of change or failure and low self-esteem—the description of her own handwriting when she had researched graphology for a homework assignment. She reread the letter.

December 13, 1955

> *Dear Bernadette,*
> *How are things at home? I miss your hot chocolate, and I really miss all the family getting together on Christmas Eve. I keep dreaming of snow and frosty nights. We have the cold days here but nothing*

like at home where your breath freezes right in front of your face. It's been busy at work with all the new shipments of manufacturing materials. I've been working twelve-hour days, and it's a strain on the family, especially with Mir and Lori fighting all the time. I have my own project to help keep peace. I turned our shelter into a Christmas room for Lori. She was so upset with Mir for buying an aluminum Christmas tree, and I couldn't bear seeing her so sad. She's down there most days after she does her homework and on weekends. It's a relief not to have the two of them at each other all the time. I think it's been building up. The tree was the last straw . . .

Lori braced herself for the remainder of the letter penned by her beloved dad.

I did discover a secret gift Lori is planning to give her mom. I was adjusting the television last night while Lori was doing her homework and almost stepped on a box. I feel a little guilty, but I opened it and read her apology note. She plans on giving the stolen buttons to Mir on Christmas, and I hope it brings them closer together. I'll keep it a secret because I don't think she'd appreciate me knowing.

I'll close for now. I look forward to hearing news from Boston. Give my love to Mom and the family. I'll send Mom a card with a note. Next Christmas, I'm going to surprise everyone with a visit, so now it's your turn to keep a secret. I haven't told Mir and Lori yet. I'll wait until next summer, maybe June.

Love, Tom

P.S. Congrats on your job as an editor. Knock 'em dead! No correcting my punctuation or spelling, please!

Lori folded the letter gently and placed it in her lap atop the other envelopes. *He knew everything.* Her thoughts tumbled like wooden blocks in a wire cage. She spent the next two hours sitting up and rereading the seven letters. She read, drifted off, woke up, tears flowing, smiling, frowning, a flood of emotions, twisting, turning, and wringing her dry.

A stream of sunlight brightened Lori's pillow and spilled across the wall. Her upraised hand danced like a shadow puppet. Life was now a shadow, the past eclipsing the present. Grandma Lottie's words pressed upon her: "This too shall pass." She was unsure of what she wanted to pass, to forget, to bury, to leave behind, maybe keep hidden.

The note from Gerald in those first fragile days came to her. *Everything happens for a reason. You'll know why some day. Be strong. Gerald.*

The hand shadow closed up into a fist and punched the pillow, releasing new sorrow and hopefully, regaining strength on the other side of pain.

Full sunlight blazed through half-drawn drapes. Perched on the windowsill, a female sparrow with stripes of buff, black, and brown feathers bobbled its tiny head and chirped. Lori had read in a poem that sparrows symbolize joy and protection and, at times, simplicity and community. She recalled "Mary's Slumber Song" that Grandma Lottie crooned to her when she was restless and overtired. "Amid the roses, Mary sits and rocks her Jesus child / While among the treetops, sighs a breeze so warm and mild / And soft and sweetly, sings a bird upon the bow / Ah, baby, dear one, slumber now."

Comfort and consolation. A voice like a silk-edged wool blanket warding off woes now the source of unrest. *The buttons. Did Gran know? Would she admit if she did?*

Lori stepped into the hallway as Bernadette exited the bathroom. She towel-dried her damp curls and gave Lori a sheepish grin.

Chapter 9

Ups and Downs

Lottie was the last to rise the morning of the letter revelation. Exhaustion consumed her. She welcomed the visit northeast but didn't expect the overwhelming desire to sleep. Rest, deep rest, had eluded her since arriving in Boston four days ago. Doors creaked in the upstairs hallway. She kept her head wedded to her pillow. The travel alarm clock pointed to eight o'clock. Rooftops bordered the urban sky, unlike the wide-open space of Texas.

Lottie raised her arms in an all-out stretch.

"Gran, are you awake?" Lori whispered into the room.

"Come in." She smoothed her nightgown.

Lori, in her yellow sundress, appeared peaked and withdrawn. She held a bundle of envelopes tied up in a blue ribbon.

"You feeling okay, darling? You look a little pale."

Lori clutched the letters. "Did you know about the buttons? Dad wrote to Aunt Bernie."

"What buttons?"

Lori plopped at the foot of the bed. "I asked Aunt Bernie if you knew. She said I'd have to ask you myself." She spread out the envelopes. "Then she got kind of mean and said I'd have to cross-examine everyone. She said the letters were personal, but she let me read seven of them."

After a long pause, Lottie spoke. "And?"

"I don't know why she gave them to me." Lori restacked the letters.

"Did you ask her?"

"No!"

"I don't know what your dad wrote, Lori. It's not my business." Lottie rose from the bed. She fitted on light blue slippers and reached for a robe on a hook behind the closet door.

"It's about your daughter. My mother."

Another knock at the door. "Anyone hungry?" Penny's melodious voice was similar to a triangular bell signaling mealtime. "We have Belgian waffles on the menu. Fresh strawberries and homemade whipped cream."

"Sounds wonderful, Penny. We'll be right down. Do I have time for a quick wash?" Lottie welcomed the interruption.

"Sure. The crew might be gone, but I'll be here." Penny peeked around the door. She sensed a bit of tension—Lottie standing in the middle of the room and Lori balled up on the bedspread like a kitten ready to pounce. Penny smiled and made a quick exit.

Lottie unhung a sleeveless celery-green linen dress from the closet and snatched undergarments from a dresser drawer with carved leaves framing brass handles. "I don't know about any buttons, and I'm sorry that these letters brought up painful memories."

Lori shook her head slowly. "I don't believe you."

Lottie froze in the doorframe. Oh, she was all too familiar with the stubborn, willful child with a scrunched-up face staring into a mirror wishing away a sprinkle of freckles. All too familiar with the angry teen, arms folded in a standoff over an aluminum Christmas tree adorning a dining room window. But distrust was new territory, uncharted waters.

"Let's not keep your Grandma Penny waiting." A dismissive remark was all she could muster in her exhausted state.

Lori was seated when Lottie entered the dining room. A fresh bouquet of blue and pink hydrangeas in a clear glass bowl added a happy note to the breakfast setup. Ben Hopkins stood to greet Lottie.

"You look smashing this morning, Charlotte." Ben insisted on formal names. Ed was Edward. Bernie was Bernadette. Lottie was Charlotte and so on. The exception was Lori since she refused to be called Lorraine. And he insisted on Ben. He wore a cryptic smirk, and Lori was in no mood to entertain an investigation. She spooned a dollop of whipped cream on top of her crispy golden waffle.

"So, what've you learned, Lori? I hear you're being carted all over Boston." Ben pierced his waffle.

Penny interrupted. "Let's not quiz Lori. It's a vacation not a school day, Ben."

Lori was up for the challenge. "Boston was founded in 1630 by Puritans. In May 1721, a smallpox epidemic hit, and inoculation was invented. Massachusetts was the first colony to outlaw slavery in the early 1780s. The first elevator in America was installed here in 1837."

"Really?" His smirk widened into a bona fide smile.

Lottie drank deeply from a cup of tea. "Scollay Square Hotel."

Lori added, "America's first football stadium."

"Yes, Harvard Stadium." Ben dabbed his thin lips with a blue linen napkin.

"Opened in 1903," said Lori. "Molasses killed twenty-one people." She picked apart her waffle.

"Oh dear, you shared that one?" Penny wiped table crumbs into her apron with an unused butter knife.

Lottie cut into a corner of her waffle piled high with strawberries. "We visited the area."

"I'm impressed," Ben said.

"I'm not finished." Lori fixed her eyes on Ben. "Boston. Where a young nurse named Charlotte married a handsome, tall doctor named John, and the rest is . . ."

"Our family history!" Lottie piled another spoonful of sugared strawberries on her plate.

"Charlotte, are you taking Lorraine—I mean Lori—to Nantasket?" He watched Lori sculpt her whipped cream. "You can't miss Paragon Park and the Giant Coaster."

"Oh, I could skip it, Ben, but Lori would enjoy it. We'll take a drive out there for the day, maybe tomorrow."

"When were you going to tell me?" Lori swiped at her whipped cream and licked her fingers.

"Well, I was thinking about it—and inviting your friend Tally." Lottie felt exhaustion again. The day had yet to begin.

"She's leaving on Saturday for New York." Lori jabbed at the edges of her waffle, avoiding eye contact with both grandmothers and her Uncle Ben.

"Well, we better make it sooner than later. Would you like to invite her, Lori?" Lottie questioned the prudence of their Boston trek. The letters were a new discovery and a vexing one. Oh, not that she doubted there were letters, many letters. Tom was devoted to his family, and distance wouldn't diminish the close tie. But the letters ripped apart the fragile alliance between granddaughter and guardian. Lori was Lottie's world. Lottie was Lori's world. They relied on each other to stumble through life's messiness for now. Emotional distance and an unpardonable distrust would make life harder, and it was already unbearable at times.

"Sure," Lori said. Her casual replies were difficult to interpret, even for Lottie.

Lottie examined the luscious fruit on her fork. "Ben, how's Kathy? I was hoping to see her on our visit."

"Tearing up the golf course. In a good way. Right now, she's in Minnesota for the US Women's Open. She fared well in Kansas last year. You're looking at a bona fide golf widower." Ben took note of his niece's ennui. "Lori, do you like photography?"

Lori perked up. "Uh, yes, very much."

"Why don't you come to my studio? I can show you how to develop film." Ben checked his watch. "You can spend Friday with me on a shoot, and then we'll develop your photos."

Lori's ear-to-ear grin brightened up the room. "Boss!"

"I'll be here at seven this Friday morning. Pack a lunch. We'll be out in the field. No time for anything but a quick break."

"Okay, I'll be ready." Lori squirmed with delight.

Ben to the rescue, thought Lottie. She welcomed a tide change from troubled waters. "How about the beach tomorrow?"

"Sure, sounds like fun. I'll see if Tally can join us."

Yes. A 180-degree turn.

Penny stacked up breakfast dishes and silverware. Lottie caught the twinkle in Ben's eye. He winked at her and nodded. A wink back and Lottie acknowledged a comrade in arms.

A tiny spark ignited Lori's spirit. "Where are we going on Friday, Uncle Ben?"

He grinned. "It's a surprise."

His reply peeved Lori. No more surprises!

Ben whistled and bowed with his hat, a parting gesture. Lottie selected the ripest, sugar-coated strawberries.

Lori blurted out the words. "Did you put him up to this, Gran?"

Lottie answered calmly. "No, Lori, this is all new to me. I'm hearing it for the first time." She inspected the strawberry, her ruby-red manicured nails a near match to the sweetly tart fruit.

After breakfast, Lori, rejuvenated by thought of the photography outing, helped Grandma Penny by drying dishes. She called Tally about the Paragon Park outing. Tally agreed and invited Lori over to her Aunt Veronica's to clean and hull strawberries for making jam. Lori sprung out the door as if the Boston environs were familiar territory.

Bernadette had traveled via train to Wilmington, Delaware, to interview friends and relatives of well-loved jazz musician Clifford Brown.

After midnight, Bernadette's taxi pulled up in front of the Hopkins household. Lottie listened for the slam of the cab door. She bided her time for Bernadette to get settled in. Down the short hallway, Lori sat up half-awake, with letters sprawled across her bed.

Lottie visited Bernadette twenty minutes after she'd arrived home. "Why, Bernie? Why did you give her the letters?"

"Why did I do it?" Bernadette sighed and tightened her bathrobe. "I had to give them to her. They'll be healing. She has pain so deep.

The letters will bring everything to the surface, like sucking out poison from a snake."

How dramatic, thought Lottie. "Well," she said, intrigued, "maybe I should read them too. I hope you're right, Bernie." In submission, she left the travel-weary writer.

Lori stirred with restlessness. She could barely contain her excitement, not only for the amusement park, but even more for the anticipated photo shoot with Uncle Ben.

At 2:00 a.m. Thursday, Lori awoke from a dream of her Christmas shelter. In the world of silence, before birds heralded the dawn, she replayed her memory tape of Sunday, December 18, and Joy's visit . . .

• • •

Joy bounded back up the stairs to lift the slanted door. She peeked down the steps again. "It's fab, Lori. Don't stay down here too long." She gave a shiver as if to shake off the unwanted notion of being under the earth.

"Joy!" Lori heard her own plea, not sure why she'd called out her friend's name, only knowing the visit seemed rushed.

Joy reappeared mid-step, leaning over, expectant and waiting.

"I want to give you something." Lori picked up a box and presented the newly purchased garland. "Here."

"You know I'm Jewish, right?" Charmed and surprised, Joy accepted the open box holding a string of pointy red petals.

"Wrap it around your Hanukkah bush?" Lori gave a tilt of her head and a shy smile.

Joy hugged her friend in a clumsy embrace, giggling at her own awkwardness. "Now I've really got to go!" Joy lifted the door once again and vanished.

• • •

Tally arrived fifteen minutes early for the planned outing. Penny offered her tea and raisin toast. Settled in the kitchen, Tally flipped through the June 4 edition of *Life* magazine. Shaking off her dream, Lori yanked a floral print shift off a hanger, slipped into her sandals, and bounded downstairs.

At Paragon Park, Lori and Tally gaped out the window of Penny's car parked alongside the shoreline. A perfect start to a promising day. Lori was amazed at her buoyed spirits. A mere two days earlier, she'd hated the world—at least her world. The Giant Coaster, touted as the largest in America with its tons of steel and wood frame, loomed ahead. *I am the roller coaster*, she thought. *My highs, too high. My lows, too low.*

Two hours into it, and Lori was still ride-hopping. She'd exhausted an arm's length of tickets before realizing she was famished. Her last bite to eat was an overly ripe speckled banana she'd grabbed from the kitchen fruit bowl in haste.

Tally people-watched on a bench as Lori queued up for the Giant Coaster. Not a fan of heights, Tally claimed she got dizzy on a three-step ladder. She enjoyed competitive games while Lori and Lottie waited in long lines. After a round of Skee-Ball, Tally walked away with a stuffed pink poodle tucked under her arm.

While Lori and Lottie rode "the Giant" for a third time, Tally strolled along the boardwalk and sampled fried clams and a frankfurter but longed for a Coney Island dog or a ham and pineapple pizza. With pink cotton candy in one hand and a pink poodle in the other, she watched taffy being pulled. Lori scooted up behind and covered Tally's eyes. "Don't look now, but there's a horse waiting for you, Tally!" Lori spotted a mustard stain on Tally's white linen blouse. "You ate without me!"

"Huh?" Tally brushed a few crumbs from her blouse. "Just a hot dog. Clams. Cotton candy."

"Join me on the carousel, puhleese!" Lori pulled on Tally's free arm and tossed the prize poodle to Lottie, who strolled behind.

A magnificent work of art and machinery, the Paragon Park Carousel was built in 1928 by the Philadelphia Toboggan Company. Lively organ music resounded. Riders bobbed up and down on sixty intricately carved horses and two Roman chariots festooned with cherubs and goddesses in flowing dresses with flowing tresses.

Tally forfeited her cotton candy to an attendant and hopped on a white horse with a gilded saddle. Lori rode sidesaddle, tucking half her skirt under the sage-colored seat of a tan horse with flared nostrils. After a few turns, they squeezed their hands together.

The bond was strengthened. Lori had a confidante when she had believed that no one could ever, would ever replace Joy. She couldn't bear to hear the word. Joy was taken from her, but now she had trust. She trusted Tally, the broad-shouldered, athletic, silent, giant-hearted New Yorker who missed Coney Island hot dogs and an uncle with tales of murder and mayhem. Tally was alien to Texas but made the most of her new home. Texas, home to Lori, was now alien territory. Nothing would ever be the same.

She looked at Lottie, who waved and smiled. Lori waved back, erasing resentment, distrust, and thoughts of a joyless world. A clean slate. In a few hours, she would embark on a new adventure with Uncle Ben. And a camera.

Chapter 10

Photo Shop

On a map, Cape Cod resembled a stretched-out arm, bent at the elbow, ending with a raised and curled fist. The tightly closed hand was Provincetown, a place known for its historic link to Pilgrims and the fortunes of the sea, including the whaling industry.

Lori, with three hours sleep, woke up at 4:00 a.m. Friday, waiting and watching for the sun to rise out of the pitch black. She had heard, many times, that it's darkest before the dawn. The dark mirrored the silence. No birdsong filled the blank spaces of the abyss-like quiet, as if the world hadn't yet formed.

Ahead of the first rays of dawn, Lori and Uncle Ben left a sleepy Beantown in his 1953 Buick Roadmaster Skylark, a two-door convertible. He named her Rosemary, after Rosemary Clooney, believing his pride and joy on four wheels matched the singer's limpid blue eyes.

The day, even at 7:00 a.m., was warm and muggy. A few hours later, Lori screened her eyes from sunrays as they drove along the recently constructed Mid-Cape Highway. She worked her way through a wax paper sleeve of Ritz crackers to break the early morning fast. Penny had packed corned beef on rye sandwiches, a small container of cottage cheese, and a thermos of iced tea for the road.

Ben, freckled hands at ten and two o'clock on the steering wheel, whistled with jazz singer Ella Fitzgerald. Her sweet voice rippled over the airwaves like a pebble across stagnant waters. Lori recognized the tune and recalled a moment on a sizzling hot day in August a year ago . . .

• • •

Tom Hopkins sung "Hard-Hearted Hannah" to his wife, Miriam. She teasingly shooed him away with a flip of her starched apron. Lori planned a stayover with school friends, a girl's pajama party, celebrating Joy's fourteenth birthday. Joy honked the horn in her dad's car. Lori said one last goodbye before heading out the door. She caught her mom and dad in a tight embrace in the dining room threshold. Miriam's head rested on Tom's shoulder like an orphan in a storm. Lori felt oddly comforted by a sign of affection between her parents. Miriam, with a peaceful curl of her lips, beckoned Lori, who raced to give them a bear-like hug. No words. The language of familial love.

• • •

Lori listened to the engine's hum and kept silent by her Uncle Ben's side as they fell into a comfortable quietness together.

A mist of clouds eclipsed the full sun. In a flash, Lori thought of the letters. "Uncle Ben, can I ask you a question?"

"What if I said no?" He grinned.

"Then I wouldn't ask." She crossed her arms and peered out the window.

"I couldn't refuse you, Lori. Ask away." He turned onto a deserted stretch of road with a panorama of rocks, sand, and water.

"Did my dad write to you?" She focused on the passing scenery.

"Christmas cards with notes. Why?"

"Oh, Aunt Bernie let me read her letters from my dad. That's all." She turned away, self-conscious about her investigation.

"We talked a lot on the phone."

She paused. "Did you know about the bomb shelter?"

"Sure, yes. It's common in your area, right? Having a fallout shelter?"

Lori nodded. "I guess. Did he ever mention me decorating it for Christmas?"

"He did tell me about the television experiment."

"It was cool how he got it to work in the shelter."

Ben's face lit up. "Cool? Now you sound like your dad. Thomas was a wunderkind with electronics. A genius kid."

Ben parked the car in the middle of nowhere, at the end of a wide expanse of sand and sky.

Lori wiped cracker crumbs from dry lips. "There's nothing here but sand." She reached for her last cracker and examined the salty surface.

"It's your blank canvas." Ben rested his hands on the steering wheel.

"It's film, not a canvas, Uncle Ben."

"You're the camera's eye, Lorraine."

No one called her Lorraine. Ever. Even her mom wouldn't resort to the full name under a barrage of teenage tantrums. Yet, she was too flustered to defend the only moniker she recognized—Lori.

Ben handed over his camera. "Before I show you the complicated process of speed, lighting, and lens types, I want you to look at the world through the camera's view finder until the glass disappears and your eye is the only eye."

Lori peered through the lens. "Okay, I see sand. Lots and lots and lots of sand." She placed the camera in her lap. "You want me to take photos of sand?"

Ben gave his trademark grin, or smirk, as Lori silently referred to it. "I don't want you to snap any photos. Just look for now." He jumped out and was at the passenger door in a heartbeat. "C'mon, Lori. Let's discover. But keep the camera in front of your face."

Lori combated directives and authority. But Uncle Ben's voice was commanding yet gentle. And she respected his talent. Award-winning photographer. And maybe it was time to stop resisting instruction and change. It was resisting change that led her to an underground retreat. But, as Tally had reminded her at Paragon Park when they traded secrets, the underground shelter also led to her survival.

Lori stepped out, the camera pressed to the bridge of her nose. No pavement, no traffic signals, no sidewalk curbs, no tripping hazards to mar her way. "I hate to say it, Uncle Ben, but this exercise seems pointless. There's nothing but sand, a few rocks, some grass."

"Wait it out, Lori. Just wait it out." Hands in his trouser pockets, he gazed out upon the clear horizon. "I can't teach patience. It's a choice and a practiced habit."

A quarter of an hour passed. Lori's sandaled feet sifted through grains of sand and what she considered "nothingness." Her arms were tired, her spirits flattened. The seashore was not the excursion she'd anticipated during the darkest hour between night and day. Ben breathed in the salty air. A screeching seagull soared in search of a meal or any morsel washing up on the shoreline.

Lori sensed something crawling up her left arch and met the stare of a baby box turtle, newly hatched, that clambered across her foot. "Ah, Uncle Ben!"

"Don't move, Lori. Look through the camera."

"It's so small. It could fit onto a teaspoon," she said. "Wait! There's one in my lunch pail!"

"It's in the car. I'll get it," Ben said.

And then it happened. The baby box turtle climbed onto a teaspoon Lori placed underneath it. She clicked photo after photo, capturing nature and creating art. "Uncle Ben, it has bits of eggshell on its shell. It must have just hatched!"

The turtle peered at the lens with steady curiosity. The lone screeching seagull came close by. Lori kicked sand over the vulnerable turtle and snapped photos of the winged creature as it circled. An orange iridescent starfish washed up in a foamy wave.

"Uncle Ben, it's a starfish. It keeps twisting." Lori pressed the camera to her face.

"Probably devouring its meal, maybe a hermit crab. It pushes its stomach through to the outside of its body and injects its prey to kill it."

"I'm watching a murder here?" Lori moved the camera from her face.

"It's part of nature, Lori. Life and death. Moments on the continuum."

His words held no comfort. "Ready for a break? You've been steady at it for a while now."

"Okay, I am a bit hungry." She matched his mischievous grin. "Well, not as hungry as that starfish."

They slowly walked to the car. "Uncle Ben?"

"Yes, Lori?"

"It never leaves me. Everything destroyed. Sometimes I see it even before I open my eyes in the morning or before I go to sleep at night. It's like a camera. I'm the camera, and I can't ever make it disappear."

"I'm sorry, Lori. Maybe if you become a photographer, you can have enough other images to sort through and file in your memory bank. It's what we do. Photographers. The images never really leave us, but they can be crowded out. There are images I don't like, but they've become more distant. And there's time. That's all we have. Time and distance."

Lori grabbed the thermos and poured iced tea into paper cups. They raised them, rejoicing. She reached into the metal box for another silver spoon that caught the sunlight on its rim. A seagull circled above them and finally rested a few feet away.

Chapter 11

Turtle Beach

*L*ori and her Uncle Ben traveled through Beantown and its environs the next few days like two detectives searching for clues to an unsolved mystery.

On her second foray to the seashore, Lori watched and waited as the world came into focus through her lens.

Ben instructed, "Don't snap a photo yet. Be the camera."

After her third outing, Lori phoned Tally visiting family in Brooklyn.

"Hi, Tally. Thanks for accepting my call."

"You can thank my cousin, Vincent. He was curious to find out who was calling long distance."

"It is kind of late, but it's the cheaper rate."

"Seven thirty isn't too late."

Lori rearranged the bit of straw inside a crate on her nightstand. A baby box turtle poked out its head. "What's Brooklyn like?"

"Different from Boston. We had a block party last night. All the neighbors came out. How's Boston?"

"It's been a blast, Tally. I'm going to study photography in college. Maybe I'll be a teacher."

"Yeah, me too."

"I have a pet turtle."

"Really? What are you going to do with it?"

"Leave it here. My Aunt Bernie will take care of Sandra Dee until I come back."

"Sandra Dee? Like the model?"

"Yeah, and my first model."

"Okay, I better go. Thanks for calling."

"See you back in Texas."

They both smiled. *Texas really was home.*

The novelty of photography transformed into a full-fledged obsession for Lori. At sunrise, she pointed the camera beyond her bedroom window throughout the early hours. On their fourth foray, Uncle Ben whisked her away to a marketplace replete with vibrant plants, vegetables, and people. In the late afternoon, they motored again to the Cape Cod seashore with its expanse of sky, sand, and isolation. In between each photo shoot, Ben advanced her knowledge in camera complexities. She developed her own film in his darkroom and waited patiently for images to emerge, every one piecing together new memories.

Life pushed aside the pain. No time for it. Lori jotted in her diary. *Monday, July 9, 1956. Dear Diary, Time is a funny thing. Some days are filled with pain, some with peace, and then back to pain. Now I understand that pain can be a choice if I choose to relive it. For now, I choose to forget it, but, for certain, it will return.*

On their final excursion, Ben and Lori traveled to Provincetown, at the tip of Cape Cod, to a quaint community possessing art studios, community and professional theatre, wooden piers, and weathered fishermen. Ben pointed out the Cape Cod School of Art. "The first outdoor school of figure painting in America. And some famous actors walked the boards here. Bette Davis, Henry Fonda, Ruth Gordon, Humphrey Bogart, and Gertrude Lawrence."

While strolling down a narrow street, Lori spotted an artist painting the portrait of a lady with cream-colored skin and a lofty expression.

Auburn hair framed her fine cheekbones. A perfect subject. The model wore an apricot-colored cotton sweater with off-white pearl buttons. The aloof painter had a mass of blond curls piled high on his head, Cupid's bow lip, and sensitive brown eyes. He remained oblivious to Lori. She disagreed with his interpretation of the woman's likeness. Her eyes needed depth, more color, any color. They appeared gray, cold, and shallow. Maybe he saw an intangible quality unknown to the casual observer.

Lori stood there until the model gave a placid smile and a flick of her wrist, the same shooing motion Lori's mom used when annoyed. In a flash, Lori conjured up Miriam waving away her grumbling over the aluminum Christmas tree last December. Dejection hit Lori like ice-cold water thrown in her face. Her heart was newly pierced with remorse for her childish ways.

"Uncle Ben," she whispered. "I feel kind of sick. Can we leave?" Lori made an about-face and ran up the winding street to a nearby dock, tears streaming down her face. A fisherman secured his boat and rearranged nets. He was unaware of her watchful eyes. *Invisible*, she thought. *I just want to be invisible.*

She fixed her eyes on the fisherman. Before long, Ben was by her side. Neither spoke for several minutes. "Ready to go?" Ben asked.

"No. I'd like to stay here on the dock." She silently added *and be invisible.*

"Okay," Ben replied. "Hungry?"

"Not really."

"How about fresh fish?" He wasn't giving up.

"I'm not hungry." She heard the quiet rage in her voice.

Ben was indefatigable, and this was no exception. It's how he plowed through any photo assignment, whether a crying baby for a family portrait or an exotic bird that made rare appearances. "Mind if I eat?"

Lori wiped her teary eyes and faced Uncle Ben. "That woman." She choked on the words.

"A lot like your mom." Ben scanned the surroundings for an eatery.

"You noticed too?"

"Of course!" said Ben. He gazed intently at the fish shack near the pier.

"She shooed me away." Lori stepped closer to the pier's edge. Fishing fleets anchored after a predawn catch.

"I guess you were a distraction maybe." Ben watched the boats draw nigh to unload their nets. His stomach grumbled.

"I'm trying to get away from memories."

"Memories are tricky business." He sighed. "I'm ready to dive in and catch a fish myself and eat it raw."

"Well, that's kind of silly," Lori chided. She pointed to the fish shack.

"What are we waiting for, then?" Ben held out his hand. "You've got to try some. Okay?"

And, out of the blue, a caught fish leaped off the deck of a docked boat and plunged into the water, swimming with abandon.

"Look! It got away. I can't believe it," cried Lori. "How could that happen?"

Ben looked at his watch. He was due in the office in two hours to review a magazine spread of his Arizona dude ranch shoot from last month. "He's a lucky one. Let's go sit and introduce ourselves to a not-so-lucky one. Eyes and all."

"That's disgusting, Uncle Ben. A whole fish?"

"Okay, then. No eyes." They walked toward the fish shack.

At dinner that evening, Lori reported on the flopping getaway fish and nothing more about the artist's model. Sorrow dealt with and dismissed, like the flick of a wrist.

Chapter 12

Swan Song

Treasured moments filled the remaining days in Boston, but the swan boat ride capped the summer on the Thursday before their Sunday departure. At noon, Lori strolled the Public Garden with Lottie. A fleet of pontoons lined the pond like peacefully moored marine creatures.

Bernadette suggested the outing and, as always, conveyed a historical note. "They started operating in 1877."

"They're beautiful," exclaimed Lori. She and Lottie leaped on board.

The boat ride took place on a remarkably calm afternoon. The pond resembled glass. Lori rowed the oars, barely stirring the water. Lottie closed her eyes and soaked up the warm, soothing early afternoon rays. Two boats coasted by while keeping a safe distance. One had its oars lifted out of the water, a blonde head resting on a broad shoulder. The other held a young couple guarding twin toddler boys bent forward to splash the water.

Lori continued her gentle, rhythmic rowing. "If you throw in your feed, Gran, the swans will come closer. That's what Tally and I did on her last day here."

"Well, I'm glad we have this time together, sweetheart. You've been very busy in the last few days."

Lori slackened her oars and watched the two boys giggling and flapping tiny fingers in the pond. She gleamed. "Yes. I'm glad we're here."

Lottie polished her Ray-Bans with a cotton cloth. "You've got quite a mentor." She pushed the sunglasses in place as the sun heightened. "You've spent most of two weeks behind that lens."

"Yes, Gran." She inspected her camera. "It does whatever I tell it to do."

"Like an assistant." Lottie relaxed and propped up her slim legs covered in mint-green capris.

"It's that too!" Lori snapped a photo of two swans touching beaks. Every moment, she searched for the next moment to preserve.

The swans drifted closer to Lori and Lottie's pontoon. Lori disturbed the water to get their attention. She sprinkled a handful of feed, and they approached the boat, their stretched-out necks bobbing for grains.

"Gran? Do you mind me living with you?" Lori looked down into her lap.

Lottie lifted her sunglasses. "Lori, how could you even say such a thing?"

"It went through my mind this morning, and you told me not to keep things to myself." The feeding ended, and the swans floated away.

"Lori, we're a team. You're the best part of my life. You are my life."

With a door opened, Lori continued, "Why didn't you ever remarry when Grandpa died? You were kind of young."

"Kind of young?" She chuckled. "I wanted one love. I don't need anyone else in my life, dear. Besides, I have plans for us."

Lori proceeded with caution. "Like what?"

"Travel plans." Lottie readjusted her sunglasses.

"An adventure. Like Auntie Mame in the book. But you're not eccentric. So where to next?"

"We'll start out in New York and catch a few shows," Lottie said.

"And then?"

"Across the pond."

Lori clapped her hands. "London? Paris?"

"Yes, and Rome. Maybe a surprise or two."

Lori pondered the answer. She liked adventures. Not surprises. Not anymore.

A swan let out a plaintive cry. Lori picked up her camera and caught it, throat stretched out and upward, beak pointing to the sky and singing as if an audience were pitched forward and applauding the sweet sounds.

Chapter 13

Red Letter Day

On July 14, their last Saturday in Boston, Lori and Bernadette planned lunch while Lottie caught up with a few former nurse friends.

"You're still in touch?" Lori climbed into the awaiting taxi.

"One, but four of us are meeting up," Lottie said.

"Talk of old times?"

"That's right. Old ladies talkin' 'bout old times." Lottie pronounced her Virginia accent.

"Were any with you and Grandfather during the war?" Lori was only mildly interested. She was anxious for more exclusive time with Aunt Bernie before bounding homeward.

Both got in the taxi, which would drop them off at their respective destinations.

"Josie. She'll be there." Staring out the backseat window, Lottie erased the years in between . . .

• • •

At twenty-seven, Charlotte, an elementary school teacher in rural Virginia, responded to a Christmas card and invitation from a childhood friend, Josie Moore, to visit her in Boston. The Great War, in its third year, had decimated soldiers and civilians throughout Continental Europe. Despite the bone-chilling cold and bitter winds of the northeast, Charlotte grew an instant liking to Boston's urban life and returned to Virginia to make earnest goodbyes. Her anticipated departure was not received well by her mother, Alice.

"Leave now? Have you lost your mind?" Alice lamented.

"I met with Principal Williams. There are so few children in the third grade that they're thinking of combining them. You see, Ma, it's like it was meant to be. It's my fate."

"You call it fate?" She counted fingers. "Irresponsible, impetuous, irreverent."

Charlotte closed her ma's hand ever so gently. "Inspired, Ma. Believe me."

Mother and daughter locked eyes. Alice brushed a gray strand off her face. "It's because you don't have a beau, isn't it? You think you'll meet one up yonder? It's too far, Lottie. Move to Richmond and meet a nice fella. A good Christian man."

And there it was. The spinster card and Alice holding the winning hand. Charlotte, called Lottie by her mom, was defenseless on that one. They both knew it. Nearing thirty, with no marriage prospects in sight, was less than promising.

Still, Lottie held a trump card. "Pa gave me his blessing."

"Well, don't expect one from me." Alice unstiffened. "Call when you're settled in."

• • •

Lottie leaned against the taxi's leather bench seat and reminisced of Vassar Training Camp in early spring of 1918 and the three months of nurse training before being thrown into the bleak terrain of the French battlefront.

The taxi sped along, interrupting her ruminations. Boston's majestic brownstones, bathed in sunlight, took on a golden hue. They made a final turn at a busy intersection a few blocks from their destination. Traffic remained steady. The taxi driver whistled a show tune.

"What was it like?" Lori asked, biding her time along the commute.

"Boston? Exciting. Lots different from Virginia. Cold. Very cold."

"What about the war in France?"

"The first and the worst. I never expected in my life to see such pain and misery as I did near the trenches." Lottie tried her best to be ambiguous, repulsed by speaking what she witnessed at the side of her future husband, John, saving lives and limbs in makeshift hospitals. France sustained the bleakest and bloodiest battles. No one actually tallied the total deaths, deep in the millions. Lottie remembered hearing reports of nine hundred French soldiers dying every day.

"And then you got the flu, right?"

"It was the exhaustion." Lottie spared details of her short-term stay at Massachusetts General Hospital and how fever delirium raged within her like a burning furnace.

• • •

On April 6, 1917, the United States declared war on Germany and sent troops to the battlefront on the side of France and Britain. In May 1918, driven by patriotism and intensive medical training, Lottie boarded a ship bound for France with the doughboys, American marines prepared to fight the Huns.

Crossing the "great pond," she met a surgeon, John Mitchell. For Lottie— love at first sight. For John—a vision of grace and purity. Lottie's pearly whites, golden brown curls, and angelic face melted John's heart. She assisted throughout numerous surgeries, many without proper anesthetics. In June, the American marines marched blindly into an interminable blood bath at Belleau Wood, once a hunting preserve and a natural fortress of dense tree clusters. A battle raged for one month. The French retreated, and the contingent of doughboys pushed on. Nearly two thousand died and eight thousand were wounded. In a field hospital, Lottie worked eighteen-hour shifts. Many days, she leaned against John to stay on her feet assisting with rapid-fire surgeries. In early autumn, 1918, they returned to Boston and faced a different war—Spanish influenza.

Lottie, weakened and fatigued, fell victim to the epidemic within a few weeks. In Massachusetts General Hospital, a seventy-five-year-old priest, Father Mark Swift, offered the anointing of the sick, a sacrament reserved for patients days or even hours from death. John, wretched yet stoic, remained by Lottie's side.

"My dear boy, I'm sorry for so many losses. I hear you and the young lady saved many lives."

John said nothing.

The priest continued, "Is she Roman Catholic?"

A barely audible, "Yes," arose out of John's burning throat. He believed Charlotte, the preferred name for his beloved, would eventually join the Roman Catholic Church, or at least, he told himself so. Father Swift made a sign of the cross at the conclusion of his prayers. Charlotte wheezed. Her chest rose and fell. Her eyes flickered. She appeared to be actively listening and quietly responding to every prayer while grasping the black beads of a rosary given to her by a French soldier as a thank-you for saving his mangled legs.

Father Swift gave one final blessing and whispered to John, "I pray she lives."

The priest's expression seemed stern as John bowed his head respectfully and mumbled, "Thank you."

Father Mark Swift departed. A flood of peace staved off John's tears. In her subconscious, Lottie heard John plead for God to spare her life. He made an audible vow to remain by her side for the rest of her days on earth. By a miracle, Lottie fully recovered. By evening, she ingested clear chicken broth. By the next morning, she finished a plate of boiled potatoes.

• • •

"Gran? You hungry?" Lori said.

"What, dear?" she replied, foggy from her daydream.

"You didn't eat breakfast. Aren't you hungry?" Lori worried about her Gran's waning appetite and oft repeated motto—eat to live, not live to eat.

"I'm fine, dear." She gave Lori a peck on the cheek and held out a few dollars from her purse. "Here's your cab fare home after lunch. The hostess will call one for you."

The cab pulled up as Bernadette waited on the sidewalk. She bent into the cab door. "Thanks for getting Lori here."

Lori climbed out of the backseat. "You can thank Barnie!"

Bernadette offered her hand to Barnie the cab driver. "Pleased to meet you. I'm Bernie."

"Pleased to meet you. I can schedule a pickup at 1:30," he said. "Want to make sure the little lady gets home safe and sound."

Lori flashed a wide grin. "Is that enough time, Aunt Bernie?"

"Make it 2:00 p.m." Bernadette hugged her niece. "You're leaving tomorrow! I want as much time as I can get with you."

Lori looked jubilant that the self-admitted workaholic had devoted the afternoon to her.

"See you at two o'clock sharp, young lady." Barnie checked his side mirrors and reentered a traffic stream. He winked and deepened wrinkles etched around lively brown eyes. "Time to yourself, huh?"

Lottie smiled. "The Statler."

Barnie changed lanes. "Statler Hilton? Got bought out by Hilton almost two years ago. When were you last here?"

"It's been a while."

Lottie arrived early, ordered a cocktail, and settled into the Statler Hilton's expansive and refashioned lounge area. She sipped a perfect gin martini with a twist and equal parts dry and sweet vermouth. She twirled her spiked olive and recalled the Statler's grand opening in 1927 as the largest hotel in all New England . . .

• • •

John Mitchell discovered the demands on a heart surgeon were limitless. To safeguard his well-being, he arranged out-of-the-blue weekends with his darling Charlotte. She would telephone her confidante, Josie, and drop off an unsuspecting Miriam on a Friday afternoon. "Stealing away," she called it.

*Like lovebirds released from separate cages, John and Lottie rendez-
voused at the Statler, spotting each other in the crowded lobby, the din of
conversations swirling above, beneath, and around. The weekend getaways
rekindled their romance and the torch of desire hearkening back to their
first kiss. Many times, they held hands and said nothing, their hearts filled
to bursting. The glow of candlelight cast shadows on his chiseled face as
they wined on champagne and dined on Welsh rarebit, one of her favorites.*

. . .

Decades later, the hotel was still recognizable. Lottie sipped her martini
and reminisced. A vivid image of John's smoldering good looks flashed
through her mind.

"Charlotte?" A few feet away, a silver-haired Josie quickened her step.
The two embraced, wiped away tears and the years in between.

Meanwhile, in the North End, Lori and Bernadette found a secluded
table in the crowded restaurant. Lori studied her menu at leisure. Hints
of oregano and garlic wafted through swinging doors from the frantic
kitchen. "Why don't we share a pizza pie?"

Bernadette closed her menu. The waiter advanced, hands behind his
back, like an inspector or establishment owner. He sported a handlebar
mustache, waxed at the tips, and a red-and-gold vest of shimmering
brocade. "Are you two lovely ladies ready to order?"

"Hi, Giuseppe. We'll share a medium pizza. Hold the cheese on half
and add anchovies."

"*Bene*, Signorina Bernadette." A canyon-wide smile. "A glass of vino,
perhaps?"

"Two iced teas, *per favore*," Bernadette's hands rested on her pointy
chin.

Lori observed another side to her aunt, lighthearted and a bit flir-
tatious. She wondered why Aunt Bernie and the youthful waiter were
on a first-name basis.

"What are anchovies?" Lori asked.

"Fish. Italians have been putting fish on bread for over two thousand years."

"Oh."

"An acquired taste." Bernadette handed Giuseppe the menus and a smile to match his own.

Giuseppe performed a sweeping bow and slowly backed away. A mustached, burly waiter bustled by and nearly knocked him over. "*Guardi dove va!*" he scolded. "*El stupido!*"

"He called him stupid!" Lori whispered.

"It's his Uncle Mario. He's hard on him." Bernadette opened a compact mirror and powdered her nose.

"How do you know him?"

"I met Giuseppe when I was in college. I taught English to youth. He was fifteen and close to dropping out of high school. I worked with him. His English improved, and he finished high school. I was so proud of him."

Lori persisted in a low voice, as if speaking to a co-conspirator. "He's twenty-two?"

"Yes."

Giuseppe reappeared with a tray of tall, frosty glasses. "*Tè freddo,* Signorina Bernadette." He flashed a winsome smile and set the second beverage in front of Lori. "Signorina?"

Bernadette gestured. "This is my niece, Lori."

"*Mi piacere.*" Giuseppe's bent-at-the-waist bow seemed excessive to Lori. Her cheeks flushed. "Pizza will be up soon." He exited in haste.

"Why is he speaking in Italian?"

Giuseppe looked wistfully in Lori's direction. She noticed his wide shoulders and tapered torso, like an Olympic swimmer. Light brown hair, perfectly coiffed, gleamed with gold highlights.

Uncle Mario wrung his hands and wagged his head. "Giuseppe, *tu sei un flirt!*"

Giuseppe shrugged his shoulders before checking his lunch orders. "*E un amica, Zio!*"

Mesmerized by the interplay, Lori said. "His uncle called him a flirt!"

"I didn't know I had a Nancy Drew on my hands. You'd make a good investigative reporter. Okay. I'll give you the story. Giuseppe is going to night school to learn how to run a business. He wants to buy this restaurant. His father is the manager, but not the owner. His Uncle Mario thinks he's too ambitious. Giuseppe lives at home and saves every dollar to make a down payment and hopefully get a loan."

Almost on cue, Giuseppe set a pizza pie on a stand. Half was embedded with silvery fish. Lori wrinkled her nose in disapproval. "Those are the anchovies?"

"*Si*, Signorina. I don't like them either." Her sour expression transmitted its own unsullied charm. "Is there anything else you'd like?" Lori's bashful beam endeared him further.

"Another tea, please."

"*Si*, Signorina Lori." He removed her glass and disappeared between tables.

"He remembered my name."

Bernie helped herself to the anchovy pizza. "Care to try it?"

"Ah, no thank you." Lori reached for a piece of traditional pie with spicy red sauce and puddles of mozzarella cheese.

"Let's eat! I have something to tell you, about the letters."

Meanwhile, Lottie listened to the chatter of valued friends catching up on private matters. Sitting quietly, an image came to mind of Miriam, her only child. When Miriam was born, Charlotte had believed her joy would be complete. But a colicky baby had set her on edge, even more than a soldier screaming out from a nightmare.

As a three-year-old, Miriam had exhibited a restless and fretful demeanor. She was a pretty girl with rich auburn hair, rosy cheeks, and eyes like glinting sea glass washed ashore. The charming exterior had concealed her demanding nature. She'd rock back and forth chanting her wishes until a favorite doll or treat materialized. Countless times,

Charlotte had longed for her days as a nurse, especially when John was on call for emergency surgeries.

Before wedded bliss and Miriam's arrival, they had worked side by side in makeshift hospitals. Both possessed a deep passion for saving lives, no matter how torn or disfigured the victim in their skilled hands. Their faith had grown strong. God was using them as instruments.

In the hotel lobby, the former nurses chatted as Lottie retreated, sunk down in the lounge chair, and disappeared into her private recollections. She never imagined pain from rekindling these friendships. *Oh, how fragile we are*, she thought, cradling her empty glass.

Bernadette relished her pizza with anchovies. "So here we are, back where we started. Good choice."

"I like it here. I mean the restaurant," Lori replied. "I'm not sure about Boston. I hear it's really cold."

"Well, I can't argue that one," Bernadette said. Giuseppe checked back on them. "Giuseppe, what do you think of Boston winters?"

He served a second round of iced tea. *"Troppo fredda!"*

"Hmm, that doesn't sound good," Lori said.

"You don't speak Italian? I could teach you, Signorina Lori."

"Lori's from Texas. She's visiting," Bernie said.

"Ah? Texas? The Lone Star state? Buddy Holly."

Uncle Mario lurked behind.

"You know Buddy Holly?" Lori gasped in mid-chew. "He's from my town. We went to the same high school." She clasped her hands in sheer delight.

"Everything okay, Signorina Bernadette?" Mario asked. His manner was grave while giving Giuseppe the evil eye.

"Uncle! A spill, so I came to wipe it up. Enjoy your pizza and your day." He bowed like a magician after his final trick and vanished.

Mario apologized. "Giuseppe talks a lot."

Lori, miffed at the interruption, came to his defense. "Not at all. He's very attentive, right, Aunt Bernie?"

"Everything's fine, Mario," said Bernadette.

Mario backed up and made his way to another table of customers.

Lori sprouted a fondness for Italian ambiance and fare in contrast to the Hopkins household that served up Yankee pot roast, baked beans, brown bread, or bland variations of meat and potatoes.

"Lori, before you leave, I want you to know that I never mentioned to anyone what your dad wrote to me." The somberness in Bernadette's voice was unbearable to Lori. She wanted the past to remain in the past, at least for now.

"Do you have to bring that up now?" Lori scanned the dining area for a distraction.

"I don't want you to think I mentioned the letters to anyone, okay?"

"Doesn't matter anymore." Her feigned insouciance created a slight barrier between them. "I do have a favor to ask, though." Lori kept the topic of letters buried. "Will you take care of Sandra Dee? Until I come back?"

"My granddaughter is the same age as yours, Charlotte." Josie spoke between bites of veal cutlet and golden mashed potatoes with a sizeable pool of melted butter. Lottie picked at her salad. She'd lost her taste for meat dishes after battleground surgeries and preferred leafy greens and crisp julienne-sliced vegetables with a simple olive oil dressing. Josie dug into her handbag and pulled out a fat wallet stuffed with receipts and family photos. She flipped to one, drew a picture from its sheath and passed it to Lottie. "Elizabeth, my granddaughter, but she goes by Betsy."

Lottie examined the pocket-sized portrait—a profile of an ethereal blonde with an upwardly tilted nose, pouty lips, and a lush fringe of eyelashes.

"She's lovely." Lottie passed around the photo.

"Betsy wants to be a stage actress. Studies voice, dance, and acting at Juilliard in New York."

"We'd love to see Lori's photo!" Martha said.

Lottie should've been prepared. Family photos were compulsory when visiting friends rarely seen. She placed a radish rose on her fork. "Actually, I don't have any with me." She suppressed an apology, an automatic reaction to disappointing others.

Josie folded hands with Lottie and held on in a tight and reassuring clasp. "Charlotte, I know words can't express how sorry we are for you and Lori. What happened to Miriam and Tom was such a shock to all of us. I didn't want to bring it up, but I couldn't let this time go by without saying something."

Lottie blinked back tears, her hands enfolded in Josie's. Lottie communicated without words—*we need to talk.* The message came through as Josie released her grip.

"I must say, Charlotte, you have a figure of a teenage girl. What's your secret?" Martha asked.

"I've come to believe you are what you eat." Lottie quickly adjusted to the formal name she hadn't heard so regularly since John passed away five years ago.

"Well, imagine that," Martha said. An attentive waiter set a generous block of Neapolitan ice cream in front of her nose. He poured her a second cup of coffee and added a splash of cream. "Three more forks, please?"

Bernadette reached for another slice. "I can pick off the anchovies if you'd like . . . ?" Lori listened with half an ear and eyes on Giuseppe wiping a nearby table. ". . . as I was saying, southern Italians came to Boston and other cities. Very poor, couldn't speak English. They worked hard and organized labor unions . . ." Bernadette placed her half-eaten slice on the plate. "Lori?"

"Hmm? What?"

"You're not listening." Bernadette traced Lori's focus to a cleared table behind her.

"Yes, I am." Lori picked up a string of mozzarella cheese sprinkled with oregano flakes. "You asked if I wanted anchovies."

"Okay, topic change. Wait until you see the music center tonight. The best students from every state and international. Perfect send-off."

"Aunt Bernie, I'm really sorry to be leaving. I like Boston." She confided in a low, almost hoarse voice, choking back emotion. "I have nothing left in Texas."

Giuseppe reappeared. "May I interest two beautiful ladies in a dish of spumoni?"

"Spumoni? Is it anything like anchovies?" Lori was instantly mortified by her silly remark.

Giuseppe answered with a mischievous grin. "No, but I can add some if you like, Signorina Lori."

"Sure, we have time for spumoni," Bernadette said.

Lori blurted out, "What does *Giuseppe* mean? In English?"

Brown eyes, glimmering with gold specs, held their own version of a smile. "Joseph. It means Joseph. Hebrew for, 'Jehovah increases.'"

"Well, someone's listening, because your customers had increased," replied Lori, enchanted and emboldened.

Uncle Mario seated ten bankers and waved frantically at Giuseppe.

Martha, Fannie, Josie, and Lottie bid their goodbyes with affectionate hugs and kisses.

Josie lingered behind. "I'll catch up with you later, Fannie. Martha it was wonderful seeing you. We must get together again soon."

"It was wicked good seeing you, Charlotte. You haven't aged in thirty years. I want to know your secret," said Martha.

Fannie was all merriment, her usual demeanor. "She told us already. You are what you eat. Let's go and let our two southern ladies spend time together."

They exchanged one last round of heartfelt embraces and parted ways, leaving Lottie and Josie alone in the lobby lounge.

"Do you know how much I miss you, dear southern lady?"

Lottie signaled the waiter. "I'm still in shock, Josie. Both of us are."

"Tell me more about Miriam. You were so concerned in your last few letters."

Their waiter appeared instantaneously. "Gin martini, please. Stirred. Make it dry. A twist of lemon." Lottie's melodic voice brought an automatic smile to anyone she greeted.

The waiter turned to Josie. "And for you, madame?"

"An iced tea, lemon and sugar on the side."

Tyrone made straight for the bar, and Lottie confided, "She was a nervous wreck, especially when everything was fine. She thrived on chaos, even buying that damn aluminum Christmas tree that upset Lori." The waiter reappeared with a tall glass of iced tea, a saucer dish of lemon quarters, a porcelain sugar bowl with a decorative silver spoon, and an extra dry martini on his tray. He carefully placed all the items on the table and made his exit.

Lottie continued, "The more things she bought, the unhappier she was, like a void that couldn't be filled."

"And Tom?" Josie squeezed lemon juice into her beverage.

Lottie un-skewered the lemon slice into her cocktail. She relaxed with Josie, no guard up, no pretense. "Oh, he was pleasant enough, too pleasant." Lottie inspected her glass. Ordering one martini, let alone a second, was a rarity. She discovered alcohol a disturbing form of relaxing the mind, making her judgment foggy.

Josie waited patiently for more story. "Poor Miriam. Did she ever settle down in Texas?"

"Miriam was never comfortable in her own skin. It didn't matter where she lived or what she was doing." Lottie examined her drink. "Josie?"

"Yes, Lottie?"

"Remember soldiers screaming and shaking from nightmares or moaning in pain?" Lottie set down her glass.

"Do I? Fists pounding into walls or bed frames. Kicking and screaming. I don't think I met one who slept through the night." Josie shivered.

"I had dreams of the fields. They'd start out peaceful. Wheat shafts waving in a breeze. And then the trees in the woods would move, and the sky would go dark gray, and raindrops would fall. But it wasn't rain. They were drops of blood and then a torrent, a downpour. I'd wake up soaked in sweat. So afraid." Lottie paused. "You know, I had those dreams when pregnant with Miriam. I think that's why she was such an anxious child, Josie. My dreams. The terror and fear. I was communicating it all to her."

"Charlotte, you're a nurse. You know that's highly unlikely."

"Yes, I know, but the flu weakened me. I think Miriam was born with stress from my trauma."

Josie studied Lottie's lovely visage burdened by worry and sadness. "Charlotte, you were the best mother."

"I wasn't, Josie. I wasn't the best mother. You know that." Lottie swirled her martini. "I was bored, restless."

"You did your best. She was your life. Lori is your life. My goodness, you moved to Texas!"

"Because John died." Lottie took a hard swallow of her drink.

"You're looking at all of this in hindsight, Charlotte. And the shock of losing Miriam. You'll question everything now." Josie pitched forward with concern for her troubled friend.

Lottie put down her martini. "No, Josie. I've had these thoughts for years now, ever since moving to Texas and observing how anxious she was and the prescription bottles filling the medicine cabinet. It's like she created her little wars with Lori, buying that fake tree. Such a silly thing, but that was it. They'd battle over the silliest things."

"Teenagers and moms, Charlotte. They'll find something to fight over. Remember the good times for now," Josie consoled. "I mourn Ernie's death every day. I even speak to him out loud. Of course, he hasn't answered me yet."

Josie and her light touch, shining humor into a dark corner. The two Virginians sat in silence, survivors of change, soldiering the battle against loneliness and the loss of loved ones. She plopped lemon slices into her iced tea. "I wasn't the best mother, Charlotte. I have two children who hate each other. They don't even speak when they visit on holidays. They sit in separate rooms. It's horrible."

"What? You can't blame yourself for that one. People are stubborn and unforgiving over the slightest infractions, especially in families."

Josie resisted a grin. "There you go again, using those fifty-cent words. You always were smarter than me."

Lottie brightened up. "Well, Josie, that's the first time you've ever admitted it."

"You mean you agree with me?"

"Not at all!" Lottie relaxed. "But I don't mind hearing it."

"Well, I guess not," Josie said. "Now that we've bared our souls, let's make a pact to meet again. In New York."

Lottie raised her glass in a grand salute, shoulders and spine aligned. "New York."

Josie straightened up at attention. They were two girls from Virginia—innocent, wide-eyed, patriotic. The years in between collapsed somewhere in time and space. She lifted her glass. "In . . . Indu . . ."

"Indubitably!" Lottie curbed a chuckle that reached her very soul.

Bernadette revisited the subject at hand. "Are you angry with me for sharing the letters?"

"Why would I be?" Lori attempted a casual and unaffected response.

"I don't know. Maybe because I'm now questioning it myself."

"It's done." Lori dabbed a paper napkin across her lips.

"I hope you come back. I really do." Bernadette signaled Giuseppe.

"I have to for Sandra Dee."

"Oh yes, Sandra Dee, my new acquaintance. I promise I'll read up on turtle care." Bernadette dug for her wallet.

"I'll be back soon. Maybe for Christmas. We'll see." She didn't reveal her tentative arrangements to accompany Uncle Ben on an assignment for a *National Geographic* feature photographing the best ski resorts in Vermont. She'd try to convince Grandma Lottie to return to Boston so she could firm up her plans.

"Christmas?" Bernadette took the bill from an attentive Giuseppe. "That's not far off and a long way to travel for a few days."

"Not if it's five days. We'll see."

"I hope you do come back soon, Miss Lori." Giuseppe made a final bow. "Maybe we'll have a white Christmas for you."

Chapter 14

Texas Toast

Throughout Lori's Boston stay, Ben had a second shadow. She was an exceedingly eager apprentice, throwing herself into tasks with unbridled enthusiasm. Partly, it was an escape from the pain of loss. Nevertheless, she was hooked from the moment a baby box turtle stared up from a teaspoon.

For the five days he traveled on special assignment, she visited a local library and researched theories on photography and studied the proper techniques for black and white versus color. She absorbed information like a sponge. Grandma Penny described it as "a blossoming in Boston." No one in the Hopkins family was happier than its matriarch, Penny, to behold Lori's transformation—more like an epiphany. Lori's worldview shifted. The ordinary held the extraordinary. Don't give up. Never give up. But on what, she didn't know. Maybe people, maybe plans, maybe life itself.

Fourteenth of July. One final evening in Boston. The entire Hopkins family—Bernadette, Olivia, Portia a.k.a. Rose, Edward, Farley, Ben, and their families—jammed around tables in the kitchen, dining room, and living room.

Following an early dinner of franks and beans, Lori confided in Lottie as they dried and stacked dinner plates. "I'm going to be a photojournalist."

"A journalist?" Lottie witnessed the instant attraction to photography in her granddaughter, but not to writing. As a freshman, Lori had agonized over homework papers, whether they were three hundred-word essays or lengthy research projects.

"How else can I describe what I see?" Lori asked.

A concert at the Berkshire Music Center, sponsored by the Boston Symphony, was Penny's idea as a last night celebration in Beantown. Lori sat between her two grandmothers and fanned herself with a neatly pleated concert program. She whispered to Grandma Lottie. "Feels like Texas."

Penny, seated on the other side of Lori, overheard the comment. "It's the hottest day on record. But I'll take it after three snowstorms last March."

Lori reverted attention to the sweet, powerful resonance and vibrations of the finishing piece, maybe Beethoven, possibly Mozart. She didn't recognize or pretend to know classical music. The airy sounds evoked an emotional response. The plucking of violin and harp strings, the blasts of trumpets, the trill of a flute, all blended or singled out with imageries of swans, turtles, and molasses pouring down a city street. And then red-haired models wearing pearl-encrusted wedding dresses. And, finally, the letters from her dad. They materialized like clef notes and melody lines on music sheets. The letters she'd carry back to Texas. And for what? They were read, exposed, anything but secret, now uncovered. What would she do with them?

The musical protégés from all over the country and the world bowed to thunderous claps and shouts of "Bravo!"

Penny and Lottie, separated by Lori, leaned in to each other.

"They're kids!" Lottie searched the ground for the program that had slipped out of her lap.

"Nineteen from out of the country too. Four hundred study every summer here at the Music Center. Did you enjoy it, Lori?" Penny asked.

"Let's visit again at Christmas. Are there more concerts then?' Lori restrained her enthusiasm.

"Christmas?" Lottie was taken aback. "So soon?" *Yes, too soon,* she thought, the first anniversary of a Christmas without Miriam and Tom. "We'll see."

"Fair enough." A seed planted and left to fate, she drew each grandma into a soul-satisfying embrace.

Lori packed clothes in her Cape-Way blue leather suitcase, a gift from Aunt Bernie. She held up the red dress, an impulsive purchase, and considered how unstylish it would look in a year or two. Thoughts turned to Tally and their awkward, self-conscious disrobing behind a makeshift curtain. They had formed an easy bond and promised to be in touch back home.

Lori left Boston changed in mind, body, and spirit. A shift took place, and she didn't know exactly when. Maybe the moment Tally had walked through the Hopkins kitchen archway and filled the tall and small space with her magnanimity. Oh, she'd resented it at first, like Texas and all things tormenting her and chasing her to Boston. Maybe it was the carousel ride. Maybe Grandma Lottie's sad yet serene face. *How miserable I've been,* she thought. *I lost my mom. She lost her only child.* Lori made a pact with herself to ease up on Grandma Lottie, even if it meant keeping her mouth shut tight until she exploded.

At touchdown, the plane skidded to a screeching halt. The beleaguered passengers gasped a collective sigh of relief after intermittent turbulence throughout their flight. They stepped off the plane, and a hot wind welcomed them back to Texas. Lori stuffed five hastily written postcards, compliments of the flight, into her skirt pocket. Lottie prayed for continued peace in their household.

The two weary travelers were anxious to arrive home. Their neighbors Betty and Sam Spencer picked them up from the airport. Lori shuffled through her United Airlines postcards and reread her greetings.

"How many postcards did you write?" Lottie inquired.

"Five. Grandma Penny, Aunt Bernie, Uncle Ben, Tally, and Joy's sister, Ruth. She's eight years old."

Lottie kept quiet. She remembered Joy's grief-stricken parents, blaming themselves for her death by granting a visit to Lori's Christmas shelter. The "if only" sentiment was a difficult one to remedy, and Lottie decided it best to leave them be as they dealt with remorse, confusion, and deep sorrow.

"That's nice," Lottie replied now, at a loss for meaningful words.

"Joy's parents aren't speaking to us. I have to start somewhere." Lori sighed. "I think I'm ready for school. I miss my friends."

Lottie thanked Betty and Sam for the ride. Lori collected their bags, luggage, and one prized possession—the Kodak Tourist II camera strapped around her neck. She snapped a photo of Grandma Lottie's house. "This one's for me. I'll call it the house of love."

Lori bounded through the front door. Lottie wiped away an unexpected tear.

"There is an appointed time for everything, and a time for every affair under the heavens. A time to be born, and a time to die . . ." Gerald read the passage over and over before closing what his Aunt Merle referred to as "the Good Book," the family Bible, passed down from three generations of Rogerses, his mother's surname. God spoke to him, leading to daily prayer, scripture, and hopefully, keeping his mind off Lori, who had wormed her way into his heart throughout the summer. Warring thoughts. God called him in the morning during prayer. In his mind's eye, he blinked away Lori, the girl with strawberry blonde hair framing her hauntingly sad visage. He read again. *"A time to weep, and a time to laugh, a time to mourn, and a time to dance."*

He intended on asking Lori to the Lubbock High Homecoming Dance and hoped beyond measure that Tally mentioned his hello during her Boston visit. If Lori had thought of him once over the summer, he'd be happy, for it was torture to think she was indifferent to him. If absence made the heart grow fonder, he was living proof!

Gerald closed the Good Book for a third time. He zipped up the leather-bound cover and set it on a redwood table. The day was sweltering and dusty, a film of fine dirt on everything in sight, especially the wood railing and steps. From a distance, his older sister Barbara's hazy silhouette drew closer. Home from college, she worked as a manicurist in a local hair salon. Her own nails were bitten to the quick, not much of an advertisement for her summer trade as pointed out by the salon owner. But a winning smile dazzled customers, and her attentive ear made them feel special as they unloaded their stories, secrets, or bits of gossip. Barbara studied psychology and wanted to work as a high school counselor.

"Still mooning over your sweetheart?" Barbara stepped onto the front porch.

"She's not my sweetheart, and how do you know about her, anyway?"

"Don't you remember, Gerry? The note you wrote? You wanted my opinion." She rubbed her neck, sore from brushing nail polish on a few dozen hands per day.

"That was months ago, and you're jumping to conclusions."

"Lighten up." She curled up on the glider's overstuffed chintz cushions made of a sun-faded yellow rosebuds print. Barbara was a younger version of her mother, Norma. She cropped her hair, while Norma's snowy white tresses flowed to mid-back. Barbara dreaded the Rogers curse of silver or white hair fringing an unwrinkled, twenty-five-year-old face. For now, at eighteen, she had no signs of what she'd termed as "inhairitance." Even so, she kept her crowning glory razor short with little evidence of its silky, straight-as-a-pin texture. At age fifteen, she'd worn it shoulder length, the longest ever. At least two dozen barrettes slipped through during a hot, dry summer, and she'd adopted an annoying habit of head jerks to keep a black curtain of hair out of vivid jade-green eyes.

"Thumping that Bible, huh?" Barbara dangled a long, muscular leg, prompting the glider back and forth. "Count me out, preacher."

Gerald deflected her slight. "How's Mom?"

Barbara swung wildly, the glider creaking and whining. "Crazy as a bedbug. She's in a confinement room. They should pad the walls and put bars on the door."

"She's getting worse?" He rested the book of Scripture on his lap.

"What? You think that book is going to make her sane? I don't know what she did to God, but he sure isn't smiling down on her, or us for that matter."

"How can you say that? We have a roof over our heads and a good family here."

Barbara knew he was right. *Life could be much worse.* Their Uncle Preston had stepped in when his sister, Norma Wilkins, returned for a final time to a revolving door existence at a nearby state-run mental institution. Richard Wilkins, a traveling encyclopedia salesman, had convinced himself he was unequipped to care for his children. He had abandoned Gerald and Barbara, affectionately known as Babs. Gerald was eight and Babs was twelve when they resettled to Preston's sprawling ranch with livestock and the resplendent riches proffered from Texas gold. Uncle Preston's wife, Merle, had incorporated the orphaned duo into their family of three children, Jake, Mary Ellen, and Samuel, all grown and ready to launch their own destinies.

Barbara inspected her bitten nails. "They've started electric shock therapy. I'm against it, but Uncle Preston signed the papers, so it's a done deal. She's had two treatments."

"When can I see her?"

"Gerry, we've been through this too many times. She said she doesn't want you there. She barely speaks to me. I don't know why I visit!" Barbara swung fiercely. "Just forget it, okay? Forget her! She wants us to forget her and move on."

Gerald looked out at the horizon. The blazing hot sun bleached the landscape white, almost as white as snow. Back to Ecclesiastes. *"For in much wisdom, there is much sorrow; whoever increases knowledge increases grief."* He bent his head low. "I want what's best for her, that's all."

Barbara eased up. She loved her brother as she would say, "to pieces." Remorse tightened her chest knowing Gerald remained cheerless and broken-hearted by not seeing his mom. "She has the best doctors, and she does ask about you, Gerry. She doesn't want any visitors. She only sees me for family updates, and she doesn't get along with Uncle Preston, so there you have it."

Gerald flipped pages to Paul's Letter to the Ephesians. *"Blessed be God the Father of our Lord Jesus Christ, who has blessed us with all the spiritual blessings of heaven in Christ."* He looked up. "I'm going to ask her to the Homecoming dance in September. Don't tell anyone."

"Who would I tell?" She stopped the glider. "I leave in two weeks for college."

"I know."

"I'll miss you." Her voice cracked with emotion. "You know that, right?"

Gerald, unblinking, attempted a brave smile. "Yeah, I know."

She stooped down and put her head on the chair's armrest.

Gerald touched the top of her bristly scalp. "Are you going to keep the crew cut?"

"It's not a crew cut! It's the gamin look. All the rage in Paris, London, and New York. Write or call if you need me. Don't even hesitate, do you hear me?"

"But you'll be in Houston."

"Close enough," Barbara said.

Chapter 15

School Daze

A new school year, and Lori met Tally the night before to size up their first-day outfits. Lori decided on a light gray blouse, navy blue A-line skirt, and oxblood penny loafers. Tally wore a yellow shirtwaist dress.

"That's something I'd wear," Lori said.

"And the gray and dark blue looks like something I'd wear." Tally twirled barefooted. "I'd switch with you, but I'm at least two sizes bigger."

"No, I like the change. I'm tired of pastels."

"You'll be a smash at the homecoming dance in that red dress." Tally made one last turn.

"If I go." Lori dove onto her chenille bed cover.

"If you don't go, I'm not going." Tally folded her arms.

"What if someone asks you?"

"Who me? No one's going to ask me. I'm not even sure I fit in here." Tally rubbed sleepy eyes.

"Well, you better start!" Lori tossed a sampler embroidered pillow Tally's way.

Tally hugged the cross-stitched pillow to her chest. "Gerry's going to ask you to the dance. Will you go with him?" She danced with her improvised partner.

Lori reclined on her bed and tucked both arms under her head.

"School hasn't even started yet, and the dance isn't until next month. How do you know he'll ask me?" She had little interest in the topic.

Tally threw the pillow back to Lori, hitting her square in the face. "Why else would he ask about you and make sure I told you hi? He must be thinking about you."

Lori jolted up. "But that was in June."

Tally maintained her stance. "I'm sure he's thinking of you all the time."

Lori suffered an unexpected wave of exhaustion. "Can we change the subject? Shoes! What shoes go with maize?"

"Maize?"

"Like corn or butter. Wait, I've got it. A pair of black flats!"

"Perfect!" said Tally. "Sorry I hit you."

"That's okay. If I didn't know better, I'd say you were jealous."

"Ouch! That hurt." Tally bristled before brightening up. "Okay. Even…"

Lori reclined again. "Steven."

The following morning, Lori attempted a confident stride while repeatedly tucking in her silky blouse. Suddenly, she felt distant, plain, and hollow. She had barely made it through the spring semester before escaping to Boston. Now, on the other side of summer, she proceeded to a new homeroom with doubts and fears consuming her.

And then, turning the corner in the hallway and in her life, she pictured her Boston family. A calm overtook her like waves folding and curling against a sandy shoreline. She'd make it through the school year and back to Boston and Sandra Dee.

At lunchtime, Lori sighted the maize-colored dress in the crowded entrance to the cafeteria. She caught up with Tally and tugged on her sleeve.

"Hi, remember me?"

"Lori, I looked for you in between classes. What happened?"

"I vamoosed for a while, that's all."

Tally was incredulous and whispered back, "You could get suspended. Where'd you go?"

"I hitched a ride."

"You what?" Tally shrieked.

Lori and Tally worked their way into the line. "I hitched a ride to my old house."

"But why?"

"To make peace." Lori's eyes searched the crowd, unsure of who or what she was looking for, or if she wanted further interrogation.

They entered the cafeteria and joined the pack of students picking up trays.

"What'll ya have, sweetie?" said Marge Lyman, a school institution for thirty years. Her mousy wisps of hair, caught in a net, gave her a severe look softened by kind gray eyes.

"I'll have a hot dog and fries." Tally tapped her feet, impatient to hear more of Lori's truancy.

"How 'bout you?" Marge asked.

"Same," Lori said.

Marge slid two identical plates in front of them.

Gerald stood like a sentinel at the end of the line, a bowl of chili on his tray.

"May I sit with you?" Gerald asked.

Lori hemmed and hawed.

"Sure, for maybe five minutes," Tally replied. "We have to run off."

He hesitated. "It's the first day back. Where are you heading?"

"Checking into a class," Tally added. "We might want to change an elective."

Lori was vexed by his interrogation. *Let it go*, she told herself.

"Okay, I'll check in with you tomorrow. Hope it all works out." He vanished into the crowd.

Lori and Tally dashed for a table's empty corner. They gobbled down hot dogs and split an order of fries. On the way out, Tally spotted Tim Gordon seated in close range. A few times, she'd seen him searching sidewalks and streets for crown bottle caps to trade for pocket change. The Gordons were dirt poor, and Tally guessed, many nights, Tim went without dinner.

"Hi, Tim. Would you like my fries?" Tally asked.

Tim bit a bruised apple and whiffed the thick, deep-fried potatoes. "Fries? Sure!"

With purposeful strides, Lori and Tally headed for the vacant school courtyard. Tally sat on a low brick wall. "Okay, so tell me why you went back there. I mean there's nothing left, right?"

Lori pointed to Tally's shoes. "Black flats."

"I was up till midnight looking for them. But you're off subject." Tally stretched out her legs and flexed her feet. "I hear they're turning the tornado site into a park."

"My birthday's coming up. Fifteen on the fifteenth. My first alone. Without Mom and Dad. It's not even been a year."

"Yeah, I know. You're off subject again. Why did you go back, and who gave you a ride?"

"I needed to see it and . . . Okay, I'll tell you because you're really being pushy," Lori said.

"I'm not being pushy." Tally folded her arms in defiance.

"You are!" Lori's tone was shrill. "Okay, the day of the tornado, Joy came to see me."

"Yes, I know," Tally said.

"Would you let me tell it?"

"Okay, go on."

"I gave her a strand of garland. Poinsettias. Cotton velvet ones. I found the garland. I thought maybe she threw it away, and I was mad at her. I didn't know she was in my house when the storm hit until a few days later. I kept the garland. Now I don't want it, but I can't throw it away. I can't." Lori sat next to Tally. "So I clawed at the spot where the underground shelter is, and I buried it right there. Like a marker. Maybe a memorial. I'll always know it's there."

"Will you go back?"

Lori answered as if she anticipated the question. "No, never. It's done. There's nothing more."

The school bell rang, interrupting their tête-à-tête.

"C'mon, let's go." Tally jumped from the wall. "What about the ride?"

"Oh, Abi's sister. She had her dad's car." Lori examined the dirt under her fingernails. "The maize dress looks nice."

"Cut it out!" Tally brushed off her skirt. "I feel like a big corn husk."

"Okay. Lemon."

"Why not plain old yellow?" Tally slipped on a tight black shoe. "Tomorrow, we sit with Gerry." She jabbed Lori's ribs. "Didn't I tell you?"

Lori rearranged her skirt. "Honestly, he's the least of my problems."

"Yeah, I can see. How many times are you going to tuck in that shirt?" Tally said in mock seriousness.

"News flash. Your shirtwaist is maize."

"Even!" Tally exclaimed.

"Steven!" Lori replied.

The following day, when the lunch bell rang, Gerald sprinted down a stairwell to the dining area. After five minutes with no Lori in sight, he joined the growing line and grabbed a hot dog and bottle of Coke. While carrying his tray between neat rows of tables, he heard Lori chatting with friends.

He casually approached Lori's lunchtime enclave of Tally, Abigail, and Jane. "Hi, I didn't see you come in." His look of surprise, if not shock, didn't go unnoticed. The soft, loose reddish-gold curls framing her face were gone. She appeared nothing like the teenage girl in his daydreams during idle summer days. "Lori? I didn't recognize you."

She held up a spoonful of Texas chili. "Oh, yeah, I cut my hair."

He scratched the back of his neck and blurted out, "Why?"

"Why not?"

"It looks fab," Jane said. "Like Audrey Hepburn."

"Actually, I did a hack job. My grandma straightened it out." Lori plunged the spoon into the spicy meat and stifled a chuckle. *I have my own bowl of red, the one above my shoulders!*

Gerald shuffled. "Well, uh, I can see you're busy right now. Can you meet me at the library after school?"

Lori scraped the last bit of chili. "Sorry, can't do."

"Then tomorrow? After school?"

"I guess. I'll let you know if I can't make it."

"Your hair, it looks a lot like my sister's."

"Is that a compliment?" Lori pushed away the empty bowl.

"Well, my sister likes it. Uh, okay. Have a nice evening, ladies." With haste, he searched for a seat at any table away from Lori and her friends.

Jane chortled. "*Ladies*? What's that all about?"

"He's going to ask her to homecoming. He didn't want to do it in front of us," Tally said.

"I barely know him." Lori dabbed the corner of her mouth and tossed the napkin into the bowl.

Tally countered. "It's not like you're going to marry him. It's a dance."

"Besides, he hates my hair."

"Yeah, what's with the wig chop?" Tally propped up her elbows.

"I needed a change." Lori rubbed her bare neck. "I've been thinking about it for a while. All summer, actually."

"What are you going to say when he asks you to homecoming?"

Lori rolled her eyes. "Are you writing a book? I don't know! He hasn't asked me yet!"

"But he will."

Lori combed both hands through her shorn hair "He said I remind him of his sister. I'm betting he changes his mind."

"Oh, the bet's on!" Tally gathered the four lunch trays. "How much?"

"My red dress."

Jane chirped. "What dress? Can I see it?" She grabbed a handful of M&M candies stuffed in her skirt pocket.

"Don't be silly," Tally replied. "It would never fit me, and what would I do with it? No one's asking me to the dance."

"You can go stag," Abigail said. She held out her hand. Jane dropped a few candies into Abigail's palm.

"Stag is for boys," said Jane.

"Who knows, Tally?" Lori said. "Homecoming's a month away." They shook hands until Tally turned it into an arm-wrestling match. A flush-faced Lori got the upper hand, bending Tally's forearm closer to the table.

In mid-wrestle, Tally quizzed her contender. "What's that word we learned last spring? Ah, *insouciant*."

"What does it mean?" Jane inquired, fixated on the wrestling match.

"It means *indifferent*." Lori ran her free hand over her scalp and conceded.

"And your picture should be next to it in the dictionary." Tally kneaded her palms.

"What? About Gerald Wilkins? If you're interested, why don't you meet him in the library?" Lori said.

Abigail, the peacemaker, chimed in. "Okay, let's lighten up. Day two and we have an entire school year to get through. I've had an algebra tutor all summer, so heavy topics aren't cool."

Lori simpered. "Well, that sure lightened things up, Abi."

The foursome sat quietly for a moment, adjusting skirts, belts, and attitudes. Abigail cleared her throat. "To solve the equation *x plus eight equals twelve*, you must get x by itself on one side. Therefore, subtract eight from both sides."

"And the answer, Professor Abi?" Tally said.

"Let's see, if Gerald, or Gerry, is the eight, that leaves the four of us remaining!" said Abi. She brushed fingernails across her chest.

The four, Lori, Jane, Tally, and Abi, giggled and clapped hands, shaking off private qualms in the hopes and promises of a new school year.

Lottie arrived at the usual time for school ride pickups.

Lori tossed her books in the back, jumped into the front seat, and dropped down the visor. "Gran, do you know why I cut my hair?"

A Buick wagon packed with high schoolers pulled out in front.

"Not unless you tell me."

"Because I don't want to end up like my mom, patting my hair all the time."

"When she wore it tied back? I've never seen you do it." Lottie waited to join the stream of cars heading out to the road.

"I don't want to turn into her."

"Fair enough," Lottie said with no intention of provoking further discussion.

The days since returning to Texas had been turbulent, with emotional highs and lows. Lottie did her best to be, as Shakespeare described, the *"ever-fixed mark, that looks on tempests and is never shaken; the star to every wandering bark."* In essence, she was love and would bear out all the insults, the accusations, the hostilities, and lead Lori out of the despondency she entered at a moment's notice.

"Hey, Gran, can you pick me up later tomorrow?" Lori sounded whimsical and lighthearted. The ride home, away from the pressure of school and classmates, comforted her. She caught a breeze with her extended arm.

"Sure, what time?" Lottie imagined Lori on the Paragon Park roller coaster mere weeks ago as she thrilled and screamed with each dip. The highs and lows on the iron rails didn't compare to what she'd brought back to Texas.

"Hmm, a half hour," Lori answered. She framed her fingers as if preparing a photo shoot. "Well, aren't you going to ask why?"

"Why?" Lottie stopped at the only homebound red light.

Lori kicked aside her flats. "I'll tell you later."

Lottie glanced at her granddaughter, now the cat who'd swallowed a canary. Oh, how her heart ached for Lori! She recalled her own rushes of deep sadness and loneliness months after John disappeared in North Korea. Lori was new to grief. For both—mother and daughter—the devastating shock changed life in a heartbeat and seized them in different ways. Lottie remained stoic and at odds with her southern spiritedness.

Minutes from home, Lori blurted out her secret. "Gran, I think that boy Gerry is going to ask me to the homecoming dance."

"That's nice," Lottie said. The ever-fixed mark, quietly stirring her inner turmoil and releasing it with a simple, barely audible sigh.

"Gran, let's eat out tonight. A drive-in, but no chili," Lori said, now cheerful.

So many moods in the length of a car ride. Lottie remembered her own hormonal teen years and the resulting drama. Yes, they'd weather the storm, every storm. She would see to it.

Later in the evening, Lori sat at the kitchen table and finished the last chapter of her summer reading assignment, John Steinbeck's *The Grapes of Wrath*. The phone rang. Oddly enough, Lori expected the call.

"Lori, I don't want your dress. Really, I don't."

"How about a Saturday afternoon double feature?"

"Deal."

The midafternoon sunlight streaked through Venetian blinds lending a film noir feel to the library's main room. Gerald sat at the end of the long oak table closest to the reference section shelves. He flipped through a *Life* magazine from July 11, 1955, and mentally rehearsed his homecoming proposal. The librarian, Mrs. Carson, appeared anxious. Eyeglasses dangled from a beaded chain across her expansive bust. She approached Gerald. "May I help you?"

"No, thank you. I'm waiting for someone." He wore a sheepish grin.

"I see. I'm closing up fifteen minutes early today, which gives you—" She checked her wristwatch. "Fifteen minutes."

As if on cue, Lori breezed in. "Sorry I'm late."

Mrs. Carson focused on her watch. "You do know there's no talking in the library."

Lori, hugging books, managed a shoulder shrug. "But we're the only ones here. I promise we'll be quiet, Mrs. Carson."

Mrs. Carson softened. "Okay. I'm closing in fifteen minutes." She adjusted the blinds.

Lori settled into an oak chair next to Gerald and noticed the magazine cover. "Where'd you get that magazine?"

Gerald scratched his head. "Uh, from the magazine rack."

"Can I see it?" Lori flipped frantically through the pages to a sidebar including an article and photos of John Christmas and his family. "It's them. They lived in a bomb shelter like my dad's. Part of a government experiment. He mentioned it at breakfast one morning, and I asked if I could use his bomb shelter for Christmas . . ." She trailed off so deep into memories that Gerald could have been orbiting the planet.

"It must be hard . . . the reminders," said Gerald with trepidation.

She kept her nose in the pages. "Every day is a reminder."

"We really miss Joy. She's the one who got Elvis Presley to our Christmas dance last year."

"She showed me his name on a slip of paper. She'd forgotten it. Joy was so . . ." Sudden emotion choked back Lori's words, leaving her lightheaded and dizzy.

"Uh, now he's everywhere! Do you like Elvis?"

Lori closed up the magazine. "Who doesn't?"

"Did you see him on *The Steve Allen Show*?"

She chuckled. "Singing to the hound dog? That was nowhere!"

"Quiet please!" Mrs. Carson locked up her desk drawers. "We're closing."

Gerald leaned forward. "Lori, would you be my date for the homecoming dance? It's in two weeks."

Lori steadied his folded, shaky hands. "I know when it is. Okay." She released her gentle hold.

"*Okay,* meaning *yes*?"

"Okay, meaning yes."

"Swell, that's really swell! My sister Babs, I mean Barbara, can drive us. She's at college, but we squared it away."

"The one you said I look like?" Lori tilted her head in a pronounced manner.

"Well, yeah, your hair."

Mrs. Carson, a shell-colored cardigan draped across her forearm, flickered the light switch.

Gerald shot up and pulled out Lori's chair. "Would you like to see the Elvis movie?"

"Love Me Tender?"

"It comes out in November." He returned the *Life* magazine to the periodical rack.

"Hmm. Let's get through homecoming." She gathered her books.

Mrs. Carson walked to the exit with Lori and Gerald in tow. She turned off the lights and locked the door. With Lori a few feet ahead, she tapped Gerald's shoulder. "Don't be so anxious, young man."

Gerald whispered back, "You were listening?"

"All you students break the silence rule. I could write a book with what I've heard!" She bid them adieu, waved at Mr. Dugan the history teacher, who was closing up his classroom, and headed for the parking lot.

"What did she say?" asked Lori.

Gerald shrugged. "Something about writing a book."

At the Saturday matinee, Lori and Tally joined a sizeable crowd outside the Lone Star Theatre.

Lori griped. "I didn't think you'd pick a Western. You know I hate Westerns."

Tally read the marquee. "Natalie Wood is in it. She's my fave."

"It's a Western."

They moved up in line. "Did popcorn come with the bet?"

"Only if it's a movie I like." Lori rummaged through her wicker handbag.

"Is that a new pocketbook? What color is it?"

"Uh, corn yellow." Lori sorted through a comb, wallet, a pack of tissues, and cosmetic mirror.

"Like my shirtwaist!"

"Oh, so now I owe you my purse too?"

"No, silly. How did he ask you to the homecoming?"

Lori offered a stick of Wrigley's Spearmint chewing gum. "He said, 'Lori, would you be my date for the homecoming dance?'"

"And what did you say?" Tally unwrapped the gum.

"I said, 'Why don't you take your sister?'"

Tally dropped her hands to her sides. "You did not!"

Lori giggled and moved in front of the ticket booth. "Two tickets, please."

"That's one dollar," said Sarah Grogan, the theatre maven who had managed the Saturday matinees for the last twenty-five years.

Tally persisted. "Tell me what you said!"

Lori handed Sarah a dollar and grabbed the tickets. "Why do you have to know everything, Tally?" She loathed Westerns, and Tally's prying sent her over the edge. In a huff, she passed the ticket to her friend and stormed through the lobby. Tally, stunned, stood at the booth holding the ticket. She entered the lobby and bought popcorn.

With practically every seat filled, the curtains parted, and the screen brightened up with coming attractions. Squeals of delight echoed. The words, *Here He Comes, Mr. Rock 'N' Roll Himself*, appeared on screen, then a larger-than-life Elvis Presley strummed a guitar and crooned "Love Me Tender." The audience clamored as Lori and Tally, sitting in separate aisles, suffered loneliness, hurt, and confusion, the opposite of a joyful day.

Tally rhythmically ate her popcorn. Lori sat, crumpled in her seat, tears streaming down her face, anger and remorse flooding her senses.

A fidgety girl with thick glasses and sandy-colored hair nudged Lori's arm. "'Love Me Tender!' And it's a Western! Isn't Elvis a dreamboat?"

Lori grunted between a yes and no and sunk deeper into her seat. She chewed tasteless gum and missed plot points as her mind wandered to thoughts of remorse. Ten minutes into the movie, the resilient Tally licked buttery fingers while engrossed in the unfolding story of John Wayne as a Civil War veteran on a mission to rescue his niece from Comanche Indians.

The two reunited in the lobby before the second movie of the double feature. Tally initiated the peace offering with the half-eaten container of popcorn. "I'm sorry. I ask too many questions."

Lori took the popcorn. "No, I'm sorry for snapping like I did. I don't know what got into me."

"It's okay. I'm a big goof." Tally scooped out a handful of popcorn.

They walked to the exit with a skip in their step. Mrs. Grogan yelled out from her microphone. "Aren't you girls staying for the double feature? It's the new Dean Martin and Jerry Lewis Western comedy, *Pardners*."

Lori looked pleadingly at Tally.

"No thanks, Mrs. Grogan. Can't stay today," Tally said.

The afternoon walk home was hot, hazy, and dusty, but they didn't notice. They mended the sudden tear in their budding friendship.

"Here's what happened. He asked. I said, 'Okay.' He said, 'Okay, meaning yes?' and I said, 'Okay, meaning yes,' and then he kissed me."

"He didn't!" Tally, open-mouthed, stood at an intersection.

The traffic light changed, and they proceeded into the crosswalk. "That's all of it," Lori said. She raced ahead and pelted Tally with popcorn. "Other than trying to kiss me." Tally caught the last few kernels and threw them back at a lighthearted Lori.

Tally was equally blithe. "Maybe we can see the next Elvis movie together!"

Lori hesitated. "Maybe."

On homecoming day, Lori steamed out the silky layers of her red petal dress. The gap of a few months had diminished the excitement when she first slipped it on in a space between long aisles of designer clothes and high-end fashion. Now, it was another ironing chore.

From Uncle Preston's midnight blue Cadillac Coup Deville, Barbara watched a nervous Gerald, a white rose wrist corsage in hand, approach Lottie's front door. Her heart ached and soared all at once. It ached because she couldn't replace their fragile mom with the broken brain. It soared because she loved Gerald like her own son.

Gerald rang the doorbell.

"Hi, Gerry. I'm Lori's Grandma Lottie."

Gerald entered the main area with cozy furnishings and wallpaper of light blue and gold leaves.

Lottie gestured to a settee of gold brocade under a large picture window. "She'll be right down. Would you like a glass of tea?"

He pulled at his collar. "No, thank you, ma'am."

Lori entered looking every bit the homecoming court's sophomore rep, bestowed by the class majority vote.

"You look . . . boss!" Gerald wiped a sweaty palm against his trousers and handed Lori the white rose.

Lori felt glamorous, even if unsure she was up for the occasion. Lottie reassured her in an embrace, and she stepped out the front door led by Gerald.

"Hi, Lori. I'm Barbara. Gerry calls me Babs." Her arm rested on the open window. "Cool dress. Where'd you get it?"

"Boston."

"Filene's Basement?"

"How'd you know?" Lori pressed her fingers against the petal layers.

"Lucky guess. Hop in," Barbara said.

Lori liked the big sister instantly, so friendly and casual, not formal and serious like her brother. "Thanks for taking us to the dance."

"Anything for Gerry. Let's burn some rubber." Barbara winked.

The drive was relatively quiet. Gerald reached out a hand to Lori, who reluctantly accepted an encouraging squeeze that seemed to say, *It's okay. You look swell!* How could anyone say so much with a light touch?

At the school's front entrance, chicly dressed girls clustered around boys in slicked back hairdos and jackets pushed up on their forearms. Barbara smiled. "I'll be back in a few. Have fun you two!"

The homecoming court theme was the semblance of a crown with the homecoming queen as the diamond center and two precious stones on each side representing the senior, junior, sophomore, and freshman classes. The carpentry class had built an elaborate crown structure painted gold with five life-sized portals, one for each court attendant representing a jewel. For the ceremony, the homecoming court's companions would escort them to the stage, helping them on and off their platforms as mandated by the school's safety committee.

Two weeks earlier, Tally had lobbied her classmates to vote for Lori when it was announced that the sophomore rep would be a ruby. She had pleaded with her recalcitrant friend, who was ready to decline her victory. "It's meant for you. The dress from Filene's is perfect for the homecoming court."

Lori had capitulated.

The homecoming court assembled. Lori appeared as the evening's star in her tulip-red sheath and shiny, cropped hair. Paulette Mason, the senior homecoming queen who donned a silk diamond-collared blouse and a hip-hugging skirt of white lace, eyed Lori, who was clearly a scene stealer and more than an attendant in her fashionable ensemble. The other girls—Marsha, the emerald freshman; Georgette, the topaz junior; and Veronica, the sapphire blue other senior—paled in comparison to Lori, the sophomore ruby.

Gathered at the stage's wing, Marsha cried out, "Wow, Lori, you look fab! Like a queen in that dress." Georgette and Veronica nodded in acknowledgement of Marsha's compliment. Paulette frowned with resentment and smoothed her stiffened collar, cumbersome for her tiny shoulders and thin neck.

The music was cued, and the school band played, "Pomp and Circumstance" in a boisterous rendition that quelled the auditorium crowd.

"Why graduation music?" Marsha asked.

"Because it's played for the show *Queen for a Day*," Veronica said. "The one where the winner has the saddest story."

"Then you're the real queen, aren't you, Lori?" shot Paulette without blinking an eye. Lash One.

Lori deflected by remaining silent. The students clapped, awaiting the jewels to take their places. First, the emerald, Marsha was escorted by Jimmy, her next-door neighbor who she asked in confidence. Next, Georgette, the topaz, took a demure approach with a catlike walk to the platform and stood next to Sam, her boyfriend since freshman year. Then came Veronica in sapphire blue, an astonishing look-alike of Veronica Lodge, the debutante with blue-black hair immortalized in the *Archie* comic books. Toby, her date, had a red shock of hair similar to Archie, but slicked back in a ducktail.

Lori, the last jewel, preceded the diamond. Even with the rumble of applause, Lori heard the words whispered near her ear by the vulnerable queen. "We really miss Joy." Lash Two. The venom made its strike. Lori wilted like a flower desperate for water, baking in the sun, bent down to the awaiting clay-like earth. "She didn't even make it to the Elvis dance she organized." Lash Three. Lori straightened up, feeling each painful thrust. And then something inside swelled up and made her strong. *Be Strong!* She visualized a portrait of Jesus in Grandma Penny's parish church and the words *Jesus I Trust in You* printed underneath.

Gerald heard Paulette mumbling but couldn't understand what she said. He repeatedly glanced at Lori and monitored her expressions.

Paulette went in for the kill like a lion who detects a faint breath of life from its prey and pounces with mighty claws outstretched for a final jab. The band's music crescendoed as they awaited the two jewels—the ruby and the diamond. Lori imagined a ruby and diamond transforming to liquid, pouring over her and Paulette. Blood and water. Jesus on the cross, a lance piercing His side. Yes, blood and water. Her spirit quieted.

Paulette moved closer to Lori as she made her first step from the side curtain. She spoke loud enough for Gerald to hear her vitriolic words. "Do you ever feel guilty about Joy?"

The three stood, lifeless and frozen. Gerald was speechless. Paulette shuddered at the pure hatred that had escaped her mouth. Lori, with great peace, spoke to everyone and no one in particular. "All the time."

She and Gerald calmly linked arms and walked out onto the stage.

Lottie waited up and reread an old novel, *So Big*, published in 1924 by Edna Ferber. The door creaked, and she was taken aback by Lori's bright and cheery manner. "I had a wonderful time, Gran. I made new friends, and I danced, and . . ." She sniffed the white rose at her wrist.

"And?"

"And," said Lori. She summoned up, with a satisfied look, the half-hearted I-don't-know-what-got-into-me apology from Paulette over a half-empty bowl of Hawaiian Punch and melted orange sherbet. "I made peace."

Part II

Middle Ground

(1959 – 1976)

Chapter 16

Fall Back, Spring Forward

Gerald shoved a folded note into Lori's skirt pocket as they lined up for senior class graduation practice.

Lori grabbed his hand and squeezed it. "Passing notes to me? Isn't that how we started?"

His head hung as if bearing a heavy weight. "They're not my words. Much better . . ."

"Should I open it?"

"Maybe later."

Senior classmates shuffled into order. The principal, John McDowell, gave a disapproving look to Gerald and Lori. Gerald nodded in his direction and moved to the back of the line.

The fledgling musicians, all underclassman, assembled and tuned up. Graduates rehearsed walking the stage and receiving their diplomas. Some were enrolled in college, others were ready to make tracks on their own, and still others had no plans beyond the actual ceremony. All were banded together for a few more days.

After the run-through, seniors were dismissed. Gerald and Lori caught up at the school exit doors.

"I haven't opened it yet," Lori said. She turned over the envelope in the pocket of her navy dirndl skirt. Sudden turmoil rose within her. *I won't like this message,* she thought. Lori unsealed the envelope. Gerald stood by, his own hands deep within the pockets of his cuffed denims.

The handwriting was impeccable. It read:

"The Song of Songs 8: 6b–7a Stern as death is love, relentless as the nether world is devotion; its flames are a blazing fire. Deep waters cannot quench love, nor floods sweep it away."

Lori closed the card. "You're writing to me about natural disasters? Deep water, floods, and blazing fires?" She verged on handing back the note.

Gerald laughed. "Leave it to you to put a negative spin—"

"Negative spin?"

"Never mind." He focused on his buffed saddle shoes. "Lori, I'll love you forever. There's no other girl for me." He held out a blue suede pouch. "It's my pledge, my promise of, you know, not being with anyone else."

She opened the pouch and examined the gold locket's inscription. *Always in My Heart.*

"It means a lot, and I hope you accept it." He spoke with a boldness that she'd rarely witnessed before.

"I don't know what to say, Gerry." She held the locket.

"I'll love you forever."

She looked profoundly into his kind, almost saintly countenance. "I can't commit to the same feeling. I'll keep the locket, but I feel like a hypocrite because I don't know—I mean, I don't think I can wear it." *What a horrible thing to say,* she chided herself.

"It's okay. The fact that you accepted it will be enough. I'd be honored if you wore it, but I understand if you don't."

An awkward silence. Chatting students passed by.

Lori stammered. "I like you, Gerry. You're kind and strong, I mean, in your faith. You're the best friend, even boyfriend, a girl could have. But I'm not sure when I'll be back to Texas. It's not fair to you."

They moved to a stairwell leading away from the exit doors. "I don't look at things as fair or not. I look at what I believe right now, and that's why I'm giving you this promise. But I don't expect the same from you."

"Okay, I'll keep it for now." She undid her necklace and added the heart locket to the chain that held a tear-shaped sapphire stone, a gift for her sixteenth birthday from Grandma Lottie.

"When do you leave?"

"In two weeks, I leave for New York City with my gran. Then we're off to Europe. She wants to show me parts of France where my grandfather and she served in the war. Where they fell in love."

"That should be a blast. I mean, lots of fun."

"Gerry, I'll miss you."

Tally signaled Lori from across the walkway.

Gerald kissed her, first on the cheek and then surreptitiously on the lips. "Uh, I'll miss you too."

Tally plonked down on the edge of Lori's bed. "What a knucklehead!"

"I think it took a lot of courage to say what he did." Lori groomed her hair while seated at her brightly lit vanity table. In the last two years, she had resumed her longer mane with its full body of waves, soft curls, and red-gold highlights. She pulled a few stray strands from her ponytail and addressed Tally through a panel of her three-way mirror. "Besides, he didn't expect the same promise from me."

"You know he's thinking of entering the seminary, right? Why would he be making any commitment to you?" Tally stretched atop the chenille cover.

"Yes, we've talked about the seminary. It's not like he proposed to me!"

Tally luxuriated in the warmth of Lori's bedroom. French provincial fittings of antique white furniture replicated childhood days. Lori had insisted on creating a time capsule of her youth when she moved to Grandma Lottie's home. The only reminder of the modern, sleekly furnished ranch home reduced to rubble was a framed photo of an unsmiling Lori and her mom and dad in front of an aluminum Christmas tree bedecked with uniformly green ornaments.

Tally stared at the ceiling. "Will you miss Texas?"

"Oh, Tally, I think I'll miss you most of all!"

"Said Dorothy to the Scarecrow. I've seen *The Wizard of Oz*."

Lori giggled and envisioned when she truly befriended Tally and sealed their bond in the summer of 1956. Three years later, Lori maintained her willowy, model-like figure. Tally was more athletic with widening hips and broad shoulders. Lori had teased Tally after gym class earlier that day. "You could balance a stone jar on your head like those women carrying water from wells."

Indisputably, Tally was a force on the basketball court and was the highest scorer on the girls' team. Lori had joined the cheerleading squad in her junior year after a bumpy and rough road throughout her sophomore year. She was a natural gymnast, mastering cartwheels, flips, and scissor-like jumps. She was the center of attraction with her fearless workouts and bouncy ponytail.

Like no other friend in their circle, Tally understood Lori. She had waded through the troubled waters and dark days, the untimely rages out of nowhere, the subsequent apologies for walking away whenever a conflict arose. Nothing had prevented them from mending ways or patching up a tear from terse words or thoughtless accusations. Tally had kept all these feelings to herself, and her admiration for Lori's tenacity, strength, and courage grew.

"I've got to go," Tally sprung up from the bed. "Don't take him too seriously."

"It's just a locket." Lori shrugged.

"Well, now you have two."

"I do?"

Tally held out a square white box. "It's my going away gift."

Lori rose from her vanity bench and accepted the gift. Engraved words read *Friends Forever* on an oval-shaped locket with a gold chain. She slid open the cover and chuckled at the photo booth image, remembering the giggle fest and rush of dizziness following her third ride on the towering roller coaster at Paragon Park in 1956. Both had made crazy eyes, acting like children and forgetting, for a few seconds, the anxieties of teenage life.

"Tally, it's perfect." She promptly placed it round her neck and pouted. "I don't have a gift for you."

Tally shuffled her feet in an unrehearsed dance. "Yes, you do. You made me feel at home in Texas. Even with all you were going through. That was gift enough."

Lori clasped the sapphire stone and the two lockets. Her heart let go of the icy clutches of anger, disappointment, and hurt that gripped and squeezed out any semblance of joy at any given moment. Happiness, the intangible made tangible, lingered for the first time in over three years.

Chapter 17

Roamin' Holiday

Charlotte Mitchell was her own version of Mame, the unconventional character of book and movie fame who took charge of raising her orphaned nephew. In the same vein, Lottie introduced Lori to the wide world beyond Texas. First stop—the Big Apple.

"Why is New York City the Big Apple, Gran?" Lori packed her mint-green suitcase and coordinated cosmetic case—high school graduation gifts from Tally's mom. She folded a freshly ironed navy-and-white linen shift after examining the classic lines and dark hue. "No more puffy skirts," she said beneath her breath and tucked a pair of matching sandals under the toiletries. For chilly evenings, a Kelly-green linen blazer completed the outfit.

"What did you say, dear?" Lottie kept packing.

"Big Apple," Lori repeated. "What does it mean?" She minded her suitcase for a final inspection.

"It started at the racetracks in New Orleans. A reporter heard stable hands call New York the big apple. Years later, jazz musicians picked it up." Lottie inspected her traveling wardrobe. All her clothes, from casual slacks to evening wear, had simple lines similar to fashions by her favorite designer Coco Chanel.

"Broadway and the theatre. That's New York." Lori's confidence had grown, and her emotional highs and lows had evened out like a seesaw at mid-level.

Their odyssey began with three nights at the Hotel Piccadilly in the heart of Manhattan's Theatre District. Following a matinee of Ethel Merman's impressive performance in *Gypsy*, Lottie and Lori dined in the Piccadilly's Club Room and watched the people parade.

"Your mom and I used to come here on her spring breaks. We'd book a room and catch a string of Broadway shows."

Lori swished a straw in her Shirley Temple cocktail and stabbed a maraschino cherry. She toyed with her food, a discomfiting habit since high school days. "I wasn't hungry, Gran." She shoved aside the remains of her chef's salad—hard-boiled egg slices tucked under romaine lettuce.

The waiter returned with the check and cleared away the plates. Lottie surreptitiously studied the blonde at a table for two across the room. She was certain the young lady was Betsy, her friend Josie's granddaughter— the one in the photo who studied at Juilliard and rarely went home for holidays or vacations while absorbed in the hustle of theatre life and auditions. The one who, at this very moment, was stashing a silver spoon in her purse before the older gentleman returned from the men's room. Lottie vacillated between introducing herself and remaining anonymous.

"Gran, I remember the song."

"Yes, dear, which song?" Lottie watched the actress and the man get up to leave. She gave him a light kiss on the cheek. He took out his wallet and handed her a few bills as they walked to the reception area. The man shook hands with the head waiter.

"'Three Wishes for Christmas.' I memorized the lyrics." Lori cleared her throat and recited two verses.

"Very nice . . ."

"There's more," said Lori. "My favorite part about the snow falling silently." She recited the final verse and added, "Gran, this trip is your early Christmas present. The perfect gift!"

Days later, the travelers traded theatre districts by leaving behind Hotel Piccadilly in the Big Apple for Piccadilly Circus in the Big Smoke.

"The Big Smoke?" Lori unpacked her suitcase in the luxurious room at the London Ritz.

Lottie stretched a sinuous arm. "The coal fires and fog from the river. Fog and smoke."

"Like smog?" Lori admired the regal fireplace, one in each hotel room to her astonishment. Heavy gold-threaded brocade drapes drawn back revealed a dreary morning.

"Exactly." Lottie touched her toes. "I was visiting a friend, Polly, in 1952. It was a pea souper, fog so thick you couldn't see two feet in front of you."

"You never mentioned Polly. Is she here?"

"Polly lives near Paris now. I wrote to her in May. She plans to meet us when we arrive." Following her morning exercise regimen, a glowing Lottie adopted a sprightly attitude. "Ready to explore London?"

"What happened in 1952? Here in London?" Details of disaster stories now intrigued Lori.

Lottie donned a white terrycloth robe in the opulent bathroom with gold-plated fixtures. "A lot of people died. Now there's the Clean Air Act."

"How did you survive if you were here?" Lori shook off the moodiness that overtook her like a storm cloud out of nowhere. Goose bumps surfaced on her bare legs as she pictured the deadly fog.

"I headed for the hills!" Lottie exclaimed. "Polly and I hightailed to Paddington Station and left London the same day the smog rolled in."

"You might have saved her life, right?"

Lottie remembered insisting that Polly and she leave the Big Smoke on December 5, 1952. She woke up that morning and knew the air was poisoned, with ill effects to her weakened lungs. She booked a train to the coastal city of Brighton leaving before noon. The creeping fog and coal fumes mounted their toxic mix. No one foresaw the effect that lasted until December 9. Lottie's alacrity for sensing danger was sealed on a French battlefield and resealed in Texas on Black Sunday . . .

• • •

On that fateful day, April 14, 1935, a dust storm of sand, wind, and debris rolled across barren fields. Lottie thought she saw a storm cloud from her friend Lucille's porch on a peaceful morning. Lucille shoved her inside the front door. The hollow sound of wind and grains by the thousands, maybe millions, rained down on the roof, spraying against windows and leaving her shaken to her depths. Lucille's words had etched their indelible mark. "If we were out there for one more minute, we might all be blind."

• • •

Lori sat cross-legged on the expansive bed with its silky, soft-as-butter covering. "Gran, do you think you saved Polly's life?"

"Maybe."

The nascent photographer insisted on towing her camera when they pounded the pavements. In London, skyscrapers and Broadway glitz were replaced by antiquity and a chapter of European history at every turn.

"Why is it Piccadilly Circus?" Lori noted the neon lights, billboards, theatres, and restaurants. "It looks like New York!"

They waited at a crosswalk. "*Piccadilly* is for piccadils or frilly collars from the seventeenth century. Roger Baker, a tailor, lived here and made piccadils. *Circus* is Latin for circle." Lottie pointed out a lit sign. "Coca-Cola has been here since 1954, the last time I was here."

While crossing the busy intersection, Lori espied a woman with champagne-colored hair smoothed under and molded to perfection. Huddled inside one of London's ubiquitous red-framed phone booths, her unrevealed face heightened the mystery of the private conversation. She wore a red velvet cape with several folds, giving it a costume-like quality. *Perfect,* thought Lori. Her telescopic lens closed in. Phone receiver in hand, the woman's profile revealed aristocratic features—high cheekbones, strong chin, well-arched eyebrows. A long red leash was attached to a Cavalier King Charles spaniel waiting patiently on the sidewalk. Lori focused on the dog, who beheld the camera's eye, even from a distance, as if ready for its close-up. The woman was now the backdrop for the main attraction—the faithful, four-legged companion. Maybe the dog knew the routine. Maybe the woman made a date. A clandestine rendezvous with her lover and the only witness who couldn't give her away!

Lori studied the woman and let the camera hang loose from her neck as she and Lottie joined a throng of tourists, denizens, and those with destinations unknown. The woman stepped out of the iconic booth, so unreservedly British. The pale blond pageboy caught a ray of light. Lori guessed her subject was nearing middle age and well preserved. Tears, streaked with black eyeliner and mascara, muddied her cheeks. She resembled a clown following a circus performance, the real sadness lingering behind smears of paint. The woman scooped up the dog in a tight embrace and wiped her face in its soft, long hair. Transfixed, Lori wondered. *A broken heart?*

Lottie fought a coughing spell, a byproduct of weakened lungs, and raised her lilac silk scarf to stave off the endless fumes from double-decker buses and the steady stream of autos. She held Lori's hand and half dragged her along the sidewalk "Please, Lori, can we step it up? We'll hail a cab to St. Paul's Cathedral. We have a show tonight."

"Another show?" Lori whined. She hid her true feelings—a desire to walk, watch, and record the sidewalk show and real life in a pulsing, frenetic, smoke-filled city. Scars on masonry and bricks from a not-too-distant past. The blitzkrieg. Relentless shelling, air raids, fiery destruction. Less than two decades ago. Scars on human hearts.

Lottie recognized Lori's all-too-familiar faraway gaze. The stare fed by a tumult of thoughts. Lori's camera hung from its strap. Lottie softly replied, "We planned this one. *My Fair Lady* on the London stage."

"But no Rex Harrison as Professor Higgins." Lori moaned.

Lottie's lungs filled with the assault of traffic fumes. The number of cars had tripled since her last visit. "But Julie Andrews . . ."

"I'd rather see Audrey Hepburn in anything. She's still my favorite!" Lori's fears mounted. Losing sight of her subjects—the crying woman and the faithful dog—in the pointless prattle. She realized Gran was doing her best to make a memorable holiday. When they returned stateside, she would head directly to Boston for college. The span of distance seemed intolerable, at least right now. Life would change, two thousand miles apart for long stretches of time. Lori's own petulance always annoyed her. Yet words of contrition escaped her, even when aware of her sudden spate of willfulness. She consented. "Okay, you're right. I'm just . . ."

And then the moment arrived. Lori breathlessly snapped photos—tears, laughter, and the spaniel's wet tongue—all at once! The woman's teeth—perfect, straight, superbly white teeth. A tear-stained, smiling face. And the dog, the delightful, loyal friend licking the salt from her cheeks! A profile shot, a series of profile shots, obscure enough to keep the subject anonymous. Those perfect teeth framed in red lipstick. Her silhouette framed by a multitude of red-framed windowpanes. Fresh tears with bits of mascara; the dog's black, moist nose sniffing; its pink tongue lapping at her cheeks. Perfect, and all recorded in a series of photos. Her first taste of London from the tunnel of her lens.

A steady stream of honking automobiles nearly slowed to a halt, not that Lori noticed. She reentered her surroundings, as if from a hypnotic trance. "Okay, Gran. I'm ready. Why don't we hail a cab? Oh, here's one!" Lori was exuberant. She signaled a taxi, and they climbed in. "We can take the tube back, right?"

"Yes, dear." Lottie was relieved to escape the oppressive smog. "Did you get what you wanted, dear?" She rearranged her scarf and gestured to Lori's camera.

The woman in the red velvet cape, her beloved pet tucked under an arm, crossed in front of them. Lori was struck by a notion—she would never see the woman's full face or meet her eyes. As a voyeur, maybe for the best.

"I think so, Gran." She squeezed Lottie's hand with gratitude from every fiber of her being. Nothing gave her more comfort, more peace than an understanding heart. Lottie's heart.

In the afternoon, St. Paul's Cathedral towered above them on the City of London's highest point. Limestone, flying buttresses, magnificent domes, neck craning wonderment, all part of the Anglican Church, a pinnacle of British heritage that represented 700 years of faith and worship. In awe, Lori and Lottie strolled the whispering gallery with its circular walls. A proper British gentleman with a handlebar mustache, bowler hat, and walking stick bowed. "Americans?"

Lottie smiled. "Yes."

"Been here before?"

"Many years ago. After the war, actually both wars."

"You weren't here in 1913, were you?"

"No, that was a little before my time." Lottie, mindful of a restless Lori, inched away.

"Jolly good. You know the suffragettes tried to blow it up." He pointed with his cane. "Planted a bomb beneath the bishop's throne."

"Well, we're certainly glad it failed," Lottie said. "Good day." She caught up with Lori.

"What did he want?"

"Not sure. Mistaken identity?"

They entered the tube, a subterranean passage deeper and darker than Lori anticipated. She balked at the endless descent and suggested they ascend at the next stop and hail a cab. On the platform, Lori sorted out her emotions of being underground in a subway system that served as shelter from air raids during the Second World War. She thought about her abandoned shelter back in Texas. Commuters gazed off, waiting for trains. A deafening silence.

She turned to Lottie. "Do you know where we're going? Maybe we can get off at the next stop and walk the rest of the way."

"We have a few platform changes, and it's too far to walk," Lottie replied. "Remember we have a show this evening."

Lori sighed and buckled down for the set course. A girl, maybe three, inched up to her as she held on to her mother's hand. She wore black Mary Jane shoes, a light summery jumper of a calico print, and a matching bow in her brown curls. With a Raggedy Ann doll in her other hand, she watched Lori's every twitch. As children are wont to do, she bade Lori into her make-believe world and presented her doll. "This is my friend."

Lori, surprised by the encounter, forced a response. "She's very pretty. Does she have a name?"

She answered in a childish, breathy voice. "Yes. It's Joy."

The train arrived. The girl in the calico dress hugged her doll named Joy to her tiny frame. Lori dealt afresh with a trail of memories, back to Texas, back to her own Joy, the friend of a lifetime, brought back to life by a child on a train platform. Underground. A place where she had last seen her Joy. And for the first time in four years, her heart didn't ache at hearing the name.

Back at the Ritz, the famished commuters decided on afternoon tea in the plush Palm Court with its mirrors and sparkling chandeliers. The host, reserved and friendly, greeted them with a slight bow. "Ladies. Welcome to the birthplace of the Afternoon Tea. Are you guests of the Ritz?"

"Yes," Lottie said.

The host bowed again and stepped aside. "This way please."

In the following hour, the two indulged in finely cut sandwiches with minced fillings and glazed currant scones slathered with Cornish clotted cream and strawberry preserves. Lori surveyed the tray of leftover pastries and teacakes. "I'll be ready for a nap if I eat more of these pastries. But I can't resist!" She reached for a lemon tart.

Lottie's teacup was dutifully replenished by their server, a slightly built youth with auburn tresses caught up in a hairnet. Her pale face, without a trace of makeup, was a match for the porcelain tea kettle.

On their last full day in England, the travelers hopped a double-decker and took in all the usual touristy sites—Big Ben, Buckingham Palace, and Tower of London. They exited at Covent Gardens to explore alleyways and unique shops. At a quaint restaurant, they ordered afternoon tea once again. Lori slathered orange marmalade on a plain, buttery scone. "I think I'll be back, Gran. I'm sure of it."

In Paris, the City of Lights, Lori consumed enough French pastries to loosen her wide leather belt a notch. The sable brown belt accented the cream-colored A-line dress she'd discovered in a boutique in London's Carnaby Street, an epicenter for nightspots and trendy fashion. "How do French women stay so trim?" She scrutinized her thickened waistline in the full-length closet mirror.

Lottie examined her granddaughter, who had grown an inch taller since spring. "Exercise, riding bikes, walking. Oh, and baguettes instead of chocolate croissants. You look beautiful, dear. The belt is fine." She clapped her hands. "Today, we have a special plan."

"The place where you and Grandpa met?"

"We met on the ship."

"Okay, where you and Grandpa fell in love?" Lori punctuated her words with a few waist-whittling twists and turns followed by deep knee bends.

Lottie brushed her natural waves. "Polly is meeting us here at the hotel and driving us to Belleau Wood. It's an hour or so outside of Paris. On the way back we can visit—"

"Please say Versailles," Lori said, hands folded in a prayer.

"Versailles."

Lori clapped. "I'm having the time of my life, Gran. The best. And I'm glad you're not coughing anymore."

"Yes, dear. I can't take the smog, I guess."

"I like Europe. There's so much life!" Lori picked up her camera. "Can I take your photo?"

In full sunlight, curtains drawn, Lottie assumed a translucent quality, the Basilique du Sacré-Cœur of Montmartre as a backdrop. Her golden-brown hair had no gray, no betrayal of her age. Her sea-green eyes were a deeper shade, more akin to a jade stone, at least this morning. Beams of light had a halo effect.

Lori framed the striking image. "Say cheese!"

"*Fromage!*"

Polly arrived at the hotel at the precise time of the planned rendezvous. The porter swiftly opened the car doors, and Lottie climbed into the front passenger side. Lori plopped into the backseat. Lottie and Polly quickly exchanged cheek-to-cheek kisses, and off they sped, bypassing bicyclists, mopeds, and taxis.

"Lori, I'm so glad to finally meet you." Polly glanced in the rearview mirror. Lottie removed a compact from her tan leather purse and dabbed powder on her nose. "The souvenir compact I gave you from the queen's coronation in 1952."

"You went to Queen Elizabeth's coronation?" Lori gasped.

"No, dear," Lottie said. "Queen Elizabeth became the monarch when her father died in 1952, but her official coronation was on June 2, 1953."

"Yes, and I moved to France in 1950. Charlotte and I decided to meet in England," said Polly. She resembled a cabaret singer, in full makeup and side feather hat.

"During the Great Smog!" Lori was pleased she knew one of their stories.

Polly broke free from an early morning traffic snag. "Yes, that's right. What's your Gran's secret? She looks the same as she did back in—"

"Long ago." Lottie closed up her compact mirror.

Within an hour, they ambled along the once blood-stained paths of the Belleau Wood. Locals claimed that the trees remembered, the ones still standing, like sentinels that had guarded and protected French and American soldiers.

"Were you a nurse too?" Lori's tone was hushed in deference to hallowed ground.

"I was a Hello Girl. Switch board operator." Polly lifted her spiked heel out of the pliant earth. "Let's head to a café."

Lottie was lost to them, deep in the past as she strode the carnage path of war . . .

• • •

Bodies barely alive, barely breathing. Coming out of the woods. Out of the brush with dreams of returning home. Without limbs. Keep the heart beating! Yes, keep the heart beating! Stop the bleeding! John's words and her reply. "We can save him!" His words. "We do our best, Nurse Charlotte." Nurse Charlotte. So formal. So dedicated. A doctor headed for the seminary. "Discerning," he told her in private. Love at first sight for Lottie.

· · ·

Lori snapped photos from behind. Lottie's head bent low, reliving, reviving the ghosts of soldiers torn apart. And then Texas, 1955. Another carnage. The storm that had ripped apart Miriam and Tom's suburban rancher. And Lori. Precious Lori, asleep in the sunken hideaway. And now back to France. What? Forty years? A mere blink of an eye. War was in her DNA, her life story. It had brought John to her in 1918 and took him in 1950. A far-off land. North Korea. And then the war with nature! Her own daughter swept away by an unrelenting tunnel of wind.

"Gran, are you okay? You've been looking at the ground for the last fifteen minutes."

Lottie returned, eyes ahead at the bright green leaves, the fields of fragrant wildflowers and grass, and Polly's reassuring smile. Yes, Polly understood. She'd lived it. And so had Lori. A different bond, but a shared marker on their timelines. "Yes, the café sounds good."

A vase of daisies and baby's breath enlivened the café table. Polly resumed her story to an attentive Lori. "I was a volunteer under a call to action from General Pershing." She sipped a cup of home-brewed coffee, the heady smell of roasted beans filling her nostrils. "We were the Hello Girls. We took maybe one thousand calls per day and communicated with the front line."

"How'd you get the job?"

"Easy. My grandmother, my mother's mother, was French. She taught me as a child."

"And you met my gran here?"

"Yes. After the war, I married a British soldier." Polly lit a cigarette on a slim gold-rimmed filter. Her drawn lips accentuated fine lines. "I haven't been back to the states in nearly forty years. I'm a war bride in the other direction, I suppose. Paul and Polly Brittingham. I usually go by Polly B. or Mrs. B." A ring of smoke curled around her. "Paul died in 1950. I moved back to Paris . . ."

Polly's story echoed in the background as Lottie drew deeper into the past . . .

• • •

The Great War, by 1918, was desperate for skilled doctors and nurses. Charlotte and John met their shared destiny on the way to France and the pure hell of trench warfare. Sprays of ocean water and a bout of seasickness resulted in both retching off the side of the ship crossing the Atlantic. After heaving, they wiped their mouths in unison and laughed out loud.

"John Mitchell. I'd shake hands, but . . ."

Lottie laughed again. "Charlotte Brookes. So, you're the doctor I've heard about."

"What've you heard?"

"That you're the best." She was surprised by a sudden blush to his cheeks.

"Well, I hope I can live up to it, Charlotte."

Later that evening, scrubbed and refreshed, they sat together in the barren lounge area as the ship tossed and pitched. Both forewent dinner and decided on a repast of soda crackers and tea. She learned a great deal about her future husband in a few hours. John was a six-foot-four surgeon, fairly recent to his practice. He ministered at Ellis Island before a reassignment to a Boston hospital. A native Bostonian, he was grateful to return home, removed from the hopelessness of immigrants with illness and disease arriving to American shores. He loathed the idea of breaking up families.

Children were deported, and a parent accompanied a sick child back to the deplorable conditions of their homeland. One percent of those entering Ellis Island were turned away, many times due to physical deformities, not only disease. "I witnessed a family split apart," he confided. "A child of five, hysterical, stretched out her arms. The mother tore her from the father's arms. I still see the tears streaming down the man's face."

Lottie listened. His tender heart captured her own. Yes, she was certain— love at first sight.

"How did you find your way to Boston?" John asked.

"A friend from Virginia invited me. She's a teacher. I taught back home. I've been in Boston less than a year. Not sure why I uprooted myself. I'm a tad homesick and don't like the cold."

John nodded. "It's an adjustment."

"Josie, my friend, encouraged me to be patient. She thinks my new life in Boston's for a reason."

Lottie mused that John Mitchell was her destiny. While crossing the "great pond" to the warfront, she grew fonder of the likeable doctor. Not because he was the most handsome man she'd ever met. Not because he was respected in the medical field. Not even because he looked at her as if he'd never seen a woman before. The fondness was due to his humble spirit, a rare trait for most of the doctors she encountered in her training days. Humility appealed to her quiet, Virginia sensibility. Lottie had confided to Josie: "He's the most likeable doctor."

"You're forgetting handsome," Josie said.

"Oh, no I'm not!" Lottie replied, her cheeks flushed.

As a surgery nurse by John's side, her heart filled with love, brimming and extending out to soldiers with limbs blown apart. What she didn't realize was how John Mitchell would change her life, even her faith life.

Dr. Mitchell found time to visit a chapel and attended mass when a priest was available. He possessed a peacefulness at battlefront operating tables mending broken bodies and despairing souls.

A fellow surgeon, Stephen Malone, called him Father John. Word was out that he'd considered leaving medicine for the priesthood. As a youth, John looked into a seminary instead of high school. But his love of science took hold, and he discerned that he could serve as God's instrument with surgeon's hands. That's the story Lottie got from Dr. Malone, who noticed the spark between the two of them.

• • •

"Lottie?"

Polly waved her hand like a hypnotist bringing an audience volunteer out of a trance. "Lottie?"

"Sorry, I'm daydreaming."

Polly inserted a cigarette into her filter. "Yeah, memories are like an avalanche. Beware of falling rocks." She struck a match.

Lori observed the two of them, stone-faced, sifting through imaginings of love, war, and the years in between. Polly drew on her cig. Smoke circled her head like a lopsided halo. Lori inspected a forkful of quiche Lorraine.

"I've perfected my quiche recipe." Polly flicked ashes into a crystal tray. "But not puff pastries or croissants. Too many layers."

"And butter," Lottie added.

Polly peered down at her substantial waistline. "You still look like you danced out of a Coco Chanel ad."

"As in dated?" The sun warmed Lottie's shoulders and bared arms lifting the weight of memories.

"Hey, do you think we'll make it to Versailles?" Lori's mission—a visual tour de force of the palatial grounds.

"I'm ready. Charlotte? Seen enough?" Polly brushed a few pastry flakes off her lap and inspected her cotton sweater for oily stains.

"Yes, let's go." Lottie drained her coffee cup.

"By the way, I mentioned you to Francine."

"Who's Francine?" Lori asked.

Polly, surprised, glanced at Lottie. The two exchanged information, not saying a word.

"Francine is a girl I adopted. We adopted her." Polly lit another cigarette.

"We?" Lori perked up.

Lottie nodded for Polly to continue.

"Your gran and I adopted her. She was two years old."

Lori searched Lottie's face. "Why didn't I know? Did my mom know?"

"Your grandfather knew."

"I have an aunt? Aunt Francine? Do you see her? Where does she live?"

"I'll tell you on the way to Versailles," Lottie said.

"I have another aunt? My mother has a sister? Where is she?" Lori's questions piled up like bales of hay dotting the French countryside.

Polly snuffed out her cigarette after a few puffs. "It was during the war. Both her parents were killed. Her mother was a spy for the French resistance. Francine's father was a soldier. He died first. We befriended her mother, Simone, in Paris on our way to the front, here in Belleau Wood. She liked Charlotte. Trusted her. Simone knew she was a marked woman. Spies didn't last long. Her husband, Michel, was on the front line. They had doomsday assignments."

"We signed co-guardianship papers, Polly and I. My plan was to bring Francine to the United States."

They volleyed the story to each other. Lori followed as if watching a tennis match in the final round. "I received a telegram that Charlotte was near death with influenza. Francine and I grew close."

"And Polly spoke French. Francine was French. I had to let go."

Lori mused. "She'd be close to my mom's age."

"A few years older," Lottie said.

The three drew closer as Lori caught up on missing chapters in Lottie's personal history. She often wondered why her gran was secretive. Was she also Mata Hari, a spy for both sides of the war? More secrets. Part of the Hopkins-Mitchell hushed saga for God knows what reason. Lori had the mind and curiosity of an investigator. She liked details. Her camera's telescopic lens picked up laugh lines rimming her subject's eyes and features that an artist may erase with forgiving strokes of a paintbrush.

"Can I meet her?" She directed her question to Polly.

"Francine? She lives in New York. Well, half the year. And London the other half."

"Gran, would you recognize Francine now?" Lori's thoughts reeled, spun, and whirled like a toy top spinning out of control.

"I haven't seen her since she was a little girl. We've written to each other," Lottie said wistfully.

"You're pen pals?" Lori spat out the words. "I'd like to meet her."

"We're heading back soon, Lori . . ."

"But when she comes to New York. Where is she now?"

Polly and Lottie eyed each other like unmasked co-conspirators.

"In London," Polly answered.

"And what does she look like?"

"Blonde—"

"Does she have any pets?" Lori waited an eternity for the answer.

"Yes, a dog named Susu."

"A King Charles spaniel?"

"Why yes." Polly tossed her cigarette pack into her black purse. "How did you know?"

"I didn't."

Versailles appeared lifeless behind the camera lens. Lori imagined the pompous Queen of Hearts in the Alice in Wonderland tale parading through the formal shrubbery and manicured lawns.

Lori was dissatisfied with her postcard-like pictures. The Eiffel Tower, a formidable structure, transformed into iron lace at night, the glow of lights illuminating its considerable intricacy. But no stories. She hungered for a story.

What are the odds? Her thoughts were jumbled with news of Francine. *Maybe it isn't her. Maybe it is.* She'd find out. She'd visit Francine, the aunt she'd never met. Or maybe she had, through her lens.

Back at the hotel, the exhausted travelers turned in early. Lori lazed in their hotel bed next to Lottie. "Why'd you never mention Francine?"

Lottie unfastened her necklace of blue moon glass beads gifted by Miriam fifteen years ago. "I wanted to forget. It's too painful Lori. Please let it go."

"Gran, the woman in the phone booth in London. Maybe that was Francine?"

Lottie raised her eyebrows. "That's almost absurd enough to be true."

"Can we visit Francine?"

"Not now."

"Did my mom know?"

"No, dear, she didn't. Only your grandfather."

"Would you recognize her? In my photos?"

Lottie, fully clothed, lay on the bed. "I don't know."

Hours later, the dawn brightened their room. Lottie stirred.

"Gran, you rest. I'm going to the corner bistro for a chocolate croissant. Would you like anything?"

Lottie turned to her side. She woke up earlier with a slight headache and thanked God it wasn't a migraine. The day in Belleau Wood had proven to be an emotional maelstrom. She resolved to rest her brain before resuming their travels.

"No, Lori, I'll order at the hotel. Are you all packed?"

"Yes, back in a jiff."

"Don't get lost, sweetheart. The streets are winding."

"I'll leave a trail of bread . . ." Before Lori finished, Lottie was asleep, a damp washcloth smoothed across her forehead.

The Montmartre section reminded Lori of Provincetown with its enclave of artists and painters on narrow cobble streets. A violinist plucked a sweet, heartrending piece in solemn celebration of a brand-new day. Portrait makers, lining the sidewalks, set up their paints and easels. Lori gamboled, avoiding contact lest an artist beckon her for a caricature or sketch. She mouthed, *"Bonjour,"* and made tracks to the bistro.

Turning a corner, she nearly stumbled over a solitary painter, a man in his seventies wearing a black felt beret. Wirelike gray hairs escaped his white V-neck undershirt. A cotton vest of French blue was splattered with paint, like a palette. He had a thin, determined mouth and a beaky nose and black eyes set close together—a human crow. A hefty cat with white fur and enormous blue eyes like sapphires sat upright on a café chair of three wire legs and a heart-shaped wire backing. Nothing stirred the cat from its pose or interrupted the project, until Lori's unwavering presence.

"Mademoiselle, you are an American, *oui*?" he inquired without breaking his concentration.

"Ah, yes, *oui*." Lori kept still as the bushy, snowy feline maintained its regal bearing.

"And how do I know?" The artist dabbed final touches of azure to the eyes.

"My clothes?"

He chuckled and remained fixed on his work. "No, no mademoiselle. It's the camera. You are in pursuit of a photo, but not a *touristique*. *Tres different, oui*?"

"Yes, *oui*."

"And you are wanting to take a photo *du le chat, oui*?"

"*Oui*."

"*L'artiste* painting *le chat*?" He pulled away his brush from the canvas. "Giselle, shall we allow the mademoiselle to take a picture while we work?"

Giselle, *le chat*, let out a high-pitched meow.

"*Oui*?" said the artist.

A second meow.

"Ah, mademoiselle. Giselle says *enchante*."

"That means 'nice to meet you'?"

"*Oui*, and she has agreed to the photo. *Tu es chanceux!*"

Lori caught a ray of sunlight on the impassive feline's frosty coat, the artist's back, and exactly the right angle to capture his work on the portrait. She was thrilled—natural light and the artist's right hand brushing slight touches to the cat's eyes on canvas. The worn beret and mottled hand were the only references of him on film. Three stories in one frame.

"You are wondering why she does not move, mademoiselle. *Elle est ma preferee*! I painted at least fifty portraits. But, please, merci, I must finish."

"Merci beaucoup." Lori reached into the pocket of her black pencil skirt, a purchase at a Montmartre boutique. She placed the francs on a side table.

"For your breakfast, mademoiselle?" He focused on the canvas.

Lori nodded incredulously. *"Oui."*

"Giselle, our visitor, *elle est gentille."*

Giselle meowed a third time. Lori curtsied and inched from the "*le petite monde*" inside the world at large. La Villes des Lumières. A posing cat. A moment captured for eternity. Voila!

In the hotel lobby, Lori scuttled to the closing elevator doors. A hand waved them open, and she stood face-to-face with Elvis on a fifteen-day leave from his German military base. Lori murmured, "Good morning, Mr. Presley."

A lip curl emerged. "Call me Elvis."

They shook hands. The bell announced her floor, time cut short by a ten-second ride. Lori heard her voice. "What's it like, Elvis?" She meant the fame, the Army stint, the future itself.

He halted the closing doors. "Like I say, do something worth remembering." He grinned, put on dark glasses, and released the button.

Rome. Bold, brutal, and breathtaking is how Lottie described it.

"Next, we'll go off the beaten track." Lottie pinned her ultra-sheer, taupe-colored nylons to a garter belt, so foreign to her these days, as foreign as the cities on the Continent, experienced a lifetime ago. She pulled the stockings up her slim, hairless calves. No ravaging marks from age or her early years of nursing and endless days on her feet. "I've booked a surprise." She donned a pair of camel-colored pumps, her trademark shoe for the last five years. Although worn, she preferred their low heel and rounded toes for comfort. As planned, their morning jaunt included four hours of hoofing it around the Eternal City.

Lori was anxious to seize the day—*carpe diem*. They'd retrace locales of her favorite movie—*Roman Holiday* starring Audrey Hepburn. Lori wore a taupe-colored swing skirt, dusty pink blouse, and light brown flats similar to ballet slippers, and pirouetted like the Sugar Plum Fairy or principal dancer in a staged performance. "I'm going back a few years, Gran! Audrey and I are one today! I'm Princess Ann breaking away from royalty for adventure!" Their hotel, Hassler Roma, overlooking the Spanish Steps, was favored by the actress throughout the film shoot.

"You remind me of Doris Day, Gran." Lori fell back on her bed and wiggled her toes. "Not that you look like her. You don't have freckles. She always looks concerned about everyone, like you." A map of Rome was beside Lori. Thirteen circles identified their destinations.

Lottie hummed the tune to "Que Sera, Sera" and daubed on light coral lipstick for daytime. She turned to her granddaughter, the one who was so vexed by her own freckles five years ago that she had bought a jar of vanishing cream. Now the "kisses from the sun" were disappearing as a young adult, now eighteen, emerged from the child who once slept with a Raggedy Ann doll and a tangle of stuffed animals.

"Sounds like a compliment to me. Who doesn't like Doris Day?" She prayed the day would be a joyful, whimsical, serendipitous exploration.

From the first step of their odyssey, it seemed as if traveling angels escorted them. Lottie attributed it to a psalm she learned back in Virginia from her Sunday school teacher. She had connected to the psalms—supplications to God. Mrs. Marshall, the preacher's wife, had informed her students that Holy Scripture should be "written on their hearts." Lottie couldn't quote from random Bible verses, but she had memorized Psalm 139: *If I rise on the wings of dawn, if I settle on the far side of the sea, even there your hand will guide me.*

The concierge ordered a cab. "I'm ready, Gran." Lori stashed her personalized treasure map, creased and folded a dozen times, into her camera bag. They'd begin their walking tour at Santa Maria in Cosmedin. At the final site, they'd flag a taxi or wait at a bus stop. A leisurely dinner at their hotel would cap off the evening.

Lori retraced Audrey Hepburn's steps and recreated scenes from *Roman Holiday*, taking on the persona of the sheltered princess in search of chance. "Here it is!" she called out. "La Bocca della Verità. A person will lose a hand if they tell a lie. Remember in the movie how Gregory Peck as Joe pretends to lose his hand?"

A tour guide, hearing the remark, added a bit of real history. "Signora and Signorina, *per favore*." He gestured to a side altar. "Do not forget to visit the skull of St. Valentine and say a prayer for those whose hearts are broken."

Lori conjured up the woman emerging from the London phone box, her wet cheeks buried in her spaniel's fur. "Yes—I mean, *Si! Grazie!*"

As they progressed, Lori drew Xs through the circles. "Let's have champagne at the Caffe Rocca. This is fun!"

For a blissful moment, Lottie witnessed in Lori the smile of a child that could light up a curtain-drawn room.

After a few sips of champagne, Lori's wanderlust kicked into overdrive. Lottie did her best to keep pace. They planned the best locales for last—Colonna Palace where Audrey Hepburn/Princess Ann held a press conference and resumed her royal duties with an admiring Joe in the press pen; Trevi Fountain, with a toe dip; and the Spanish Steps, near their hotel, as a finale. They walked beside the Tiber River, and Lori got a brainstorm. "Gran, if we walk back to the train station, we can rent a Vespa scooter. I have a wide skirt and flat shoes, so I can do the driving."

"Lori, you don't have a license."

"Yes, but you do!" countered Lori. "Let's do it. Please! Then we can drive to the barber shop in *Roman Holiday*." She consulted her map. "Here it is! Via della Stamperia 85. We'll ask for directions. Puhleeese!"

Lori's hands wrung in begging fashion, and Lottie chuckled with reminders of her own youthful exploits. "Fine, but I'll drive!"

"But Gran, my skirt's full. See?" Lori twirled. "It's much easier for me."

After umpteen wrong turns, near misses, alarmed gestures from pedestrians, and motoring against traffic, Lottie wished she hadn't weakened to Lori's insistence to drive. They pulled up to the iconic barber shop. Lori was rattled and apologetic. "I thought it would be easy, like in the movie. I feel kind of silly."

With renewed sanguinity, Lottie jumped to her feet. "We're here. And in one piece. Let's make the most of it."

Her high spirits dampened, Lori entered the barber shop with Lottie close behind her. A spry male attendant greeted them. *"Ciao a voi due bellezze!"*

Lori combed a hand through her disheveled hair. She whispered to Lottie. "He called us 'two beauties.'"

"Remember, we're in Rome."

"*Mi chiamo* Giuseppe, and I know best the style for you, Signorina." He snapped his fingers and clicked his heels. "*Seguimi, per favore.*"

"Uh, we're . . ."

"Yes, yes, Signorina. You are here because of the movie. *Si, si.* You and hundreds more, maybe thousands soon! But Giuseppe, me, am telling you. *Destino!*"

"Fate?" Lori said.

"*Per piacere*, Signorina! Giuseppe will make you more *bellissima* than Miss Hepburn or Princess Ann!" He patted a parlor chair, its leather worn thin and shiny by women of all ages seeking a makeover or discovery of untapped beauty à la a new hairstyle.

The stylist made quick work of his subject, tilting Lori's head one way, the other, up and down. He studied her face from a few feet's distance, turned away and back, as if by surprise. "It's *la fantasia*! I need to visualize how the world should see you, but first through my eyes!"

"I understand," she said. "I do the same. Uh, with my camera." Lori lifted up the bag at her side.

"*Perfecto!*"

Twenty minutes later, Giuseppe handed the ingénue a mirror. She swiveled to inspect a twist swept up from the nape of her neck. Flirty bangs framed her face, and tendrils flowed loosely at her temples. "You look like a goddess, Signorina! Loosen the hair for *la será*. A few shakes will do it!"

"Like the French actress, Brigitte Bardot. *Oui?*" Lottie monitored from a striped canvas folding stool.

"*Oui, oui*, Mademoiselle!"

They bade farewell to Giuseppe, a kiss to both cheeks, and mounted the Vespa scooter for a final spin. "I'm dog-tired, Gran." Lori sported a new pair of sunglasses and unpinned hair, shaking it loose as instructed by Giuseppe. At the Trevi Fountain, Lori dipped each toe in the cool, flowing waters and fantasized about plunging in headfirst.

"No coins?" Lottie referred to the popular film of three American women seeking adventure and romance in Rome.

"Different movie. I'm Princess Ann, remember? With a new do," she said playfully.

Their agenda complete, they nestled into the Spanish Steps with gelato cones, lemon for Lottie, a double scoop of chocolate and hazelnut for Lori.

"Gran, do you remember me mentioning Giuseppe? The waiter in Boston?" Lori crunched her cone.

"Of course." Lottie savored the last few licks of her citrus-flavored confection, a perfect blend of icy and creamy textures.

"Do you think he'd remember me?" Lori pinned strands, a haphazard version of her Italian stylist's creation.

"I guess you'll find out." Lottie was accustomed to Lori's positing a scenario with every intention of carrying it through. "Shall we climb the Spanish Steps, dear?" And so they did, holding hands, a faintly hot midafternoon breeze behind, a brilliant sun in front, and rekindled hope encircling its invisible force.

Lori, with a tinge of sadness, prepared to leave behind the Eternal City and her *Roman Holiday* adventure. The final curtain on their European odyssey signaled the near end of summer and the beginning of life without Grandma Lottie, her ever fixed mark.

Lottie kept their ultimate destination secret until they arrived at the airport. Lori read the boarding pass. "Czechoslovakia? I can barely spell it! Why?"

"It's the heart of Eastern Europe. We're heading to Prague."

For Lori, Prague was European in its opulence but less romantic. The language was unfamiliar, nothing like the bits of French and Italian she understood. The world, once again, seemed a daunting place, and she cleaved to Lottie's hand like a child at a fairground. Lottie, in turn, sensed the nervous energy pulsing through the fragile teen's palm.

Taxis lined the ground transportation sidewalk. A brash young man watched in amusement as Lottie read aloud her hotel to a confused driver, who shook his head.

The cabbie bellowed, "Over here, lady. I speak English." Lottie sighed relief. With Lori in tow, they made their way to the cheeky driver leaning on his cab door, one muscular leg crossing the other.

"Do you know this hotel?" Lottie handed him a business card.

"It closed five years ago."

"What?"

"It changed names. I can take you there."

"There's a big difference between closing and changing names," Lottie said, agitated, as he piled their luggage into his trunk.

"If you insist, lady."

"You alarmed me, that's all." Lottie's exhaustion fueled her pluckiness.

Settled into the cab, everyone's manner improved. "I'm an actor. Spent time in New York. Did a few plays and returned to Czechoslovakia last year. Trying to get film work now. I drive the cab to pay the bills."

Lori took note of his profile—dark features, black hair, and hazel eyes, not a typical fair-haired, blue-eyed Slav. "Why'd you leave New York?"

He raised a hand and rubbed his fingers together.

"Oh, yeah, money. It's expensive," Lori said.

"What brings you to Prague?"

"I start college in Boston." Lori rested her arms and chin on the passenger seat ledge. "It's my last holiday. We traveled to London, Paris, Rome . . ."

"And now Prague." He switched off his meter as they approached the hotel's main entrance and glanced back for Lori's reply.

"Before returning to Texas, and then, well . . ."

"Yes, yes, Boston," he added.

"My gran surprised me with this one."

"Well, I hope it turns into a good surprise!"

"Well, the first surprise was good, right?" Lori said. "Meeting you and that you speak English."

"Yes, yes, and maybe I will return to the States. Maybe I gave up too quickly. We'll see."

Another silence. Lottie sighed. "Oh, I'm terribly sorry. I didn't change my money. I see a bank on the corner. If you'd like to stop, I'll pay extra for your time."

"No, no forget it. This is my uncle's cab. I like to give a free ride every now and then. Your hotel is right here."

Lottie pulled a ten-dollar bill from her wallet. "You can change this or keep it for your next stay in New York. Something tells me you'll be back on stage."

"My name is Ari Novak. Look for me." He touched the rim of his cap.

"Lori Hopkins. Thanks for the ride."

After a brief respite, they ventured to the Church of Our Lady Victorious located in Prague's Lesser Quarter district.

"Why did you bring me here?" Lori asked.

"It's where God wants us right now." Lottie spoke with a truth she didn't fully understand.

Lori gravitated to the ornate, gold-adorned shrine dedicated to the Infant Jesus of Prague, a sixteenth century wax-coated wooden statue. The child-like prince wore a diamond-encrusted robe and a golden crown on his curly crop of hair. The right hand was raised in a blessing. The left one held an orb. At fourteen, Lori learned that the orb was a globus cruciger representing the world with a cross atop. The dominion of Christianity and the triumph of Christ.

Lori glared at the statue in royal robes holding up the world as if to say, "This is mine." Her hardened heart answered, "But I'm not." The hurt was a scar easily ripped open with a summoning up of what was destroyed on a Sunday afternoon four years ago.

Lottie appeared in deep meditation, head bowed. Lori wondered what prayers she uttered in her silent pilgrimage. For the few years following the storm, Lori attended Sunday mass to appease her grandmother. Now she was convinced she was even further from the Savior who didn't save her life from ruin. She understood why her grandmother, a woman led to share her faith, brought her to the Infant Jesus of Prague. And, maybe, in an inexorable way, she even appreciated being here.

She sat with Lottie as tourists knelt, venerated the wax figurine, and lit candles. After a few minutes, she wandered off near the side altars. A girl, thin and angular with a plain face and luminous eyes, nodded a greeting. Lori nodded back. The young teenager handed her a pamphlet printed in Czech, Hungarian, Polish, German, Italian, and English. She read the panel in English. *Come back to me.* Without a word, the girl disappeared through church exit doors. Lori folded the paper in half. "I'm here. Where were you?" Words spilled out like tears as she whispered to the Infant of Prague, his eyes fixed on everyone and no one in particular. She returned to Lottie and grasped her hand. But the question resettled in her heart, like a stone weighing it down.

Chapter 18

Cape Crusade

The restaurant was revamped. Tablecloths of red, white, and green plaid replaced the checkered ones. The new décor, light oak, was more buoyant than the former dark mahogany wood.

"Welcome to Slice of Italy." The waif-like hostess, twenty years old, greeted Lori. Her bleached hair, dry and brittle, contrasted black roots. Strikingly blue peepers and perfectly arched brows all but made up for the disastrous coiffure. She grabbed menus from her hostess stand.

"I'm waiting for someone," Lori said.

"I can seat you while you wait. How many?" She clenched a cherry Life Saver between tea-stained teeth. Before either spoke, Bernadette was behind them.

"Well, look at you, Brigitte Bardot."

The hostess patted her hair. "Yeah, I get that a lot."

"Could we have a booth, please?" Bernadette said.

"Yes, ma'am." She searched for an empty booth, as if any of them were filled.

When seated, Bernadette shook her head. "Oh, no, I'm a ma'am now. By the way, the Brigit Bardot comment was meant—"

"Yeah, I know. Thanks." Lori perused the daily specials.

"Give me the highlights. I'm guessing Rome not Paris for the do."

"How'd you know?" Lori scanned the room.

"Okay, so what was *the* highlight?"

"My photos. Stories in frames, Aunt Bernie."

The waiter, all swagger, rocked back and forth on Italian leather shoes. "My name is Tony. Can I interest you lovely ladies in our lunch specials?"

"I'll have a glass of wine, the house red, and an antipasto" Bernadette said.

"I'll have today's special, cheese ravioli. Is Giuseppe here?" Lori asked.

"You mean the owner? Gio? He's away this week. He'll be back on Monday."

"Oh," Lori said nonchalantly, feeling foolish for mentioning his name. "I'll have an iced tea."

"Very good, ladies." Tony brushed his hairy, stubby fingers against Lori's hand as he took her menu and strutted off.

"Cheeky fellow," said Bernadette. "Tell me the highlights. What was your fave?"

"Too many highlights. Okay, the first, a dog in London, a cat in Paris, and a man in Rome named Giuseppe who restyled my hair after a scooter ride with Gran."

"Okay, that was a quick trip."

Tony arrived with their beverages and lingered for a few more seconds. "May I tell Giuseppe who was asking for him?"

"Uh, Lori from Texas. But that's okay. I'll stop by some other time." Lori wished she'd kept quiet, certain the brazen waiter would mention her inquiry. Tony bowed and backed away.

Lori refocused. "What's new with you?"

"I think I met someone." Bernadette lifted her glass of wine.

"No, really?" Lori spooned two sugar cubes into her iced tea. "Where'd you two meet?"

"He's a reporter for the *Boston Globe*. We were both covering the same story. Anyway, enough about me. So, are you settled in yet?"

"Are you kidding? I miss Gran already! How will I survive without her?"

Bernadette offered a comforting hand. "Hey, what am I? Chopped liver?"

The lunch crowd rolled in. Aunt Portia a.k.a. Rose approached their booth. "Well, Heavens to Betsy, where have you been? And it's our darling Lori."

"Hi, Aunt Rose," Lori answered. "I'm in Boston now for college."

"That's right. I heard all the latest from your Grandma Penny. Well, I'd join you, but I have a lunch engagement. Don't be a stranger, Lori. You too, Bernadette. We never see you." She trotted off, coppery hair swaying against her chartreuse slicker.

"Why does she call her own mother Grandma Penny?" Lori asked.

"It's the Portia protest again. Someday, maybe she'll actually like her name."

Lori stacked three pasta squares. "I'm buying lunch. You took care of Sandra Dee. I can't thank you enough, Aunt Bernie."

"No, don't be silly. You're a poor college student now. You need to watch your budget."

"I have a souvenir for you." Lori presented a package wrapped in pink tissue paper.

"A stenographer's notebook? Just what I need."

"No, Aunt Bernie. Don't be silly!"

Bernadette tore off the wrapping. A framed canvas of a large, downy white cat sitting on a pink silk pillow stared back at her.

"Giselle. She's from Paris. The artist knew I'd be back. I think even before I did."

"She's . . ."

"The cat's meow?"

A broad smile from Bernadette. *"Belle."*

"I thought you'd like it."

"Thank you, Lori. I can tell it's very special."

"I'll be by to pick up Sandra Dee now that I'm settled in."

"She's ready and waiting."

Tony returned with the check. "Signorina, Gio called. I mentioned you. He said he would very much like to see you next week, and lunch will be on us."

Lori blushed. "Uh, that wasn't necessary, but thank you."

Tuesday of the following week, Lori's afternoon classes were canceled. Her roommate, Connie, a Bostonian, offered to accompany her to the Slice of Italy. She thanked her graciously. "I'm getting used to your public transit. In Texas, we drive everywhere."

"What's it like in Texas?" Connie polished off a crisp McIntosh apple.

"Big. Miles and miles of nothing." Lori combed her long, tapered fingers through a fringe of bangs.

"Do you miss it?" Connie tossed the core into a wastebasket under her dormitory desk.

"With every heartbeat." She was shocked at her instant response. Four years ago, she was beyond determined to leave behind the Lone Star state. But the heartbeats were for Grandma Lottie. She ached to be reunited with her one source of comfort. "I'll be back soon. Maybe we can meet up at study hall."

Connie stretched her arms. "I plan to study the back of my eyelids."

Upon entering the restaurant, Lori felt the tension. Parties waited for tables. Loud voices from the kitchen penetrated the walls. A short, stocky man wearing a toque, white coat, and checkered pants stormed through the dining area. He threw down the toque. A frantic Giuseppe rushed out of the kitchen. He yelled out, on the heels of the chef, "You can't quit, because you're fired!"

At the bar, the chef raised a wine glass to Giuseppe and smashed it on the tile floor.

Two customers ducked and spun off their bar stools.

"You'll pay for that, Ricardo!" Giuseppe said.

The bartender swept up the broken glass.

Giuseppe addressed a few stunned witnesses. "A slight mishap. Angela, please seat our guests." He noticed Lori in the skirt and blouse she wore in Rome, her day as Princess Ann. "Is that you? Lorraine, right? Bernie's niece?"

"Yes, Lori. I see you're busy. It's a bad time."

"I won't disagree." He oozed charm. "I'm the chef for today. Good thing I know my way around the kitchen." He took stock of customers settling into booths and tables. "Lori, I am so happy you remember me.

Is it okay if we meet for dinner? Maybe your aunt can go with us if you need a chaperone."

Lori wanted an escape hatch, although she was thrilled by the proposition. "I can ask her."

"Please do. I'm counting on it. Now I must get back to the kitchen." He caught her hand and kissed it. "Princess Lori."

Lori waited for the call from Lottie. She sat between Grandma Penny and Uncle Ben at the kitchen table. Bernadette sat across from them. The phone rang, and Penny grabbed the receiver. "Lottie?"

Lori cheerily jumped up to share the receiver. "Hi, Gran!"

"Everything okay, dear?"

"Yes, Gran." She ignored meeting eyes with the Hopkins ad hoc committee.

Penny said, "Thanks for calling me back, Lottie. We want your advice. There's a man—"

"Young man," Ben interjected.

Penny raised a finger to silence him. "Well, he's a bit older than Lori."

"He's under twenty-five." Ben winked at Lori. She pretended not to notice.

"Let me finish, please." Penny's round, invincible eyes silenced Ben. "Giuseppe, now owner of a pizza restaurant."

Lottie sounded tinny across the phone lines. "Yes, I remember. Lori mentioned him."

"He remembered me and asked me out, if it's okay."

"As long as there's a chaperone," Lottie said.

Penny covered the receiver. "See, what did I tell you? She needs a chaperone." She tipped back and talked into the phone again. "That's exactly what I said, Lottie."

"Penny, I'm kidding. Put Lori on the phone, please."

Lori clutched the receiver. "I'm here, Gran. I miss you."

"I miss you too. I trust you dear. Be sensible. Stay in a crowded area. Have him pick you up and drop you off at your dormitory. No long drives."

"He's meeting me somewhere in walking distance."

"Even better. Have fun. So how are your classes going?"

Ben whispered. "Are we done?"

"Let them talk," Penny said. She swooshed Ben and Bernadette out of the kitchen.

Lori spoke, her voice low and raspy. "I miss you, Gran. I can't believe I'm saying this, but I miss Texas. I never thought I would, ever again."

"I miss you too, sweetheart. Is school going okay?"

Lori twisted the phone cord. "My classes are fine. Sandra Dee's in my dorm. I like my roommate, Connie. Are you coming up?"

"No, I wasn't planning on it. You'll be home at Christmas?"

"Yes, Gran." Lori lingered. "It's good to hear your voice."

"You too." The distance shortened with each passing second. "Okay, I'll let you know how my date goes."

"Give your Grandma Penny a big hug from me."

After Lori hung up, Penny poked her head through the archway. "Lori, you have a visitor."

"Tally?" Lori yelled out.

"How'd you know?" Tally beamed in the archway.

Lori embraced her. "Who else would be visiting me in Boston?"

"My mom's taking care of my aunt. She had a bad fall and needs help, so I came with her."

Penny exclaimed. "Oh, dear. I hope she's okay! Please let me know if there's anything I can do to help!"

"Thanks, Mrs. Hopkins. She'll be fine, but I'll let my mom know."

"Please do! I'll let you two girls talk." She took flight like a winged creature.

Tally dropped into a kitchen dinette chair. "Where's the clock?"

"It's in the repair shop. One of the grandkids threw a baseball and hit it. Right when the bird came out. It's so good to see you!"

"I'm here overnight. I fly back to Texas in the morning."

"Wow, that's quick. Time for a cup of tea?"

"No, I'm zonked out, and I have an early flight."

"I have a date!" Lori batted her eyelashes and glanced over one shoulder.

"The Italian waiter?"

"He's not a waiter anymore. He owns the place!"

"What about Gerry?' Tally circled her foot.

"He's a friend, Tally. Nothing more."

"Well, I'm sure he misses you. He asks about you."

"And what do you say?"

"That we had a big fight and we don't speak to each other."

Lori threw a dish towel at Tally, who volleyed it back. "So really, what do you say?" Lori asked.

"What can I say? That you're in Boston until you finish the semester, and you'll be home for Christmas. Right?"

"Right. What's your story?"

"My story? Schoolwork. What else?"

"No love interest?"

"No." Tally paused. "Okay, yes. Basketball player."

"Aha!" Lori paced like an inspector putting clues together. "Not surprising."

"Why?"

"You play basketball too, right? So you have the common interest." Lori flared up the stove burner under the copper tea kettle.

"And what's your common interest with the Italian waiter?"

"You mean owner. I don't know yet." Lori grabbed a copper canister filled with tea bags in a corner of the countertop. "Oh, would you do me a favor when you get back to Texas?"

"Sure." Tally pulled on her elbow for an extended stretch.

Lori picked up a packet of photos on a phonebook stand under the wall phone.

"Oooh, pics. Can I take a peek?" Tally studied the first image. "Who's the woman with the dog?"

The tea kettle gave a piercing whistle. Lori clicked off the burner. "Don't know."

"A face in the crowd, huh?" Tally tucked the photo back in the packet.

"For now." Lori pulled out the photo of the woman with the dog. "Would you give this one to my gran?" She poured hot water into her choice porcelain cup rimmed in pink rosebuds. Images of London, Paris, Rome, and Prague hid behind her blank stare as she rhythmically dunked a tea bag.

Life at Boston University's urban campus was underscored by freshman growing pains. The week started with Lori's favorite class Monday morning at 8:00 a.m.

Professor Leonard Portico lectured. "Photography is both art and business. Learn them both." He sat on the edge of the desk. His boat sneakers dangled, and he appeared more like the captain of a fishing vessel than a college faculty member. A balding pate and graying whiskers and mustache topped off his nautical persona. He peered at a clipboard. "Miss Hopkins?"

"Ah, yes." Lori squirmed behind her desk.

"Tell us why you're here." His feet swayed.

"To be a better photographer." She straightened up in her seat.

"Oh, so you're a photographer?" Professor Portico jumped down from the scratched and worn desk.

"Yes, I am. That's how I got accepted here. With my portfolio." She regarded her contemporaries. "Like everyone else in this class."

Giggles rippled through the cavernous space of a hundred students.

"Miss Hopkins, do you know the rule of thirds?"

"In photography?"

"What else, Miss Hopkins?"

"Yes, uh, it'd be easier to draw."

Professor Portico extended a piece of chalk and pointed to a slate board on wheels.

Lori drew a square and two vertical and two horizontal lines inside of it. "When framing a photo, divide the scene into these blocks and position your subject at or near the intersecting lines."

"That's an adequate description. Thank you." The professor cleared his throat, an intentional pause. Lori resumed her seat. "Many of you will fail my class. And I will be doing you a favor. You will go on to work in financial institutions filling out mortgage papers. You will bake cookies for PTA meetings, and a few, very few, will become professional photographers. And by professional, it could be anything. Studio work with babies and grandparents for their pictorial archives. Oh, you will all fill your family albums. Fine prints of good times, 'Say cheese!' and all of that nonsense."

Professor Portico circled the lowered center stage and put a hand to his chest to continue his soliloquy. In a pin-drop silence, Lori placed her pen on her tablet and immediately got his attention.

"Are you writing this down, Miss Hopkins?"

"No, Professor."

He picked up her notepad and chuckled. "Well, if it's me, it's a damn good likeness." He ripped out the page, balled it up, and threw it to a proximate waste can. "But this, Miss Hopkins, is not an art class." He continued, "Your first assignment is to photograph yourself. In a mirror. I want them all back here by the next class. That's all for today."

The students packed up books and ascended the stairs in hushed voices.

Professor Portico yelled out, "Miss Hopkins? May I see you for a minute?"

"Lucky you," said the sweet-natured freshman seated next to her. "I'm Nina from Boston. Maybe we can get together." She passed a note to her. "Here's my dorm room. Look me up."

"Thanks. I'll do that," said Lori.

Professor Portico dug out a binder from a leather carrycase, worn and thin at the edges. "This is your work?"

"Yes."

"You are on your way, Miss Hopkins. I rarely see talent such as yours. But you need to work on depth. There's no depth, although you have a good eye."

"Uh, thank you." A sudden elation and a calmness filled her spirit.

"That's it. You may go." He raised a knuckle to his mouth. "Question. The photos you sent after you were admitted. The woman and the dog. In Britain. Did you know them?"

"No, sir. I used my telescopic lens from across the street."

"Yes, I can see that much. What could you have done differently?"

Lori brought to mind the milieu of a busy London street mere months ago. "Well, I could have gotten a better sense of story, I guess, if I had captured what was going on around her?"

"Sounds like a productive choice." He clapped his hands in a dismissive manner.

She paused before leaving. "But then no one would have noticed her perfect teeth."

"So it's a toothpaste ad?" He collected his books and shoved them in the bag. "Miss Hopkins, that's all for now."

Ben observed a wall clock marking a half hour beyond their meeting time in Provincetown at the fish shack they discovered in the summer of 1956. "I could've picked you up, Lori."

"Sorry, I'm late. I missed the first bus out." Her chair scraped the rough wooden floorboards. The strong odor of raw fish filled her nostrils.

"Peter Pan?" said Ben.

"Yeah."

"Did you buy a round trip?"

"No, I wasn't sure when . . ."

"Good, I'll take you to Boston."

"Thanks, Uncle Ben. You were coming from a different direction, so I didn't—"

"It's fine, Lori. Are you hungry?"

"Famished! I miss Gran's cooking."

"We'll get you a healthy supply of Bernadette's brown bread," Ben said with a mischievous grin.

"Gee, thanks Uncle Ben." She matched his smirk. "I've got lots of questions for you."

The waiter approached.

"Two orders of fish and chips. The freshest piece of cod for the lady," Ben said.

The waiter winked his approval. "Anything to drink?"

"Seven-Up, please," said Lori.

For a solid hour, they traded stories—the fledgling student and the seasoned professional, both sharing a passion for life behind the lens.

The following week, a Saturday night, Lori went through half her wardrobe, undecided on what to wear on her first date with Giuseppe. She chose a pair of black slacks and a white cable-stitch sweater. Lori grabbed her navy peacoat, a gift from Grandma Penny for Beantown's brisk autumn afternoons. "How do I look?" She executed a quick spin.

"Well," Connie said. "Just wondering when you joined the Navy."

"The coat, huh? Too drab?" Lori brushed off a few pieces of lint from the dark blue wool.

Connie sidestepped a pile of laundry and opened her closet, barely the width of a yardstick. She pushed aside blouses, skirts, slacks, and a red flannel nightgown and pulled out a pink satin bomber jacket. "Try my jacket. It's the living end, don't you think?"

Lori switched coats. "Well, it's certainly pink."

"Pink is perfect with your black slacks. You look hip!"

"I look like a greaser," Lori said.

"Better than a longshoreman!" Connie's hint of a pout displayed hurt feelings.

Lori threw her head back and exhaled. "You're right." She hugged her roommate. "Thanks a bunch, Connie."

"Where's the rendezvous?"

"Oh, the deli around the corner."

"Gee, how romantic," quipped Connie.

Giuseppe was late by ten minutes. Lori was taking off the shiny pink jacket as Giuseppe raced to her side. "May I?" He helped her out of the jacket and handed it back to her with an apologetic look. "I'm so sorry for being late."

"No chefs walked off?"

"Not yet." He checked his watch. "But it's still early."

"I figured a lunch date would be a challenge for you."

"In the restaurant business, every hour of the day is a challenge! So how do you like living in Boston? How's Bernadette? I don't see her much lately."

"Boston is no Texas, I can tell you that. I never knew how much I'd miss it."

Giuseppe leaned back, arms folded. He was all focus, like a reporter holding an interview. "What do you miss the most?"

Lori didn't have an answer. Not an immediate one. She thought of Gerald.

He wagged his finger. "You have a love interest, Lori. *Si?*"

"I have friends." She diverted attention to the menu to hide a grin.

"What's his name?"

Lori grinned broadly, a few beats shy of a full-out laugh. "He wants to be a priest. Well, maybe. I don't know. He's confused. But I'm not. Can we order?"

"Lori." He reached out for her hand. "It's okay. Let's have lunch. No more questions. Do you recommend anything?"

Lori got his humor and liked his company. "Do you like salad?"

"Yes, antipasto! American salads are for rabbits, Lori. How's the hamburger here?"

"Well, nothing like Texas."

The waitress rushed up to the table and put down two glasses of water. Giuseppe smiled and winked at her. Full focus. *He makes everyone feel special,* thought Lori. The waitress smiled back bashfully and pulled on her silver-streaked ponytail.

"We'll have the hamburgers," Giuseppe said.

The waitress glanced above her glasses directly at Lori. "How would you like yours, sweetie?"

Lori was stunned. "Uh, medium."

"Same here." Giuseppe closed his menu.

The waitress collected the menus. "Fries?"

Lori whispered in an admonishing tone, "Do I want fries too?"

Giuseppe winked again. "We'll split an order."

Back at the dormitory room, Connie anticipated a report as Lori tossed her the pink jacket. "Well?"

"He ordered my lunch without asking! I mean, this isn't the old country."

Connie examined her jacket. "Okay, then he's sophisticated."

"Well, it's not like I fell off the turnip truck!"

"What?"

"Never mind. And how would you like a guy ordering your food?"

Connie shrugged. "Depends on how cute he is." She hung up her jacket. "Why didn't you tell him?"

"Tell him what?" Lori fell into her bed and pressed fingers against her temples.

"That you didn't want him ordering for you."

"I will. Next time." She rolled to her side and put a pillow over her head.

"Next time?" Connie plunged on her mattress. "Aha, so it wasn't that bad?"

"It was a nice time. Other than him ordering my food."

"Did he kiss you?"

"Connie, I don't even know him."

"When's the next date?"

Lori spoke through the pillow. "Two weeks from tomorrow."

"A Saturday night date? Plenty of time to shop."

"I'm on a budget. We're going bowling."

Connie clapped her hands and headed back to her crammed closet. She pushed aside clothes and displayed a shiny black satin bowling jacket. Faux diamonds and a ring of rubies resembled a bowling pin. "Isn't it the coolest?"

Lori uncovered her head. "I'm kidding. We're going to a French restaurant and an Italian opera."

"Okay, can't help you there. You're two sizes smaller than me."

Tired of chatting, Lori, like a lead weight, sunk deeper in her bed. She missed Texas, Lottie, Tally, and maybe Gerald. *Maybe.* "I already know what I'm wearing."

Her favorite topic, fashion, piqued Connie's interest. "Let's see!"

Lori winched her pillow and studied it like a crystal ball. "Can't. It's in Texas."

The package arrived three days before Lori's follow-up date with Giuseppe. Lori had asked Grandma Lottie to ship the red dress to Grandma Penny. Lottie had discovered fruit punch stains from the homecoming dance in 1956. She phoned Penny that she'd have the dress dry-cleaned before mailing.

"Okay, let's see it!" Connie crunched on the celery stalk and its chewy fibers. She'd read that eating celery burned more calories than the stalk contained.

Lori slipped the red tulip dress over her slim silhouette.

"Wow! Wicked good!" Connie chomped on her fourth stalk. "This celery's making me hungry." She reached under her bed. "Did you hide my Cheetos?"

"Why would I do that?" Lori checked her appearance in a full-length mirror hanging from inside the closet door. "You know Cheetos are from Texas."

"Yeah, and what's that got to do with the price of tea in China?" Connie snapped a crispy stalk in two. "You do look fab, Lori. Knock 'em dead!"

She appeared elegant and cultured beyond her years. Giuseppe had switched plans to a performance of Tchaikovsky's *Swan Lake* after she'd confided it was her favorite ballet.

"I thought we were going to an opera?"

"I wanted to surprise you, Princess Lorena."

"Well, you sure as shootin' keep me on my toes. Any more surprises?"

"If I told you it, wouldn't be a surprise," he answered.

As they settled in, Giuseppe whispered in Lori's ear. "I'm the luckiest man here tonight."

"And why is that?" she asked coyly.

"Because I have the most beautiful woman in Boston sitting next to me."

He raised her hand to his lips and kissed it gently.

The restaurant business afforded precious free time, but Lori lifted Giuseppe's spirits, a welcome departure from a tight-knit lineage tied to Italy. And he found her enchanting in a way he couldn't describe.

"*Bella*," he confided in Tony, his waiter, cousin, and paisano.

Tony raised his shoulders. "I dunno, Gio. *Lei e carina, si!*"

"No, Tony. *Bella! Bella!*" He grabbed Tony's face in a teasing manner.

Tony slapped away Giuseppe's hands.

Two weeks before Thanksgiving, Giuseppe and Lori arranged their fifth date. They met at the same delicatessen for college students from their first date. Lori, demure and subdued, drifted in wearing her navy pea jacket and black slacks. Giuseppe checked his watch. She was five minutes late.

"Do you always carry the camera?" He gave her a light peck on both cheeks.

"It's how I learn."

"You've never photographed me."

"I thought about it." She held up both hands to frame his face.

He waved her hands away. "I don't like myself in photos. What if there never was a camera invented? What would you do then, Princess Lorena?" Mock seriousness. *His stamp*, thought Lori.

"Cavemen drew pictures on walls. Egyptian hieroglyphics captured everyday life. Humans will always use images to tell stories."

"Lori, you may take my picture."

"Where?"

"Right here!"

The real Giuseppe filtered through the poses. Goofy faces, childish antics, silliness. Nothing she ever expected and all elicited by simply uttering, "Be yourself!"

He draped a white scarf over his head, imitating his *nonna* in Italy. Next was a smoldering pose like heartthrob actor Rudolph Valentino in *The Sheik*, all done with the same prop. Lori clicked away. He flirted with the camera, and the camera, in turn, fell in love with him. The last pose was "The Mummy," his head completely wrapped in the scarf, his penetrating eyes staring out. He mumbled, "Are we done?"

Her riveted eyes moved from the lens. "Maybe."

"Good. Let's eat." He unraveled his scarf bandage.

"On one condition. I choose my own food."

He shrugged. "Deal, as you Americans say. But I must inform the waitress."

"Deal. On one more condition. You don't change what I tell you." She bent forward. "I'll have the French onion soup."

When the waitress approached, Giuseppe winked at her. "The lady will have the French onion soup." He winked at Lori. "A thin slice of French bread and an extra layer of the Gruyère cheese."

Aware of Lori's opposition, Giuseppe lightened the mood with a scarf wrap as he mimicked Nonna and babbled in Italian.

"You look . . ." She paused. "Fabulous." She laughed at his antics until the soup arrived. It was perfect, and so was the evening.

Connie sat cross-legged like a summer camper waiting to hear a fireside story. "Are you in love?" Her words spilled across the dorm room like a risky dice roll.

"I don't think so. He's charming and fun."

"What about the guy back home?" A second dice roll.

"He's my friend. Why?"

Connie passed over an envelope.

"Well, I hope you didn't steam open this one."

"I never—"

"I'm kidding." Lori slit the envelope and read the letter to herself. "Hmm . . ."

"Good? Bad?"

"A visit," Lori said. "I better let Grandma Penny know."

"From Texas?"

Lori reread the letter. "He's visiting New York with friends. Driving to Boston after the Macy's Thanksgiving Day Parade . . . to visit me."

Wednesday afternoon before Thanksgiving, Lori got a phone message pinned to her dorm room.

She called. "Hi, Gio."

"Can you steal away for a movie tonight?"

Two female students lined up behind Lori.

"It depends . . . I've got an exam in a half hour."

"*A Summer Place.*"

"Sandra Dee and Troy Donahue?"

"*Si,* Princess Lorena."

"Okay, if you can drop me off at my gran's house afterward."

"I'll pick you up at six."

At ten that evening, Lori and Giuseppe pulled up to the Hopkins townhouse. Lights were dim. They tiptoed into the foyer. Lori wrapped her pink angora scarf around Giuseppe's neck and pulled him closer for a kiss.

"Hi, Lori!" Gerald stood in the foyer's threshold.

His voice struck a chord.

"What? What are you . . . ?"

"My plans changed. We're heading to Manhattan at four in the morning to see the parade. Your grandmother left a message with your roommate."

"I haven't been at my dorm since early afternoon. Gio and I went to a movie."

Giuseppe offered a hand and wrapped the other around Lori's waist. "You are Lori's friend from Texas? She's mentioned you."

Gerald gripped his neck and shook Giuseppe's hand. Lori grew uncomfortable with the unexpected arrival. "Ah, Gerry meet Giuseppe. So when did you get here?"

"Your grandmother said she expected you at six, so that's when I came by."

"You've been waiting four hours?"

"I better go, Princess." Giuseppe kissed Lori and brushed her cheek with his fingertip. He addressed Gerald. "Enjoy Boston." He whistled the tune "Oh What a Beautiful Morning" from the musical *Oklahoma!* and vaulted into his red Alfa Romeo Giulietta.

"Who's the Romeo? Your boyfriend?"

"Yes, you could say that."

"I just did."

"Gerry, we're apart. I'm here."

"And the locket?"

Lori entered the living room area, kicked off her shoes, and set down a train suitcase. "I still have it. Are you staying for a while? I didn't know you changed your plans."

"Sorry, but your grandmother expected you at six. She was very worried."

Lori, tired of explanations, wished the surprise visit would end. Her mixed feelings wore her out. She missed Gerald, even when in Giuseppe's company, but was bothered by his questions and the nagging notion that he was checking up on her.

"I wish I knew you'd be here early. We could've had a real visit, Gerry." She gave a tender look, a friendly vibe. "Is my grandma awake?"

"No. I told her I'd wait up for you."

"I'm not a child."

"Then why are you acting like one?"

"Gerry, let's be kind. It's been a long day . . ."

"I'm sorry, Lori. I should leave."

"Why don't you stay? We have room." A thought struck home. "Gerry, why are you here?"

Gerald bent forward on a leather ottoman. "I'm joining the seminary. I wanted to tell you in person."

Lori froze. She wanted to embrace him. Tell him she understood even if she didn't. Mixed emotions flooded her senses, and she wasn't sure what she was feeling. *Betrayal? Sadness? Joy? Relief? Surprise?* No words. Nothing to say. Only questions and a deep yearning to hold him.

"Lori, dear? Is it you? I was worried." A thin, brittle voice emanated from the staircase.

"I'm sorry, Gran. I didn't get a chance to call right after my exam. Gio and I went to the movies, and he dropped me off."

"Gerry, sweetheart, do you want to stay? It's so late."

"No thanks, Mrs. Hopkins. We're heading out early."

"Okay, I'll let you two say goodbye. Lori, bright and early."

"Yes, ma'am."

Alone again, Lori and Gerald made awkward attempts at a goodbye.

"Lori, your boyfriend. Are you two . . . intimate?"

"None of your damn business, I would say!" She released a neck chain and tossed it to him. "Your locket."

"I'm sorry, Lori. That was rude and insensitive of me."

"Hey, no one's perfect. I wish you the best." Of what, she wasn't sure as he walked through the door.

In bed, she ruminated over the night's events. Gerry's words, *Be Strong*, projected onto the ceiling from a torrent of thoughts. Too much thinking. She loved him because he'd helped her when she needed it. Years ago. What would happen to their friendship was too troubling to ponder. She dragged over the carrying case by her bedside and felt around for a small bottle, a sedative recommended for insomnia by Nina, her college friend. It was an over-the-counter antihistamine, mainly for allergies, but caused drowsiness and a temporary cure for sleepless nights. She'd taken it once after an all-night exam review. Desperate for shuteye, she trudged toward the bathroom and downed a couple antihistamine tablets. In fifteen minutes, blissful slumber took hold.

Gerald grew sullen on the early-morning drive to New York City. He lost all interest in the parade he'd anticipated since childhood. His two buddies, Matthew and Donald, had generated a to-do list before entering the seminary.

Matthew spoke first. "Still thinking about Lori?"

"I'm not sure why I told her right before I left. Maybe to hurt or shock her. Why would I hurt Lori, if anyone?"

"The Song of Songs," Matthew said. "Were one to offer all he owns to purchase love, he would be roundly mocked."

"Or maybe I wanted to keep her heart and not give mine in return." He clutched the locket. The truth of his words left its mark on his own heart and deep remorse in his soul.

After the Thanksgiving holiday, Lori was anxious to dive back into school. Any distraction from personal quandaries would be a relief, although there were a lot of expectations, chiefly from Professor Portico's deeming her his protégé. Ben cautioned about perfectionism, a byproduct of the arts. "Don't beat yourself up, Lori. We're always perfecting our craft. It's never-ending."

Before returning to Texas for the Christmas break, Lori had one wish—to attend the Boston Symphony's annual Christmas concert with Bernadette, Grandma Penny, and Uncle Ben. The foursome headed out on a Saturday night, December 5. Lori wore her red tulip dress for the final time. First with Gerry as a sophomore homecoming queen, second with Giuseppe at the ballet, and third for no reason other than she preferred to end on the number three. She hooked arms with Ben and slanted against his shoulder. "Wow, Uncle Ben. You missed a Boston Bruins game for me?"

"Eh, didn't feel like flying to Detroit anyway. Merry Christmas to my favorite family member."

Bernadette escorted Penny. "I'm listening, Ben!"

They settled in for a night of sweet and, at times, rousing music. Later on, Lori slept soundly, her lips curled as if sugarplums danced in her head

On Sunday morning, she phoned Grandma Lottie. "I'll be home soon, Gran, after finals. Miss you!"

"Miss you too, sweetheart. Everything okay?"

"Did you know Gerry's going into the seminary?" She already knew the answer. Grandma Lottie was good—too good—at keeping secrets.

"Yes, dear, he stopped by and mentioned it to me."

"Before or after he visited me?"

"Why, it was before Thanksgiving."

Lori sighed. "It doesn't matter. We're on different paths. I'll miss him though."

"It's very hard saying goodbye to friends."

"I don't like goodbyes, Gran. Any goodbyes," Lori said and added lightly, "Okay, uh, goodbye!"

Back at her dormitory, Lori was restless with fleeting images of Giuseppe and the white scarf photo shoot. He was like an intoxicating elixir.

On a rainy Saturday afternoon, before fall semester finals, she confided in Connie. "I need to break up with Gio. For now. If it's meant to be, it will last, right?"

"Do I look like an expert?" Connie munched on Cheetos. "Okay, I'm listening." Connie paid half-hearted attention. No boyfriend. No prospects. But Lori grew on her. They shared a room, dreams, and hopes for a bright and dazzling future.

"I see his face through the lens."

Connie licked her fingers. "That's weird. Maybe if you two hang out more, it'll disappear."

"Or maybe not."

"I think you're trying not to get too close."

"I'm already there." Lori sighed. "Thank you, Connie."

"That's it?" She rubbed fingers coated with cheese powder on her natty, hitting-the-books cardigan sweater. "No more discussion? It was just getting good."

"I know what I should do."

On Monday afternoon, Lori stopped by the restaurant with a note for Giuseppe.

Dear Giuseppe, I return to Italy next spring. It's best if we remain friends. I will see you when I return. Until then, I think it best that we not see each other.

Lori made her way back to the dorm in a stupor, drained from wondering how her letter was received.

"You did it, huh?" Connie busied herself. "I'm rearranging my clothes by color." Her tiny closet resembled a rainbow. She rarely wore black, a reminder of her Nonna, a withered, dour matron less than five feet in height who still grieved the loss of her husband twenty years after his death.

Lori watched her roommate with renewed appreciation for her listening ear. Connie—unpretentious, joyful, and ready to make the best of every situation.

Back in Texas, Christmas break promised movie outings, Lori's favorite pastime, and a reunion at a drugstore soda shop with Abi Jenkins and Jane Patterson. The threesome caught up on all the news from Lubbock High School.

"Mr. Dugan proposed to Miss Higgins!" Abi said.

"Our health class teacher? He was always gaga over Miss O'Donnell, the math teacher," Jane said.

"He did ask her. She said no." Abi slurped her chocolate malt. "She's joining the convent."

"No!" Lori, bemused, wondered how anyone discerned a vocation.

Gerald didn't bother to contact her. She was certain he knew she was in town. Word traveled fast, mainly by Abi, who spread news like wildfire.

On Christmas Eve, Grandma Lottie and Lori cozied up in the parlor beside a short-needled Virginia pine with its dense foliage and thick limbs. Colorful lightbulbs of red, green, blue, and gold bounced off the ornaments, many made of hand-blown glass from Germany. The Victorian angel topper was a family heirloom from Lottie's childhood days in Virginia.

Lori breathed in the heady pine fragrance. "Gran, you said Grandpa was thinking of joining the seminary. And you came along and changed everything."

Lottie chuckled. "I'm not sure it was all my doing!"

"But he fell in love with you and made a commitment."

"He did make a promise. If I survived, he'd marry me."

"You think he'd have become a priest if . . . ?"

"We'll never know. It doesn't matter. He served the Lord. Always."

"Gran, the photo I sent back with Tally. Is it her? Francine?" Lori curled up on a brocade settee and rested her head on a gold satin pillow.

"Well, I looked it over several times. It's possible. Very possible."

Lori expected her semester in Italy would wipe the slate clean. No Giuseppe. No Gerald. No roommates. Only romantic and remote locations evoking her time with Grandma Lottie less than a year ago. Yet, she'd changed. All the naivety of the *Roman Holiday* summer altered by making hard choices.

During her Roman spring, Lori visited the other Giuseppe, the

Italian hairstylist. He recognized the strawberry blonde Americana, so distinctive from his regulars and tourists.

"*Ben tornato*, Signorina!"

"You remember me?"

Giuseppe clapped his hands like a hummingbird batting its wings—his signal for an attendant to ready a spot. "I always remember my creations!" He cleared a chair in seconds. Lori took the seat. He analyzed her mirror image. "There's someone special in your life?"

"Yes."

"What's his name?" He examined the outline of her face.

She glanced away from the mirror. "Giuseppe."

"I like him already. Let's give you a *stile molto speciale!*"

"*Speciale!*" echoed Lori.

She left the salon with a style at least one year ahead of the States. Americans would classify it as the bouffant flip popularized by the soon-to-be president's wife, Jacqueline Bouvier Kennedy.

For the Boston homecoming, Ben was the first to greet her. "Lori, you look quite sophisticated."

She radiated self-confidence. "I'm ready to take on the world, Uncle Ben!"

"So you return and I leave for Rome. Come with me to the Summer Olympics. A special assignment. You can be my apprentice."

"But I'm just back! And I have some personal business."

"I suspected. You know what they say about absence."

"I know it can go either way. Make the heart grow fonder or out of sight, out of mind. I missed you and everyone. But the stories in my photos. So many. I'm making my way! It's coming together!"

The restaurant closed at 10:00 p.m. Giuseppe, thinner and wearier, mopped the tile floor as Lori walked through the unlocked door.

He leaned on the mop. "I've been waiting for you Princess Lorena."

They embraced for what seemed an eternity and rekindled a blissful romance that swept them through the summer.

The delicate, long-necked swans—a backdrop for a love story. Their graceful presence created a peace-filled, natural sanctuary within the Boston Common area. Beeping cars, traffic, and pedestrians faded into a distant backdrop. Lori pictured the moment lasting forever. Giuseppe, despite his machoism, was special to her—vibrant and intelligent—and she felt exceptional in his company.

A whirlwind romance had sparked since her return from Italy and competed with her passion—the art of photography. A silent battle raged over a gnawing desire to end the love affair before it overshadowed all else.

"Lori, I need to say goodbye." He focused on his Italian leather shoes, hands buried in the pockets of pleated trousers.

"You brought me here to say goodbye?" Lori choked on her words, made raw in her constricted throat. *How could this happen?* She was the one who'd considered the goodbye. Would she have had the same blunt, brutal approach?

His gold-flecked eyes softened and met her flinty expression. "I have an arrangement. A marriage. It's how we do things."

"So, this was never meant to be." Oh, how she knew it, a reckoning with the truth.

"I'm happy to be with you, Lori. You are *magnifica* and very wise. You're so different from other American women . . ."

"I'm not wise. I make mistakes all the time."

"I do not believe our time together was a mistake."

Lori watched the swans that hearkened back to the summer of 1956 with Grandma Lottie.

"We can still see each other." He looked hesitant, his thick brows knitted.

"Whatever for, Giuseppe?" She sounded abrupt and unkind. "Do you know who she is?"

"Of course."

"Okay, then. We say goodbye."

"Lori, I had to tell you before I grew any closer to you."

"I see. It was purely physical."

"No, it was beautiful . . ."

"Don't talk about it." The hardness of heart she fought resettled. "I'm okay with your decision. Actually, I'm relieved."

"Let's not be bitter . . ."

"I'm not bitter."

They gazed at the swans.

"Giuseppe. Be kind to her."

"I am, Lori. That's why I'm here now."

And they parted with a clumsy, half-hearted embrace and a tattered love story too easily dismissed.

Lori assessed her losses on the T back to campus. With college graduation soon approaching, Boston was behind her, and so was Giuseppe. She wanted it to end, but endings were abrupt and, many times, sad. Too many final goodbyes. The rhythmic sound of cars chugging down the tracks soothed the sting of rejection. And she consoled herself. It would never work. The train stopped at her destination. She stepped out and shook off the last pang of her first genuine heartbreak.

Chapter 19

Sighs and Whispers

Her skin was like white tissue paper, smooth and transparent. A tiny blue vein pulsed in her eyelid. "So you're the budding photographer I heard about."

"Thanks for meeting me, Betsy. My gran is like my public relations agent."

They settled into a tan leather booth at the Chock Full o' Nuts in Greenwich Village. Lori picked up a small sign propped against the napkin holder that read *Heavenly coffee*. She ordered coffee and date nut bread slathered with cream cheese.

"First, it's not Betsy. It's Bette. B-e-t-t-e." She paused. "Yeah, so is my grandmother Josie. What brings you back to New York?"

"An assignment." Like magic, the waitress breezed by with a sweet, moist sandwich and mug of coffee. "Split this with me?" Bette glanced at her watch, a dismissive action. Lori discounted the slight. "Are you in a show right now?"

"Off-Off-Broadway." Bette devoured the half sandwich in one bite. "I'm making my way uptown. So what brings you to New York?"

"Uh, like I said, an assignment. I was an intern for the *Globe*. They kept me on when I graduated from college. I'm photographing Central Park."

"Avoid the drug dealers. They prefer not to be photographed."

Lori wondered why she'd contacted the testy, preoccupied stranger. She had hoped to get some insight into locales off the beaten track.

Bette continued, "Why did you want to meet me?"

Before Lori could answer, Bette's mood swung in the opposite direction with renewed enthusiasm, her hunger abated. "When you finish your heavenly coffee, I'd like to show you something. Don't rush though. Why'd you want to see me?"

Bette repeated her question. Lori rationalized she was preoccupied. Maybe waiting for an audition callback. Maybe worn down by endless competition for acting roles. Maybe a bad review. Maybe nothing and everything that rattles nerves. Lori sipped her coffee, intrigued by the pale blonde with gossamer skin living out her dream. "What's your show?"

"I'll tell you when it opens. If I tell you now, it may not happen."

"That's pretty superstitious."

"It's me. Are you going to finish your sandwich?"

"I can order another one." She pushed the plate closer to Bette.

Bette pointed a frail finger at the sandwich. "You know they assemble those in Secaucus, New Jersey." She finished the remains in one bite. "I'm low on cash, if you could lend me a few dollars." Unblinking eyes.

Lori ordered a sandwich that arrived, wrapped in wax paper, in a few seconds. She pulled out a twenty-dollar bill from her purse. Bette nodded and murmured a thank-you. Lori perceived, in the struggling thespian, a different hunger. Maybe a hunger for fame, but definitely for the half-eaten sandwich between them. Lori suddenly realized she should've offered to buy her something to eat in the first place. But, it was all new. The theatre crowd. Actors waiting tables in restaurants, living hand to mouth, lining up for auditions, and giving way to an all-consuming passion to walk the boards. Lori sorted out coins from her change purse.

"No tipping policy here," Bette said in between sandwich bites. "Owner thinks it's degrading. Employees have a health plan and fair wages. Do you know Jackie Robinson?"

"Of course." Lori snapped her purse shut.

"He's VP." The mercurial Bette shot up from the booth. "Let's blow this joint!"

"From *The Wild One*! Marlon Brando."

Common ground, if shaky at best, Lori thought.

Bette turned the catchphrase "a New York minute" into thirty seconds with a purposeful stride and disappearing act as she descended a subway stairwell. Lori, the reflective photographer, dogged her trail and feasted her eyes on a melting pot of the human condition. She addressed Bette inside the jam-packed train. "Where are we headed?"

Bette gripped a grimy metal pole. "You'll see."

As a rule, Lori abhorred surprises. She suspected Bette didn't know her story, and she wasn't sure she cared to know any intimate details of Bette's story.

They ascended the subway stairs and headed for Grand Central Terminal at a fast trot.

"Where're we going?" Lori kept pace with the light-footed, ethereal actress.

"You'll see." Bette stepped up her stride. She pointed to a large archway near the Oyster Bar & Restaurant. "Stand over there at the corner and face the wall."

Lori followed instructions. Bette stationed herself at the opposite arch. Noisy herds of commuters piled out of trains and rushed by, heading for street exits.

"Lori?" Bette's voice was loud and clear as a bell.

"Yes, I hear you. It's like you're right next to me."

"Sighs and whispers. See you there."

"What do you mean?" Lori pressed her ear to the archway. She spun around. Bette was gone.

Back in Boston, Lori surmised that Bette had revealed the show's title before vanishing at Grand Central two months earlier. She boarded a train and arrived one hour before opening night of *Sighs and Whispers*, the Off-Off-Broadway play. The actors never faced the audience and spoke into an archway resembling the one at Grand Central Terminal. Eight characters weaved their stories—an assassination plot, a marriage proposal, a heist plan, and an illicit love affair played out in lines whispered into the arches. A sound system amplified what each character heard as they faced the wall.

Bette spotted Lori in the fifty-seat space filled with thirty people. After curtain call, she invited her backstage to a dressing room bigger than the stage itself.

"Well, what did you think?" Bette took a drag from a Winston offered by the actress who'd played the mistress in the love affair.

"I liked it."

"What's she gonna say, Bette?" The actress sucked in her half-spent cigarette. Her Brooklyn burr reminded Lori of Tally's mom.

"I did wonder what happened to all the story threads. They were sort of hanging out there."

Bette tossed her powder blue sweater on a lighted makeup counter and rolled deodorant under her arms. "That's the idea. Life. Nothing's tied up like a neat little package. Where're you staying?"

A voice bellowed. "You decent in there?" Three actors barged in. One gawped at Lori. "You a critic?"

"No, I'm a photographer." Lori extended a hand that went unnoticed.

"Everyone's a critic, luv." The bearded actor had a heavy Londoner accent. "Where's your flat?"

"I'm at the Gramercy Park Hotel. Uh, I better get going."

"We're just getting started, luv." He tore off a perforated square of blotter paper. "I've got some 'Wow.'"

Lori's guard went up. A few students she'd met at Boston University experimented with hallucinogens.

"White on white tablet, luv. LSD."

"Not interested. Thanks for the invite. I better go."

No one bothered to introduce themselves or see her out. Bette snatched up her sweater. "I can walk you to your hotel."

"No, that's okay. It's not that far."

"Maybe we can crash at your flat," said the Brit.

Lori ignored the comment. "Break a leg, everyone. I enjoyed the show."

Bette escorted her through the empty theatre. "Lori, thanks for coming. We let off steam."

"I'm not judging anyone."

Bette's eyes betrayed her disbelief. "Keep in touch."

"What were the sighs?"

"Sounds from the audience most likely. That's showbiz." Bette put on a sad-happy, all-knowing smile. Lori recognized it in herself.

The following morning, Lori strolled to Gramercy Park. She bought a pouch of bird seed to feed pigeons. A homeless man slept on a park bench under a sheath of old newspapers. Drool escaped his mouth. The British actor from the previous night was at the far end of the park exchanging money for a baggie. She spied on the transaction. The actor walked past and didn't recognize or acknowledge her. With a sudden sting of cold air, she zipped up her red corduroy jacket and tossed Bette's phone number into the nearest trash can.

Sighs and Whispers ran for two weeks, longer than anyone anticipated given the horrendous reviews. One forgiving critic called the play "inventive."

At the *Boston Globe*, Lori learned the ropes as a stringer, what Ben Hopkins cautioned her was "a tough way to make a living."

"But you freelance, Uncle Ben."

"The *Globe's* a great place to start. But don't get stuck there. Get your name out. Everywhere. I'll give you leads and intros."

Bernadette was her other ally. The Boston bookends—Ben and Bernie. Their esprit de corps bolstered her, fed her assurance, and minimized the stress of life as a photographer. Her impressive portfolio expanded. At the *Globe*, veteran staffers dubbed her Brenda Starr after the wildly popular comic strip, the stylish redheaded reporter with a penchant for escapades and glamorous assignments. Lori insisted she was no Rita Hayworth, the sex symbol Miss Starr was modeled after in the 1940s. "Where to now Miss Starr?" would resound from rows of desks rising above the pounding of typewriters. Editors told her she had a gift, an eye for a story. The more critical types confided that her writing was passable but her photos remarkable. One feature editor advised, "Stick to pics."

On Friday morning, November 15, Lori was summoned to a meeting with a handful of department editors and the chief of staff.

"Thanks for joining us, Lori. Coffee?" The newsroom staff editor wore the same gray sweater day in and day out. Press corps rumors circulated that he couldn't write without the sweater, his creative cape. Cub reporters referred to him as G.S. for "gray sweater."

"No thanks." Lori, a bit jittery, thought she was called in for a minor infraction, although she couldn't think of a single misstep she'd made. Poised with pen and stenographer's notebook, she awaited instructions. A handful of names filled a slate chalkboard under the heading *Holiday Vacations*.

G.S. poured coffee in a Styrofoam cup. "Lori, we got word the Dallas Citizens Council is complaining about the president's upcoming Texas tour. He's going by motorcade in other stops, so they're insisting he do the same in Dallas."

The chief of staff chimed in. "Lori, you're one of our best photographers. Inexperienced but damn good. We'd like you to cover the Dallas tour on a photo shoot. No interviews."

"We have a lot of reporters out since we're close to Thanksgiving." G.S. stroked his sweater sleeve as if it were a lucky rabbit's foot. "It's a crackerjack assignment."

Breakfast was earlier than usual. Lori crunched on a half-filled bowl of Corn Flakes and headed out to an awaiting taxi. Her four-hour plus flight was at 6:00 a.m., the exorbitant ticket paid for by the *Globe*. The photo assignment: capture the Boston-bred president as he proceeded down a wide avenue in Dallas.

When Lori arrived in Texas, she first called Grandma Lottie from a pay phone at the Dallas airport. "Hi, Gran. I'm here. Well, sort of . . . I'm on assignment."

"I've sent you a letter, dear. Mailed it yesterday. I'm going to Boston."

"When?" Blaring loudspeakers and the shuffle of travelers competed for attention.

"Christmas." Lottie poured tea into her Wedgwood teacup. She switched back and forth from tea to coffee each day. Friday morning was tea and lightly buttered toast.

"That's great. Were you going to surprise me?" A line formed behind her. A portly woman resembling a bear in her brown coat pointed at her watch with grim determination.

"No, I wrote it in the letter. What's your assignment?"

Lori signaled one more minute to the grizzly traveler behind her. She looked at her watch. 10:30 a.m. "The president and first lady arrive soon, in an hour. I'm here to take photos for our paper. He's big in Boston."

Lottie's laugh trickled like music over the phone line. "Yes, I imagine so. I'll see you next month, dear."

Lori clicked the receiver and slightly bowed to the anxious woman. She bounded outdoors into a taxi and headed downtown.

On November 22, 1963, a sunny day, Lori stood on the curb's edge at Dealey Plaza, a city park in Dallas. Photographers and spectators lined up, awaiting the presidential motorcade. A departure from her portfolio of nature photos, Lori enjoyed the parade-like atmosphere. She positioned her camera's lens like a spyglass. The four-door Lincoln Continental convertible limousine, painted black, moved slowly down the wide avenue. People cheered in the bright daylight. Lori swung her camera round and round, capturing exuberant profiles and the spirited cheers. She focused on the slim and stylish first lady in a fitted and fashionable pink suit and matching pill box hat. Glossy, dark hair framed her patrician features and wide-set eyes.

In a split second, chaos broke out. Time slowed and sped up all at once. Images forever frozen behind her camera. First, the gunshot. Or was it gunshots? Maybe a tire blowout? Through her camera lens, the president's head jolted backward in one violent thrust. Lori watched his head go limp in the first lady's lap before she scrambled behind the seat, nearer to the limo's trunk. Then screaming sirens. Cries of hysteria. Lori's camera dangled from its strap. Words echoed throughout the crowd. "The president's been shot!" She picked up her camera and recorded shocked eyewitnesses. A dumbfounded world went silent amidst pandemonium.

On Sunday morning, Lori returned to Boston haunted by images. By Sunday evening, she'd lost nearly three nights of sleep. Jacqueline Kennedy's pink suit, imprinted in her mind, kept her awake until early dawn. Her eyes, when closed, made the mental pictures sharper. The following day, she and the *Boston* editorial staff watched President Kennedy's funeral.

On Tuesday morning, with G.S.'s recommendation, she saw his doctor, Ralph Taylor, for anxiety, mainly insomnia. He prescribed Valium, a newly marketed sleeping pill. He gave her a few package samples from a drug company rep that called on him monthly.

"Try it first. If they help, here's a script," said Dr. Taylor.

Lori knew of her mother Miriam's proclivity for prescription drugs and was at first hesitant. She recalled, at the age of twelve, checking out the medicine cabinet in their house. There were at least five pill bottles. One had *Miriam Hopkins* neatly typed on a label. She had asked her mother about the contents. A nonchalant Miriam had replied, "Vitamins, aspirin for headaches." Lori had pointed to another bottle with *Miriam Hopkins* printed on it. "Oh, that helps me sleep."

Lori drifted back to her mother's words, like a warning.

"You'll be fine." Dr. Taylor patted Lori's folded hands like a Dutch uncle. "This will help you sleep."

Thanksgiving was a somber occasion. Instructed by Grandma Penny, no one asked Lori about Dallas. Her bloodshot eyes and quiet manner bespoke the tragedy she witnessed firsthand. After two nights of taking the sample drugs, she appeared groggy and distant.

Twenty of the Hopkins family congregated on November 28, 1963, to hear President Lyndon B. Johnson address the nation: "Tonight, on this Thanksgiving, I come before you to ask your help, to ask your strength, to ask your prayers that God may guard this Republic and guide my every labor." The words wafted through to Lori, who nodded off, exhausted by her travels and adjustment to the medicine. President Johnson continued, "We are not given the divine wisdom to answer why this has been, but we are given the human duty of determining what is to be, what is to be for America, for the world, for the cause we lead, for all the hopes that live in our hearts."

Within two weeks, sleep was easy. Too easy. Nights of easy. Lori day-dreamed about sleep and the comfortably numb sensation it offered. But she woke up tired and irritable, robbed of REM sleep from the prescribed sedative. Caffeine tempered drowsiness.

One day, Ben inquired about Lori's muddled state. "She's in a fog. What's going on?" He sat with his mom on a cold December day with Christmas two weeks away.

"I think it's the sleeping pills." Penny absentmindedly flattened a tea bag against her cup.

"Sleeping pills?" Ben's reaction was like a sounding alarm.

"Yes, Valium." Penny pressed on the packet to the point of tearing it. "I'm hoping when Charlotte gets here, they can talk."

Ben sipped his barely brewed tea. Water with a hint of flavor. "I can talk to her. I don't think we should wait."

"Do what you think is best. Charlotte will be here next week."

They listened in silence to "O Come All Ye Faithful" from an album *The Great Songs of Christmas* with recordings of various artists. Penny tossed her spent tea bag into a saucer and drank her strong, lukewarm tea in one swallow, letting the loose tea leaves settle at the bottom.

Later that evening, Penny fell asleep and snored soundly on a Chesterfield sofa of russet brown. Ben picked up the latest issue of *The New Yorker* dated December 14, with artwork of lush green Christmas trees lined up for sale on a city sidewalk on its cover.

Lori tiptoed into the parlor. "Uncle Ben, do any of your photos haunt you?"

"No, not really. Is it Texas?"

"It's everything. Insomnia. The images never leave me."

"Lori, the sleeping pills aren't the answer."

"Yes, I know. I'll be okay."

Lottie arrived three days before Christmas in Boston—where she'd once made a life, a home, and a family. But it would never be the same without John and Miriam. Husband and daughter now gone like ghosts of Christmas past. Yet in the Dickens's novel, a morality tale, Ebenezer Scrooge learned lessons about forgiveness and charity. She wondered what lesson she had learned with the loss of those dearest to her, except for Lori.

Lottie was immediately alarmed. Her beloved granddaughter appeared spent and visibly nervous. After a long-awaited embrace, she appraised her at arm's length. "Lori, are you okay?"

"A little tired." Lori's weak smile revealed her listlessness. "Thanks for being here, Gran."

"Of course, darling." Lottie nodded to Penny, who had phoned her earlier in the week to discuss Lori's exhausted state.

"Gran, I'm sleepy. I think I'll go to bed. We can catch up tomorrow." Another half-hearted smile so contrary to the beaming one, like a lit candle in a dim tunnel.

Christmas Day, 1963, fell on a Wednesday. The Hopkinses gathered for their traditional brunch. They filed into several areas, including the main dining room and card tables set up in corners for younger ones. Lori and Lottie took their mid-table spots, where they'd sat in the summer of 1956. Ben Hopkins passed a plate of brown bread to his niece. "Here, Lori. Your favorite."

Lori added a slice to her dish. No repartee or comeback. Blissful sleep—a few hours away—was her unremitting wakeful thought, even when surrounded by loved ones, even Lottie. She managed a feeble "Oh, boy" and passed the tray.

After brunch, generations crammed into the family room. Bernadette served her fabled hot chocolate. P. Rose's daughter, Lily, flattened out gift wrap and neatly folded it for her mother. Any paper beyond salvaging got balled up for a toss. Merriment and hugs abounded from children receiving cherished toys on their lists. Uncle Ben's gift to Lori elicited the most excitement they'd witnessed from her in weeks. "Wow, a Color Demi."

"That's nice, dear," Penny said with encouragement. "It's a camera, right?"

"The Color Demi came out in October. It's compact, and you get twice as many pictures per film," Ben said.

"Perfect for my new job," Lori said.

"Where?" Lottie batted a paper ball to Farley's son, Brian.

"New York. It's where it's happening!"

They met without pretense. No long goodbyes. Separate ways. Maybe a few sentiments that you'd find in a greeting card.

"I'll miss you, Lorena."

"Until your blushing bride arrives. How long has it been now?"

"Too long. It's a family matter. An arrangement. *Matrimonio combinato.*"

Lori reached for her blouse beside the bed. Giuseppe was never meant to last. How did she know? How could two people share so much intimacy and time together with no future? The affair was better dismissed, happy memories as a keepsake. He was old-school, she an unsettled soul desiring to roam the world and lose herself in capturing another person's story. But not his story. Nothing permanent.

It was a disquieting feeling, but no heartache remained for their final tryst. She avoided clichés. Even *I'll miss you* would've sounded vapid, insincere. "I'm moving and won't be back."

"You'll be back, but not for me." The truth accepted with one last goodbye.

Bidding a decisive farewell to Giuseppe was parting with her old life and beginning anew.

Saying goodbye to prescription drugs? Nearly impossible. Dependency on drug-induced sleep led to foggy days. She packed up everything but the pills and threw away the half-empty bottle.

Boston prepared her for urban living at its zenith in Manhattan. Her impression—busy sidewalks and vacant eyes. New York life was punctuated by freelance work and long stints away from a six-floor walkup in the Chelsea neighborhood. It was her hub, not what she bargained for, but far enough from Boston and Texas for now. Until loneliness seeped in the walls of her New York apartment.

Lori considered herself street-smart for a Southerner with firm roots in Lubbock, Texas. She missed Grandma Lottie, especially following the Christmas reunion, and wrote postcards from every photo shoot.

Her images were raw in a natural way. She rarely, if ever, enhanced photos with what she referred to as "magic tricks" before they hit print. "Don't touch up the photographs, okay?" she repeated to publishers she worked with in her vast array of growing business contacts. Life as a freelancer was good, if not great. She didn't mind the stress of living paycheck to paycheck, stretching her budget for monthly bills. The real home base was Texas and the comfort of Grandma Lottie's nest when she wasn't traipsing across the country or continent.

Lottie missed her granddaughter, the bright little star with a tinge of sorrow in its shadow fringe. She noticed the sadness every time Lori returned from her travels, as if she fought symptoms of a cold or flu. And then she'd be okay again as she geared up for an assignment mere days later. She'd remark, "I'm becoming a gypsy." A glint of wanderlust in a faraway gaze.

Local publishers and national magazines prized her creative choices. She built a solid reputation in the print industry. Many clients referred to her as an "award winner" when the perfect nature subject came along. What they didn't know, what she didn't yet know, was that she had a growing appetite for human stories.

Lori's naked eye recorded more than anything revealed to her on the soft or harsh focus of a camera lens. Stored in her subconscious, the images caused more restless nights, like the starfish in the summer of '56. How innocent, fixed on its sandy table before Uncle Ben threw it back into the salt water. Underneath the burnished armor was a set of spiny teeth surrounding a mouth in continual search of food. So much going on without noticing.

In a long overdue lunch date with Uncle Ben, on assignment in New York, she shook off her starfish dream from the night before. "It's your fault, this obsession of mine."

"And it all started with a turtle." He cherished serendipitous moments with the budding photographer. Her future was secure, her talent immense. She discovered the story in every image.

Lori inspected her club sandwich, each quarter impaled with a cellophane wrapped toothpick. "Sandra Dee. Did I tell you I met Sandra Dee? The real one?"

"I think I would have remembered that story." Ben methodically dipped French fries into a puddle of ketchup.

"You're the last person on earth who hasn't heard it, Uncle Ben."

"I'm all ears."

"Tally got me in to see the premiere of *Tammy and the Doctor* in Dallas." Lori un-skewered her turkey club and ate one quarter in two bites.

"And you brought Sandra Dee with you?"

"How'd you know?" She picked apart a three-layer sandwich quarter.

"I was joking."

"Tally dared me. I pushed my way to the front of the line, and there she was, so pretty and slim, with Bobby Darin."

"And?"

"I said, 'Miss Dee, I'm a big fan. Meet Sandra Dee. She's named after you.' I raised her up in her carrier, my Sandra Dee, and she stuck out her head. I'm telling you, Uncle Ben, they locked eyes for a few seconds, one Sandra Dee to the other."

"Then what happened?" He was surprised he hadn't yet heard this story. Or maybe he did around the family table and wasn't listening. It wouldn't be the first time.

"She laughed and said, 'Pleased to meet you, Sandra Dee.' I saw real kindness in her eyes, like she appreciated me naming a turtle or anything after her. Then I got kicked out. The ushers wouldn't let me bring Sandra Dee into the theatre."

"How discouraging."

"Actually, it's okay. I got to meet Sandra Dee. I went back the next week. Not my favorite Sandra Dee movie. I didn't see the love interest with the lead guy, Henry Fonda's son—not like the one with Bobby Darin."

Ben pushed the fries in front of Lori, who'd been eyeing them while retelling her story. She swapped with the remaining club sandwich quarters.

She was still the teen with itchy feet, irrepressible at times with her enthusiasm, sullen at times with her great loss, but perpetual motion in seeking the next adventure. They traded lunch, photography tips, and impressions of life through the camera's eye.

"I dreamt about the starfish. How it looks so peaceful while killing. We do that to each other, sometimes. Giuseppe and I were like starfish consuming each other."

"Lori, you're too hard on yourself."

"If I don't admit the mistakes, I'll never learn."

"Get some rest. The travels can run you down." Ben examined the check. "At least no starfish here."

"Unless New York is the starfish!" She winked and squeezed his arm.

Two years out of college, Lori continued building a solid portfolio with freelance business, hopping from job to job. Her assignments fostered a love for nature. She crossed the country, coast to coast, in search of the forgotten or near extinct.

When possible, Lori brought Sandra Dee on an assignment. A rented car was easiest for transporting her sidekick. She believed Sandra Dee liked the road trips, and it gave her solace that she wasn't abandoning her yet again. Her favorite assignments were in the Southwest. She reveled in her travels along Route 66 through ghost towns, stretches of desolate landscape alive in ways unseen to the eye. The quiet expanse comforted her, much akin to Texas but less barren.

In Arizona, she pulled over for an impromptu photo shoot of cactus flowers. Sandra Dee munched on a medley of beets, carrots, and corn. The sun was a luminous yellow in a sapphire blue sky. Lori fixed the perfect lens and made adjustments to light filters. The Christmas cactus spawned red and white petals bursting forth from smooth, succulent leaves. Satisfied with the shoot, she reclined on a cluster of large rocks and soaked in the tranquility.

Lori never heard the rattler sidewinding her way. The sting was like hundreds of bees attacking a single target. The venom restricted blood flow and caused shortness of breath in an instant. She limped to the station wagon packed with camera equipment, a suitcase, and Sandra Dee. A cursory examination revealed one puncture, not two, on the side of her ankle. Maybe the bone prevented the second fang from sinking in. Swelling and bruising occurred instantly, then faintness as she hobbled into the backseat of her rental in search of a package.

One week before Lori headed westward, Ben gave her three vials of antivenom serum . . .

• • •

"It's enough to fight off the venom before you get to a hospital. You'll have thirty minutes. You may get deathly sick from the medicine, but you won't die from it. You could die without it."

"Sounds a bit over the top. I'm always careful." She shook the contents.

"Trust me on this one. Snake bites are quick. You won't know until it penetrates. You'll be focused on the shoot."

• • •

Lori veered into a gas station for directions to a hospital. Beads of sweat and her distended ankle alarmed the owner.

"The medical center's about forty-five minutes away," he said and insisted on driving her. She agreed if Sandra Dee could accompany them.

The emergency center staff injected additional antivenom drugs. After a restless overnight stay, the resident doctor wrote a script for sleeping pills before releasing her.

Lori frowned at the medical note. "Thanks, Doc, but I don't need it."

He answered, "Just in case."

Before leaving town, she headed to a drugstore and filled the prescription for Valium.

In New York, Lori missed three assignments in a row from different publishers and stopped calling family and friends. She blamed recuperation from the snake bite. The first missed shoot was "New Life at the San Diego Zoo." The second was the Portland Rose Festival and Starlight Parade. The third was a pictorial overview of Yellowstone National Park in Wyoming.

She normally cherished her westward assignments, an escape from the metropolis. Publishers complained of having to hire another photographer in a pinch. The snake bite recovery led to flimsy excuses, lies, and apologies. They varied from "Sorry, there was a death in the family. I won't be able to get there" to feigning a long-term illness short of cancer. Words came out of her mouth that corrupted her principles, leaving her defeated and demoralized, like the alibi for the Yellowstone project, the final blow to her self-esteem.

Lori popped a Valium and dialed the phone on her nightstand. "Roger? Lori Hopkins. Well, you'll never believe this one. I have mono. I'll be out of commission for at least a month or so." Roger whined about no one being available up to her standards and told her to get better soon.

Three weeks of missing paychecks and a shrinking budget drained her savings to pay rent and utilities. Sleepless nights returned, and the

Valium lost its potency. A physician prescribed methaqualone, a synthetic, safe barbiturate-like depressant to lower anxiety and induce sleep.

As fellow Manhattanites, Bette and Lori became fast friends. Their acquaintance opened doors for Lori to New York's murky underground of drugs, art, and punk rock bands. After Bette's closing night performance in another flop titled *Dress Rehearsal*, she and Lori headed for a party at a SoHo club. Lori downed a glass of champagne offered by the play's producer, who was convinced he had a hit on his hands. Lori flattened out like a dead weight from the drink and the Quaalude she popped earlier. The British actor, Malcolm, from *Sighs and Whispers* spotted her collapsed on a black velour chaise in the lounge area.

"Bette, your friend's fagged out."

"She's into ludes. Has trouble sleeping." Bette snorted a line of cocaine and wiped her nose.

The British actor loomed over Lori. "I've never introduced myself. Malcom. And you're Lori?"

Lori lifted her head, a leaden weight. "And you're the drug dealer."

Malcolm grasped his black silk shirt. "I'm an actor, luv. Artists, poets, writers throughout the ages used drugs." He offered a colorful slip of paper with pink hearts like a valentine. "Aldous Huxley, author of over fifty books, said LSD was his most profound creative experience. You could use a stimulant, luv. C'mon. One hit."

Within the hour, Lori's euphoria took hold. Pulsing music from the Velvet Underground transformed to shades of red, white, and blue. The American flag materialized, melted, and dripped before her eyes. She touched an electric halo fixed above Bette's shimmery, light-infused hair strands. Partiers and cast members had electricity coursing through their veins like fluorescent pink liquid. In her haze, she repeatedly pressed the button on her Polaroid Land Camera and developed a pile of photos to record every distorted shape and transcendent image.

Six hours later, in Chelsea, Lori paced back and forth in the few feet of her living space. "I'm climbing the walls," she muttered. She picked at her itchy forearms and sorted the Polaroid snapshots. Blurred and undiscernible silhouettes. Nothing like the hazy electrified humans she'd witnessed a few hours ago. Jittery and wide-awake, she headed for the medicine cabinet and downed a Quaalude to escape the waking world. She drifted off with the chirps of a starling on her windowsill, like the one in Boston when the world was simpler and her mind much clearer.

Ruth Lieberman followed Lori's meteoric success and collected photos of prairie dogs for her tenth-grade project—research on nineteenth century pioneer life. Lori's nature shots were dramatic and stunning. Wild horses racing along unmarked paths as if celebrating their harness-free existence. Bison so still they seemed like statues. A red fox guarding the entrance to her den.

Lori's subjects were either oblivious to being subjects or captivated by her presence. A photography magazine referred to her as "Lori Hopkins, Svengali with a Camera." Ruth first read Lori Hopkins's bylines with disdain. Lori had killed her sister, Joy—a simple truth as interpreted by a stubborn-hearted hurting child. But her unrelenting spirit yearned for peace since Joy's death, and Lori was an integral part of it. In moments of truth, she realized that Lori was hurting too. Yet, a resentful eight-year-old wanted no part of Lori, the Grim Reaper.

The airline postcard had arrived on a sweltering afternoon in the summer of '56. *Dear Ruth, I'm thinking of you and hope we can keep in touch. Joy was my world and my best friend. I'll always miss her. Lori.* She had read the hastily scribbled note three times and tore it into minute pieces. But the words had lodged within her. *Keep in touch . . . Joy was my world . . . I'll always miss her.*

Only years later would Ruth even consider that Lori had hurt as much she did over the sudden, irreparable loss. Ruth's mom had told her that Lori and Joy were like sisters of different mothers and urged her to extend a gesture of peace and forgiveness.

"Write to her. Send a greeting card," Mrs. Lieberman had said.

"Why should I? I don't even know where she lives." Ruth, at sixteen, was weary of harboring resentment. She wanted to clear the air but kept it to herself. Until she spoke to Abigail Jenkins—now Sawyer—Lori's friend. Ruth babysat the Jenkins's two children. Abigail's husband was a mailman, and Abigail—or Abi—the center of all Lubbock gossip.

"Hi, Mrs. Sawyer."

"Girls are asleep. Should be an easy night. I made chocolate-marshmallow fudge. Help yourself," said Abi.

The Sawyers headed out the door for bowling night. Ruth settled into Mr. Sawyer's La-Z-Boy recliner of army green cotton velour. Abigail rushed back inside. Ruth seized her golden opportunity. "Mrs. Sawyer, I'm trying to contact Lori Hopkins, the photographer. I have a homework assignment, and she may be able to help."

The honking car interrupted. Abigail searched a desk drawer for hand lotion. "What? Oh, Lori. Here!" She tossed over an address book from the desk drawer and ran out the door.

Lori didn't recognize the voice that greeted her over the phone. "Yes, hello?"

"Hi, this is Ruth Lieberman. Joy's sister."

"Ruth?" Lori shook off her fuzzy state.

"Uh, I meant to contact you earlier."

"It's okay. How've you been?"

Ruth coiled the phone cord around her wrist. The call was harder than she ever expected. "Um, I wanted to tell you that, um, I really like your photos. I have most of the magazines with your photos, and I, um, used your prairie dogs for a school project on prairie life. I got an A."

"Well, thanks for letting me know. I'm grateful you told me." Lori paid no mind as to how Ruth obtained her number. It didn't matter.

"And to tell you that, uh, it's not your fault what happened to Joy. Please forgive me if I hurt you. I know you loved her like a sister."

Lori's whirlwind of emotions rivaled any storm. Ruth threw her a lifeline attached to a phone cord and the words: "You loved her like a sister." Tears streamed. Tears for Joy. Tears of Joy. Tears that cleansed.

"Ruth?" Words caught in her throat.

"Yes?"

"Thank you."

"Okay. I look forward to your next photos. Where will they be published?"

The conversion was sudden, like St. Paul being struck by a blinding light. "*National Wildlife.* I'm doing a spread on red wolves in Mississippi. They're really scarce."

"Okay. Uh, Happy Easter."

"Yes, and Happy Passover, Ruth. Tell your mom I said hi."

Lori inhaled a fresh attitude and exhaled her demons. Ruth was waiting to see her work. Maybe others were waiting. She knew her publishers were waiting. With sudden resolve, she opened the mirrored medicine cabinet, uncapped prescription bottles, and emptied sleeping pills and sedatives into the toilet. Temptation flushed away and a life renewed.

Chapter 20

Barb Wired

Barbara Wilkins never intended to make a living as a spy. After college, she moved on to graduate school for her master's degree in education, a two-year program required for school administrators. She was committed to being "the best high school advisor to come down the pike" as she confided to faculty and mentors. Until the country came calling, in the middle of the Cold War.

By 1963, Vietnam was an awaiting bloody cauldron stirring up unrest in American universities. Her brother Gerald was in the seminary getting closer to God. President John F. Kennedy was assassinated months after Barbara started her guidance counselor career. She set her sights on R. L. Paschal High School in Fort Worth, Texas, drawn to its history as Fort Worth High School, which opened in 1882. Briefly known as Central High School, it moved to its new location in 1955, where Barbara planted herself for a career challenging students to realize their dreams.

In June 1964, a recruiter from a high school in Roanoke, Virginia, called her out of the blue. "Hey, nothing wrong in checking it out," she said to Gerald on one of her weekly phone calls. "Maybe I need to get out of Texas."

She remembered every beat of the fateful day that reshaped her life, distorted it beyond anything rational. The recruiter, Mr. Mark Latchford, asked to meet June 7 in Houston. Barbara mentioned the recruitment meeting to her Uncle Preston. "You're as smart as a whip, Barbara, and I'm sure he'll try his darn best to win you over."

On June 6, Barbara finished up her school year, sending seniors into the wild blue yonder. Some graduates set their sights on college, others trade school. More than a handful received best wishes and hugs on their wedding plans. Barbara's calendar marked the appointment—Christie's for lunch at 11:45 a.m. She commenced her four-hour drive at 6:00 a.m. with a scorching heat rising from paved roads. By noon, Houston would be "hot enough to fry eggs on the sidewalk," Uncle Preston warned.

"Miss Wilkins?" The gentleman stood up from a table for two, displacing his napkin and oblivious to it. Barbara immediately picked it up.

"Mr. Latchford?"

"Yes." He pulled out the other chair. "Please sit. Thank you for accepting our invitation."

A waitress in a cornflower-blue uniform and hair pinned under a net showed up on the spot.

"I think I'll have the steak platter. How 'bout you, Miss Wilkins?" Mr. Latchford directed full attention to his guest.

"Fish platter, please."

The waitress collected both menus. "I'll be back with two waters. Care for anything else?"

"Iced tea, please. Plenty of ice." Barbara squirmed and settled in.

"Sounds good. No sugar," Mr. Latchford said all businesslike.

The waitress shifted her wide hips from one foot to the other. "It's swate tay." She pushed a pencil behind her ear.

"Uh, that's fine."

Barbara read his body language—anxious and abrupt.

Latchford tucked his napkin under his collar. "Been in Texas for three days and consumed enough beef to last a lifetime." He resembled Don Knotts, the slightly built, bug-eyed actor who played a deputy sheriff on television's *The Andy Griffith Show*. Even his choppy delivery was right in character with Barney Fife wearing a police badge and holster in a small town like Mayberry. He continued, "Ate at Brenner's Steakhouse on recommendation from a colleague who said I'd chomp down the best steak in Texas."

"Well, you came to the right state for steak." Barbara was lost for engaging conversation and wondered why she drove four hours to rendezvous with the thin, socially awkward man.

The waitress returned with two large glasses of sweet tea, extra ice for Barbara. Left alone, Mr. Latchford tipped forward, his oversized orbs unblinking and penetrating. "Miss Wilkins. Let me get right to the point. I'm from the CIA. We are in a recruitment phase."

The refreshing tea quenched Barbara's thirst. "No, this is for a position as a high school counselor, right?"

"Made up. Your country would like you to serve."

Barbara laughed self-consciously. "How on God's green earth did you find me?"

"We can find anyone, and your name came into our data search."

"But why me?" Barbara drank deeply from her frosted tumbler.

"Many reasons, but I must stop right here. If you have no interest, I will terminate the appointment before lunch is served. I will inform our waitress that you weren't feeling well and left. You will not tell anyone about this meeting. Absolutely nothing to no one."

"Well, Mr. Latchford, as we say, 'Lettin' the cat outta the bag is a whole lot easier 'n puttin' it back.'" She paused. "And if I'm interested?"

Mr. Latchford now appeared less like the comic actor and more like a secret agent. He relaxed his posture, a crooked smile on his face. Nothing nefarious, only a professional who knew his mission, knew how to recruit, and sensed another victory. "Well, then, I hope you enjoy your lunch, the fried catfish platter. That would have been my second choice."

Barbara downed her iced tea. The waitress brought over a pitcher and poured a second glass. Mr. Mark Latchford checked his watch. All business again.

The plates of food were set in front of them. Mr. Latchford sniffed his steak like a dog wary of tainted raw meat. He speared the center of the prime cut, inspected the morsel, and chewed it slowly with total concentration. Barbara looked on with morbid fascination.

"Poisoning. An unsophisticated attempt I can spot immediately by an acrid smell or taste at first bite." He ate his lunch with relish as if it were his last meal. "We'll neutralize your speech. We don't want to pin you to a locale."

"Ready and rarin' to go." Barbara placed the napkin in her lap and picked up her fork.

Mr. Latchford dabbed his chin. "Precisely!"

"Precisely?"

"Yes, that's precisely what we don't want." He pointed his fork. "Nothing to trace you to Texas. You'll have several hometowns. You'll learn three languages."

"I know a little Spanish."

His smile broadened. "It's a start."

Chapter 21

Red Badge of Courage

In the frosty night air, Lori's shallow breaths hovered like wispy clouds. Depleted and chilled to the bone, she unlocked the front door and heard the faint playing of a jazz piano.

"Come watch," Grandma Penny said. "It's a new Christmas show."

Lori bent from side to side fighting mental fatigue, feigning interest in the animated special. The television screen illuminated the dimly lit family room with bookshelves from floor to ceiling. Like a child eyeing candy jars, Penny followed Charlie Brown's search for a Christmas tree. The incorrigible Lucy, a bully prototype, chose the gaudiest in the lot, all sparkly and pink like a frosted cupcake. Charlie Brown approached a withered tree branch spasmodically shedding a few of its remaining needles, as if shivering in the cold.

The bumbling Charlie Brown, always on the brink of a failed mission, gave the story line its predictable yet charming direction. The gang, led by Lucy, vetoed his tree choice. Oh, how he would ruin Christmas!

"Join me, dear. It's almost over." Penny patted the space next to her on the tweed love seat in a color she referred to as oatmeal. Lori collapsed on the cushion and stretched out tired, aching legs. The credits rolled. The Peanuts gang caroled, "Hark! The Herald Angels Sing."

Ben thundered in. "Hello! Where's my favorite niece?" He entered the archway, hands hugging the frame.

"Welcome home. We didn't expect you before Christmas." Penny rose and hugged him. "Don't I get a mention in your favorites?"

Ben, more jovial than usual, hugged her back. "I only have one mom." He beckoned Lori, and the three-way hug lasted through a string of commercials. "Lori, I'm glad you're here. I'll cut to the chase. Can you take over an assignment for me?"

"Depends, Uncle Ben." Lori stooped down and chucked off her brown suede boots. "I'm leaving soon to spend time with Gran, and I could use a break from the cold."

"Then you won't mind the assignment. A shoot in the Florida Everglades. Flora and fauna."

"Fauna? You mean crocodiles, alligators and snakes?"

"I thought you liked reptiles. Anyway, it's not until the new year, so you have a few weeks to think it over."

Lori shuffled photo assignments like a casino card dealer. At twenty-four, still a fresh-faced college grad, she'd already acquired clout as a freelancer and, now drug-free, met all her deadlines.

"I'll give you a ring when I get to Texas." She removed the other stylish boot, rubbed her sore feet, and mumbled, "These should've stayed in the display window." She'd spent the last few days traipsing around Boston on a shopping odyssey and had loaded up gifts to leave under Grandma Penny's Christmas tree. Her heart ached for Texas and Grandma Lottie. Her plan was to pack up Sandra Dee and head home.

"Where are you going, dear?" Penny bent her twig-like calves over the sofa's armrest.

Ben hesitated. "Saigon."

Lori glanced at Sandra Dee burrowed in hay with only her shell visible, a water-filled drinking tube clamped to her wire cage. She rented a poppy-red Ford Mustang and traveled the length of the eastern sea coast on Route 1. Before swinging west to Texas, she planned an overnighter in South Carolina and one in Florida. "You know, Sandra Dee, you might like Florida. Maybe we can head back that way and take Ben's assignment in the Everglades? What d'ya think?"

Lottie Mitchell busied herself preparing for Lori's return. The tree was up, a soft pine needle. Childhood ornaments and happy times with John, now gone fifteen years, hung on each branch. Lottie set Lori's eighth grade project, a gingerbread house, on the dining room buffet table. Tom Hopkins had shellacked its roof trimmed in red and green gumdrops, white icing framing each window and two candy canes bordering the entranceway. Lori had won first prize and gifted the confectionary to her grandmother the year before the storm.

The slam of a car door interrupted Lottie's musings. Lori ran up the walk and into an awaiting embrace.

They settled in for a quiet night of reminiscing.

Now, days before Christmas, one cherished memory sparked another.

"Remember when I tried on that dress in Filene's Basement? The homecoming one?" Lori asked.

Lottie sipped a cup of Mexican hot chocolate. "You called it your Red Badge of Courage."

"I never told you, but I felt like I was covered by angels that day."

"What do you mean?" Lottie inquired so breathlessly she barely got the words out.

"The raincoat you wrapped around me, like wings, angel's wings. You were all like angels to my rescue, giving me shelter."

Lottie leaned against the chair's spindles. "We can be surrounded by love in the strangest of places."

"Yeah, Gran. Even in the basement of a department store. I love you, Gran. You helped me weather everything, every storm in my life."

"You are my life, Lori. I'm so glad you're here for Christmas."

The following morning, they finished a leisurely breakfast of strong, brewed coffee and a cinnamon swirl cake piled high with buttery crumbs. Juicy sections of tangerines gave the minor feast a healthy component. Lori browsed celebrity headlines from the *Lubbock Avalanche* announcing Elvis Presley's annual donation of $50,000 to a variety of Memphis charities.

"Gran, I kept a secret from you."

"Yes, dear?"

"When we were in Paris, I rode the elevator with Elvis Presley."

"Really? Did you talk to him?"

"I called him Mr. Presley. He said call me Elvis."

"Did he say anything else?"

"Yes. He said do something worth remembering."

"It must have meant a lot to you."

"It means more sharing it with you. Merry Christmas, Gran."

They interspersed lively conversation of the Boston family tree branches with giggles like schoolgirls enjoying the last few minutes of recess. Lori planned to take Grandma Lottie shopping at the new department store in Lubbock that had opened over the Thanksgiving weekend.

"You go without me, dear. I woke up with a bit of a headache. I'll sit and read, and maybe we can go out for dinner." Lottie curled up on the seat cushion. To Lori, she seemed like a porcelain doll in her pink chenille robe and pale complexion.

"Are you sure?" Lori said. "I don't need to go shopping." She lingered. "What are you reading?"

Lottie displayed the cover—*I Never Promised You a Rose Garden*.

Lori looked baffled. "Isn't it about mental illness?" She picked up a green tote bag beside the sofa. "Here, I brought the *Selected Writings of Truman Capote*. It has 'A Christmas Memory' in it."

"Yes, I remember, from *Mademoiselle* in their December issue. 1956. I still have the magazine." Lottie flipped open the book. "I'll read it again. It's been a while. See you when you get back, dear. Leave the dishes. I like my little chores."

"Now that's the difference between us, Gran. They're all yours." She checked her watch. "I might stop by the Kress store too, for sales." She kissed Lottie's translucent cheek.

By noon, Lori arrived home with packages and a half gallon of Breyers ice cream—vanilla bean for root beer floats.

She recognized Tally's mom's car, a white Pontiac Catalina, parked in the driveway. A surge of joy went through Lori at the unexpected visit. Hopefully they were stopping by for lunch. *Maybe Tally's with her*, thought Lori. She bounded toward the front door. Maybe they organized a surprise. She pictured Tally springing from behind the couch or through the parlor archway.

Lori juggled shopping bags and opened the door. Tally's mom jumped up from the couch.

"Hi, Mrs. Marconi. Is Tally with you? Where's Gran?" Her wary eyes searched the room.

Tally rushed in, tears streaming down her face.

Lori ran to her and grabbed both arms. "What's wrong? Are you okay?" She was close to shaking out an answer. Tally's lips trembled. She brushed away a steady flow of tears.

"Lori, sweetheart, sit down," said Mrs. Marconi. "I've got plain horrible news, and this isn't easy."

"What? Where's Gran?" She pointed a finger accusingly. "No! Don't you say it! Don't you tell me!" Lori appeared frozen, speechless, like a victim of shock, her eyes lackluster and unfocused.

"Tally!" her mom hollered. "Get a blanket! Dear God, I think she's having a seizure."

On Saturday, December 18, ten years to the day of the storm, her beloved Grandma Lottie died. There was no warning, similar to the sudden loss of her parents, Miriam and Tom Hopkins, hit by a tornado blast on Sunday, December 18, 1955.

By Divine Providence, if she even believed it, Lori was home for the holidays and had spent a few wondrous moments with her gran two hours earlier, soaking up all the love she could hold and letting go of bitterness for the approaching Christmas season.

Lottie died of an aneurism at the foot of her bed. She was dressed in her pink chenille robe. An open magazine, *Mademoiselle*, December issue, 1956, was splayed across the floor beside her. A model, reminiscent of Audrey Hepburn, wearing a lilac blouse and skirt under a silvery evening coat peered out from the cover, glamorous albeit outdated. The words, *A Christmas Memory by Truman Capote* were printed across from the photo. Lori imagined her gran revisiting what she'd read aloud a year after the devastation of 1955. And now she wondered what would've happened if she were there at the instant of death, what futile efforts to save Grandma Lottie's life she would have made. The doctor said she died instantly.

But Lori went over the morning, image by image, how Gran rubbed her temple and complained of a building headache. Died instantly, the doctor said, and the words were now an indelible mark, an imprint of the fragility of life. A woman who defined courage in her youth, wisdom in age, and understanding, one of the greatest gifts of all, was now dust unto dust. Courage, Wisdom and Understanding. Her tombstone would reference Psalm 139, the one written on her heart since childhood days in Virginia.

The Texas funeral was a brief service. Charlotte Mitchell's body returned to Boston, far from Virginia, her original home, and even farther from the home she'd made in the Lone Star state.

Uncle Ben and Grandma Penny met Lori at the airport. Ben was solemn. Penny was tearful at the loss of her best friend, a tenderhearted soul that gave birth to Miriam, the joy of her dear son's life. She considered Charlotte a sister, and now she would do her best to give comfort to the little girl all grown up but still so vulnerable. Lori said nothing upon greeting them. Her grief was palpable.

"They're all waiting for you, Lori." Penny's embrace was hard and sudden. "We're all here for you." She had no other words.

Ben chimed in. "I bought you a camera for Christmas. I think you'll like it."

Penny admonished. "Ben, couldn't that wait?"

"Unless you want to wait for Santa Claus." Ben's penchant for humor punctuated any setting.

Lori clutched her cosmetic case toting a straw, a water bottle, drilled holes, and Sandra Dee. "Thanks, Uncle Ben. I'll need it for when I take over your assignment."

"Florida?" he asked, his eyebrows raised.

"No. Vietnam."

Christmas 1965 was a sad affair, cheered only by news of Bernadette's forthcoming wedding. Nearing forty, she'd met a man five years her junior, William Butler, called Bill or BB because he had a laugh like a spray of bullets. Bill introduced himself to the Hopkins brood and, as an only child, sparked an instant kinship with Lori. Bernadette was the first to hug her brokenhearted niece, her favorite, when she entered the doorway.

The funeral for Charlotte Mitchell was December 23, five days and ten years following the storm. The Hopkins family referred to it as the Storm of '55. Lori wouldn't tolerate hearing the word "tornado," which conjured up thoughts of a twister and all the good that came out of it for Dorothy and her dog, Toto, in the Kansas prairie land in the fictional story. She wasn't Dorothy and there was no Wizard of Oz. The years following the storm were made bearable by the serene presence and loving protection of Charlotte Mitchell.

But for now, the family focused on meeting Bill and the imminent wedding. Lori was happy for Aunt Bernie who could "charm the stripes off a zebra," as her dad would say.

When Bill introduced himself, Lori made a point of asking him how he and Bernadette had met, stunned that she had no news of him.

"We met on an assignment. She actually interviewed me." Bill pulled at his forest-green turtleneck sweater.

"About what?"

"Jazz. I'm a musician, and I teach music at two high schools here in Boston."

Bernadette piped in. "Not too surprising, huh?"

"Not at all." Lori gave her a quick jab and an embrace so tight that they felt each other's heartbeats.

Lori pondered letting go of all ties to her remaining family. When Penny Hopkins telephoned her in Texas, she'd practically ordered Lori to come to Boston and be "with family." Lori had conceded for two reasons—Grandma Lottie's burial and her next assignment. She'd convince Uncle Ben to allow her to accompany him to Vietnam or go in his place. If she went in his stead, her argument was one of youth versus age. Uncle Ben was over fifty and might find the assignment punishing. She made her case to him in private. "I'll take your assignment, and you can go to Florida. No threat of malaria, bullets, or politics."

Ben questioned Lori's proposition. "I'll think about it." He was the mentor, the one who ignited her passion for being the camera's eye. He didn't want to let her down but also didn't want to appear as the coward slinking away from a battleground assignment.

The morning of Christmas Eve, Bernadette and Lori rose at 5:00 a.m. for girl talk, hot chocolate, and Grandma Penny's sugar cookies in shapes of bells, stars, and Christmas trees.

"Okay, so tell me that machine gun laugh doesn't get to you." Lori got right to the center of her cookie and argument all at once.

Bernadette plopped three miniature marshmallows in her hot chocolate and watched them fizzle. "It's when he's nervous. Why? Does it annoy you?" She rarely shied away from any discussion no matter how pointedly personal or uncomfortable.

Lori reached for a handful of marshmallows. "As long as it doesn't bother you."

"Honest, Lori. I'm okay. It's just a laugh. What's this really about?"

"I want you to be happy." Lori's concern was genuine.

Bernadette and Lori clasped hands over the Formica table. The cuckoo clock chimed 5:15 a.m.

"Grandma will be up in fifteen minutes."

"Lori, I'm happy." Bernadette released Lori's hands. "I love Bill. He's not perfect, but he's for me. I know it."

"Good, I'm glad."

"Anyone in your life right now?" Bernadette chose a star cookie and a potentially troubling topic.

"I'm too busy for romance." Lori bit into a bell sprinkled with green crystallized sugar. "Anyway, I'm hoping I can go to Vietnam with or without Uncle Ben on assignment."

"Vietnam? Do you know there are already close to twenty-five hundred soldiers dead, not counting wounded and—"

"I'm not going there to count bodies." Lori swallowed the last of her hot chocolate.

"Why Vietnam?"

"Because I'm tired of photographing subjects I can't interview." Lori pushed away her plate, a habit since high school cafeteria days.

Penny stuck her head through the archway. "Girl talk?"

"Hi, Grandma. Come join us." Lori appreciated the interruption.

"What's our story?" Penny prepared the coffee pot.

"Oh, how I met Bill," Bernadette said.

"Will you be here for the wedding, Lori?" Penny measured ground coffee beans.

"When is it?" inquired Lori.

Bernadette broke off a star point from her second cookie. "August of next year."

"Sounds like a long way off." Lori wondered where she would be in a year, if not a month.

The Hopkins family, clusters of siblings and grown children, crowded into the dining room and den. Lori was, again, the sad happy girl of ten years ago when she cried in Grandma Lottie's lap on a Christmas night and Lottie's gentle hands stroked her hair as she sang "Mary's Slumber Song," an old lullaby. Now, on top of the din of Christmas cheer, she hummed the tune and gazed at her empty Spode dinner plate and the hand-painted tree in its center. Penny had been collecting the design since 1950 and was thrilled with each acquired piece like a child with brand-new fashion dolls.

"Did you say something, dear?" Penny was wide-eyed like the carved blue bird in the kitchen's cuckoo clock.

"Ah, no, just . . ." Lori noticed Bernadette's tender expression facing her fiancé, Bill, at the far end of the table. For a moment, gratitude filled her heart, and she resisted the taciturn indifference to a time of year bringing joy, peace, and good will. Grandma Lottie was gone, and she didn't say goodbye. Another strike in the strange but undeniable complexity and simplicity of fate. "Glad to be here. With family." She felt a twinge of disloyalty to the familiar ghosts in her life, warranted or not.

Chapter 22

London Calling

*L*ori made a to-do list before heading to Saigon, the capital of South Vietnam. The chores included: arrange for mail to be held at the post office in New York; drop off Sandra Dee at Bernie's apartment in Boston; return Connie's phone call; pick up birthday card for Uncle Ben; buy boots; and meet Francine. The last item involved a flight to London; a rendezvous with Polly, her Grandma Lottie's friend from Paris; and a meetup with the adopted French girl now grown and living fulltime in London.

Bernadette hugged her niece. "We can't keep track of you, Lori."

"You have the list, right? Green beans, grapes, papaya, and apples. Leave the skin on. Oh, and since I'll be gone for a long while, let her float in this tub every few weeks. Don't put her near anything you eat. Turtles have salmonella, but you knew that, right?"

"Bill told me."

"Oh, Bill. Yes, she won't contaminate you. But keep her from the kitchen and bathroom."

"And bedroom." Bernadette glanced around her one-bedroom apartment. "I'm thinking of bringing her to work."

"Good, she'll like that. Okay, no long goodbyes. I've got a plane to catch."

"Lori, I worry about you. Always on the run."

"Don't worry. I'll catch my breath." She passed Bill on the stairwell. "Hi. Remind Bernie about the apples."

"Apples?"

"Don't peel the apples. She'll know." Lori bounded down the stairs and opened the door wide to the next horizon. She tossed her list into a receptacle and readjusted her duffel bag.

By mid-January, 1966, London's deep freeze and snowfall almost canceled Lori's flight plans. When she arrived at Heathrow Airport, the temperature was minus two degrees Celsius or nearly twenty-eight degrees Fahrenheit. Polly arranged a meeting the following day at a bakery shop in Piccadilly Circus, not far from where Lori and Grandma Lottie vacationed.

Polly and Lori ordered blueberry scones and Twinings English breakfast tea. "I'm so sorry about Charlotte. You must miss her terribly."

"She was my life." Lori left her scone untouched and gulped her milky tea. "Is Francine open to meeting me?"

"Yes. She is but wonders why you want to meet her." Polly piled a spoonful of strawberry jam and clotted cream on her scone. "I miss these." She took a huge bite, letting the buttery crumbs fall into her plate. "I told her about you. Not the whole story, but enough," said Polly.

"I need to share something. It won't take long."

"Tomorrow at four o'clock. Just the two of you. She shops on Carnaby Street and can meet you at a tearoom." Polly passed a slip of paper to Lori. "I'd like to see you again before you leave, Lori."

"I leave for my next assignment on Thursday."

"Can you meet Wednesday night? Dinner and a movie? Have you seen *The Sound of Music*?" Polly pressed the crumbs to her index finger and cleaned off her plate.

"Twice. Once with Grandma Lottie. The other with Grandma Penny."

"*Doctor Zhivago*?"

"It's over three hours long," said Lori.

"One more. *The Spy—*"

"*Who Came in From the Cold*? Okay."

"Great. I'll check the times and leave a message at your hotel." Polly broke apart a second scone and resumed the jam and cream ritual. "I loved going to the movies with Charlotte."

"Me too. Thanks for everything, Polly. Your note and card were lovely."

"I'm sorry I couldn't make it."

"That's okay. It's a long way."

At midafternoon the following day, Lori headed in the tube for Carnaby Street, the fashion mecca further commercialized by the ethereal Twiggy, the model who appeared as if a slight breeze would knock her over. Lori passed by women her age wearing scads of mascara, shiny boots, and fake fur in garish colors of lime green, fluorescent pink, and bright orange.

A bell announced her entrance. She was the only café customer, a sudden contrast to the busy, hectic street life. On her heels was an eye-catching blonde loaded down with shopping bags. Lori recognized her immediately.

"Francine? I'm Lori Hopkins." They shook hands clumsily. Francine cradled bag handles like bulky bracelets.

"Yes. My mum was insistent I meet with you. She was very fond of Charlotte, your gran."

They sat across from each other at a wooden picnic table on benches painted a sunny yellow. A brass watering can decked with dainty purple asters, milkweed, and a single calla lily garnished the space in between them. Francine's stack of packages occupied the remainder of her bench.

"Yes, we sort of met before I went to college a few years ago," Lori said. She groped for an envelope in a soft-sided briefcase by her side.

A Twiggy-like hostess bounced up to them. "Hi, I'm Dorcas, the owner. Thanks for coming in. I'm closing soon, but you're welcome to a cup of tea and whole wheat rolls."

"Tea would be fine. We shouldn't be long." Francine checked her watch. Dorcas trod off to the kitchen. "It's an organic food restaurant," Francine continued.

Lori slid the envelope across the table. "I'm a photojournalist."

Francine gave the envelope a suspicious glance. "Yes, my mother told me. I didn't know Charlotte. Other than she abandoned me."

"She didn't abandon you. My grandmother and Polly took over guardianship when your parents died. She was going to adopt you and bring you to the States, but she got very sick."

"I know the story."

Dorcas put down stoneware mugs, a high contrast to the Royal Staffordshire cups and saucers in British tearooms. Francine waited until they were alone. "When did we meet?"

Lori pulled photos out of an envelope, the ones put away since college days, the ones that led to glowing comments from her peers and exacting criticism and ultimately praise from academic circles. Francine studied the photos of herself in a phone booth, a dog tied to a leash waiting on the sidewalk.

"Yes, you sent a print to my mother. Were you following me? This day. I remember it." Francine shoved the photos in the envelope and returned full attention to Lori.

"I wasn't following you. I saw you through my lens. You were crying. I've always wondered why."

An unflinching Francine paused. In the distance, Dorcas wiped a work surface, the clock ticking louder. Lori considered the visit a mistake in the ensuing moments.

"I received very bad news that day." More silence. More sips of tea, the clock ticking and announcing the quarter hour in a high-spirited voice.

"Time is fleeting!" Dorcas yelled over. "Don't mind my clock. It's 4:15 when I usually close. It's all right though. It's my mopping day."

"You looked beautiful and mysterious," Lori said. "All the red. Your lipstick, the phone booth . . ."

"I'd been trying for over ten years to conceive," Francine said. "That day, I received the news that I would never have children."

"I guessed it was bad news."

"The doctor's office asked me to call in. So cold, huh?"

"You buried your face . . ."

"Susu on her new leash!" A twinkly smile. A real one. Lori instantly liked her companion.

Francine gathered her packages and deposited a few bills on the table. "I'm glad we met, Lori. Thank you for the photos." She passed back the envelope. "If you would process one of Susu for me, if you have the negatives. The one on the sidewalk. Please edit me out." She wrote an address on a piece of paper. "Send it here. Best wishes on your assignment. Where to now?"

"Saigon."

"My, you are an adventurous soul, aren't you? Godspeed, Lori. Who knows? Maybe our paths will cross again. I don't rule anything out in life. Especially now." Another warm smile in her eyes, the windows to the soul.

Chapter 23

The Interview

On February 11, 1966, Lori Hopkins touched down in South Vietnam. The first US combat troops had arrived one year earlier with 3,500 marines landing at China Beach to defend the US air base at Da Nang. They joined 23,000 American military advisors established by President John F. Kennedy.

Lori wasn't the first or the last referred to condescendingly as a "girl reporter." Supreme Commander General William C. Westmoreland attempted barring women from overnighters as soldiers navigated Vietnam's landscape—lowlands, hills, and densely forested highlands. Only twenty percent of the terrain was level. Machetes were mandatory to hack through the jungle thickets and inch through the hellish nightmare of snipers, booby traps, and deep tunnels, an entire network or underbelly to accommodate guerilla warfare as practiced by Viet Cong.

Westmoreland didn't succeed in banning female war correspondents from the front lines. It didn't matter since battleground was indistinguishable from peaceful ground. Every village posed a threat.

Time spent with soldiers would be intensely quick like a Roman candle's dying spark. Lori had little preparation to capture what she hoped would be the body and soul of a marine. She got clearance for an interview in the middle of a jungle battleground—rice paddies, thick vegetation, relentless insects, and the occasional burnt-out village. She observed a soldier's movements, swift as blades on ice, even while hauling eighty pounds of gear.

Day one—Lori reviewed a list of potential interviewees and requested a meeting with a Sergeant Kendall from Texas, a leader of a machine gun squad.

The first thing Lori noticed were the rolled-up sleeves of his creased battle fatigue shirt, stained with blood, sweat, if not tears. On his forearms were glistening, disc-shaped marks, embedded scars, in a neat row. They appeared fresh, only hours in the making.

Sergeant Kendall grabbed a pack of Camels from the makeshift coffee table, three overturned wooden crates. He ripped open the plastic and tapped the pack on the edge of a crate. Lori waited for him to light his cigarette. He snapped the Zippo lighter shut, took a deep drag of the unfiltered tobacco, and answered her silent question. "Leech bites, sugar pie. Aren't they beauties?"

Lori nodded. The marine sergeant stretched out his arm. "Some souvenir, huh? Would you like to see what else I'm taking home with me?"

"Only if I can photograph it."

"Name's Barry," he said with a conciliatory grin. "Texas gal, right?"

Lori shook his hand, and he instantly felt her untold pain of loss. Maybe it was her steady grip. Maybe it was the profound sadness in her eyes. Maybe it was a mirror of his own private hell—jungle warfare. Whatever, it was undeniable, and his handshake lingered, not wanting to let go . . . ever. Then the interview.

"Tell me about your first day here."

"Wait, sugar, we hardly know each other." Barry inhaled deeply and blew rings of smoke above her head.

Lori, straight-faced, played along. "Lori. From Lubbock."

"Well, well." A pronounced drawl. "Lori from Lubbock. I like it." He bowed slightly. "Galveston. I guess you can call us state mates."

"I'm told you agreed to an interview." She swung a canvas bag from her right shoulder.

"Well, I didn't know it would be a pretty little thing like you. Now I'll need to mind my Ps and Qs."

Lori tilted her head. "Expression dating back to 1602."

Barry burned through his cigarette, drawing on it with harsh lips. "Separating pints from quarts in the pubs. Can you recommend one around here?"

"Sorry, I'm new to the area." She checked her tape recorder.

"I like you Lori from Lubbock. You can ask me anything."

Lori clicked on her recorder. "Let's start with your full name."

He drew the last puff. "Barry Kendall."

The first scheduled interview ended suddenly. Enemy forces were active, and the squad was called out on a search and destroy mission on the trail of the Viet Cong. Sergeant Barry headed up the machine gun squad of eight.

Lori stayed behind and dreamt of her bomb shelter in Texas. The shelves were bare, nothing but concrete like the catacomb it resembled when unadorned. At daybreak, the whir of choppers replaced the nightmare of the unseen tornado that ripped her home apart. Death was a thief, stealing loved ones while she slept or busied herself with inconsequential chores.

She wondered if the soldiers thought of death with every boot step on strange paths rigged with explosives, traps, and camouflaged dugouts lined with enemy soldiers. By day, she shook off nightmares. By evening, haunting dreams returned. Pain and isolation were a residue. They scorched her insides. Emotional scars were like a virus that hid and returned.

Day two—Lori reconvened the interview with Barry Kendall.

"You look like you've seen a ghost, little sister."

"Bad night."

She recapped the military intervention in Vietnam. He inspected and cleaned his M16 rifle.

"Is this a history lesson, darlin'? 'Cause I'm living it."

Lori felt foolish. She didn't know where to start. "Yes, you're right. How many years have we been here? Close to eight?"

"Close enough. We're between a rock and a hard place. There's no way to win. The Green Berets were sent to train the South Vietnamese and get out five years ago. We're still here."

"When did you arrive?"

"August of last year. In two weeks, I had blackwater fever, malaria. I was choppered out on death's doorstep."

"Then what?"

"We dropped bombs on North Vietnam." He examined the barrel of his M16 and pointed to an unseen enemy. "That's real war, darlin.'"

"What did it accomplish?" Lori hugged her knees while seated on a cigar box.

Barry focused on his M16 rifle inspection. "Me sittin' here talking to you."

"What do you mean?"

"Ever bet on a losing horse?" Barry dropped the M16 by his side. "We're not going to win this one, darlin.'" He winked. "You can quote me on that one."

Lori seized her camera. The sun crested above the horizon. "Don't move."

"How 'bout a beefcake shot?" Barry leaned forward and pressed his hands together, enlarging his chest and pumping up his muscle-bound biceps.

"Such a Texas boy, huh?" She smiled and clicked.

Day three—they started again.

"Okay, tell me about your first day." She set down the tape recorder at her side and the mike in between them.

"Be specific." He sounded terse, nothing like the teasing, flirty manner she'd encountered on their initial meeting.

"Okay, sorry. The first day. In battle."

Barry scanned the microphone and recording equipment, avoiding eye contact. "Same as every day. Kill or be killed."

A tough nut to crack, thought Lori. *Will I break the shell and open to a story?* "Okay. What happened on the first day of battle?"

"I'm a machine gun squad leader. I have eight men who report to me. They are my family. That's how it is here. You form a family, and you protect that family." Barry took a drag of his Camel. For Lori, the interview stopped for what seemed an eternity, and she wondered if it would end right there. But, as a survivor of her own personal demons, she knew his war memories were fresh. Not buried. Not yet.

"Go on."

Barry squashed the ashy stump into the mud. "We entered a village. Just a handful of huts—straw and bamboo houses, high above the ground. Nine of us, including me, the sarge." His gazed right through Lori, as if she were invisible. "It was too quiet. The hair on my arms spiked like quills on a porcupine." Another silence. Time running out. Lori figured she had maybe five minutes to hear the rest of his story.

She persisted. "What happened next?"

Barry pressed his boot where he dropped the cigarette butt. "A boy, maybe nine or ten, ran from one hut to another, right in front of us. I thought it was to distract us. Or maybe a signal. And then all hell broke loose."

"What do you mean?" she asked.

"Napalm hit the far end of the village. We were damn lucky to survive. We ran for cover. Found out later there was a Viet Cong nest outside the village."

Lori couldn't help but ask the next question. "But if it was targeted for bombing, why were you sent there?"

Barry shook his head slowly. "It's war, sweet thing, and I would've shot the next person, man, woman, or child that ran across my path."

"Why?" she interjected without hesitation.

"Because any three could carry a grenade. It's war. We were the backup. The badass backup. I protect my family, and there are eight of 'em. That's all." He got up from his makeshift stoop. "Time's up, sweet thing."

Lori snapped photos. Barry gulping water from his canteen. Barry readjusting eighty pounds of combat gear and artillery. Barry being a soldier.

Day four—Lori met all eight men but focused on Barry. She wanted one story. The other squad men ignored her, kept their distance, but talked behind her back, joking and laughing in her direction.

Barry squatted on a crate and held out a tin of an oily, solid paste. "Put peanut butter on those crackers, darlin'. It'll bung you up so you don't get the runs."

"They don't want me here." Lori bit into the Ritz cracker.

"The guys? They don't get why you want to be here. They hate it. We all hate it. You're a constant reminder of our hate. So, why are you here? Life not thrilling enough back home?"

"I'm a photographer. I see the world through this lens. I wanted to see more of it and hopefully share something worthwhile."

Barry revealed a dimple under his morning scruff. "Well, I hope I don't disappoint you, sweet thing. Before we go on, I need to warn you. Keep a watch on those pretty legs. I don't want them all marred from leeches. They'll crawl up, and you won't even feel it at first."

"Leeches?" Lori felt up her pant legs.

"Yes, ma'am. They're the length of a needle and as thin. You've probably seen pictures of 'em right before they drop off." He held up his pinky finger. "Then they're about this size."

Lori crouched her knees to her chest.

"Say, you're a smart aleck," Barry said. "What's the most dangerous animal that ever lived?"

"Land or water?' Lori steadily rubbed her calves and arms.

"Both." Barry ate a tin of pork and beans for breakfast.

"Crocodile?" Lori felt unsteady with thoughts of leeches.

"Not even close, darlin'. Half the human beings that ever lived have been killed by female mosquitos. Malaria, yellow fever, dengue fever, encephalitis, filariasis, and elephantiasis." He scraped the sides of his tin. Lori checked her surroundings for any winged creatures.

Barry suppressed a smile. "There are 2,500 known species and forty carry malaria."

"Only forty?" Lori smacked a mosquito on her neck.

Barry laughed quietly. "Yeah, and they're all here in South Vietnam. Welcome to mosquito central. I've seen soldiers die from blackwater fever before they even hit the trails."

A soldier sauntered over. He was shorter than Lori and nearly the same weight. His dark eyes darted like a wild coyote ready to pounce on its prey.

"Duncan, what do you think? She's as pretty as a possum, ain't she?"

"She's a looker, Sarge." Duncan's unassuming grin exposed two missing teeth in the middle of the bottom row. He looked twenty, maybe nineteen years old. "Pleased to meet you, ma'am. I'm from Alabama. Sarge tells me you're from Texas."

"Lori Hopkins. Pleased to meet you, Duncan. Yes, Lubbock."

"Did you know Buddy Holly?"

"No, but we went to the same school."

"He's one of my favorites. What kind of music do you like, Miss Lori?"

"Okay, Duncan this ain't no blind date," Barry said. "We're moving out."

"Nice meeting you, Miss Lori." He walked away with a slight limp.

"Duncan's a tunnel rat. He's lucky to be alive. My job is to get him home in one piece."

"I've read about tunnel rats."

"Well, sweetheart, you're lucky to meet one. I don't like having a tunnel rat on my team."

"Why?" Lori dipped her cracker into peanut butter resembling light brown shoe polish.

"Because I can't protect him. Search and destroy. That's what we do. The trails are the deadliest. Open targets, that's what we are. In the jungle, you got green camouflage, lots of it. And you have the tunnels. Charlie's got tens of thousands of miles of tunnels underneath our soaked, rotten feet. Sending Duncan down there is worse than suicide."

"What do you mean?"

"With suicide you decide on your own. His job was decided for him."

"What do you hope for since you've been here?"

"Hope? Honey child, I hope to see Texas again with all limbs attached and working. That's it in a nutshell. You done? Because we're moving out." Barry jumped off the crate and onto his feet in one easy motion. He picked up his M-16 and held out a hand to assist Lori. "I'll be honest, too, sweet pea. The guys think you're a couple sandwiches shy of a picnic, if you don't mind me sayin'. So what demons are you fighting that brought you all the way to hell on earth?"

The shrill screech of all winged creatures served as a backdrop to the quiet ensuing between interviewer and interviewee, tables now turned. Lori came up with nothing, no pithy or humorous reply. Barry wasn't surprised. He'd dug a deep, vulnerable pit with merely a few words. He read people, sized them up. He sensed pain like a divining stick locating water. He let it go, and they prepared to move along the trail.

Duncan sidled up. Sergeant Barry put an arm around him in a crushing embrace as they walked together. "You're right, Sarge. But we wouldn't say she's pretty as a possum." Barry squeezed him tighter, like a Big Brother with his assigned buddy. "We'd say she's as cute as a button."

Lori gathered her belongings—recording device, rations, and notebooks. Barry spoke quietly and deliberately. "Hear that, sweet pea? Duncan here says you're as cute as a button. Ever hear that one?"

Lori smiled. "Not lately."

Day five—she had enough story and images to fill several magazine columns. In the morning, they rose to utter silence, not a good thing.

"When the high-shrilled pitch of birds and insects stop, it means there's people out here," said Barry. "More people than we care to meet. We're moving out."

Lori learned to gear up more quickly than she ever imagined, spurred on by the ever-present threat of incoming bombs and snipers. The rapid pace and slowing down were random, not systematic. Chaos was integral to war. Planning was a ruse. Generals were strategists, charting out moves and setups where battalions would attack. But the surprises turned deadly when it came to war.

The same night, Lori poured sweat with the oppressive heat and unrelenting nightmares. "Mom? Dad?"

Barry drew the last of his cigarette immediately outside her tent. He'd kept guard every night without her knowing. He heard the muffled cries again. "Mom? Dad?" He stamped out the cigarette butt and peeked in the tent. Lori sat up, cross-legged. He'd seen night terrors before. In her case, it was probably exhaustion, stress, and maybe war. It damaged everyone and everything in its path. No escape from its ravages, even a reporter on the sidelines. He examined her open eyes and sleeping state. He knew better than to shake her out of it. She slumped over. Barry held her like a delicate flower. Her arms, beaded with perspiration, were like soft, velvety petals. He bore her sadness, the weight of it in his own soul. He knew she had secrets like embers singeing from within.

Lori woke with a start. "Huh? Did you say something?" She wasn't surprised to see him.

He spoke softly. "Crying on the inside, huh, Texas girl?"

She leaned against his glistening shoulder, their sweat mingled. Her voice hoarse. "Many times. The tears won't come out."

"I'll be your watershed, darlin'."

"Is that a good thing?" Her eyes closed.

"You decide." He kissed her shoulder, rose, and walked away.

She was asleep in a matter of seconds as he resumed his place as sentinel.

At early dawn, Lori remembered nothing of the previous night, not even her night terrors, as Barry expected. Her secrets remained her secrets. Besides, he had enough of his own.

Day six—in the morning, Barry was all soldier as she approached. "Let me introduce you to some weaponry, Miss Texas." He held up his firearm. "This is an M60 machine gun, the most common infantry weapon we use out here. Other than my men, this is my closest buddy. My friend keeps me alive, so there you go. It weighs close to twenty-five pounds, and a lot of gunners call it 'The Pig' but I got more respect for my friend here. I call him 'Eagle Eye' because I count on him to find my prey. I can mount this son of a gun, or it can operate from a helicopter or tank. I'm the gunner, but every soldier in my squad carries two hundred linked rounds of ammo and a spare barrel."

Lori jotted words as he prattled on. "Okay, quiz time, little sister. How many governments in Saigon since we got into this mess?"

"Uh, don't know. How many?"

"Don't know. Thought you would, being bright as a penny, huh?"

"Two different buckets of possums?"

He laughed so hard he doubled over.

"Right? One hand, you've got inept government. Other hand, fighting a war. Two different buckets . . ."

"Of possums. Next question. The guys are trying to guess your age." Barry inspected his ammo rounds and packed up his gear.

"What's your best guess?"

"My guess? Twenty-four."

"Twenty-four it is," Lori answered.

"Well, I'll be danged. Let me guess. Virgo?"

"Sure 'nuff!"

A dazzling smile and surprisingly perfect teeth. He continued his interview of the interviewee. "Any soldiers in your family tree?"

"My grandfather was a doctor, a medic. He died in the Korean War." No mention of her father.

He sensed a closed subject. He had a knack for knowing when to back off and switched the limelight. She learned that a machine gunner carried two or three belts of ammo. Everyone else in the squad carried an extra belt. If you had a choice between food and ammo, there really wasn't a choice.

Day seven—Lori held the microphone between them. "What do you fear the most?"

"Well, it isn't death, not my death. That's in the Almighty's hand." He inspected his cigarette. "I guess you'll keep pestering me if I don't answer, so I better come up with something." He folded his arms like a coach in the team's locker room. "Fear doesn't work here, little sister."

"What about the Barry back in Texas?"

"That Barry will never be the same. War changes everything. But hell hath no fury like a woman scorned. So if I fear anything, it's a scorned woman."

"Know any?" She kept to her line of questioning, unsure of what she was seeking.

"A few." He held out his hands like balances. "Women on one hand. War on the other." His left hand lowered. "War is ugly." He looked over at his right hand. "Women? Vengeful." His right hand lowered even farther, the balances out of kilter.

Lori persisted. "War is ugly because people act ugly, right?"

"War brings out the worst and the best in people. Courage, devotion. Women don't need a war to act ugly. Hell hath no fury . . ."

"Like a woman scorned." She noticed his facial muscles tighten. "What next?"

'Texas, darlin', in one piece, good Lord willing, and patch up what I left behind."

"What did you leave behind?"

"A life worth livin' out. That's enough."

Lori juggled her canvas knapsack, tape recorder, and notebooks. Saigon awaited. She had two days to make her deadline.

"What do you fear the most?" Barry, square-jawed, eyes both resolute and sympathetic, waited for an answer.

"That's a great question." Lori gave her trademark widening grin that, as Grandma Lottie often remarked, could light a candle in a wind tunnel. Lori noticed a radiant, toothy grin from the soldier who defined true grit. The perfect blend of boyish charm and bravado. "Not getting things right," she said.

"What right?"

"Anything." She shrugged. "Right timing in life or getting the real you on paper."

Barry chuckled. "That ain't fear. Sounds more like pride."

Lori considered the perceived slight. "Okay, I fear my prideful nature."

"That's pretty deep, darlin.'"

He rooted through his knapsack. He opened to a blank page in his notebook, tore it out, and scribbled a few words. "Send a copy to my mom when it's published."

"Of course." Lori read through his scrawl.

"And Miss Hopkins?" He grabbed his helmet and held it to his chest. "Bless your heart." A Texan's best twang.

Day eight—Lori interrupted Barry's writing ritual. Every week, if war didn't erupt, he sat with his stack of airmail envelopes and onion skin paper and wrote a one-page letter to home. He eyed Lori preparing her tape recorder. "So what do you know about Galveston?"

"Not much, to be honest. I've never met anyone from Galveston." She pressed the record button. "You're the first."

Amused by her persistence, he indulged her for the last interview. "So you want to see a picture of my sweetheart?"

Lori witnessed a chink in the soldier's armor. Barry held out a photo of a girl, maybe five years old, a sprinkle of freckles on her nose. She had a missing tooth that didn't hinder a sunny smile. "Meet Bonnie. She's the bright star in my life."

"Your daughter?" Lori hated being presumptuous. But, like pulling teeth, he wasn't one to give information freely, and the coaxing continued, even on her last day.

"No, ma'am."

He vacillated between respectful mannerisms and humorous jabs. She never knew which to expect. Enigmatic, yes, but a heart as big as Texas.

"She's my little sister," he said with restraint. "Born on Christmas Day, 1955. She's ten years old now. This picture is five years old."

Lori fixed her eyes on the photo, her face a blank canvas. A tumult, like waves of sadness, crashed inside her. Christmas, 1955. Her throat constricted. She restrained a wash of tears. Not here. Not now.

"You all right?"

She kept up her defense. "She's cute as a button."

The scar was ripped open with no regard for where or when—in the middle of the jungle in South Vietnam, in a cozy hotel room in Montmartre, or wading in a pool at a friend's birthday party. Sadness had no borders when it lived in the mind and heart.

He placed the photo in his wallet. "She sure is." He didn't push it. The water diviner of emotions tapped into a reservoir this time and let it lie.

With hours remaining, Lori packed up her camera gear. Instincts on high alert, Barry took charge. "Don't think I'm getting fresh, sweet thing." He reached under her fatigues. Too late. The leech had found its host and next meal. "Look at me, darlin'. I'll talk you through this one. Don't look down. Look at me. You'll feel a little pressure from my finger." He pressed against her skin.

"What?" Lori jerked away her right leg. He grabbed it with force.

"Hold still, now. Look at me. I'm going to slide my finger back and flick the leech sideways." The dislodged oral sucker attached to Barry's index finger. Lori examined her leg. Barely a mark. Barry pushed at the leech's hind sucker. "Key is to go for the small end. Most people overreact and go for the big sucker. It gets mad when you interrupt a feeding. Hand me my bag, darlin'." Within seconds, the ordeal was over. "Let's look at that leg." Lori rolled up her pants. He handed her a packet of salt. "Rub some on."

"Thank you," said Lori, sotto voce.

Barry's grin masked concern. He bandaged the tiny puncture wound. "Now if you get bit by a mosquito—"

"I'm on my own."

Feeling safe in the middle of a living nightmare defied description or logic. A soldier protecting his family, extended by one.

Lori quit Vietnam but not the war, the jungle, or Barry. She pored over her notes, photos, and recordings. In Saigon, the press room was alive—urgent and chaotic, like an emergency room at an inner-city hospital. Half-eaten bagels strewn on littered desks shared space with pitchers of coffee and stacks of paper cups. No one paid mind to trash cans piled high with crumpled paper and overall disarray. Reporters fleshed out stories with alacrity and acuity.

And Lori began, the words flowing, infused by the jungle experience that haunted and frightened like she'd never before encountered other than a day in Texas eleven years ago.

Following her assignment, Lori returned to sift through Grandma Lottie's belongings. Life at home wasn't home. Texas? Foreign land. As she prepared to leave, a car stopped in front of the house. Lori peeked out the window, and her heart raced.

"So you'll be Father Gerald soon, huh?"

"I'll be Father Gerry next spring."

"Sounds friendlier, huh?" In a girlish voice, she added, "Hi, Father Gerry!" She switched to a baritone. "Uh, Father Gerry, the school needs a new roof."

Gerald grinned. "Don't wish that on me. Actually, I'm hoping for a military assignment as chaplain."

"You know there's a war going on, right?"

Gerald calmed a nervous eye twitch. Nothing much had changed since he first asked her to the high school homecoming dance. "I know, and you've been there."

Lori thought too hard on her reply. Another war raged. Not the one she photographed. Not even the one that mourned Lottie's passing. Certainly not the one she fought throughout her dependence on sleeping pills that had put her brain in a fog for endless days. Her war was a turning away, a readiness to leave behind, toss aside, and fully negate the gift of faith for it came with pain and suffering. Oh, how peaceful and pretty, that faith Gerry or Gerald submitted to every day with his vocation. It had worked for Grandma Lottie, who lived through the ugliness of war and death. But for Lori, the gift of faith remained unwrapped in a bomb shelter in 1955. So many times, she thought she was through doubts or disbelief and had crossed over to the other side. And then it would sweep her away again, the devastating funnel of wind created by nature and God that carried away her family, her belief that God cared for her.

"Lori, you have so much pain in your eyes. I wish I could help."

Lori laughed. He sounded insincere, so incredibly insincere. "Pain? It's part of everyone's life. Why should I be an exception?" She grew belligerent. "Do you think I feel sorry for myself? I don't. I'm a survivor! Whatever danger comes my way, I somehow escape! I'm lucky, right? Just lucky."

"There's no such thing as luck, good or bad, Lori. All things are ordained by God."

"Oh, so what's free will, then? I choose every day. I chose to be in that bomb shelter."

"I know," he added pleadingly, "and now to be in harm's way. It's how you deal with pain."

Lori's green eyes narrowed. "Don't preach to me. You're not a priest yet." She consulted her watch. "I'm running late. Would love to chat, but, oh, well . . ." With a sudden surge of emotion, she embraced him.

Gerald clasped Lori's chapped fingers. "Lori, faith can't be explained. It's lived."

Stepping back, she released his hands. "I'm not looking for an explanation."

"Let me say this to you. We fix our eyes on what is unseen, not what is seen. What is seen is transitory, what is unseen lasts forever."

Lori adjusted the belt on her Burberry trench coat. She wanted to run from this man who had turned piety into a fulltime profession. "I'm a photographer. I do nothing but see. I capture what is transitory and make it permanent."

"That's true. But next time you look through the lens, see with the eyes of faith."

Lori shoved her hands deep in her pockets. "And what will that accomplish? The subject, what I see, doesn't change."

"But you will!"

"Should've seen that one coming," she rejoined. "Good luck. Oh, that's right. How about mazel tov?"

Gerald grinned. "Yes, mazel tov is fine. It's actually a blessing."

"Well, I got something right." She matched his grin. "You'll make a good priest. I can see it. No. Wait. Not see it." Car keys jangled in her pocket. "I better go."

Gerald's pulse quickened as they bounded through the doorway. Every time he saw Lori, she stole a piece of his heart. He prayed for his love to be charitable in the sight of God, as one would love a neighbor.

Chapter 24

Barriers

Camp Pendleton—an unplanned meeting ground. Serendipity or destiny. It didn't matter. The threesome from Texas—a deacon, a soldier, and a photojournalist—found themselves in California after Barry completed his first tour of duty. An off-base bar and pool hall was frequented by marines coming back and marines going out awaiting rice paddies and foliage so dense it took four hours to advance half a mile. They all had stories they kept to themselves back on American soil.

Deacon Gerry heaved a frosty beer mug. "Barry, here's to you and everyone in your squad. God bless all of you for coming back in one piece."

Barry threw back a shot of Jack Daniel's. "Wasn't my time to go, preacher."

"You believe in fate?" Lori knocked back her whiskey in one gulp, a burning sensation in the back of her throat. She slammed down the glass.

"Well, well, sweet thing, not very ladylike. I thought you bought that shot of whiskey for me. My celebration like Father Gerry here said." His carved biceps crossed over each other. "Aren't you afraid of burnin' a hole in that lovely throat of yours?"

Lori replied nonchalantly, "I have an aunt in Boston who adds a shot of whiskey to her coffee every morning. She said it kills the bad germs."

Barry chuckled and signaled the waiter. "Ready for a refill?" He had a fixed smile. The dimple in his right cheek deepened.

"One more for the road." Lori mimicked him by flexing a bicep. They giggled at their own silliness.

Gerald signaled the waiter. "Tab, please." He reached for his wallet.

"Gerry, old man, I mean Father . . ."

"He's a deacon," Lori said. Her head drooped.

"Deacon, I'm just getting started." He slid his shot glass down the bar.

"Hey, this ain't no shuffleboard. What'll you have?" the bartender shouted.

Barry bristled at the bartender's surliness. "The best whiskey you have. Crown Royal or Jameson. Not that Canadian piss water."

"You from Texas?"

"Yessir."

"We're all from Texas. I'll have a shot of tequila like a real Texan," Lori hollered.

Gerald's concern deepened with a grimace. "I think we've had enough . . ."

"You know how to drink tequila, sweet lips?" Barry egged on his drinking companion. The bartender approached with a shot of whiskey and the tequila, salt and lime.

"Lick, sip, and suck," said Lori. She licked the back of her hand and poured salt below her index finger. She licked the salt off her hand, drank the tequila, and sucked the lime wedge.

"Well, ain't that special, but you ain't no real Texan," Barry said. "You're a transplant. I'm fourth generation." Barry ate a handful of cocktail peanuts to temper hunger pangs and nausea. Feelings for Lori, his Texas flower, left him uncomfortable. Her pout made him queasy.

"My pinkie finger knows more about Texas than you do." She folded her arms and readied for battle.

Barry waved his finger. "You study Texas through your camera lens. I live it."

Gerald signaled the bartender again. "I'll settle the bill."

"Yeah, and I'll settle who's a real Texan." Lori sat straight up, eager for a repartee.

Barry grinned. "You're on."

"State flower."

Barry chuckled. "You quizzin' me, Bluebonnet? Who doesn't know that one, right, Deacon?"

"They cover the fields at my Uncle Preston's ranch." Gerald counted out money and squared the tab.

"What's the scientific name?"

"Oh, smart girl, huh?" He pitched forward nose to nose with his competitor. *"Lupinus subcarnosus."*

Gerald stood up.

"Take a load off, Deacon. This party just started." Barry refocused on his competitor. "Okay. I talk Texan, and you tell me what it means."

"You're on," Lori said.

Their volley continued for nearly an hour with added drinks. Deacon Gerry prayed for the Holy Spirit's gifts of knowledge and understanding as he played referee and tallied the score. If Lori answered correctly, she garnered a point. If not, Barry garnered a point. He saw through the sophomoric game. Barry hungered for her company, her presence.

Barry caught Gerry's stare. "Hey, Deacon, have we settled who's the true-blue Texan here?"

"Lori won, fair and square. She had every answer right."

"Okay, let's do a tiebreaker, Lora-li."

She winked at Gerry. "Okay, let's do it, soldier boy."

Barry straightened up and assumed his poker face. "Who invented Texas toast? Tell me that one, Lora-li."

"The Pig Stand in Denton, Texas. 1946. My dad took me there when I was ten years old. It was his favorite. Only thing missing was a side of Boston baked beans."

Lori polished blush-colored nails on her pink tank top, a sign of victory after the final round of verbal wrestling. She weaved around a billiards table and headed to the ladies' room.

"Why'd you let her win? You know Texas toast has been around since the 1920s, right?" Gerald asked.

Barry watched Lori navigate the room. "You love that little lady."

"I did," Gerald said.

"So God called you, huh? Did He speak from a cloud?"

"From the Good Book."

"Doesn't he speak to all of us through the Good Book, Deacon?"

"He called me to be a priest." Gerald spoke with renewed conviction. "Yes, God tested."

"Then I'm the real fool, 'cause she'll always love you."

Gerald chuckled. "Oh, I pined like a lonely pup. The crush of the century. I don't think Lori will ever marry."

"Who's talkin' marriage, Deacon?"

"You're both restless. She has her demons, like all of us."

"I knew it from the first handshake. The sadness in her eyes."

Gerald watched for Lori's return. "You know her story?"

"Nope, but she sure knows mine."

Gerald confided, "A tornado wiped out her house while she was in a bomb shelter asleep. Both parents died."

"How old?"

"Fourteen. I remember the first day of school after the holiday. She walked into the classroom, and my heart pounded so loud I could hear the blood rushing. I ached for her."

Lori washed her hands in the lavatory sink and studied her face. Skin, dry and sallow; lips, pale; cheeks, no color. Sleep escaped her at night, leaving her drained and tired upon waking. She'd make a doctor's appointment and explain how assignments gave her insomnia. She'd leave, once again, with a script for sleeping pills. Her comfort. Her torment. The seesaw, the ups and downs, would begin again.

Barry caught sight of Lori as she walked out of the restroom. "How 'bout an arm wrestle to break the tie?"

She fell into her chair. "Can't admit defeat?"

"Let's call it a tie." Gerald rose and assisted Lori.

Arms folded, Barry's stony face bordered on hostility. "I say we tie on another one."

"I paid the bill. We're leaving." Gerald put Lori's white cotton sweater around her shoulders.

"Have you always sucked the life out of a party?" Barry said. Lori appeared spent and beyond exhausted. His brash exterior hid concern for the Texas flower he'd held back in Vietnam.

"Every chance I get." Gerald softened. "Let's go."

Wisdom and understanding. Gerald prayed the gifts of the Holy Spirit informed his actions and shone through his countenance. He knew Barry cared deeply for Lori. He cared deeply for both of them. The face of Jesus in all God's children—the kind and gentle, the mean-spirited, the broken-hearted, the young and old. Anyone in his path.

Before leaving California, Lori met with Gerald to wish him well and say her goodbyes. Barry drove her to the rectory where Deacon Gerald resided temporarily. The parish was few in number, mainly of Spanish and Philippine descent. White, pink, and red azalea bushes in full bloom lined an arched pathway—a lovely reminder of springtime.

Lori strayed into a chapel. An Infant of Prague statue, a familiar sight, adorned one corner. At an ambo, she read from an open Bible.

"More bitter than death I find the woman who is a hunter's trap / whose heart is a snare and whose hands are prison bonds. He who is pleasing to God will escape her / but the sinner will be entrapped by her."

The black leather cover had *Gerald Wilkins* engraved in gold-leaf. She sensed his presence. "So I'm a trap?"

He had no answer.

"The trap is loosened." She exhaled. "You're as free as you decide to be. It's all on you. I never asked you. I never invited you into my life, Gerry. It was all on you." Her words were fresh cuts on old wounds.

"I know, and I'm a coward and a fool. I pray for mercy every day."

Barry entered the chapel. "Well, if it isn't the two lovebirds. Don't let me interrupt."

"I'm leaving," Gerald said.

"No final words?" Lori asked.

"With you, I'm chasing the wind." The words sounded hurtful, punishing.

"What do you mean? Chasing the wind?"

"You're my vanity. The end of wisdom and folly are the same. Vanity. I think of you, and it's my folly, my foolishness because I know it will come to nothing."

Lori sneered, like a wild creature caught in a trap. "How do you know?"

"Because wisdom teaches me that I'll never be satisfied."

Lori shook her head violently. "You're not making sense."

Barry hung back. After a few lunchtime beers, his buzz already impaired his better judgment. "Let him go, Lori. He's a fool."

Lori lashed out. "You'd never understand!"

Barry laughed hoarsely. "I understand he's telling you goodbye. Forever."

"I know, I know." She fixed her gaze on Gerald. "I never thought I'd say this to anyone ever again." Her words were little more than a breath. "Pray for me."

They spoke to each other without speaking.

Barry left the chapel, lit a cigarette, and cursed the day he met Lori.

On Saturday, May 4, 1968, Gerald Wilkins became Reverend Gerald Wilkins at Sacred Heart Cathedral in Amarillo, Texas. Uncle Preston, Aunt Merle, and their three adult children, Jake, Mary Ellen, and Samuel, congregated in the first reserved pew. Aunt Merle dabbed her eyes with a silk handkerchief embroidered with her initials. Her tears were partly out of sympathy for her nephew, Gerald, the family orphan and partly because she cried at any ritual or ceremony—weddings, baptisms, and funerals. Seven other deacons received the Rite of Ordination. During Holy Mass, the candidates were brought forward and presented to the assembly. They promised to perform the duties of priesthood. As the candidates lay prostrate before the altar, the congregation prayed the Litany of the Saints. Bishop of Amarillo, Lawrence Michael De Falco, laid hands on each candidate, invoked the power of the Holy Spirit, and transferred spiritual power and authority.

Following Holy Mass, the newly ordained priests entered the church hall to loud cheers and clapping hands. Mary Ellen Beauford, now married and living in New Orleans, was the first to embrace her cousin.

"So handsome." She blushed. "And holy. Handsome and holy."

With red-rimmed eyes, Aunt Merle hugged her nephew. "Oh dear, you were such a sweet boy. We're so proud of you, dear. Father . . ."

"Father Gerry."

His two male cousins, Jake and Samuel, shook Father Gerry's hand. Samuel spoke to Jake in confidence. "Two of my horses are ready to foal back in Lubbock."

Father Gerry scanned the community hall. Preston carried homemade fruit punch in two paper cups and handed one to his nephew. "She won't be here, Gerry, Father Gerry."

"Did you talk to her?" Father Gerry asked.

"I did. She's out of town and sends her love," Preston said.

"You mean your sister, Barbara, right?" Mary Ellen tilted her head.

"Who else?" Preston passed the empty cup to his wife.

Mary Ellen frowned. She took the pulse of Texas news. While visiting Lubbock, she had spoken to her friend's younger sister, Abigail, an old school mate of Lori Hopkins. She had discovered that Lori received an invitation to Gerald's ordination. Abigail's husband, a mailman, had delivered an envelope from the seminary to Charlotte Mitchell's house where Lori kept an address.

Father Gerry caught Mary Ellen's all-knowing glance.

"Lori's not in town, Gerry," Mary Ellen said.

Samuel rocked back and forth impatiently. "So where to next, Father Gerry?"

"I'm going to Nam as a chaplain. I leave next week."

"Vietnam, dear? Haven't you already been?" Aunt Merle asked.

"I'll go back as a priest."

In the evening, Father Gerry met up with a seminarian, Joseph O'Malley, two years behind him in studies. Joe had served in Vietnam and was honorably discharged from his marine battalion due to a hand grenade explosion that blinded his left eye. Texas natives, Joe and Father Gerry bonded with similar stories of growing up in Lubbock and attending the same high school, although a few years apart in age. Father Gerry unburdened his disappointment of Lori's absence to a seminarian's sympathetic ear.

"Remember, worldly wisdom is foolishness in the eyes of God."

"You're preaching to me, Joe?" Father Gerry loosened his collar.

"I have to start somewhere." Joe patted his friend's back.

"I'm not wise to this world." Father Gerry stretched out his hands and studied his fingers.

"That's good. Otherwise, you'd have to unlearn everything to become wise."

"And how did you become so wise?"

Joe O'Malley picked up his Bible. "That's it. I'm not."

Barbara Wilkins had fought in the Cold War and conversed in Russian with ease. She studied code books and manuals used by KGB agents. She memorized series of numbers and figures in a few seconds. She mastered the Loci method of retaining mental images to associate with classified material—top secret letters, confidential memos, and photographs. The brain was a highly effective memory device when properly trained. But Vietnam was unfamiliar territory, the latest enemy linked to Communism. She arrived three days prior to her assignment—track prisoners for rescue attempts. Two Central Intelligence Agency operatives, one marine captain, and an enlisted private compared notes and slurped weak black coffee from tin cups and water from canteens. Barbara and Tom Phillips, her fellow CIA agent, acknowledged each other with brief nods.

"What's going on?" Barbara said.

"We're tailing the communications mission," Tom replied.

"An open target," Barbara added.

Tom shook his head. "No, kidding."

The twenty-year-old private looked puzzled.

"Our guys are on one side of a hill," Barbara explained. "The enemy is blind to them. Dispatchers get info and report back. If the enemy gets rid of 'em, we lose our pair of eyes."

The CIA operator, Tom Phillips, conversant in Vietnamese, was new to combat fighting. He picked up Viet Cong chatter. "They shot down the radio guy."

"Any of our guys?" Barbara jotted notes on her clipboard.

The captain and commander, a rough-and-tumble World War II veteran, checked through his list. "No Spooks for the Gooks."

Earlier that day, the marine captain, Douglas, led them through flooded rice paddies and rotted jungle foliage in damp, spongy boots. Barbara yearned for the arid Texas air and tumbleweeds that collected against the fence surrounding Uncle Preston's ranch. She returned there as often as possible, in between assignments.

"Who do they have?" Barbara asked.

The private spoke up. "Well, our radio guy, two privates, a gunner, a priest, and the helicopter pilot."

Captain Douglas growled his disapproval. "A priest? What the hell is he doing there?"

"Uh, newly ordained from Texas."

"What's his name?" Barbara asked dryly.

"Father Gerald Wilkins."

Barbara formalized a plan. It's what she did now. It's why she was here—plan and scheme safe endings. Part of espionage. Part of why God sent her to a private lunch appointment with a man from the Pentagon seeking out the best steak in Texas and his next successful recruit.

The prisoners of war ate food discarded by their captors. The staple, rice, was bug-infested and moldy after sitting in soggy bags. Malnourished and beaten, the prisoners moved from camp to camp as promulgated by Viet Cong military advisors. One American soldier from another camp made a run for it on one of their treks. Gunfire opened up. The prisoner dropped to the ground. Blood poured from a gaping hole in his chest. Father Gerry prominently displayed a wooden cross to guards pointing guns at him. He raised his hands and backed up slowly facing their weapons.

He bent over the mortally wounded man, who panted quickly and spit out barely audible words. "You're a priest?"

"Let me give you absolution. What's your name, Private?"

"I'm dying." He gasped. "I don't want to die."

"Save your breath." The guards surrounded Father Gerry and the young soldier.

The nineteen-year-old POW died as Father Gerry made the sign of the cross. He never got the soldier's name. The Viet Cong wouldn't let them speak to each other to prevent lending secrets for escape or subversive activity.

Rescue missions were miraculous events. Everyone knew it, notably the rescued.

The knights in shining armor flew in on two CH-47 Chinooks capable of low altitudes. Radio chatter picked up reports that the POWs were on the move to a different location. Perfect timing. Mobility spelled vulnerability. The door gunners took aim and wiped out the Viet Cong.

A medic howled above the whirring chopper. "He's bleeding. He needs blood."

A nurse examined the battered, semi-conscious chaplain in blood-soaked prison garb. He wore a satchel and wooden cross. She shouted, "Weak pulse!"

The medic reported to the CIA agent in charge. "Two soldiers didn't make it out. The priest here gave them their last rites."

Barbara heard updates of the liberation at a remote location. Her main concern—the safe return of Father Gerry Wilkins, a prisoner of war.

"So what about the chaplain?" She ran fingers through her cropped head. Yesterday, she had removed lice with a special comb. Now she obsessed over each bristly strand and contemplated shaving it off.

"He needs a transfusion."

Barbara learned that Father Gerry Wilkins survived the loss of blood from a bullet wound during his release from captivity. He'd be shipped back to the United States when he was strong enough to travel. Fate dealt her a hand that helped save her brother. The world made sense in the midst of disorder.

Chapter 25

Fan Fare

Lori poured over travel guides and memorized a few Portuguese phrases. She read how Lisbon was destroyed on All Saints' Day, 1755. In one hour, the city underwent a tsunami, a fire, and an earthquake. She observed the plane's wing through the smudged circle of a mid-aisle window seat. Her vacation plan was to head south to Algarve beaches, away from crowds, after a stay in the capital city.

Lori landed in Lisbon at three in the afternoon. The sun, intense and hot, beat down on the mosaic pavements of basalt rock. She stepped gingerly across slippery cobblestones and hailed a cab. After a quick stop in the hotel room, she joined a guided tour of a city once the richest in all of Europe.

In the quaint lobby, Lori picked up a pamphlet of a daytrip to Fátima, Portugal. A depiction of the Blessed Mother in a long white mantle and gold crown was familiar. Grandma Lottie had an Our Lady of the Rosary statue on her bedroom dresser. The blessed image was a gift from a nurse friend who made a pilgrimage to Fátima in 1947 on the thirtieth anniversary of the apparition to the three shepherd children. Lori hadn't seen the statue since the day she stepped into Lottie's bedroom, after the funeral, and grieved the inconceivable loss.

A stylish woman, seventyish, stood next to Lori. Her emerald-colored A-line linen dress complimented her trim torso. "There's a bus leaving tomorrow at 7:00 a.m. We'll arrive before nine o'clock to join the procession." The beautiful lady's exotic features and amiability filled Lori with a sense of peace. Lori, entranced by her large, coal-black eyes and ageless countenance, listened attentively. "I'm from Cairo. Our Lady appeared there last month. The second of April. Thousands witnessed her. I was one of them." The woman raised her hands. "A white figure at St. Mary's Church. We gathered and police moved, saying it was a reflection from the streetlamps. But we believers, Coptic Christians and Moslems, realized it was the Virgin Mary. She appeared again on April ninth, and I saw her. Only a few minutes, but I have pictures." She reached into her large straw shoulder bag and extracted a photo showing the outline of a woman in a veil on the church roof. "We call her Our Lady of Light. We believe the church is where the Holy Family stayed after their flight into Egypt."

Lori examined the photo. "Remarkable. Yes, I believe it's the Blessed Mother."

"The Coptic church approved the apparitions a few days ago. I'm here to give thanks to Our Lady at Fátima. If you'd like to join us, we have a seat on our bus. We're a group from Egypt and believe the surest way to Jesus is through His mother."

"I'm heading south." Lori considered the woman's strong, faith-filled testament. "Okay. I'll see you tomorrow morning. Here in the lobby? I can pay you now?"

"No, it's paid for already. You're replacing someone who cannot come. I believe the seat was meant for you. We are all connected."

Go with it, she told herself. "Yes, okay. I'm Lori."

"Miriam."

Lori stood speechless.

Miriam continued, "Miriam was the sister of Moses and Aaron. She was born in Egypt."

"Yes, I know," Lori said. "Miriam is a Hebrew name meaning 'bitter.'"

"Yes, that's right, Lori."

"My mother was Miriam. She died thirteen years ago. And my father."

"I'm sorry, dear," Miriam said. "God is sovereign, and everything happens for a reason."

A school note from January 1956 flashed through Lori's mind. *Everything happens for a reason. You'll know why some day. Be Strong.*

In her hotel room, the sleep-deprived Lori, in desperation, reached for the vial at her bedside. Before zipping up her suitcase for Portugal, she had tossed the prescription bottle, hosiery, and light beige sandals into the side pouch. A dose of promised repose. Five pills remained. Five nights of uninterrupted slumber. The last time she popped one was three months earlier—Valentine's Day.

The following day, Monday morning, Lori woke with a blinding headache from the sleeping pill she took the night before. She'd come to Lisbon, anywhere actually, to shake the off-and-on addiction induced by insomnia.

The minibus of fifteen travelers arrived in Fátima at 8:45 a.m. Lori followed Miriam onto a side street that opened up onto an immense square with a large basilica at one end. Masses of pilgrims walked and prayed at the former site of where shepherd children, Lucia, Francisco, and Jacinta, first witnessed the lady dressed in white.

"I remember the story," Lori confided to Miriam. "My Grandma Lottie kept a clipping of what happened on October 13, 1917. Seventy thousand or more showed up in the pouring rain. The three children said the woman called herself Our Lady of the Rosary and she'd give a sign. A spinning sun. Whirls and flashes of colors. At the end, the rain stopped and their clothes were dry."

Lori watched the myriad worshippers praying, singing, and waving white handkerchiefs at a statue of Our Lady of Fátima elevated high in procession. The fervor and love for Our Lady, the mother of God, was palpable, even for Lori, who had renounced the practice of a faith life since Lottie's death. An old, wizened Portuguese woman spied Lori as she took in the scene. The woman pulled out a rosary of blue, crystal-like beads from her skirt pocket and moved closer. She nodded her head and raised up the beads for Lori to examine.

"How much?" Lori asked. She dug a hand into her purse.

"No, no. Take! Take!" The beads caught the sunlight and twinkled like starbursts.

Miriam observed the encounter. "It's a gift!"

Lori nodded. *"Obrigado."* She wrapped the translucent beads around her fingers. The elderly woman shouldered her way into the milieu.

The collective chant grew louder in the basilica square. Lori felt estranged from the ardent faithful. "Miriam, it's my fault, I know, but how long . . ."

"Until the night procession. If you like, we can meet at the basilica main door for the procession in eight hours."

"Eight? Goodness gracious, I'll never find you. There must be a million people here. Where will the bus pick us up?"

"In front of the Hotel Fátima." Miriam's kind expression lessened Lori's consternation.

"Okay, if I don't meet you at the basilica, I'll meet you at the hotel."

"You are where God wants you to be." Miriam disappeared into the crowd.

Lori took shade under a banner that said *Blue Army*. Before leaving home, she decided to forego her camera. She was on vacation and wanted no reminders of her life behind the lens. But here in Fátima, she wanted no reminders of the faith she'd forsaken. The waving banner tired her worn-out spirit.

Gripping the rosary, Lori weaved through men, women, and children chanting prayers. She felt desperate to escape without knowing why. She hurried from the plaza and meandered down winding streets to a straight, inclining path. Loudspeakers magnifying a repetition of "Hail Mary" were muted with distance. The path's incline led to a monastery in a cul-de-sac. A posted sign stated visiting hours. She pressed a door buzzer. A voice over the intercom answered. "Yes?"

Lori was elated to hear a word in English. "Is there a place I can sit for a while?"

"This is a monastery." The tone was kind and direct.

"You have visiting hours."

"Yes, prearranged."

"I'd like to visit."

Lori stood quietly at the door. Minutes went by. "Please come in." A buzzer sounded. The door unlocked.

Cranberry-colored armchairs and wooden end tables were arranged in various sections and corners of the spacious sitting area. The furniture was unembellished, not what she expected in a European domicile or convent. Ten minutes went by, and she considered leaving. At one corner, a pleated partition slid open and revealed a countertop in a smaller room. Three nuns, two elderly and a bright-faced youthful Asian, all dressed in white habits, sat in a row.

"Yes, my dear, what can we do for you?' The oldest nun had an American Midwestern accent, the gentle yet unassailable voice Lori heard over the intercom. She was tall with a ramrod spine and perfect posture, like a seasoned ballet instructor.

Lori cleared her throat. "I came here to get away from the crowds."

"There's a big procession. It's a joyful day here in Fátima."

Lori felt combative. "But you're in here."

"We're a cloistered community. We pray behind these walls. We can pray for you. What is your name?"

"Lori Hopkins."

"Miss Hopkins, Lori. Are you Catholic?"

"Yes."

The nun drew closer across the counter. "We are the Dominican Nuns of the Perpetual Rosary. Our monastery is named after Pius XII. Would you like to know more about the Dominican spiritual life?"

Lori fidgeted like a first grader ready for recess. "I'm not interested in joining anything. I'm here to get away."

"Yes, you said that." The nun paused. "Why are you here in Fátima?" The other two remained quiet, eyes downcast and appearances reflective. Lori wanted to drink in their serenity.

"I was invited," Lori said.

The woman leaned against her Spartan chair. "You were meant to be here. The Blessed Mother always invites. Through someone else or directly. I think you should join in the celebration, Lori. We will keep you in our prayers."

"Thank you, Sister."

"I am Sister Cecilia, the Mother Superior. Please visit again."

Lori rose to leave. "Sister, why are you here?"

Sister Cecilia stood and met Lori's direct gaze. "On invitation, of course. From God. I accepted."

In the crowded square, Lori pressed against people and forged her way up the steps and through the massive doorway of the Basilica of Our Lady of the Rosary. She collapsed, gratefully, in a pew near a side altar. A ceremony finished up unveiling a statue of Pope Paul VI in the church's northwest corner. Pacified by the semi-quiet of murmured prayers, she fell into a deep sleep. She awoke to the mellow light of sconces. Pilgrims of all ages and nationalities gathered at the tombs of Jacinta and Francisco Marto, the two shepherd children. Lori walked over for closer inspection. A hand rested on her shoulder. "I thought you might be in here. Were you searching for me, Lori?"

"I fell asleep." Lori straightened up. Miriam wrapped an encouraging arm around her.

"Jacinta is my favorite. She is an incorruptible. One day, I believe she will be our youngest saint." Miriam had a convincing tone. Gospel truth to her words.

They exited the basilica. "You've heard about the Fátima secrets?" asked Miriam.

Lori marveled at the light of what looked like one million candles. Miriam passed a candle to Lori and lit it with a Zippo lighter made exclusively in America. A map of Vietnam was engraved on it.

"I do remember. My Grandma Lottie told me. About the Great War. She was a nurse in France."

Miriam used Lori's candle to light her own, their faces now illuminated by a soft glow against the darkened sky. "Did you know the second one? The vision of hell?"

"No, and I'm not sure I believe in all that anyway."

They stood at the top of the basilica steps. Prayers and singing intensified. Miriam raised her voice. "I see. Do you believe in heaven?"

"I'd like to, but . . ."

"Pray, Lori. Pray for enlightenment." She held her candle high. "Why don't you join us now? We have our own banner from Egypt."

Lori was too weary to soldier on by herself. "Okay, lead the way."

Miriam was exuberant, and Lori wanted to know what fueled it. But not now. She fought exhaustion and followed Miriam into the night vigil, darkness illuminated by countless flickering lights.

On the way back to Lisbon, Lori sat next to Miriam, now her confidante. She told her about the storm, the loss of Grandma Lottie, and her recent loss of what she thought was a true love. "I'm not sure of anything now," she confessed. "I want peace for my troubled mind and sleepless nights."

"But you must believe it's possible. How can God favor you if you don't believe?" Miriam read Lori's face—fatigue and anguish, the opposite of peace. "Tell me, what's his name?"

"Gerald. Father Gerry. He's in Vietnam. He went back for a second tour after being ordained a priest. I can't imagine how his family is dealing with it. I met his sister once when I was in high school, years ago."

"Do you still think of him?"

"Yes, I do."

"I think you are here to pray and intercede for him. We will pray for Father Gerry, for his safety," Miriam said.

Lori remained wide-awake during the bus ride back to Lisbon.

"Have you heard of Alexandrina Maria da Costa?" Miriam asked. "She's a mystic from Portugal. She died in 1955 after twelve years of surviving on the Eucharist."

"That's extreme. Sounds like a self-imposed death sentence." Lori, although alert, grew tired of the talk of saintly beings.

"She was paralyzed and would drag herself to church. She's also connected to Fátima and the World Consecration to the Immaculate Heart of Mary. On her tombstone are many words ending with 'Enough with sin. Love Jesus, love Him."

"Miriam, why are you telling me all of this?"

"Well, Lori, you came with us. I thought you would be open to knowing more of Fátima, the real Portugal."

"I'm glad you invited me to Fátima. But I have other plans too." She fumbled for a few parting words. "Thank you for today. I have lots to reflect on."

Miriam backed off. "You're welcome, Lori. I'm reminded of what St. Joan of Arc said before her judges."

"Yes, I know that one, but I don't remember from where. She said, 'I have been asked to tell you about it, not to make you believe it.'" Lori felt a serendipitous connection to Miriam, the Egyptian with the noble visage.

Miriam nodded. "I'm glad you joined us."

As they entered Lisbon, its sky inky, Miriam quietly prayed the rosary and sensed a storm gathering in her new friend's life.

Lori made an overnighter to a beach resort on the Algarve coast and spent the day watching the surf curl and flatten against sun-drenched sand.

Back in Lisbon, she roamed market kiosks and stopped to admire an array of colorful hand fans and a poster for a masquerade party. A man smiled at her, a few feet away.

Adriano pushed his Ray-Ban aviator sunglasses to his forehead, catching a wave of black hair behind the stems. His irises were so dark that the pupils blended in. His teeth were straight, white, and perfectly aligned. His lips were shapely, curved enough to keep a masculine quality. "The masquerade party is quite the event. Tickets are available here."

Lori, although aloof, noticed every feature on his face. She kept her attention on the fans.

"You should be looking for hats, Senhorita. You'll burn in this sun with your fair skin. Would you like some lotion? Your nose is very red."

She wanted to say *You're annoying* or *Leave me alone*. She settled on, "Thanks, I'm fine."

"There's a language to the fans. Like life, right?" His English was impeccable, with a traceable British accent. He selected a fan, and, with one flick, the blue and gold pleats spread out, some shaded, others catching light, all in sequence. "Our years are like the folds of a fan, some with dark shadows, stormy days. Others filled with light." He flicked the fan closed. "It has a beginning and an end. But we don't, yes?"

"*Sim.*" Lori opened her fan, a vibrant, floral design with petals of coral, crimson, and mandarin orange. "But there is an alpha and omega, a beginning and an end."

Adriano pointed to his Rolex timepiece, a rim of diamonds framing the watch face. "Yes, every day, and it's now time for lunch. Most Portuguese return home, but there's a café around the corner that serves the best grilled sardines in Lisbon. Would you like to join me? I can instruct you on how to use your fan. There's a language to it!"

Lori, at first reluctant, decided a café was a safe choice for a stranger. He wouldn't know anything more, where she was staying, or even her name. The entire vacation was a solo journey, and she was craving a little company. And she was fascinated by the fan language.

"Okay, but I'm not sure about the sardines."

"Trust me. Delicious. The most typical dish in Lisbon. You must try."

At the outdoor café, Adriano sat back relaxed, secure of himself. He exuded confidence and charisma. His hands were folded on his lap, a hint of a smile. "Why Portugal?"

Lori swirled a glass of white wine. "Why not?"

"Touché. It's a great country. Did you travel much?"

"Fátima and south to the beaches."

His smile widened. "The sun is very strong. *Sim*?" He tapped his nose. "Ah, and Fátima. Millions show up on the thirteenth of the month from May to October."

"Yes, I know. I was one of them," Lori answered nonchalantly while thinking her new acquaintance a bit cheeky.

Adriano selected a cigarette out of a gold case. "What did you think?"

"Peaceful. I'm not sure why I went."

"You are Catholic?" He offered her an unfiltered cigarette.

Lori nodded her head. "Yes. Raised."

"Me too. Let's talk about something else. Religion is not my favorite topic." He lit his cigarette and inhaled.

"What is?" Lori asked.

He exhaled a ring of smoke and aimed a finger through it. "You, right now."

Lori resisted an emerging smirk. "Are you always so . . ."

"Friendly?" Adriano held up one finger like a magician readying an audience for his next trick. He pulled out a ticket from his inside jacket pocket. "I have a spare to the masquerade ball tonight."

"Short notice." Lori noted grape leaves entwined on a trellis leaning against a nearby wall. A lattice covering extended over their table, offering shade and a fresh growth of grapevine with newly formed buds. The canopy and the grinning stranger captivated her. The Garden of Eden and its forbidden fruit. *How my thoughts wander*, she told herself.

"This is Portugal. You don't have to plan too far ahead. And it's not a private affair, but you need a ticket."

Plates of grilled sardines appeared in front of them by the chef making a rare appearance.

"*Obrigado*, Pablo." Adriano rubbed his hands together anticipating a feast. "This is . . ."

"Lori." She examined the rows of tiny fish bordered by a bed of roasted peppers.

"*Aproveite!*" Pablo tipped his chef's hat and left with a pronounced jiggle in his step.

"Happy fellow." Lori sliced into a sardine.

"Ah, Lori, no, you must add more olive oil. Never too much!" Adriano picked up a cruet and sprinkled olive oil over Lori's plate. "Now try it."

Lori tasted a mouthful of drenched sardines. "Pretty good."

"So it's Lori? What is your favorite dish, Lori?" He ate three sardines without glancing up.

"I'm a Texas girl—chili, extra spicy."

"Ah, I've been to Houston, a few days before flying to the Cayman Islands. Have you been?" With a few more bites, all morsels of sardines vanished from his plate.

"Grand Cayman on a shoot." Lori separated vegetables roasted to perfection.

"Shoot?"

"Photo shoot." Lori dabbed a napkin to her mouth.

"There's a turtle stew in the Cayman Islands. I'm partial to it." Adriano ignored the remaining peppers.

Lori put down her fork. "I'm partial to turtles too."

"Really?" Adriano expressed surprise.

"Yes. My first subject was a turtle. Her name is Sandra Dee. I photographed her on the end of a spoon, and I'm so happy she didn't end up in a bowl of soup."

"How long—"

"Twelve years. I suspect she'll outlive me."

"Fascinating." His grin turned sheepish. "That concludes our discussion of food. *Sim*?"

"*Sim*. And I don't have a costume for the masquerade. So . . ."

"May I see your ticket again?" *Oh, that smile again. He must spend half his life smiling. Smiling about everything. How genuine is it?* Her thoughts swirled. The wine and heat of the day had a dizzying effect. The talk of turtles made her nauseous.

He scribbled a few words and numbers on the back of the ticket. "You can get a costume here."

Lori glimpsed at the ticket and placed it in her handbag. "I'll think about it." She wanted nothing more than a few hours of rest in the dark, curtain-drawn hotel room.

"Fair enough. And if you decide not to go, I can still give you a few lessons in the secret language." Lori offered her fan. "How you position it means a lot. Lesson one. This means 'I don't trust you.'" Adriano placed his lips on the tip of the closed fan.

"Why start with that one?" Lori tilted her head in a studied manner.

"Why not?" He shrugged.

"Okay, fair enough. Next." She maintained a half-hearted interest.

"Now, 'Yes.'" He rested the closed fan on his right cheek. "And 'No.'" He switched sides and rested the fan on his left cheek.

"Basic," Lori said.

Adriano ran a finger across the veins of the open fan. "Can you guess what it means?"

"May you live a long life?"

"You're making fun." Adriano paused. "We need to talk."

"About what?"

"No, that's what it means! Okay, a few more lessons." He placed the fan on his heart. "I love you, and I'm suffering." He touched the fan to his left ear. "Leave me alone!"

Lori grew uneasy. His stare made her restless.

"Here's one you may see if you arrive tonight." He rested the fan on his lips.

"Kiss me?"

He winked. After a few more lessons, she interjected.

"How about 'Goodbye?'"

"Very well." Adriano picked up her fan and closed it. "And there you have it." He handed the fan back to her. "Will I see you tonight?"

"Well, like we say in Texas, 'Lord willing and the creek don't rise.' That's a maybe. Thanks for lunch. And the language lesson."

Adriano gestured for them to rise. "*No me olvides.*" He slowly parted his hair with the closed fan and handed it back to her. He bowed slightly and departed.

The ruby-red gown with black lace at the hem and bodice reminded Lori of the tulip dress she'd worn to the homecoming dance over ten years ago. The vibrant color complemented her red-gold updo and pale skin. The high school home economics teacher's words rang in her ears when she chose cardinal red for a wraparound blouse pattern: "Red is for brunettes and blondes."

In her hotel room, Lori checked the bathroom mirror with the fan in front of her face. She flicked it open and practiced the fan language taught mere hours ago by a man who'd captured her imagination. An escape from everything—Texas, Boston, a soldier, a priest, and the sudden loss of Lottie. He, the man from Portugal, had an alluring quality, albeit slightly disturbing. His exchange with the fan was odd, but she conceded, he was trying to make an impression. She chose to dismiss whatever disquieted her.

Lori studied the invitation. She enjoyed Lisbon's old world European grandeur and nightlife. The masquerade ball was nothing she had in mind. But, the fan language played on her, and she was willing to play along for one evening.

She used her two complimentary drink tickets on sparkling wine. She waved away appetizers and hors d'oeuvres served throughout the crowded dance floor. A banquet table held two large porcelain tureens, one with caldo verde and the other a meaty Portuguese stew. Her stomach churned when eyeing ceramic bowls of torrid green liquid lined up next to white linen napkins and silver spoons. Watching yards of fabric swirl made her woozy on an empty stomach. Within twenty minutes, she headed for the exit. A masked man blocked the doorway. "Good evening. Have you tried the caldo verde? I hear it's quite delicious. Reminds me of turtle soup!"

Lori, stunned, flicked her fan as a sign of displeasure. "Cruel humor doesn't flatter you."

Adriano threw back his head and laughed, exposing prominent white teeth. He put a hand gently on her upper arm. "I'm teasing you."

With a flash of her fan, Lori displayed a cold shoulder. Costumed guests lined up in anticipation of the first waltz. Adriano bowed deeply, sweeping a feathered hat on the parquet wood floor. An initially reluctant Lori let him take the lead. Her red satin skirt swooshed and gave a fanciful feel to the moment, as if on a merry-go-round. All she noticed were the flashes of teeth. *Why my fixation on teeth?* she wondered. Her photos. Teeth in a tiger's mouth. Teeth from a woman in a London phone both. Tusks on an elephant. Concealed teeth in a starfish.

After the dance, they stepped out on a balcony to breathe in the warm night air. Another waltz started up in the grand hall. Guests took their places for the ritual dance. Swirling skirts on one side and masked suitors on the other.

"Why did you say, 'Don't forget me?'" She paused. "At the café?" Lori focused her gaze on the city lights hovering at a distance above the terrace railing. Although Portugal was memorable, she was ready for home. More than ever.

"Why not?" Adriano rested his hand on hers. She pulled back.

"Adriano, I leave on Wednesday. Thank you for the invitation."

"Do you remember all the fan language?" He appeared hopeful, maybe too hopeful.

"Hmm, most of it."

"May I?" He pressed her closed fan against his lips. The evocative, rousing melody of Shostakovich's "The Second Waltz" reverberated in the ballroom, a stagy backdrop to Adriano's gesture.

With a direct gaze, Lori reclaimed the fan. She spread it out in front of her face and moved it back and forth with the slightest of motions, meaning "It's no use."

Adriano snatched the fan. He rested it on his heart.

They stood motionless on the balcony. The music continued, a backdrop of spinning, vivid colors and masked suitors, flashes of silk and the persistent three counts of "The Second Waltz."

Lori moved away from Adriano. He clasped her gloved hand, the one holding the fan. In a last attempt, he let the fan fall to the balcony floor. Translation: "I'm yours!" Lori's response was more emphatic than any words. She snagged the fan with her little finger signaling "Goodbye" and didn't look back.

Inside the ballroom, Lori shook off the strange language of the fan and the intensity of their heated responses. A waiter approached with a tray of champagne glasses for a toast. A guest announced a birthday from the dance floor. She seized a glass of the bubbly and joined the special celebratory dance. Intricate moves included the champagne toast and drinking without a dribble while keeping step with the waltz. Dancers traded partners, the women with fans and champagne, the men with champagne only. Interlinked arms raised fizzy drinks and dancers were eliminated with a mere drop on a sleeve or a trickle from their mouths. Lori laughed, caught up in the delirium. Adriano leaned against a wall. He smiled approvingly as Lori passed by with an array of partners. A few couples remained, including the birthday guest, a woman with honey-colored tresses piled high on her head and wearing a red satin dress with glittery gold lace at the bodice. Lori's last swallow of champagne trickled down the side of her mouth. She made a final curtsy and joined the others on the fringes. The waltz ended, and the birthday celebrant and a new partner claimed victory. Lori glanced at the wall clock.

Adriano advanced. "May I have at least one dance?" The bartender circled the room balancing a tray of champagne. He came close and Adriano picked up two glasses.

"I think I've had enough, thank you." She curtsied. "It's been very, uh, informative."

"So formal." His eyes twinkled. "Let's have one last toast to our own folds in the fan." He handed her the glass and raised his own.

"*Prost*," she said. They clinked.

"*Prost*," he repeated and finished in one quick gulp.

He escorted her to the parquet floor scuffed by waltzing feet. The dance was a blur. The rest of the night was even more of a blur.

Lori opened her eyes to a pitch-black hotel room. The alarm clock read 3:00 a.m. Her head throbbed. She was alone, bewildered, and struggled for clarity of the evening's events. She remembered dancing to the waltz music and vibrant colors—purple, green, yellow, red. The swooshing of silky gowns, her own gown. And then the dizziness, the fainting away. The blur as she was shoved into an awaiting taxi. Or was it a taxi? Someone drove her to the hotel, but she didn't recall getting to her room. A blackout. How would anyone know her hotel? Yes, the card in her purse gave the name and address!

Her rented ball gown was draped across an embroidered chair. Bent over, she gripped her head to stop the excruciating pain and crawled to the bathroom. The mirror added more missing pieces. Makeup smeared. Hair disheveled and matted.

The truth struck like a lightning bolt, making its impression through the hazy recollection. The second glass of champagne. The ring on its stem. Was it marked? For her? Pieces, like a jigsaw puzzle, came together. A flash of a smile. A look of malice, maybe? Domination? She stood straight up and returned to the bed. The fan propped on the pillow next to her was spread out, its folds flattened.

And then she remembered his leaving, only the leaving. The crack of light entering the darkened room. The nausea and dizziness. The fan closed tightly in his hand as he very slowly parted her hair. The smile, sad but hurtful. The language of the fan, "Don't forget me."

Lori attempted to rise again. The champagne. Drugged. A moment of clarity, and another piece captured. Quaaludes? She picked up the phone and rang the front desk. Her breathing was shallow. The dizziness mounted.

"Sim?" The front desk person, a hollow voice over the phone, waited for a request.

Lori's voice was ragged. "Please, a doctor. Room 301." She fell back onto the pillow in a stupor. Heavy sleep took over.

"You were a very sick woman. You almost died, Signorina." The doctor had a heavy accent, but his English was intelligible. The white coat and black stethoscope matched his black hair, white at the temples. Lori imagined Count Dracula but desensitized to daylight hours.

"You speak English." She took in the hospital room's white sterility and pieced together fragments of the past twenty-four hours.

"Yes, of course. What happened?" His poker face softened.

"I went to a masquerade ball. I believe a man, yes, a man named Adriano slipped me ludes. In my drink. I had champagne."

"Yes, you had methaqualone in your system. Very dangerous when drinking. What else do you remember?"

"Nothing. My room. Harsh light from the hallway." She omitted the fan he used to part her hair and the goodbye.

The doctor crossed his arms like an inspector. "We'll have to fully examine you. The police may accuse you of taking the drugs. There's no proof, only your word. And anything else?"

"Your name? Where am I?" Lori gathered strength and boosted herself on both elbows.

He patted her shoulder. "Rest, Miss Hopkins, please. You are in Sao Jose Hospital here in Lisbon. I'm Dr. Ventura."

"Like the freeway."

"Yes, like the freeway."

"I understand. Only my word."

"And you don't have many details. A last name?"

She shook her head, surprised that the throbbing had dissipated.

"I'm sorry, Miss Hopkins. This is an unfortunate situation."

"Doctor?"

"Yes."

"How did I get here?"

"You called the hotel room service and asked for a doctor."

Lori fell back and closed her eyes. A tune. He whistled a tune. The light from the hallway and a song he whistled. One she couldn't remember or didn't know.

The Polícia Judiciária were unyielding. Philipe Matos, a stout, English-speaking officer, led the hospital bed investigation. Lori's past dependency on sleeping pills, her struggle for over a year to stop filling the prescriptions, and her hope to kick the habit were all uncovered with relentless enquiries. The victim was on trial. The inquisitors created an alternate scenario. Possibly undue stress and the masquerade party in a foreign country reignited her addiction and the resulting unconscious state. They intimated that she invited a stranger into her room. Questions without answers. Why else would she take an offer from someone she didn't know? Lori sensed there was no hope for restitution. No hope for finding Adriano, the perpetrator, who disappeared into a mystifying oblivion. She chided herself. *How foolish!* Was she to be punished for an unwise decision? But the invite was to a public place. Isn't that what Grandma Lottie told her years ago? Public places. They're safe.

Travel and photo assignments had changed her. She adapted a

persona that threw caution to the wind. Anything for the story. *No, I won't beat myself up*, she thought over and over. *I'm alive! I'm a cat with nine lives. How many lives have I used up?* Her silent litany—*a natural disaster, man-made war, loss of my nearest and dearest. I'll live through this one.* And she felt an unrelenting giddiness at her core of how life's twists and turns, its many folds, were nothing more than choices. Good choices. Bad choices. The choice started with a fan, a souvenir in an open market. The fan and its folds. The dark and light folds of her life, marking time.

The doctor insisted his patient get more rest. Lori pressed for further investigation and questioning. Anything to help her memory and sort out the details. The police obliged.

"When are you planning to leave Portugal, Miss Hopkins?"

"My flight is May twenty-ninth."

The portly officer crossed his legs and arms with effort. "That's in two days. We will need more time to conduct an investigation if you want to press charges."

Lori scratched her head, perplexed by her present state, although knowing the effect of Quaaludes—the fogginess and the loss of alacrity of mind. "I don't know his last name. I have no information."

Inspector Matos recrossed his legs, a sizeable paunch making it more difficult. A puffy hand rested on his cheek. "We can check the guest list of the party."

"Okay. His first name is Adriano." Lori shifted a pillow from under her back. Time was running out, and she had no intention of remaining in Lisbon beyond her departure date.

"If he purchased tickets with cash, there's no record. Did they take your name at the entrance?"

"No, just my ticket. Can you at least check any records or list for Adriano?"

The police officer and his silent partner exchanged looks that annoyed Lori. Both officers tipped their hats and headed for the door.

Lori propped herself up. "Wait. Ines, the woman who owns the dress shop. He wrote her address on the back of the invitation."

The countertop was piled high with wrinkled dresses. A tiny woman inspected the rainbow of silky fabrics. She wore fashionable eyeglasses attached to a diamond-studded chain and held up an amethyst-colored gown torn at the hem.

Lori and Inspector Matos stood at the counter.

"*Sim*?" said Ines, her voice and manner cool and unflappable.

"Hi, do you remember me? I rented this dress." Lori added the red satin and black lace gown to the costumes heaped on the counter.

"You're a day late. That's an extra charge." The woman's accent was thick, and her automatic response seemed rehearsed. She went about her business. Lori sensed the dressmaker's growing uneasiness with the inspector's presence.

"We need to ask you a few questions." Matos poised his pen and notepad.

"My English is not too good. We speak in Portuguese." Ines was direct, forceful, and businesslike, matched by Lori's equal forcefulness.

"I prefer we speak in English, if it's okay. I'll be direct." Lori thought carefully before speaking again. "A man named Adriano . . ."

Ines looked confused. "Adriano. I do not know that name."

"He sent me to you. He wrote your name and address on the back of an invitation." Lori made a motion as if writing on the back of her hand.

Ines shrugged, her expression placid, and directed attention to the policeman. "No Adriano."

Lori sensed the busy shopkeeper comprehended more English than she let on. They'd engaged in a rather lengthy conversation mere days ago. Talk of Lisbon, travel through Europe, the Big Apple, family in the States, but no mention of Adriano and his recommendation of her shop. A lost opportunity on hindsight. She persisted. "He gave me your name."

Ines replied in Portuguese to the inspector. He translated. "Miss Hopkins, she asked if he sent you here, why did you not mention him when you rented the dress? You did not mention anyone. Why are you mentioning it now?"

The dressmaker's stony expression resembled a punishing,

impenetrable wall. Lori conceded defeat. She dug into her purse for a few coins and paid the overdue fine. *"Obrigado."* She turned to the officer. "Let's leave."

"Are you sure?" Matos asked, a note of empathy in his voice.

Ines examined dresses and moved them from the counter.

"She doesn't know anyone by that name," Lori said. "Or is not admitting it. I have a plane to catch tomorrow."

The police officer tipped his hat at Ines. The shop doorbell announced their exit. Lori and Matos regrouped on the mosaic walkway that first entranced and now reminded her of an assault from a stranger. "The investigation will end when you leave. A closed file." Matos lit an unfiltered cigarette. His first of the day and another breached commitment to quit.

"There's one more lead—the café owner where we had lunch. He knew him!"

"We have nothing to go on. Your word against a stranger you met in one day and have not seen since."

"But assaults, even murders, happen with strangers every day."

Matos puffed away and inspected the ashes before flicking them between the tiles. "This isn't a murder case. You're alive." He tossed the half-smoked cigarette. "Yes, you say you were attacked. I believe you, and I'm sorry for this . . ."

Lori refrained from asking for a cigarette. "I will give you a description. As much as I can remember. But, I will not stay here in Lisbon to continue a case."

"It's your choice, Miss Hopkins. There is no case . . ."

"Yes, thank you."

They shook hands. A formal gesture of finality and dubious expression from the investigator. Or at least it appeared so to Lori. She watched him disappear down a narrow street, stepping gingerly along the basalt tiles. No perpetrator. No crime. No hope for restitution.

The bell rang again as Lori reentered the dress shop. "Ines."

"Sim?" The tiny woman leered. She won. No further investigation.

"Is he related to you? Why are you holding back from telling the truth?" Her words hit the impenetrable, unexpressive wall behind the heap of dresses.

"I'm sorry for your troubles, but I don't know this man you speak of, miss. He may know the dress shop and said he knew me. Anything is possible, right?" Her English had improved again. Lori was convinced she was hiding something, maybe a nephew or a friend's son, or maybe, she was telling the truth. Lori studied the dress she wore. It matched her fan so beautifully.

"Ines, do you believe in fate?" Lori gave a wistful look.

"I don't understand. What is this word *fate*?"

"Destiny?" Lori added, not sure why she spoke of it to the human wall.

"Ah, *destino*. Yes, of course." Ines examined dresses.

Lori lingered. "Some events are beyond our control. They are determined by a power." She paused. "They happen for a reason."

Ines stopped abruptly. She grew tired of the badgering customer. "Miss, you can see that I'm very busy. I have another ball for these dresses."

"When?" Lori's interest was piqued.

"In two weeks. Please, no more questions. How do you say? Yes, enough! *Dia bom*." Ines made a shooing motion as if swatting a pest.

Lori, too numb to feel humiliation, left and hailed a taxi. While seated in the hotel lobby, she shut her eyes and sorted out the last few days.

"Lori?" Miriam, the Egyptian woman, was standing in front of her. "You're still here? I thought you were at the resorts."

"I was, but I came back here for a few days. I fly out tomorrow."

"I'm glad to see you again. I want to give you my contact information." She wrote on stationery. "I know you travel with your job. If you're in Egypt, please come and visit me."

Adriano Peres, a.k.a. Antonio Lanzetti, had every intention of attending the next masquerade ball. He'd scope out female tourists at outdoor shops. He rarely approached a European woman. Too close to home, whether in Italy or Portugal. He had a residence in both countries with a wife in Italy and a girlfriend in Portugal.

The Portuguese girlfriend's mother owned a dress shop and rented out gowns for theatrical shows, masquerade parties, and costume balls. She warned Antonio. "Don't go to the upcoming ball. An American woman showed up at the dress shop asking questions. She brought a police investigator."

Antonio explained with ease. "A crazy lady accused me of stealing her money. I met her while having lunch in an outdoor café. She sat at a table next to me and said how much she enjoyed Lisbon. I had an extra ticket to a party that evening. She seemed anxious and bored, so I passed the ticket to her and said goodbye."

The dressmaker, Ines, the mother of Antonio's girlfriend, didn't ask any questions. She chose to believe him and left the rest, and unrest, behind.

Chapter 26

Boston Reborn

On Wednesday, Lori left for Boston. The wings of a plane lightened her wretchedness. The two-hour flight from Lisbon to Orly was rough going with blustery windstorms. She was relieved to debark the plane in Paris and board the Pan Am flight for Boston. When Lori arrived at Boston Logan International Airport, she headed for the closest bar at the terminal. She ordered a ginger ale to combat persistent nausea.

The first call was to Bernadette, who was working late at the office on her literary magazine and beating the clock to the next deadline.

"When did you get back?" Bernadette sounded surprised to hear her niece's voice late at night.

"An hour ago." Lori got quiet on the other end.

Bernadette put down her red marking pen. "What's wrong? Are you okay?" Her concern was palpable, and Lori was comforted.

"Can we meet when you're done? I don't have anywhere to go."

"What?" Bernadette leaned back in her office chair. "Are you kidding? Boston's like home. It is home."

"Bernie, I don't want to talk to family right now. Other than you."

"Okay, I'll wrap up here in, let's say, forty minutes. It's ten o'clock. Why don't you meet me at my apartment? Bill's away at a teachers' convention."

"Okay, I'll be there in an hour."

"Lori." She searched for words. "It's good to hear your voice."

The phones clicked off on both ends. Bernadette rushed through copy edits, her mind on Lori and the urgency of her call.

Lori hugged her knees on the steps outside Bernadette's apartment building. The night was balmy and humid.

Bernadette approached her huddled niece. "Have you been waiting long?"

"Five minutes, maybe. I stopped in a twenty-four-hour diner."

They climbed the stairs to a third-floor walkup, not a word spoken. Bernadette unbolted the door. Her apartment was sparsely furnished. Mounds of paper and corners piled with books, magazines, and music sheets, cramped the space.

Lori collapsed on the sofa and curled up in a fetal position. "I don't feel like talking, Bernie. I need rest. Is that okay?"

"You talk when you're ready. Get some rest."

Bernadette retreated into her bedroom and went through her night-time regiment—hang up clothes, toss wash into the hamper, brush teeth, wash face, shower and shampoo for next day, don nightgown, and lay out clothes for the morning, even underclothes, so she could slide into shoes and slip out the door without a hitch. Coffee would wait until she got to the office. Before turning in, she regarded Lori balled up on her couch. Was she simply tired? Exhausted from her travels? Her busy life? The loss of so much in Texas? Or was it more? She knew it was more. Lori was a survivor. She didn't wince at pain, physical or emotional. Bernadette cleared away all the troubling perceptions that churned inside of her. Lori survived so much personal loss, war assignments, drug dependency. What was left?

The following morning, Bernadette listened raptly to the nightmarish sequence of events and, ultimately, was scandalized by no follow-up investigation. Lori vaguely recounted the drugging and sexual assault.

"And he gets away?" A nervous tick developed in her left eyelid.

Lori slumped. "It's over. My word against a man who disappeared."

Bernadette felt the heat of anger fueled by injustice rising in the nape of her neck. "Did you leave behind a description? You're probably not his first victim, or his last."

"I turned over every stone I could in two days. I didn't want to stay."

"And you came straight here? What next?" Bernadette sipped her tea, attempting to resume normalcy to the early morning hour. Deadlines would wait. Everything could wait.

"I have an assignment in Kenya." Lori's head drooped along with her spirit. "Do you have any aspirin?"

Bernadette stretched over the sink and opened up an overhead cabinet.

Lori continued, "I may need to cancel."

"Why?" Bernadette searched the cabinet for a bottle of aspirin.

"The doctor in Portugal advised against malaria pills."

Bernadette turned to her niece.

"In case . . . Anything's possible. I'll know in three months," Lori said.

"Do you really think . . . ?"

"I don't know, Bernie," she answered, slightly irritated.

Bernadette handed out the pills and a glass of water. "So what's next?"

"Time. I can get another assignment and wait things out. Time. That's all."

"You can stay here as long as you like, Lori. I'm here for you."

Lori swigged the water. "I know, Bernie. But nothing to the family. Not right now."

"Are you telling anyone else?"

"I don't know."

After three days cocooned in Bernadette's apartment, Lori faced rearranging her life, her assignments, and the shock of the Lisbon incident. She told details, as she remembered, to Bernadette, who listened patiently, not probing beyond what she heard. And she had so many questions fueled by outrage. The advice her aunt offered was captured in three words. "Don't blame yourself."

Lori did nothing but blame herself for being so easily ensnared into a web of lies and deceit by a man named Adriano who appealed to her vanity. She recollected Gerry's oft repeated words. "Vanity, all is vanity."

She hated what happened to her, but she hated the truth of Gerry's words even more. Gerry, who'd insisted on returning to Vietnam as a priest. Gerry, who'd slipped a note to her in sophomore year: *Everything happens for a reason . . . Be strong.* Gerry, who'd broken his own heart to serve the Lord.

For two days, Lori snacked on boxes of raisins and a jar of peanuts, barely leaving the couch until she woke up on day three sick of feeling sorry for herself. Bernadette busied herself in the kitchen brewing coffee and preparing Boston fare—crusty fish cakes of flaky cod, eggs over medium, and Boston baked beans.

"Do you believe everything happens for a reason?" Lori spooned the warm baked beans into her mouth.

"I'd like to believe it." Bernadette glanced at her wristwatch. Fifteen minutes late. She'd never arrived at her office even one minute late. "Yes, I guess I do."

"Bernie, I've had a death wish, you know?"

"I know, Lori. It explains a lot."

Lori fixed her gaze at the wall behind her aunt. "It explains nothing. I don't even know why. Maybe it's who I am." She rose from the kitchen table and stretched out her arms overhead, the old Lori, the girl of fourteen only a decade or so ago. "Do you ever see Giuseppe?"

Bernadette cleared their dishes. "He moved the restaurant location. He's now on the Cape with his wife and three kids."

"Three? How long has he been married now?"

"Three years. I guess he thought life would be less hectic on the Cape. Less competition, at least for Italian restaurants."

"Sandra Dee! I forgot Sandra Dee! I think I'm losing my mind, Bernie."

"She's fine, Lori." Bernadette put the aspirin bottle away and tidied up her shoebox-sized kitchen.

"Where is she?" Lori rubbed her temples to relieve her throbbing head.

"Ben has her right now. He's in between assignments. I'm sorry. I forgot to mention it."

Sandra Dee poked her scaly head out of her body armor and moved toward Lori.

"She's been hiding in her shell for three days. She knows Bernadette, but I think she hates me." Ben welcomed a change in topic, still reeling from the Lisbon account.

"How long have you had her?" Lori stroked the shell, and Sandra Dee responded by overcoming her shyness.

"Four days." Ben adjusted the glasses on the bridge of his nose, a habit he'd formed in high school with his first pair for nearsightedness. An eye doctor had recommended not going into photography because his vision was so poor. He had mailed a note with news of his first award to the doctor that read, *Thanks for the advice. You confirmed my resolve.*

Lori concentrated all her attention on Sandra Dee. "She likes it when you pet her chin." She gently rubbed the turtle's face with strokes of her index finger.

"I'm sure she'd have bitten me." Ben gripped the nape of his neck. "What will you do now?" He folded his hands on the kitchen table. The United Nations had nothing on the Hopkins bunch for deliberating, decision making, engaging in debates, and when necessary, a pouring out of the soul.

"Well, I'm not going to Africa." Lori absentmindedly petted Sandra Dee's shell with even strokes, as if for clarity or a centering force.

"I can take over the assignment. One last adventure before I retire."

"Worst time of year."

Ben laughed. "There's no good time of year south of the equator. My opinion, of course."

Sandra Dee rolled her black bead eyes after a few more strokes on her scaly brow.

"That turtle will outlive all of us," Ben said.

"Let's hope so, Ben. I don't plan on living to one hundred!"

Lori had stopped using "aunt" and "uncle" after her war assignment. She was no longer the apprentice but a foreign correspondent, a veteran at seeing the world and all of its beauty and ugliness.

She next spoke as if reading his thoughts. "I had to tell you. You're my mentor."

"What will you do now?"

"Back to Texas, sort things out. Then Boston and England."

"England?" His curiosity was apparent.

"A visit. The woman adopted by Gran and raised by her friend."

"How'd you find her?"

Lori placed Sandra Dee on the floor. "My camera found her."

Chapter 27

London Bridge

On Friday, September 13, two days before her twenty-seventh birthday, Lori got a phone call from Daniel Freeborn, her family doctor in Texas. Her due date was late February. She counted the days—February 25, 1969. Nine months from May 25, 1968. It seemed a lifetime away.

Tally was the first to hear. Lori phoned her and asked if she could meet for lunch.

"Can you pick me up, Tally?" Lori was anxious to spill the news, but not to family. Not yet.

"Sure. Where?"

"Grandma's house. I'm packing things up, getting it ready to sell."

"Welcome to the club. Marty and I are boxing up stuff now."

"Where're you going?" Lori filed a jagged nail and kept calm, as if her world hadn't changed only twenty minutes earlier.

"Oklahoma. He's homesick. I'll finish up the school year here and join him in Oklahoma City in the spring."

"Can we go to the Hi-D-Ho?"

Tally chuckled. "Before the Saturday night cruise? You know it moved, right?"

"Yeah, but it's the same, really."

"I'll be there in fifteen."

"Tally?" Lori choked back tears, the secret she held, for now, welling up inside. Images of a carefree summer day at Paragon Park, a merry-go-round, flaring nostrils of painted horses flashed through her mind. "I've missed you. I'm sorry I didn't keep in touch."

"It's okay. I'm just as guilty." A beat evaporated time. "Even."

A beat before Lori's smile crossed phone wires. "Steven."

The years in between drifted away like clouds dispersing for the sun.

They parked at the Hi-D-Ho. The waitress on roller skates sidled up to Tally's 1964 green Mustang convertible.

"I'm Molly. What'll it be, girls?"

Lori leaned over Tally. "Two Hidy burgers, two Hidy fries, two cherry Cokes. How 'bout you, Tally?"

Molly waited with pen and pad. Tally cocked her head. "She's kidding. That should do it."

Molly skated away. Lori added nonchalantly, "I'm eating for two."

Tally gripped the steering wheel. "What? Oh, Lori, that's . . ."

"Not planned and not good. You're the first to know. I did suspect."

"What happened?" Tally's initial joy shifted to concern and near dread for hearing any further news.

"Short version? Drugged and sexually assaulted in Lisbon by a man I met the same day."

Tally remained speechless. Molly rolled up with their food tray. Lori placed a paper napkin on her lap and plowed through her fries. Tally sipped cherry Coke.

"I'm sorry, Lori. I don't know what to say."

"It's okay. I've only known for twenty-four hours." She licked salty fingers.

"What happened to him . . . ?"

"That's the biggest mystery. His name's Adriano. I tried to find out more from a dressmaker in Lisbon." Lori took a bite of her burger. "I went to a masquerade ball. I met him at an outdoor market. He invited me to lunch. Offered me a free ticket. At the ball, he slipped a lude into a glass of champagne. That's all I remember."

They sat and ate together, letting the world pass by. Tally barely touched her fries and offered them to Lori.

"If you insist." Lori tossed her empty container on the food tray.

"Will you stay in Texas?" Tally hid the remains of her burger in its wrapper. Her heart instantly ached for her friend.

"A little while. Then England."

"A work assignment?"

"No, more like R and R."

"Why England? You know, it's legal, if you don't want . . ."

"That's my Tally. Third degree." Lori winked and inspected a French fry.

"But, I . . ."

"It's okay, Tally. I know you care about me." Lori put her head on her dear friend's broad shoulder and arm that could score a three-pointer with ease on the basketball court. A dark red Pontiac Bonneville station wagon parked next to them with a mom, pop, and three school-aged kids. The mom gave a sour look at Lori, now sheltered in Tally's embrace.

"Tally? I'm not sure what I'm going to do. I'm four months."

"But why England?"

"Not sure yet. But I need to go soon. Maybe next week."

"What about your house?"

"It can wait. I can't."

They straightened up. Lori looked over at the disturbed mom in the station wagon. She waved and blew a kiss to the woman before Tally reversed and peeled away.

Their conversation on Monday, September 23, 1968, occurred in the same vegetarian boutique on Carnaby Street. The owner, Dorcas, changed the name of her breakfast and lunch shop to Thyme Travelers. She believed that people could exist in two places at once and didn't shy away from telling her customers. She confided to Lori. "There's more in the world than we'll ever know!"

At noon, Francine breezed into the shop with exuberance. "Lori!" She kissed her on both cheeks. Lori welcomed the smoothness and warmth of her touch.

"I got word that Susu is fine. She had a nasty spell, but it wasn't a seizure. Dehydration. You did receive my thank you for the lovely photos, yes?"

"I did."

"And you survived your war stint. It must have been nightmarish."

"Yes."

"And here we are. When did you arrive?"

"Yesterday." Lori choked on her one-word answers. So much to reveal and she didn't know where to start.

"How long is your stay?" Francine perused the menu. "I'm famished. I think I'll have the French onion soup with gobs of Gruyère cheese melted on top." She set down the menu. "It's been quite a horrific year in the States. The assassinations and riots. What's the world coming to, right? Sorry, I interrupted myself. How long are you staying?"

Lori scarcely recognized the loquacious woman across from her. She expected a demure, rather sullen woman who only brightened up with her radiant smile. She's quite the magpie. And then it was like Francine heard her thoughts.

"Sorry I'm rambling. I'm so incredibly relieved, you see." She fingered her collar akin to Lori's mother, Miriam, who pawed at clothing or buttons nervously. How strange to witness the habit yet again! "Susu is all I have, really."

Dorcas greeted a couple, both with tousled manes, Nehru jackets, and large medallions. They nodded reverently as if entering a church.

"Francine, I'm here for a few months, through February of next year. I'm renting a flat month to month until the baby arrives."

"Oh, my. Congrats, dear." She reached for Lori's hands and flashed that sublime beam and flawless teeth.

"I'm signing adoption papers. I'd like you and your husband to be the adoptive parents. I know it's asking a lot, but I hope you will consider. You have time."

Francine withdrew her hands. A look of deep concern and a creased brow replaced the cheerful countenance. "I see. You don't want the child." She reposed and surmised the state of affairs. "Are you sure you want to go through with it? You know that abortion is legal here in England. You do have an option."

"I know. I considered it. But I've had too much sadness in my life. I don't want more."

"Yes, that's probably wise on your part. And the father?"

"I don't know him. I met him earlier the same day. And, no, it wasn't a one-night stand."

"My goodness, then you were assaulted. You're lucky it wasn't worse!"

"Believe me, I've considered all the possibilities. I'll get through this and move on with my life. All I ask is that you consider my offer. When I found out I was pregnant, you came to my mind almost immediately. You said we'd most likely meet again. And here we are. It's fate. I believe it."

Church bells rang in the distance. "Noon day mass is over. They are ringing those bells for Father Pio of Pietrelcina. He died earlier today. You've heard of him?"

"No," Lori answered, relieved that her proposition was not immediately refuted.

"He will be a saint one day. He received the stigmata, the terrible wounds of Jesus, on his hands. He also had a saying. 'Reach up as high as you can today, and God will reach down the rest of the way.'" Francine offered her hands again to Lori, who trembled at the faith of the woman she hoped would be the mother of her child. "Thanks for reaching out to me, Lori. You are brave, and I admire you."

Lori spent the holidays in England anticipating birth, letting go of resentments, anger, all things that vexed her soul. Peace filled her with each passing week as the child grew strong, kicking and stretching its limbs in growth spurts. Francine was by her side, spending Christmas with her, giving comfort and space when she needed it.

The expectant mother signed the adoption papers on a day wet with heavy snow, a messy slush throughout the streets of London. She trudged to her flat. Icy water filled her boots. A wool scarf and poncho kept the wintry incursion from the child within her womb.

On February 22, 1969, a mild winter day, Lori gave birth to a baby boy, a British midwife named Judith by her side. The adoption agency arranged the transfer. All papers were reviewed and signed by the adoptive parents before she went into labor. Lori chose a setting in an innovative birth center. No reminder of the hospital in Lisbon.

He weighed seven pounds, five ounces. The midwife swathed the wailing newborn in a thin cotton blanket. Francine was there and coached Lori through the birth, tears of joy streaming down her face. "Thank you, Lori, for letting me be here."

The new mother, exhausted and exhilarated, closed her eyes and listened to the pounding of her heart coursing blood through her spent body.

"I've chosen a name," said Francine, the other new mother.

"Please not now. Not now." Lori's eyes remained closed. The cries of her son caught hold of her beating heart. They were one again. How could she? How could she let go of this child?

Francine's face was pure joy and sheer agony. She worried that Lori, her bridge to maternal bliss, would lose sight of their adoption agreement and decide to keep Louis, even though she'd have a legal fight on her hands.

She chose Louis, after King Louis of France, the canonized Catholic and Anglican saint to honor her French extraction and her British home.

Lori made three choices the day she gave birth. She chose not to say hello or goodbye to her newborn son. Her body yearned to give sustenance to her child. She chose to take a pill to dry up her milk production. Her breasts, hardened with her baby's first nourishing meal, were an unrelenting summons to motherhood. Her third choice was not to hear the name Francine chose for her son.

Francine was saddened by this choice yet tried to understand and put herself in the shoes of a young woman she'd met by chance but had a connection to through an American nurse who'd saved lives on French soil.

Three choices on a February day in England, but the first choice was made months ago when she proposed adoption to a barren wife she'd met at a tea shop two years earlier. A French orphan who married a Brit and longed for a child.

On Saturday, March 8, 1969, two weeks after giving birth, Lori boarded a plane for Boston, her new home base. Bernadette met her at the arrival gate and drove her to the apartment and the couch Lori had curled up on less than a year ago. She slept fitfully, tossing and turning, waking to the imaginary cries of a newborn over three thousand miles away. The second night, she dreamt of Miriam in the Old Testament, putting her infant brother Moses in a basket and waiting for Pharaoh's daughter to notice him. Lori put a baby in a basket, like Miriam, but with a big difference. The child was her own.

On the fourth morning, Lori started her life over knowing her son was wrapped in caring arms, if not her own. She recognized her death wish, but not for the life of another. By the seventh day, she said goodbye to Bernadette and Bill.

On the eighth day, the sixteenth of March and eleventh Sunday of the calendar year, Lori embarked on a new assignment, "Prairie Lands of the Wild West." She read that the calendar for 1969 would not be replicated until the year 2025. Absurd, she thought. Who would even consider time so far-flung? Today was enough with its troubles.

NASA prepared for a spacewalk, and she formulated an interstellar layout and found remote regions resembling alien planets. The world, particularly the United States, was consumed with space exploration.

She was consumed with escaping behind her camera's view finder. The perfect hiding place. She preferred roaming assignments with Sandra Dee, her traveling companion. Eight days in the west. Eight days. The number without beginning or end. Her own series of octaves and never-ending new beginnings.

Chapter 28

To the Moon

Lubbock High's class of 1959 tenth reunion committee searched for a theme. No one was interested in the "Battle of New Orleans," the number one song throughout June in their graduation year. The committee chose "Venus," a hit song by Frankie Avalon in March 1959 to celebrate July's moonwalk mission. The reunion date was set for August 9, 1969, a Saturday night, at the school gymnasium. Many graduates were moms, dads, and a few teachers, like Tally, who wanted to steer clear of the school year.

"Back to school" was on the minds of many former classmates with school-age children and scores of war protestors headed for college. Lori had an assignment to cover an outdoor event in upstate New York the weekend following the reunion. She replayed the week-old phone conversation with Tally while driving to Lubbock High School . . .

• • •

Tally pleaded. "It won't be the same without you."

"I never sent a response."

"You can be our surprise guest."

Lori wrapped the cord phone around her index finger. "Okay, I'll go because I'm here in Lubbock to sell Gran's house."

"Well, it's . . . Do you need my help cleaning it out?"

"Only if you can get this stuff hauled away. I don't have any room or place for it." She counted empty boxes.

"Lori, you know I don't live here in Lubbock."

"Then I don't need any help."

Tally paused a few seconds. "Lori, did you see . . ."

"No. It's a boy, and no, I didn't." She hesitated. "I'll let you know if I need help."

"You'll be there? Next Saturday, August ninth?"

"Yeah, if there's a full moon."

Their smiles traveled across the wires. "I'll arrange it for you."

"Tally, it's okay. I'm okay."

"I know. I mean, I guessed."

"Are you so persuasive with your students?" Lori stretched the phone cord into the living room.

"They're second graders. They think I walk on water."

"That's good. What's the theme?"

"Planets."

"Plants?" Lori finished counting boxes.

"No planets. Like the moon."

"The moon isn't a planet, Teach."

"I know. Our song is 'Venus.'"

• • •

A banner hung high above the dance floor: *Welcome Home Father Gerry!*

The banner reminded Lori of the one hanging in her classroom when she'd returned after the storm. The one that read, *Welcome Back Lori!* The morning bell, the classroom door she opened thirteen years ago, remained with her. All the vapid faces, not knowing what to say to the orphan girl. On that day, she had wanted to run into Grandma Lottie's embrace, the only comfort she knew for the next ten years. Even now, she mused why banners were hung when people arrive on the other side of a tragedy. Why is it a cause for celebration? Banners are for birthdays and anniversaries, not for surviving conflict, war, disease, and devastating events. She mentioned her sentiment to Tally, one of the chief reunion organizers.

"We did it for you in high school." Tally checked planets of vibrantly colored Styrofoam balls hanging by strings from the gymnasium ceiling. Gold and silver stars glittered on midnight blue velvet curtains, transforming the sporty environment into a galactic feel.

"That's my point," Lori replied.

Father Gerald appeared at the entranceway. Party goers, sipping punch and sampling hors d'oeuvres and snacks, dropped their refreshments at nearby tables. At least half of the Lubbock High's graduating class of 1959 disapproved of the war in Vietnam. Many demonstrated and joined rallies with college students, hippies, and self-professed peaceniks. Yet, a round of applause greeted their fellow classmate as he worked his way into the room. Lori noticed his hollow cheeks, the sorrow in his eyes, and a perceptible limp in his gait. His spark was a little dimmer. She raced up to hug him before giving it a second thought.

"Father. Welcome home." After a second embrace, she whispered, "Be strong. Everything happens for a reason."

He studied her face at arm's length. "It does. Care for punch? I'm buying."

The way to the punch bowl table parted like the Red Sea for Father Gerry and Lori as they walked hand in hand. Tally poured cherry-colored fruit punch for them ceremoniously as if they were the uncrowned king and queen of the Lubbock High ten-year reunion.

"How'd you get out?" Lori sipped punch and nibbled on a Ritz cracker topped with cream cheese and a thin slice of cucumber.

"A CIA operative. I have the government to thank. Although I never met any of them."

"As it should be, right?" Lori dabbed the cracker crumbs from her mouth.

"It's a crazy world. Wars going on even in so-called peaceful times." He placed his punch glass on the table. "It's good to see you, Lori. You look different."

"Must be my maternal side coming out."

"Maternal?" Hands in pockets, he bent his head as if awaiting a confession.

"I'm a mom." She loaded a potato chip with French onion dip.

"Congratulations. I didn't . . ."

"How would you? He's not with me."

"The father?"

The "Venus" refrain blared through speakers. Lori spoke over it. "No. I gave up my son for adoption." A few classmates, in close range, hovered. She lowered her voice to a whisper. "I'm okay. You don't have to say anything."

"Okay. Will you have this dance?" Father Gerry held out a hand.

"Priests are allowed to dance? It's a slow one."

"I won't tell anyone."

Lori observed the expectant stares. "You won't have to."

Father Gerry led Lori onto the parquet wood surface overlaying the gymnasium floor to protect the basketball court from high-heeled shoes and scuff marks. Once again, the roomful of partiers divided, and they had the dance floor to themselves. Floating planets twirled above them, reflecting light from glittery facets.

"To the moon, Alice." Father Gerry batted at a Styrofoam star.

"The moon's not a planet, you know."

"I know, and we're not the Honeymooners."

Lori let out a laugh that educed full-out stares and side glances from former classmates inclined to spin stories like the fake planets spinning from their strings.

The following morning, before the sun was high in the sky, the party lines were abuzz. Tally drove Lori to the airport. Neither was privy to the grapevine and words spilling across phone wires.

Line One: "Did you hear Lori at the punch bowl? She said she was a mom!"

Line Two: "And was she telling the father?"

Line Three: "The real father? You mean . . ."
Line One: "He always had a thing for her."
Line Three: "But he was a POW. That's impossible."
Line Two: "Maybe it was before. Anything's possible."
Line Three: "True."
A voice interrupted. "Excuse me, can you all please hang up? We have an emergency."
Click. Click. Click.

Woodstock was a drug fest on farm ground owned by a man named Max Yeager. Lori pushed her way through the mud and madness. More stories than she dared to tell. More than worth telling. There was a collective mind to the whole scene that begged for anonymity. She was close to walking out, packing up at the hotel, and calling it a day.

The music ramped up. The soulful, melodic voice of singer-songwriter Richie Havens from New York City led off the jamboree. Lori was transported, lulled back to her "days of wine and roses" in the Big Apple. Neurons and synapses connected with whiffs of marijuana, calling up not-too-distant accounts that haunted, thrilled, and enticed.

A college-aged woman danced barefoot. Her gold, sunlit hair flowed beside naked, bronzed shoulders. A red halter top bolstered her sloping, pendulum-like bosom. She passed a joint to Lori, who refused with a wave of her hand. The young woman's movements became more frenzied. She shook her wide-open arms in an interpretative dance. Lori guessed pot and LSD—à la stoned and tripping—and trudged forward, mud seeping through her sandals.

Blankets spread over acres of fields created the semblance of a patch-work quilt. Lori wished she had an aerial view. Objectivity. No personal stories. The crowd itself was the story.

A towering fellow in his midtwenties sidled up to Lori. He wore a leather spike choker around his giraffe-like neck that offset a red-orange afro. His eyes were lizard-like, hazy slits fringed with blond lashes.

"You a reporter?" he mumbled in an inarticulate rush.

"Camera a dead giveaway?" She inspected her apparatus.

"Do you want to interview me?" He weaved, unsure of the ground.

"Actually, no. I'm leaving."

"Hey, what about your story?" he replied in a moment of clarity and coherency.

"Lori, is that you?" A pale blonde tripped over a blanket and fell into her.

"Bette?"

The blonde righted herself, brushing off her white gauze blouse. She carried a bottle of Boone's Farm Strawberry Hill wine. "Lori, it's you. Come join us." She waved the bottle as if signaling a ship at sea. The red-haired skyscraper, head and shoulders above Bette, wrapped sunburnt forearms around her torso.

"Well, what do you know? Fate that you two kindred spirits would meet here."

Lori was surprised by his sober response. She directed her attention to Bette. "I'm clean."

Bette giggled, her head leaning into the redhead's torso. "Yeah, me too. For another ten minutes. C'mon, join us."

Sex, drugs, and rock 'n' roll? Not the story Lori wanted to tell. *The concert performers? Leave them to the music reviewers. The girl in the red halter top? Lost sight of her. The story? No story. Not for now.*

Chapter 29

Surrender Lori

The festival began August 15, 1969, and ended three days later on a six hundred-acre dairy farm fifty miles from Woodstock, New York. For eighteen dollars each, attendees camped, danced in mud pits, soaked up sun, rain, drugs, and grooved to a phenomenal lineup of musical talent. Lori ditched her assignment and joined the fray. Her contract with *Rolling Stone* magazine was already tenuous. She was not a music reviewer. They assigned a pictorial essay, and that's what she planned to deliver. Until Bette. *Not a safe bet.* She chuckled to herself. Running into music reviewer Daryl Martin cinched the deal. He'd take over the assignment, copy and photos, for *Rolling Stone*. Everything fell into place. The easy road made easier. And the sliding back one wrong step away.

Lori visited acid tents set up throughout the concert site. Opium, cocaine, psychedelic mushrooms were freely dispensed. She smoked marijuana laced with LSD for her first high all over again. Signs of sobriety and a cleaned-up life wiped out with one joint. The festival was extended by one day—Sunday, August 17—due to rain. Word spread that there were two casualties. One person died of a drug overdose and the other while sleeping under a tractor trailer and accidentally run over by the driver.

On August 19, Lori traveled to New York City with the ragtag assortment of actors, drug dealers, prostitutes, and runaways, fifteen in total.

The commune was housed in a dilapidated East Side brownstone like a rotting sponge, soaked in the filth of mildew, food scraps, dirty bongs, used needles, and soiled clothes piled up in corners. Led by a handful of concertgoers, Lori sensed her undoing. The hell she'd escaped awaited her reentry, and the New York State party scene was as good as any. Demons returned tenfold after a clean sweep. A useless fight. The trap was set for the willing, nonresistant prey. Drugs were an easy out from self-inflicted pain. The lows of despair assuaged by euphoric highs. Part of her wanted to live, and a dark corner of her spirit wanted to die. Not suicide. In waves of desolation, she succumbed to the drugs that slowed down the pulse of life.

A dim overhead lightbulb flickered. Lori lay on a cot after a heroin fix. The man with the red afro spoke gruffly. "Move over."

"Go away." Lori turned from the light.

He leaned forward and held a knife to her pulsing neck. "Move over."

She was too high to scream or fight. The gleam of the knife's blade sparked a flashback to the hallway light at a Lisbon hotel.

"I'll kill you if you scream." He pulled at her jeans and souvenir T-shirt emblazoned with a guitar-playing Carlos Santana until a sharp blade went deep into his thin, pale chest.

"You're under arrest, Lori Hopkins, for the murder of Scott West." Handcuffs tightened on her wrists. Two police officers shoved her past the vacuous eyes of three commune dwellers who remained behind. Bette and everyone else at the party were out of sight. No witnesses to the crime.

On a midnight ride to the police station, a stunned and bewildered Lori lowered her head to stem the bile rising in her throat. Her blood-soaked T-shirt heightened her nausea. Disbelief cleared away to harsh reality. She remembered the choking sensation. The pressing knife blade twisted and turned away. And the sharp edge and point no longer against her vulnerable skin.

The interrogation room had a bare rectangular table and five chairs.

Lights were low. A man walked in. He appeared Lori's age, clean cut, prep school polished. He wore a gray suit that matched the walls. His tie was pale blue, like a robin's egg. She focused on the tie, anything but the depressing gray, a cloud of doom. He pushed back a chair directly across from her. The guard stood at the door.

"I'm your attorney. Mark Feinstein."

"He's dead."

"As they get. You hit a main artery."

"He was on top of me." She gripped her bare neck.

"Choke marks," the lawyer said, relaxed and confident. "We'll go for self-defense." The guard shuffled his feet and propped himself against the door. "Let's build our case." Mark Feinstein took a pad and pen from his breast pocket. "You were using drugs and living there?"

"For three days. I met them at Woodstock. I knew one. Bette. An actress." Lori grew fidgety. "What happens next?"

"Trial and sentencing." Mark studied his court-appointed client. Smart. Attractive. Self-destructive, maybe? "You won't get sympathy from the jury, and you have no witnesses."

"Any good news?"

"I've never lost a case."

"Well, there's a first for everything."

The trial lasted one week. Character references lined up, including Tally and the Hopkins supporters from Boston who populated the courtroom. Even P. Rose, referred to by nieces and nephews as Aunt Portia Pig, came to Lori's defense.

The jury filed in. Judge Morris's gavel hit its mark. "How do you find the defendant, Lori Hopkins?"

"Guilty, Your Honor, for the death of Scott West." The jury leader, a short, slightly built man, waited for the murmuring to subside. "But we ask the court for a reduced sentence of ten years since it was not premeditated and the defendant has no previous convictions."

Judge Morris spoke up. "The case will be reviewed for the possibility of a commuted sentence and transfer from Rikers Island to a prison in the defendant's home state of Texas." Bernadette, Ben, and Grandma

Penny Hopkins sat in silent remonstration. No words described the depths of their shock at Lori's prison sentence. With a timorous smile, Lori glanced at Bernadette and mouthed, *"It's okay."* Yet nothing in the depths of her soul believed she'd spend a decade behind bars.

Judge Morris arose with a final pound of his gavel. The bailiff approached the bench. "Your Honor, may I speak with you for a moment?"

"This is highly out of turn." Judge Morris resumed his seat.

"Your Honor, it may be important," the bailiff added.

Lori leaned to her attorney. "What's going on?"

"I don't know."

The bailiff conferred with Judge Morris, whose voice was a loud whisper. "Closing statements were made. The sentence issued." The judge looked up at the defense attorney. "Mr. Feinstein, there's a gentleman who says he has evidence. Would you like him to testify?"

"On behalf of my client?"

"Well, who else?"

Lori discussed with her attorney. "But there weren't any witnesses."

Mark Feinstein whispered, "We'll go with it."

The prosecuting attorney, Murray Stewart, screeched: "I object."

"Objection overruled. Bring in the witness. Character witness."

"Your Honor, this sounds like a ploy." Stewart stood as if sitting would lose the firm ground of his triumph.

Judge Morris considered the objection for one precarious moment. "A future life is being decided here, Mr. Stewart. Bring him in."

A tall, good-looking man with dark curly hair and thick eyebrows entered the courtroom. To Lori, he appeared somewhat familiar. He approached the witness stand for the swearing in.

"State your name." Mr. Stewart, prosecuting attorney for the deceased, paced the floor, hoping for a quick finish.

"Ari Novak." His steadfast gaze belied his nervousness. He'd never been in a courtroom.

"Mr. Novak, where do you live?" Stewart, in a monotonous tone, slowed the pace.

"Here in New York," Ari said.

"And where are you from?" Stewart paused his pacing.

"Your Honor, I object. The questioning is out of line and unrelated to the case against the defendant." Feinstein wanted to break the spell of extraneous information.

"Mr. Stewart, get to the point." Judge Morris peeked at his watch.

"Mr. Novak, may I ask what you do here in New York City?"

"Yes, I'm an actor."

"So you are trained to make up stories . . ."

"Objection, Your Honor. A leading question . . ."

Judge Morris pounded his gavel. "I remind you, Mr. Stewart. Get to the point."

Stewart accomplished his goal—disruption. "How can you shed more light on a closed case, Mr. Novak? The murderer has received sentencing." He paused. "You were not a witness to the crime."

"I knew the victim, Scott West. He acted in a few shows with me."

"Get to the point, Prosecutor." Judge Morris was known for a quick pound on the gavel.

"Why are you here?" Stewart pronounced words like arrows in a bullseye.

"Scott West was not in his right mind."

"Mr. West is not on trial here." Stewart loosened his tie.

"Continue." The judge's interest was piqued.

"He told me several times that he planned to kill someone. He said he wanted to cut someone's throat. I didn't believe it. I thought he was playing a part, one he played in one of our shows."

"Your Honor, this is pointless. I have no further questions." Stewart's aim was to remove Ari Novak from the witness stand and a prospectively disastrous detour.

Mark Feinstein acted swiftly on the cross-examination. "Mr. Novak, how long ago did Scott West mention this to you?"

"The day before Woodstock. I saw him that morning. He showed me the knife."

"Could you identify it?" The jury slanted forward. Lori's attorney was euphoric.

"Yes. It had his initials on it."

"Your Honor, this is new evidence. A description of the knife was never disclosed throughout the trial. The witness would have had no prior knowledge."

Murray Stewart folded his losing hand as Mark Feinstein continued, "Your Honor, instead of an appeal, I would like to submit the testimony of Ari Novak. The weapon used against Scott West was the same weapon he intended to kill my client with on the night of August 19, 1969. This is a case of self-defense."

The jury returned after one hour of further deliberation. "We find the defendant guilty of involuntary manslaughter in self-defense. We recommend a three-year sentence."

"The defendant will be sentenced to Rikers Island for three months until transferred to Texas for the remaining three-year sentence."

Lori opened the letter, the envelope pre-opened by a prison guard.

Dear Miss Hopkins, Thanks to you and your grandmother, I'm pursuing my acting again in New York. Sometimes our paths cross in strange ways. You will be fine, and I was glad to testify at your trial. God has a plan for you too. Be courageous in the face of all things good and bad. The good will always triumph. Ari, your Taxi Driver from Prague.

Rikers Island—Lori's version of the lost world. Even so, she saw more of the Boston Hopkins aunts and uncles while in prison than she had during all the holidays and random gatherings combined. Weekly visits became their routine. Aunt P. Rose baked a chocolate fudge Bundt cake. Once it was examined by the guards, a few crumbs remained.

Three months became six months before she was transferred to the Huntsville Penitentiary in Texas. Her lawyer fought for the time to be counted toward her total jail sentence. But the court ruled the sentencing would begin in Texas. The bargaining was that she would do eighty-five percent, roughly two and half years, until her release in January 1973.

The Boston family had mixed feelings, especially Grandma Penny, who was intent on traveling regardless of her children's protests. Although a sad reality, completing her prison sentence in the Lone Star state meant weekly letters instead of four-hour treks to Rikers Island.

Texas behind bars—the never-ending nightmare—until fate dealt her a new hand.

Disappointment penetrated the block walls. So many lives off track for years, even decades. The inmates lined up awaiting visitors. Some anxious and visibly excited, others bored, angry, and disillusioned. Bitterness surfaced in hateful expressions and venomous, spite-filled words.

In this milieu, Barry and Lori were reunited, a glass pane invisible to the touching hearts. The years in between evaporated like a puff of steam.

"How did you find me?"

"Texas isn't that big, and I know half the inmates. Word gets around. And females make up less than four percent of the population here." He folded his hands. "I do prison ministry."

"So you came here as part of your ministry?"

"As a friend."

"Barry, do you remember the question I asked you in Vietnam?"

"You asked me a lot of questions, darlin.'"

"I asked you what it was like to kill. You said it was 'kill or be killed.' You have peace."

He shook his head. "Ain't no peace there, Bluebonnet."

Lori searched his immutable smile for answers. She spoke as if divulging a secret. "He had a knife . . ."

Barry leaned forward. "And he would've used it."

"But I'll never know."

"Yeah, and you live to tell it."

Their bond was resealed. A bond they'd denied in a war-torn country three years ago. Now, in a prison meeting room, the partition window gave way to their silent communication—a deep alliance and a caring she hadn't experienced since Grandma Lottie's loving embrace.

"You're a wild card, Barry. Like one of the feral animals I capture on nature shoots."

His smile remained fixed. He was euphoric in her company. Nothing could compare, and he knew he'd never understand why. Some things in life remained a mystery. "Is that any way to treat a visitor? I come in peace."

"Will you be back?"

"I'm a prison minister. It's what I do. You'll be sick of me before your time is done."

"Barry?" She touched the glass. She wanted to ask him what his life was like now. Married? Children? Secret desires? Questions, unspoken, tumbled over each other.

For a moment, sadness reached his eyes. She'd seen that melancholy look framed with tenderness before. She was certain the war furthered it, filled it in, and made it permanent. His hand reached up and matched hers. He spoke so softly she barely heard it. "I've got you, Lori. I've got you."

"I know."

A piercing bell rang like an unexpected alarm clock. A guard yelled, "Visiting hours over!"

Barry tipped an invisible hat. "Next time I see you, no glass between us."

"I'll be waiting. Pretty sure I'm not going anywhere."

Barry gave a sober, unsmiling stare she hadn't noticed before. "Lori, you're alive. That's all that matters. We start from there."

Lori continued in their last few seconds. "Barry, do you think I have a death wish?"

Barry smiled, his dimple and boyish charm intact. "Sweetheart, you don't need a death wish to die. When it's your time, it's your time."

"Wrap it up," the guard yelled at everyone and no one in particular.

"I'll leave you with this." Barry straightened up and took his minister stance. "The Lord is near to all who call on Him, to all who call Him in truth, Psalm 145, verse 18."

"How about a priest? I know at least one."

"He's back in Nam." Barry intuited a flicker of pain cross over Lori's otherwise staid expression.

With no reply, she smiled her goodbye, bowed her head, and counted blessings as she walked away. A priest on one side, at least in spirit, a prison minister on the other, and a family in Boston praying vigilantly. A tear of joy traced down her cheek as the guard led all the inmates away.

Barry, the soldier—tough, resilient, tireless, and deeply remorseful of his own faults—climbed into his Chevy pickup, gripped his steering wheel, and wept.

Wake-up call was 3:30 a.m., breakfast served at 4:30 a.m. Work assignments started at 6:00 a.m. Lori's chores rotated between cooking and doing laundry. Inmates received no pay. Food, clothing, and hygiene products were provided. Lori made efforts to gain privileges, specifically extra time in the dayroom. She read voraciously—magazines, newspapers, books. Her goal—a book a week, fifty-two in a year, at the very least. Fictional or real characters between the pages of a story passed the time and made life tolerable. The Boston-bred Hopkins patrons wired regular deposits for Lori into the offender's trust fund. She purchased her books at the commissary with money from her account.

Barry, the prison minister, kept her sane and nurtured her creative spark in the midst of drudgery and mind-numbing monotony. Prison was made bearable by his attentive nature to everyone in his path, but especially Lori. She knew it. His eyes sparkled when he looked at her, even in her reduced state, physically, if not mentally. She thanked God for him every night before her early rise.

She numbered days on a wall calendar, marking each block with a diagonal line. She met Barry at every opportunity presented to them. They crisscrossed stories and finished each other's thoughts.

"My mom liked the article." Barry tapped a pen in his palm.

"You never wrote."

"Dealing with my own demons, darlin.'"

They sat in a blessed stillness.

"You gonna thump that Bible over my head?"

"No, but I'm gonna open it and read."

"Well, you might as well thump it over my head." She accidentally kicked over a chair, alerting the guard.

"Wrap it up, you two. This ain't no dating service." Arms crossed over his chest, the guard's impatience swelled. His stomach rumbled, close to mealtime.

Lori spoke above a whisper. "How did I end up with so many preachers in my life?"

"Lucky, I guess." Barry opened his Bible. "Isaiah. He's my man. And I quote, '*do not fear, for I am with you; do not be dismayed, for I am your God.*'"

"You're on the outside. Easy one for you."

"You're right. I'm on the outside. And you'll be out soon enough. Change something while you're here."

"Wrap it up, you two." The guard paced, a signal that their time was up.

Lori righted the upended chair. "Change what?"

"That's up to you darlin'."

At night, Lori faced the iron bars from her cot. A thin cover sheet sopped up her tears. *I'm afraid, God. Are you listening?*

Loud snores from adjoining cells stifled her cry.

Every ninety days, Lori made a five-minute prepaid phone call to Boston. She alternated between her Grandma Penny, Uncle Ben, and Bernie. She made life tolerable but avoided any friendships with fellow female inmates and kept at a congenial distance. They called her the "Bookworm," "Walking Dictionary" or "Red." The guards recognized she was an anomaly to their experiences of dealing with prisoners. But she had time to do. Nothing or no one could change the reality of doing time.

Chapter 30

Starting Over

In her solitude, Lori was reminded of the self-imposed prison of an underground Christmas hideaway and awoke in her sweat-soaked jail cot at least once weekly. She would never know the look on her mother Miriam's face when she had realized the deadly tornado would end her life. Her father? Maybe he had tried to protect his loving wife. Maybe they had tried to run down to the bomb shelter to escape the devastation. And the reoccurring most horrible noise—the pounding on the door. Were they trying to open up the bomb shelter door to safety? Could she have saved her parents' lives? The nightmare always ended with the pounding filling her ears.

Saturday, December 25, 1971, the warden let inmates watch football. The Kansas City Chiefs played the Miami Dolphins, who won in double overtime. The game gave Lori and Barry time together outside the confines of a prison cell. They discussed their faith, their failures, and their dreams. Barry admitted to waking with night sweats, fist-pounding nightmares in his bedroom, and binge drinking. "My demons get a little thirsty, sweet thing."

"Better not let the guard hear you talkin', minister. Besides, I think she has a crush on me."

Barry reclined, hands clasped behind his head. "Who doesn't?"

Lori confided about her descent into drug dependence—sleeping pills, LSD, and one-time use of heroin. Barry was the ultimate listener. No judgments. No opinions. No questions.

Joyce, a prisoner sporting a tattoo of Texas on her forearm, yelled out. "Hush up over there! We're trying to watch a game."

The wall phone rang over the groans and hubbub from inmates glued to the television. The guard cupped a hand over her ear. "Yeah, Warden. The game ain't over. What should I do?" She hung up and announced, "Okay, y'all can stay until the game's over."

Christmas Day on a warm December afternoon. The longest game in NFL history clocked in at eight-two minutes and forty seconds and interrupted holiday dinners in many homes. Lori and Barry spent the evening in each other's company.

Amidst the cheering and booing football fans, Lori and Barry made small talk. She cherished the serendipitous moments, so mundane to the outside world and precious in prison. It helped the confined space and iron bars disappear for a while. "Do people still say *groovy*?"

Barry wagged his head. "No self-righteous Texan would, darlin.' And don't look for any hippies when you get out."

"Wasn't planning on it. I do read the papers. Anything else?"

"Yeah. *Pong*."

"*Pong*?"

"Video games. What's happening to the real world?"

"Maybe it's too real." They spoke without speaking, their silence more meaningful than words.

At 4:30 p.m., they ate chili, Texas toast, and Christmas cookies donated by a local church group. The two kindred spirits united minds and hearts. They sat on metal benches in a dayroom as inmates watched football. Prison, yes, but not behind bars or glass panes. As absurd as it seemed, Lori believed, at that instant, it was her best Christmas.

Routines made for swift days, weeks, and months. With jail time exhausted, Lori prepared for her exit. Saying goodbye to Barry was unthinkable, but rational. The week before Christmas Day, 1972, the nightly news broadcasted the latest on the Christmas bombings of Hanoi ordered by President Nixon. The goal of the relentless air raids was an expedited conclusion to a most unpopular war. Lori and Barry lightened the dismal tenor in their early evening session.

"It's not like we're courting each other." Lori wore a coquettish, half-serious grin. Life with Barry was part and parcel of prison life. What would it be like in the world beyond the bars?

Barry chuckled. "No, but at least we're not courting death. You take care, Bluebonnet." The guard waited at the door while the other inmates filed out. Barry continued, "You ready to throw your hat over the windmill?"

"Like Don Quixote? I'm not that crazy!"

Barry yelled out to the guard. "Bobbie, don't get your panties in a bunch 'cause I'm gonna hug this prisoner here. She gets sprung next Tuesday, and it's Christmas."

The guard shouted, "Ain't seen nothin' yet."

Barry and Lori embraced. He whispered, "You're my Christmas gift, Bluebonnet. Take care of yourself and remember to whistle before you walk into a stranger's camp."

"And you?"

"Church is out, sweet thing." He kissed her forehead. "How it's meant to be." He stood and bellowed to the inmates packed inside the dayroom. "If I could have attention from y'all, I'd like to sing a Beatles song. It came out a few years ago, so some of you might've heard it."

Barry picked up an acoustic guitar leaning against the wall. At a bench, he adjusted the guitar on his thigh. The strumming and sweet message filled the space as Barry sang "Let It Be."

A new inmate yelled out. "I know that song!"

A lifer shouted, "Shut up, fool! Let the man sing."

Barry crooned the words as if he'd composed them. The appreciative audience clapped and whistled. He beamed at Lori from halfway across the room. The dimple surfaced, the one in a photo she'd captured what seemed a century ago.

He didn't return after Christmas Day. She waited for him as she counted the final days. 1971—a happy Christmas Day. 1972—a sad day after Christmas. Another loss. But she had peace. Barry said he would pray for her. Every day. The brash, flirty soldier was now her source of peace. On New Year's Eve, 1972, she joined the other inmates in the dayroom for a farewell gathering. No friends, other than Betty Lou. They'd shared the dayroom but never spoke to each other, their heads buried in worlds between pages and outside the prison walls.

Betty Lou acknowledged Lori on her last full day. "Hear you're gettin' out. I got three more years in this hellhole." They'd never traded personal stories. There was no reason. It made the time drag on. The key to getting by on the inside—live for today and focus on the future, not the past. Lori did one more head sweep of the entrance and exit. No Barry. Let it be.

Three years in prison, and freedom was a sensation to taste, touch, see, hear, and smell. Life behind bars had its routines and ways of survival. Visits and letters made it tolerable, but not the food. Many times, she told Barry her taste buds experienced their own version of a near-death experience only resuscitated by his rescue meals. He'd convinced the guards and warden of the redemptive role of nourishment, Texas-style, similar to the Word as sustenance for the soul.

On Tuesday, January 2, 1973, Lori spent the morning in the warden's office going through paperwork. "We have funds from the trust set up."

"The money for the commissary? There's more? From where?"

"Can't disclose. We'll get your belongings together. You're scheduled to be escorted out of here in an hour."

Lori walked out and didn't look back, not for one second, at the Huntsville Unit. Beyond the massive brick wall, she charted her course to civilian life, one step at a time. The one piece of information she retained was that the facility housed the only execution chamber in the state of Texas. Inmates sentenced to death served their last day at the Huntsville Unit. Period. Thoughts of human fragility made her stronger.

The next destination—New York City. Purpose—reestablish a career. Competitors, hearing of her release, billed her as the ex-con photojournalist. Those who recognized her gift for telling stories in photos welcomed her into their creative corps.

Lori checked in at the Hotel Chelsea in proximity to her former walkup. On a brisk Saturday night, she strolled Midtown Manhattan and absorbed the essence of humanity. Times Square—a feast for eyes dulled by the confines of a drab, gloomy prison. The theatre district appeared seedier than she remembered. Prostitutes, pimps, and peep shows proliferated. Litter lined streets. Flashy neon signs and lewd billboards obscured the nighttime stars. Homeless men, covered with cardboard and blankets, huddled in corners. She recognized a few drug dealers from her past years and wondered how they stayed alive or out of jail.

Her final stop—Lindy's on Seventh Avenue for a twelve-inch-high slice of cheesecake and mug of piping hot coffee. Snowflakes, no two alike, drifted across the large picture window. Silent night. All calm. All quiet. For the first time since childhood days, she folded hands, murmured a prayer of grace, and savored each creamy forkful. Everything new again.

At the hotel, Lori sifted through a week's worth of newspapers stacked on a lobby credenza. Former President Harry S. Truman died the day after Christmas. His memorial service occurred on Friday, January 5, the day she arrived in New York City. A criminal trial was to start in Washington, DC, involving a break-in at the Democratic National Committee's headquarters at the Watergate complex on June 17, 1972. Police discovered burglars hiding behind the secretary's desk outside Chairman Larry O'Brien's office.

The Supreme Court was poised to make a decision on legalizing abortion in the case of Roe v. Wade. Soaking up news in one sitting exhausted Lori. She retreated in her hotel room for the weekend. The sounds of sirens, beeping cars, and traffic in general produced enough fumes of the real world. She coveted God's nature—the trill of a bird, the scent of roses, cloudless blue skies. For now, a soft pillow and a decent bed sufficed.

By mid-January, she contacted every publisher she'd worked with since college graduation. A few of the seasoned editors were gone, replaced by younger, brash ones. Lori realized she wasn't that much older than the college recruits. And she had a solid, high-quality portfolio. And a past, an intriguing one, that didn't hinder success. Former colleagues wanted sordid details of prison life. But she wanted to forget Huntsville. Everything but Barry, the former soldier who'd saved her from a private war.

To her surprise, she experienced a wealth of assignment choices. At lunch, she broached her top choice with the story editor of *Venture* magazine. "Egypt: Yesterday and Today. I'm the one for the story."

"Hold on, Lori. I've already assigned it. I've got one in Paris." Maggie Jenkins was new to the managing editor position. She liked Lori and respected her work. But she didn't make waves. The Egypt assignment was in the hands of the chief editor's niece fresh out of New York University.

"I've done Paris. All of Continental Europe. Switch us. Give the other photographer Paris."

Maggie did have misgivings about the novice photographer. Paris seemed easier, and the recent graduate spoke French. A possibility. "I'll think it over."

Two weeks later, Lori boarded a plane to Egypt to meet Miriam, her acquaintance from Fátima, at Cairo International Airport. All arrangements were made one week earlier. Miriam mentioned awaiting Lori's call. She was sure she'd hear from her. Only a matter of time.

While en route, Lori read through a guidebook describing Egyptian mythology and the phoenix, a female bird displaying scarlet red and gold plumage associated with worship of the sun. An eagle-like phoenix rises from the ashes of the old one, symbolizing renewal and rebirth. Lori imagined herself as the mythical creature and her rebirth the day she walked through the prison gates and the other side of "the wall" in Huntsville, Texas.

Miriam waited at the bustling terminal in Cairo, the "mother of the world." She waved her arms in case Lori didn't recognize her. Nearly five years had passed since they met in Portugal, but Miriam knew their paths would cross again. Fate. Destiny by another name.

"I'm glad you kept my contact information." Lori's disturbing appearance contrasted with the vibrant young woman she'd met in a Lisbon hotel lobby.

"You've had troubles." Miriam took stock of her. "Come, let us go to my home." She kissed Lori on both cheeks and hugged the weariness out of her for a few brief seconds. "My son is waiting for us." They navigated their way through arriving passengers greeted by friends, family, or business associates.

"You never mentioned a son." Lori absorbed the exotic ambience of Cairo, an ancient city, a melding of old and new and divergent religions banded together by social customs and traditions. The home of pharaohs and phoenix birds—history and mythology.

"He's a filmmaker. I look forward to you meeting him."

Lori tasted the freedom of sheer movement as life's elixir. Every step, anywhere, added a spoonful of the restorative tonic and, more emphatically, distance from prison. Outside the terminal, she caught sight of a dark-haired male with a thin, clean-shaven face waving and leaning against a silver coupe. "A Fiat? I feel like I'm in Italy."

Miriam laughed. "Believe me, you're not!"

"Hi, I'm Rami." He was all bright-eyed and enthusiastic, a male replica of his mother. "Please, let me help you." He grabbed Lori's suitcase.

The ride through Cairo's streets offered glimpses of the Nile River. Exhilarated, Lori craned to look at the passing scenery. Rami noted her obvious interest. "The Nile River is the world's longest. It runs all the way from near the equator and flows into the Mediterranean Sea north of here."

"We shall go on a felucca ride, and you will see all of antiquity." Miriam, an ebullient soul, consoled Lori, so far away from home and all things familiar. Lori was getting back in the groove. To her sadness, Barry, her lifeline and light of hope, became distantly associated with jail time. When in New York, thoughts of him had resurged.

"You are far away from us, Lori." Miriam clasped her guest's hand, a gesture of friendship and understanding.

"No, I'm right here." *So much had happened. How much to divulge?*

"You're a photographer? That's wonderful." Rami's upbeat personality indicated his optimism. Irrepressible joy.

"Yes, I'm here on assignment." Lori got a whiff of Rami's musk oil and Italian leather seats.

"Mama, I've invited my film partner, Peter Anderson, to join us for dinner. Lori might enjoy meeting him. May I call you Lori?"

"Of course." *Impeccable manners. Kind to his mother. Good company,* thought Lori.

The apartment was spacious, clean, and luxuriously appointed. A circular couch wide enough to fit twenty people governed the living room's core. An ornately carved coffee table was favored with woven tapestry and a sterling silver tea set. Tile floors, a blue and white design, complemented the gold threads of the couch like the sky's backdrop for the sun. A large, cement-floored balcony offered a stunning view of Cairo's Pyramids of Giza. Miriam replaced her shoes with house slippers. Lori removed her shoes. Miriam nodded approval. "I have a new pair of slippers if you'd like to try them."

Lori stretched as if in her comfort zone. "Sure."

"Why don't you rest, and we can talk later at dinner."

Exhausted, Lori slept through the Salat, ritual Islamic prayer at two intervals, the Asr, afternoon prayer, and the Maghrib, prayer at sunset. The chanting of muezzins echoed from minarets and mosques calling Muslims to prayer. She awoke, startled by the quiet and dark. Seconds later, she heard a knock. "Lori, it's Miriam. We will be serving dinner in half an hour. Is that enough time for you?"

"Uh, sure!" Lori wiped the sleep from her puffy eyes and dried spit from her chin. Her hair was a tangled mess, her skin sallow.

After a thorough body wash, reapplied makeup, and combed hair, Lori unpacked a navy blouse and matching skirt. She bounded through the living room with renewed energy. Miriam, Rami, and another man, midthirties, rose to greet her.

Rami bowed slightly. "Lori, please meet my filmmaker colleague, Peter Anderson." Peter dazzled like the sun at midday with blond hair to his shoulders, a light brown beard, high cheekbones, almond-shaped ocean-blue eyes, and broad shoulders—an incarnation of Prince Charming. His voice was deep, sonorous. She expected it to be light and airy like his appearance. *A paradox.*

"Lori Hopkins." Unfamiliar with customs, she bowed similar to Rami's greeting.

Peter peered into her eyes unabashedly. "You look familiar. Have we met?"

"I don't think so. I don't know any filmmakers."

Rami shuffled his feet and glanced at his mother.

Peter shook his head slowly. "Your face . . ."

Miriam intervened. "Our guest is a photographer. Most likely your paths have crossed. Shall we enter the dining room?" She directed her gaze at Lori.

Peter scratched at his beard. Like film, her image developed, and he instantly recalled where he'd seen her. A few minutes after seven, the night call to prayer rung out from mosques.

"Isha prayer. There are up to seventeen rakats or movements in Isha," Miriam said. She motioned for her two guests to be seated. Rami pulled out a chair for Lori.

"We have customary dishes for you to try, Lori," Miriam continued. She passed the tray of Egyptian flatbread to Peter. "Aish baladi. Aish means life."

A teenage girl with soft, dark brown eyes and a jet-black ponytail entered through the kitchen area. She jostled a steaming platter and placed it on a buffet server.

"Thank you. Rashida. My niece. She likes to cook and welcomes you to my home."

A diffident smile emerged from the nervous chef. *"As-salam alaykom."*
Lori responded, *"Wa Alykom As-salam."*

Rashida beamed and returned to the kitchen with a spring in her step.

"You know Arabic?" Rami performed the honors of serving dinner.

"A few greetings. Whatever I could pick up in the two weeks before my assignment. A Muslim greeting for peace be upon you?"

"Yes, but it's not exclusively Muslim." Rami noticed his mother picking up her napkin, her cue for switching topics. "We are serving koshari made with lentils, macaroni, rice, and chickpeas. We were not sure if you eat meat."

"Well, I'm from Texas, so I've eaten my share."

Peter studied Lori. "Have you been to New York?"

"Lori's a photographer. I'm sure she's been many places," Miriam said.

Rami, sensitive to his mother's irritation, chimed in. "Lori, do you have a favorite subject for your photos?"

Lori wished the conversation would lead far away from her, as far away as Texas.

"Faces. Animals. Even certain flowers have faces."

Rami nodded. "When I was a child, I imagined faces on cars. You have many more varieties in your country."

Lori giggled. "I used to think the same thing."

Rashida reentered with her homemade baklava. Spirits lifted.

Dishes cleared, the foursome reassembled in the living room. Spent by table talk, Lori stepped out onto the balcony to get a feel for the ancient city and the assignment ahead of her. "Cairo: Yesterday and Today."

"May I join you?" Peter stood at a polite distance.

Lori bristled. "Looks like you have."

He moved closer. "I filmed a short at Woodstock. The focus was on the crowds, not the music. It was twenty minutes of interviews and candid moments. Life at a concert. A microcosm of our culture."

"Are you pitching it to me?" Lori kept her eyes on pockets of light illuminating darkened facades.

"You were coming out of an acid tent. I watched you through my camera. You looked right at it, so beautiful, so vulnerable . . ."

"I'm in your film?" Lori suppressed her rising anxiety. Another ghost from the past.

"No, I cut you out. But your face, your eyes, stayed with me."

She stared straight ahead, unmoving and made of stone. A balcony in Lisbon haunted her. A balcony in Cairo sent a shiver. She ached for her very soul in a Huntsville prison. So many lives in a short span of time. How could they follow her to Egypt? All composure, she confronted the filmmaker, the sun god, brilliant against a night sky and at one with the stars. "Thanks for letting me know." She decided against revealing her story following Woodstock that wound its way back to Texas, but not home.

The following morning, she and Miriam had time to themselves. Rashida served a breakfast of eggs, feta cheese, pita bread, and falafel made with pulped fava beans.

"*Sabā il khayr*," greeted Lori.

Rashida delighted in Lori's attempt at "good morning." She liked the American woman and welcomed a new diner. Miriam coddled her niece in the hopes that she would pursue her dream of establishing a restaurant.

"*Sabā in noor*," replied Rashida with clasped hands. "I hope you like."

Alone with Lori, Miriam wasted no time. "Lori, when I last saw you in the hotel lobby, you were disturbed."

"Yes." *Where to begin and how much to reveal?* Sympathetic eyes from across the table gladdened her soul. "After Fátima, I met a man. He invited me to a masquerade party. He drugged and raped me." She stopped. The words set her insides on fire, scorching her tongue and causing her to relive the sketchy nightmare that changed her life. "I got pregnant and gave up my baby for adoption."

"You are a brave woman, Lori. God will bless you for it."

"Bless me, Miriam? I'm wrecked. A shell." She stood up and paced. "I'm sorry. I don't mean to sound so dramatic. I killed a man and went to prison. I was released a month ago, and here I am. With you, in Egypt."

"In self-defense?" Miriam collected the bits and pieces of shattering experiences.

"Why do you think . . . ?"

"Your prison sentence was not long. Three years or so? After your baby was born?"

"Yes."

"And do you know who has your baby?"

"Yes, yes. I know. But I know nothing as to why all this happened to me. Have I made wrong choices? Of course. But I don't know what's next. I ruin everything in my life."

"Lori, listen to me. You have done nothing wrong. Nothing! Fátima made you strong. It helped you get through what was your fate."

"I came to you, Miriam, to find out . . ."

"What, Lori? What are you searching for now?"

Rashida entered the room, soaked in the heavy atmosphere, and quickly receded into the kitchen. The break in conversation gave Lori breathing space.

"Why do you believe, Miriam? Because you've seen a vision on a church rooftop?"

Miriam had a serene expression on her face. "Lori, I understand your pain. Rami is not my husband's son. We had no children. At forty, I was violated and became pregnant. Seth, my husband, was a devout Christian. He insisted on keeping the child. We raised Rami as our own. My husband died the year before I met you in Lisbon. He was a good man, a saint. I was on pilgrimage to give thanks to God and to Mother Mary for such a faithful husband."

"Oh, I'm sorry, Miriam. I think you're a saint. I feel such peace in your company. Maybe that's why I am here. To seek out peace."

"There's no peace in the world. Only souls can carry it. We are the peace in the world, Lori. I'd like to tell you more about Fátima."

Minutes turned to hours. The Islamic noon prayer, Dhuhr, rang out from nearby mosques. "Dear me, Lori, I've taken up too much of your time. You have an assignment."

"That's okay. I'm devoting all of tomorrow . . ."

"Let Rami be your guide. And Peter if you like."

"Okay."

"I can rearrange things. They will be at your beck and call."

"Such an American phrase!" Lori teased.

Miriam shrugged. "Too many influences in a lifetime."

"I meant to ask you, Miriam. When we met, you carried a Zippo . . ."

"Yes, I still have it. An American friend gave it to me. Her son lost his life in Vietnam. She asked me to pray for him in Fátima. There's an inscription. 'I know I'm going to heaven because I've spent my time in hell.'"

Rashida reappeared. "Lunch?"

Miriam and Lori, confidantes and soulmates, replied, "*Aiwa!*"

Throughout the afternoon, Lori reviewed maps, guides, and pertinent information for her photo assignment. She was anxious to explore Egypt, especially Cairo. Exuberance and expectation filled a cavity of disappointment. *Maybe God had a plan. Maybe Miriam was part of it.*

At dinner, Lori, Miriam, and Rami chattered like old cronies. "Has Mama been hitting you over the head with Fátima news?" Rami winked affectionately at his mother.

"It's what brought us together. Talk of secrets." Lori anticipated any meal lovingly prepared by Rashida.

Rami un-skewered eggplant, tomatoes, and mushrooms onto a bed of short-grain rice and lentils. "Ah, yes, the secrets. I'm not sure, although the church has recognized them. So you know there's a third one that's not been revealed?"

Lori savored the spicy vegetables, grilled to perfection. "Sister Lucia, the remaining visionary, requested the letter be opened and read by the pope in 1960."

Rami continued, "And he decided not to disclose the contents. Seems ominous?"

"Possibly."

"Rami, I'm surprised you speak of Fátima." Miriam added another kebab to his plate.

"The concept of salvation history is interesting, Mama. Whether I believe it or not."

"Are you familiar with St. Augustine? He wrote that there are two worlds, the City of God and the City of Man," inquired Miriam of Lori.

"Brace yourself for this one, Lori." Rami folded his arms.

"Those belonging to the City of God resist the world and its temptations. The City of Man are those who hold God in contempt and pursue self-love and sinful—"

"But we're all sinful, Miriam." Lori instantly regretted interrupting her host.

"That's true, but God knows what's in the heart. That is why we don't judge."

"I'm thankful for my mama, who prays for me every day." Rami pushed his empty plate aside and rubbed his hands together. He enjoyed playing host and sought to know more about America and, maybe, move there and make feature films.

Miriam lightened up. "Lori, you must visit the church where Our Lady appeared."

The next morning, Lori woke before the first call to prayer. She grew accustomed to the rhythms of the day, five Salat prayers—dawn, noon, afternoon, sunset, and night—chanted in Cairo's mosques and homes. Following a breakfast of pita bread and mashed fava beans, Lori met up with her two guides, Rami and Peter.

With Rami behind the wheel, Peter and Lori chatted.

"If he's a distraction, I'll let him off whenever you want." Rami winked in the rearview mirror. Peter reminded Lori of her carefree days studying photography at Boston University and meeting up with shutterbugs nurturing a passion for images on film. As in former times, the camera and Lori were one. She was all business and focused on her shoot as Peter divulged his family background. "Both my parents are Swedish. I dropped an S in Andersson to make it simpler. I keep apartments in Philadelphia and New York and visit cousins in Sweden on a regular basis. My parents paid for the New York apartment so they could share it when in town." He gabbed while she absorbed scenes of antiquity and modern life in Egypt. So much story to tell in frames and show the world!

"May I join the conversation?"

"Jealous, Rami?"

Bickering boys, thought Lori. She enjoyed every minute, especially Rami's humor.

"A caution to both of you. Friends from the States think they have mastered our language, Egyptian Arabic. Never rely on the literal translation."

"That's anywhere, Rami, even Sweden." Peter rolled down his window for Lori to get a better view.

"*Enta hatelbes fel heta* is translated as 'you're going to wear a wall.'"

"We've done this one, Rami. Lori, your thoughts?"

"Hmm, an accident waiting to happen?"

"Close." Rami stopped at a busy intersection. A pedestrian thumped his car for being too close to the crosswalk.

"It means 'you're going to get in trouble or fail at something,'" Peter said.

Lori scrunched her face. "I hope not. A more positive one, please!"

"*Jameela*," Peter said, twinkle-eyed and bashful, another contradiction to assertive coolness.

"That means beautiful."

Rami added, "It means much more. It refers to something inside, for someone with inner beauty." He winked at Peter.

Lori checked her camera settings to hide an irrepressible smile and slight blush.

Dinner with Miriam highlighted every day, five in all. On the final evening, they made a pact to remain in touch, no matter what the circumstances.

"I want to show you a copy of the Qur'an given to me by a dear friend of the Islam faith." Miriam, as if sprouting wings, flew to a corner book-case. She opened the book and read aloud. "O Mary, God has chosen you and purified you, and elected you above all the women of the earth!"

"Don't know why, but I'm not surprised." Lori reflected on the honor bequeathed upon Mary, the mother of God.

"We have much to learn of each other. Muslims, Jews, Christians." Miriam grew silent.

Lori kissed her hostess on both cheeks. "If you don't hear from me, I'm either in prison or dead."

Miriam regarded Lori's renewed spunk and trusted the Cairo project was no coincidence. "Same here."

Lori coordinated a ride to the airport with Rami. To her surprise, Peter was with him. Upon arrival at the terminal, he insisted on helping Lori with her luggage. Rami gestured to honking horns and irate drivers jostling for a parking spot.

At the curb, Peter reached into his shirt pocket. "I'd like to see you, Lori, when you return to the States." He handed her the note. "Here's my contact number. I can't believe I found you."

Lori shoved the note in her camera bag and said goodbye. No hugs and no promise that she'd call. She took a mental snapshot. Peter in close-up. Rami in long shot. Miriam in her heart. How could anyone replace her own mother? *Betrayal? A twisted fate?* She moved away from the curb and headed for the doorway. Rami blew his horn and waved Peter into the car.

"Where can I reach you?" Peter yelled and a few passersby took notice.

Lori turned and shrugged. "Don't know yet."

"I'm all over the place, but I call Philadelphia home."

Mind, body, and spirit renewed and strengthened, Lori waved a final goodbye.

Her days in New York were infrequent as she stacked up assignments. She was spoiled for choice, the crème de la crème of photo shoots and favored road trips with Sandra Dee. Nature, flora and fauna, remained her favorite subjects. The center of a flower, the eye of a coyote at dusk, anything and everything away from the urban trap of traffic lights, screeching sirens, potholes, uneven pavements, and rushed lives.

A rosy sunset filled the windshield of her rented Buick Skylark on the way to her next shoot, "Wolves of Wyoming." With a free hand, she rearranged Sandra Dee's shredded paper and water bottle. "You might prefer Boston, but I'm a Texan. Yessirree! Wide open spaces."

Days were imbued with peace, happiness, and life behind a lens. Boston was her benchmark. Texas was her heart, even if broken. She thought of Barry doing his prison ministry. *Leave well enough alone, ol' girl*, she told herself. He was there for her when she needed mending. She'd never forget his care and comfort, and that he chose not to say goodbye. Sandra Dee poked out her head and sipped water. "You'll outlive me, you know." A gravel road led to a motel in the middle of nowhere for a nomad and her muse.

Chapter 31

Leaning Towers

*G*iuseppe's receding hairline enhanced his chiseled chin and timeless features. Their rendezvous played out like a scene from a soap opera script.

Setting—Small café.

Lori (expression of surprise and twist of her head) "She did what?"

Giuseppe (bites at knuckles) "She went back to Italy with all four children."

Lori (repeats) "Italy?"

Giuseppe (eyes heavenward) "Pisa."

Lori (sincere) "I'm so sorry."

Giuseppe (head lowered) "I have nothing, Lorena. Nothing."

Lori (sideways stare) "You should be with her."

Giuseppe (direct gaze) "I cannot! I have a life here."

Lori (direct gaze) "Your life is with your family."

Giuseppe (innocent grin) "I can start a new life now."

Lori (stern gaze) "Is that why I'm here?"

Giuseppe (insouciant shrug) "You tell me."

Lori (heartfelt gaze) "Giuseppe . . . I can't go back. I won't go back."

Giuseppe (troubled eyes) "I know I've hurt you . . ."

Lori (insistent tone) "No you didn't. We . . . It wasn't meant to be."

Giuseppe (candid expression) "I believe we could have a life. I'll miss my children . . ."

Lori (rises) "Stop. I want to remain friends, if nothing else. Goodbye. Reconsider reuniting your family."

Lori turns to leave.

Giuseppe lights a cigarette. The waiter returns. Giuseppe inhales. "A campari spritz, *per favore*." The waiter exits with a final bow. Scene ends.

Lori paced the floor at Bernadette's apartment. "He wants a divorce and acted like he's carried a torch for the last ten years."

Bernadette marveled at her niece's theatrical gestures. "What did you tell him?"

Lori was lost for words. "I walked away."

Chapter 32

A Man Called Peter

The Spirit of '76. The USA's birthday bash descended on Philadelphia with a yearlong celebration from New Year's Eve through October 1976. Thousands witnessed the Liberty Bell's move from Independence Mall to a nearby pavilion. Freedom Week, leading up to July 4, lent itself to street parties, concerts, picnics, and parades. Fireworks lit up the sky every evening for one week. A 2076 time capsule buried at Second and Chestnut Streets and a 50,000-pound Sara Lee birthday cake served at Memorial Hall offered media-worthy sidebars to main events. Peter captured the 1976 fever for his documentary. His second agenda—a bicentennial date with Lori.

On Friday, July 3, 1976, Lori met Peter at Old Original Bookbinders, one of the first restaurants in the City of Brotherly Love. While awaiting their table, Lori studied a wall of celebrity photos. Waiters in red jackets zigzagged across rooms covered in mahogany paneling.

The host, neat and compact, greeted them. "Thanks for your patience. Right this way." He gestured to Lori. "Maybe we'll have your faces up there. What are your names?"

"Peter and Lori."

"Like the actor, Peter Lorre. *The Maltese Falcon. Casablanca*," humored Peter.

During cocktails and appetizers, Lori examined the king crab legs piled in front of her. "Not the average dish for me."

"Why not?" Peter cracked a claw and offered a tasty morsel.

"I'm a Texas girl, and I've eaten enough barbeque for a lifetime. Although my parents were from Boston."

"Where are they now?" Peter, at ease with the warmth of her company, felt heady from a Tanqueray and tonic, his favored summer drink.

"I guess you don't mention family without inviting questions. They died when I was fourteen."

"I'm sorry. An accident?" He snapped open another shell.

"If you call a tornado an accident."

"Were you away?"

"In a bomb shelter sound asleep. My gran found me. The tornado touched down and destroyed five homes."

"That's a lot to deal with as a teenager." Peter drained his tonic glass. "Do you ever wonder . . . ?"

"How my life would be? Who wouldn't, right?"

"Right. We can talk about something else." The red-coated waiter, Walter, arrived with main courses.

"And you? Ritchie Rich kid?"

"Ouch!" Peter rearranged the lobster on his plate and picked up a set of seafood pliers.

Lori observed. "Boy, you really work for your food. Anyway, no slight intended. Only child?"

"Yeah, same as you."

Lori grinned. "Touché." They pinged glasses and feasted on crab cakes, lobster, fried shrimp, and coleslaw.

By dessert, they were like old chums telling knock-knock jokes and confiding childhood antics. "After a good dinner, one can forgive anybody, even one's own relations," Lori said.

"Oscar Wilde from *A Woman of No Importance*. Do I need to be forgiven?" Peter appeared serious or sincere, Lori wasn't sure.

"Believe me, it comes in handy with my family."

Lori ordered cheesecake topped with blueberries, strawberries, and two forks.

"I'm not much for dessert."

"It's bicentennial cheesecake."

Peter sliced into the thick, creamy confection. The restaurant's window flashed with brilliant fluttering sparks from distant fireworks.

"Early day tomorrow. I better get you back."

"I'm feeling a little tipsy." Lori applied an uneven layer of coral lip gloss with her finger.

On the eve of the Fourth of July, Philadelphia was one big block party. Peter and Lori chuckled over the host's Peter Lorre connection, rushed by the celebrity wall, and exited Old Original Bookbinders. Skipping along, they happened across an acapella trio singing on a street corner and joined an impromptu audience dancing and snapping fingers.

"Why don't you stay at my apartment? I don't bite or anything." Peter shoved his hands in his pockets. Lori imagined him as a male Adonis or a fairy-tale Prince Charming with his square jaw, dimpled chin, and blond curls.

"You seem harmless, but that's okay. I have a hotel room for two nights."

"I'm sorry."

Lori observed her host. "You say that a lot."

"Sorry?"

"Yes."

"I meant I should have arranged a stay at my apartment."

"That's okay. I would've declined."

Peter shuffled his feet like a schoolboy. *An enigma*, thought Lori. Worldly. Lonely, maybe? "Tomorrow is my toughest shoot. All day and most of the night. Can you meet at 11:30 in the evening?"

"At midnight, I'll turn into Cinderella!" Lori couldn't resist the storybook reference in the company of her prince from Philadelphia.

They caught a cab to Lori's hotel. Peter kissed her on the cheek. A sweet, innocent goodbye. "Can we have coffee tomorrow?"

"What time?"

"Five a.m.?"

"For coffee? I'll meet you close to midnight. Where?"

"A nightcap at Old Bookbinders? Or you could come along for the shoot."

"I thought you'd never ask! I'll see you at five! I'll be waiting in the lobby."

"Wow, I finally asked the right question! Good night, lovely Lori."

He kissed her again on the opposite cheek and worked his way effortlessly to her lips. The cab driver cleared his throat. Peter peeled out a few bills from his wallet. The taxi drove off with Peter, the prince, a little bewitched, and Lori, the princess, a little bothered and bewildered.

The following day, the USA's 200th birthday, President Gerald Ford attended a ceremony including Pennsylvania Governor Milton Shapp, Mayor Frank Rizzo, and Charlton Heston as Master of Ceremonies. Forty thousand marchers and floats from every state took part in a five-hour parade. An estimated two million visitors came to Philadelphia to attend events. Lori snapped away as Peter filmed. They worked side by side, absorbing the scene and capturing the Spirit of '76. Following a full day of filming, Lori and Peter unloaded equipment and crew at midnight, the official end of the fourth of July but not the festivities. Fireworks flashed and faded as they walked down South Street heading for Pat's King of Steaks at 1:00 a.m. The line was a block long. Once inside, they waited another fifteen minutes.

"Wake me when we get a table." Lori snuggled against Peter's shoulder.

Bliss arrived with a cheesesteak, fried onions, ketchup bottle, and side of fries.

"There's a Swedish folktale, 'The Princess on the Glass Hill.'"

Lori bit into her cheesesteak and wiped a smear of ketchup from her cheek. "The one where she holds three golden apples and the suitors have to climb up the glass hill and get the apples. Yeah, I love that one."

"But one captures her heart, and she throws him two of the apples." He leaned back, glinty-eyed. "Throw me an apple, Lori."

"How about a French fry?" Like giddy high schoolers in a lunch cafeteria, they threw fries at each other's wide-open mouths.

On the way to the hotel, Lori and Peter embraced. Their good-natured romance was ending, happily without strings. Peter offered to drive her to the train station the next morning. Lori, sleep deprived and exhausted, planned to doze off, lulled by the drone of wheels on railroad tracks.

Promptly at 9:00 a.m., Lori checked out of her hotel and stepped outside to an awaiting Peter in his metallic gold Datsun 280Z.

"How goes it, Lovey?"

"Lovey?"

"It's lovely without the L."

"If you insist, although I'm reminded of Mrs. Howell, the socialite on the *Gilligan's Island* TV series."

He smiled radiantly like a Scandinavian sun god.

She caught sight of red roses behind the passenger seat. "Are those for me?"

Peter grabbed hold of the flowers. "Do you remember the mosque we visited in Egypt? Rami told us the meaning of flowers. Three means I'd like to marry but can't. Eight means forever."

Lori didn't bother counting as she climbed into the car.

"I've been thinking of you, Lori, since we met in Egypt."

"Three years?" Lori stared into the bouquet.

"I'm a self-centered, selfish person . . ."

"Who isn't?" She remained fixed on the roses, not wanting to hear any confessions, especially of love.

"Let me finish. I'm an old-fashioned kind of guy, and I'm married to my work. But, I think we have lots in common. I'm convinced after spending time with you."

"Hold up. Are you asking—"

The doorman came up and interrupted. "Can I help you? We have cars trying to pull up here, please."

Peter waved and proceeded into traffic. "I think about you a lot. All the postcards I've sent. They could fill an album. You're so special, Lori. We could share a life together. Will you marry me?"

Lori, limp as a spent dishrag, let the flowers drop to her feet. "To end your perceived loneliness? No thank you, and our prolonged date is officially over."

The ride was deadly silent, the air thick enough to slice. Lori gathered her belongings, shook Peter's hand—an intended slight—and thanked him for the ride. She walked away and didn't look back—her practiced exit when troubled, in doubt, or determined to close a chapter.

In New York, Lori rang Bernadette.

"He wants to marry you? I mean, you hardly know him, right?" Bernadette fixed a glass of iced tea and cradled the receiver.

"I know. It's whimsical. I do like him, but for the rest of my life?"

"Stranger things have happened. Who knows?"

Lori twirled the cord. "I'm sorry I went to Philadelphia. I could have avoided the whole thing."

Bernadette cooled her cheek with the ice-filled glass on a blistering hot day in Boston. "So how did you leave it?"

"By leaving."

"You'll be here for Mom's eighty-fifth birthday, right? It's in September."

"I know, the eleventh. Four days before my birthday."

"Thirty-five?"

"That's right. Older and no wiser."

"See you in September, Lori. Keep me posted on Prince Charming."

"Why Prince Charming?"

"I dunno. Just a hunch."

Part III

Odds and Ends

(1977 – 2019)

Chapter 33

Sand Castles

Their budding courtship resumed with an apology and ended with a marriage.

The first step, the apology, followed news of Legionnaires' disease that plagued the City of Brotherly Love.

On Monday, August 9, Lori woke up at 4:00 a.m. after a chain of nightmares. One remained with her—meandering down twisty corridors of a cavernous hospital, searching room after room, not knowing who she was searching for and only finding strangers. Five hours later, she dialed Peter.

"Hi, Peter, it's Lori, calling to see if you're okay. I read the dispatches about the epidemic. Sounds scary."

"Oh, hi, Lori. Yeah, it all started at a convention. Bacteria through the air vents in a hotel. How are you?"

"I'm good. Keeping busy. I also wanted to say, I like you, I mean, as a friend. I'm sorry I was so harsh. I mean, you were saying you wanted to spend a lifetime with me, and I should be, well, flattered, you know . . . this isn't going very well."

"It's great hearing your voice."

"Thank you. Okay, then, that's it. Goodbye now."

"Goodbye, Lori. Thanks for calling. You're still lovely."

She hung up. His voice rung like a bell. *You're still lovely.*

In early October, Peter followed up with an invitation to his documentary premiere covering the July 4 events. Two months to the day of the August 9 phone call, Lori rented a car with Sandra Dee in tow for a jaunt to Philadelphia. She intended on driving back the same evening.

When Peter got wind of her plans, he insisted she spend the night at a friend's pad. She appreciated his decorum of not offering his apartment.

Lori slept on a daybed in an artist named Sofia's studio apartment. Sandra Dee chomped on a carrot in her cage set up on a low coffee table. Life seemed good. No commitments. No strings. No decisions. And then a conversation starter stirred her thoughts, maybe options, once again.

"How do you know Peter?" Lori was mildly curious.

"He started a fund for aspiring artists. I was a recipient," Sofia answered.

"A fund?"

"I had no money, no future really. My family didn't have any money to send me to college. I worked at a coffee shop and learned about the funding from another artist. It supported my tuition, books, and supplies. He's helped so many artists."

"Oh." *What now?* Lori thought. Handsome, chivalrous, generous. *What's missing?*

Sofia set out a jar of instant coffee, pineapple juice, and toasted English muffins. She hunted through her refrigerator. "I have apple butter." She set the jar on the cozy kitchenette's butcher block table. "Peter talks about you all the time. He admires your work."

"Really?" Lori spooned apple butter on a crispy English muffin.

"He buys copies of publications that feature your photos. He says you're a real artist."

Lori wished the topic would change as she pondered the words—*a real artist.*

"So do you have a showing of your artwork?"

Sofia swilled a half glass of juice. "Yes, next January my exhibit opens in a gallery on South Street. I'm finishing up a few pieces in a workshop for new artists. Peter rents the workshop too. For artists that don't have working space."

"Thanks, Sofia. Sandra Dee thanks you too. She likes carrots."

"Come and see my exhibit next January." Sofia hugged Lori, unexpectedly, with warmth and exuberance. Lori drove away from the City of Brotherly Love with kinder reflections of Peter and a recollection of the movie *A Man Called Peter*, a true story about a preacher from Scotland that was appointed Chaplain of the United States Senate. Lori had always cherished the book by Catherine Marshall. In the spring of 1955, Lori's mom had surprised her with theatre tickets. Movie day had been perfect. They took in an Easter Monday matinee and had stopped for chocolate sundaes at a soda shop before dinner. In the evening, they ate peanut M&Ms and watched *Topper* on television. All of these images projected on Lori's windshield as she drove to New York. *A Man Called Peter*. A movie and an indelible memory of happier moments with Miriam. Minutes away from home, Sandra Dee's head emerged from her shell.

"What do you think? Should I call him?" Sandra Dee retreated to her shell. Lori chuckled. "That's what I thought."

Two weeks before Thanksgiving, on a dreary, gray morning, Peter met Lori for espresso in a SoHo café. They arranged the tête-à-tête via hastily written notes mailed as if they were worlds apart. Their relationship of sorts was like an old-fashioned, side-stepping, elusive romance.

"Thanks for showing up." Peter pulled out a bistro chair for her.

"Did you think I wouldn't?" Lori picked up a menu. She hadn't slept well and had skipped dinner the night before.

"Well, if you changed your mind . . ."

"I wouldn't have accepted if I changed my mind."

"Fair enough. My treat. I insist."

Lori's eyes met his above the menu's edge. "Fair enough."

They laughed and joked about their first meeting in Egypt and Peter's insistence that Lori ride a camel.

"Do you remember how upset Rami was about his car?" Peter, the sun god, grinned like a Cheshire cat.

"Yeah, because I smelled like a camel! Are you two still in touch?"

"Yes, he's a good friend."

"You have lots of friends. The artists you support . . ."

"I try to help."

"I can see that." Lori, comfortable and content, made a quantum leap and surprised herself. "Hey, uh, interested in a Boston Thanksgiving?"

"Only if you spend Santa Lucia Day with my family. December thirteenth."

"I guess so. Is that where a girl wears a wreath with lit candles on her head?"

"That would be my sister, Brigit."

They sealed the deal. Lori walked away and turned to wave. A man called Peter and a destiny unknown.

Peter spent most of the fall season at his New York apartment on the Upper East Side. Lori visited in between her own assignments. She employed a student from New York University as a sitter for Sandra Dee when photo shoots with a rented car weren't manageable. Lori preferred long stretches of scenery and the feel of the road as she readied for the next project. Highways and unbeaten paths were visceral and more tactile than staring out at clouds and an airplane wing.

With one job left before Thanksgiving, Lori unlatched Peter's apartment door. He dozed on the sofa with a letter in his hand and awoke startled. "Hi, I drifted off."

"Yes, I see." She set down Sandra Dee's cage on a sofa table. "A love letter?"

"Hardly. It's from Rami."

A prickly sensation ran through her forearms. "Oh? And?"

"He's coming here in March of next year."

"And Miriam?" A twinge of guilt seized her for not keeping in touch.

"He said everything's fine. No news is good news, right?"

"I need to call her." She stored away Sandra Dee's stash of vegetables and fruit.

"You don't have to buy all that. I know what she eats."

Lori leaned over the sofa. Peter traced her nose and kissed it.

"Okay, before things heat up, Lovey has to leave. I'll be late for my flight. Oh, I made up a lunch bag for you."

He pulled her closer. "Oh, how kind of you. I think you deserve a special treat yourself."

She stood up. "Okay, that's it. I'm outta here. I don't like racing through airports."

Later that morning, Peter noticed his name on a brown paper bag next to the milk carton in the fridge. He opened the bag. Two golden apples. He murmured, "Well, the princess has spoken."

Thanksgiving countdown and the Hopkins household was on pins and needles.

Ben and Bernadette shopped for a turkey and trimmings. Penny insisted on cooking but relented at Bernadette's insistence.

"You make the gravy this year. We'll do everything else, okay?" Bernadette kissed her mom's cheek. Penny seemed smaller and more birdlike with the passing years. At eighty-five, she had a slight bend in her usually straight posture. Her legs were twigs, strong if not as flexible from years of ballet and tap in her youth. But if she sprouted feathers and wings, it wouldn't surprise any of her children.

The cuckoo clock tolled the noon hour. "I'll make crescent rolls too. We have Lori's suitor coming." The phone rang, competing with the clock.

"Hello." Bernadette yelled over to her mom. "It's Lori." She nodded her head repeatedly. "Uh-huh, yeah, I understand. No, don't worry. It's fine. We'll talk when you get here. Happy Thanksgiving." She replaced the receiver and busied herself with scissor-cutting a frozen butter stick for pumpkin pie pastry. "She can't make it. She's flying to San Francisco."

Penny was visibly disappointed. "My goodness, why?"

Bernadette observed an eighty-five-year-old's pout—as effective as a five-year-old's. "The Band is playing their last concert on Thanksgiving, and a documentary's being filmed."

"What band?"

"I'll explain later." Bernadette mixed butter bits into flour. "She and Peter will be here on Saturday."

"But everyone will be gone . . ."

"Mom, we'll be here!"

Ben stepped in the kitchen archway with an overflowing grocery bag, celery stalk leaves peeking out. Neither heard him come in. "Garden fresh from the farmer's market."

Penny and Bernadette quieted down like kids caught with their hands in the cookie jar.

"What's going on?" Ben dropped the bag on the kitchen counter and kissed his mom on the cheek.

Bernadette sorted out groceries. "Lori can't make it for Thanksgiving. She'll be here for the weekend."

"Okay, so what's the problem?"

"Everyone won't get a chance to meet him." Penny's pout underpinned her disappointment.

"We'll be here."

Bernadette stocked up the refrigerator's vegetable bin. "That's what I said. We don't want to scare the guy away."

"I hardly think so. Anyway, we can always serve them leftovers." Penny clutched the table's edge before standing. She refused to use a walker or cane, even though her legs stiffened up when she sat for more than fifteen minutes.

Ben side-hugged his mom. "I'm looking forward to meeting this fellow. From what you say Bernadette, he idolizes our niece."

Bernadette shrugged. "I guess that's a start." She had misgivings. Not concerning Prince Charming. He seemed sincere enough. But Lori, the elusive, the will-o'-the-wisp, like the pale flame over marshy ground that disappeared when approached.

On Thursday, December 16, 1976, they headed for Elkton, Maryland. The fifty-mile drive from Philadelphia took just an hour, even with an assault of snow and sleet.

At the town's courthouse, the eloping couple filed for a marriage license. Peter pulled out a black velvet ring box from his goose down jacket and got on one knee.

"A little late for that. We just filed our license." Lori instantly bemoaned her acerbic remark. She meant it jokingly, to ease the tension of their rash decision. She resolved to bite her tongue more often.

"Don't ruin the moment." Peter displayed a two-carat, six-pronged diamond solitaire ring.

Lori gasped. "It's exquisite. I feel like a princess."

The fairy tale's penultimate chapter—the prince climbed the top of the glass hill to claim his princess.

Two days later, on a Saturday morning, they stepped into the Historic Little Wedding Chapel in Elkton for the scheduled ceremony.

Ten years earlier, Lori had visited the chapel on an assignment, "The Hidden Charms of the Eastern Shore." She knew its history and that baseball star Willie Mays got hitched at the Historic Little Wedding Chapel on Valentine's Day in 1956. Actress Joan Fontaine also got married there. Elkton had become known since the 1920s as the "wedding capital of the East Coast," second only to Las Vegas worldwide, because licenses were easy and quick to obtain.

"Never dreamt I'd be back here." Lori's ring finger sported the diamond solitaire. Sofia, the Philadelphia artist, and Stanley, a cameraman from Peter's crew, joined them in the waiting area. The ceremony lasted twelve minutes—the bride's walk down the aisle, recitation of vows, wedding rings exchange, a prayer, a blessing, husband-and-wife pronouncement, and traditional altar kiss. The chapel photographer snapped enough pictures to fill a slim wedding album.

On Christmas Eve, they had their first argument.

"Lori, you'll be giving up that hovel—"

"Hovel? You're calling my apartment a hovel?"

"We can't live there. We're married. And your reptile." The wished for storybook romance turned into the grimmest of Grimms' fairy tales. Peter harbored a grudge over the Sandra Dee argument and resulting stalemate that lasted until after midnight.

On Christmas Day, Lori crept out as Peter slept soundly. She attended a morning mass at the Our Lady Chapel at St. Patrick's Cathedral. Afterward, she rode the subway to her Chelsea apartment and ran into a neighbor. From the hallway's opposite end, Harry, a retired tailor, greeted her. "Merry Christmas! Haven't seen you since spring."

"Hi, Harry." She hugged his feeble frame. "Busy with assignments. I'm married now."

"Ah, so you're moving?"

"Not yet."

"Oh. Why not?"

"Don't know, Harry."

She sorted through stacks of neglected mail, mainly greeting cards from Boston, Texas, and one from Oklahoma. She ripped open Tally's card. Two cardinals alighted on a snowy branch with a sentiment of "miles not separating" and Tally's scrawled message. *Call me!*

In all her haste, Lori didn't mail any Christmas cards. An unopened box of them sat atop a pile of papers on her living room desk.

On the way back to Peter's, she bought corned beef sandwiches from 2nd Ave Deli. He greeted her with a grand sweeping gesture and a black magician's cape.

"I've been waiting for you, Lovey. Watched out the window and saw you coming."

"What's with the cape?"

He swooshed it and stood aside. Sandra Dee rested in a cage large enough for a lion cub. An ornate plastic castle, decked with a string of white lights, was positioned in the middle surrounded by a simulated moat filled with water. Carrot shavings, sliced beets, radishes, and chopped apples were piled up in each corner. A sign, pinned to the front, said, *Merry Christmas, to Sandy from Peter.*

He draped the magician's cape around Lori and bowed.

"I don't know what to say. Uh, Merry Christmas?"

"I hope she likes it. Her new home. Our new home."

"But, Peter, it's enormous. I don't think we have the space."

"Nonsense. You like it, right, Sandy?"

Lori bit her lip. No arguments on Christmas Day. The cage conjured up a prison cell in Texas and Barry. Her best Christmas? No. It defied logic.

Peter and Lori noshed on corned beef sandwiches and listened to *A Christmas Album* by Barbra Streisand, his favorite vocal artist. They weren't like teens throwing fries at each other. No Independence Day antics. No joie de vivre.

"Why won't you give up your apartment?"

"I will, Peter. Give me time."

The Chelsea apartment was a security blanket. Sandra Dee stared at her from inside the immense steel structure. Lori whispered to her trusty companion, "What are we doing here?"

In January 1977, Peter flew to Hawaii to film a documentary, a history of the fiftieth state's royalty. He was gone for three weeks, long enough for Lori to sort through her harried and hasty decision. Every day she sat in a pew at St. Patrick's Cathedral, unsure of where to search for answers. While Peter was away, Lori moved into her apartment with Sandra Dee. She rifled through her desk and unearthed an address book.

"Connie?"

"Yes?"

"It's Lori."

"My goodness gracious! Where are you now? I've lost track of you!"

"New York. You're still in Boston."

"And don't plan on moving. How are you?"

"Good. And married."

"Congrats! Who's the lucky fella?"

"A filmmaker." Lori redoubled her steps, anxious to get to her point. "Connie, we talked a lot as roommates."

"Oh, my goodness, don't quiz me on anything."

"You said you would know when the right one came along."

Connie chuckled. "Easy to say since no one came along back then. I do remember one thing . . ."

"The look of love?"

"You remembered, and I said it before the song came out."

"The eyes speak love. You said I would know . . ."

"Lori, I was a psychology major. Always full of opinions and theories."

"But you were on to something."

"The look of love. Better than any words."

"You're right, Connie. Thanks."

"That's it?"

"For now. Happy New Year."

"Don't be a stranger, Lori."

Peter brought souvenir gifts from Hawaii—a necklace and bracelet of rare Niihau shells, a ukulele, and Kona coffee, labeled the best in the world. He didn't share news of his work and grew distant with passing days awaiting his next project. Two people sharing an apartment, not a future.

On Valentine's Day, they attended the Broadway revival of *Fiddler on the Roof* and stopped by Sardi's for a late-night snack of port wine and a cheese platter. Lori picked at a wedge of aged cheddar. "I'd rather have cheesecake at Lindy's."

Peter screwed up his face. "You and your cheesecake. Happy Valentine's Day, Lovey."

"Peter. You don't look at me."

"I always look at you, Lovey." He fidgeted and combed through his tangle of curls.

"You look through me. An indirect gaze. Hostile."

"Nonsense. Psycho-babble. You ready?"

The argument escalated throughout the evening. "It's that damn apartment. You won't give it up."

They both knew why. Lori processed a mental checklist.

Time apart? Peaceful.

Time together? Apprehensive. Combative.

Intimacy? Less frequent since their reunion.

In March, Peter spent a month in Japan filming the marathon monks in the Kyoto mountains. The monks of Mount Hiei run a thousand marathons in a thousand days. In the last one hundred years, less than fifty men completed it. Lori offered to take an assignment in Japan so they could be together.

"Peter, we never had a honeymoon."

"There's time. What about Sandy?"

"It's Sandra Dee! I'll get someone to take care of her."

With no words of encouragement, she dropped the notion. Time and distance added clarity—a separation of hearts never truly united. Lori dreamt of a sandcastle worn down by each breaker until it disappeared.

In six months, she filed for an annulment on the premise that she was not of sound mind when they married. After reviewing her prison record, the legal court accepted her claim. Peter didn't contest.

With solitude came serenity. Lori realized her heart belonged to no one. Until the other prince beckoned with an orb and a blessing. *Expect the unexpected.*

"Laurie?" She heard a whisper and turned to solemn faces and praying hands looking up reverently at the child statue. Hearing voices. Drugs had done this to her before. Almost destroyed her life, taking everything good and wholesome out of her path. But she'd kicked it! Was she hallucinating? She turned her head again. No familiar faces. And why would there be? In Czechoslovakia? It had been nearly twenty years since she'd stepped foot in the church. She questioned why on earth her path led back to this place. *I've survived so much without you*, she thought. *Why did I come here again? Why?*

A girl sat next to her in the pew.

On impulse, Lori asked, "Did you say something?"

The girl, perplexed, answered, "No. Why?"

"Oh, nothing." She continued, "Excuse me, what's your name?"

"Laurie. What's yours?"

"Lorraine, but I go by Lori."

"Oh, you heard my mom. She called me to point out something. That's really funny, huh?"

Lori sighed relief. "What a coincidence. I mean, your name sounds like mine. American?"

"Yes. I'm visiting my great-grandmother. She lives here."

A middle-aged woman with gray streaks at her temples approached. "Laurie?" Worry lines deepened on her brow.

Lori hadn't slept in two nights and appeared disheveled. Her light auburn hair, pulled in a ponytail, gave her a severe mien without makeup on her pale complexion. "Hi, I'm Lori. I heard you call your daughter."

"Well, isn't that amazing? Where are you from, Lori?"

"Originally, Texas."

The woman's disposition altered. "Well, we live in Texas, for heaven's sake. Name's Hanna. Come have dinner with us! I mean here!"

The following evening, Lori took up Hanna's invite. Brick row houses with red-tiled roofs were indistinguishable. Lori double-checked the address before paying the taxi driver.

"We're so glad you could join us!" Hanna Petruska graciously ushered their guest into a dim hallway leading to a parlor. Her daughter, Laurie, sprung up from a two-seater sofa in a room so tiny that an area rug spread wall to wall. Lori and Laurie shook hands.

An elderly woman rocked quietly in a corner, and Lori nodded at her and smiled. The sound of silence competed with a ticking wall clock, clanking bracelets, and the steady rhythm of a rocking chair.

"My grandmother baked Hungarian country bread. It's her specialty. We also have goulash. I hope you like it." Hanna retreated to the kitchen.

The wizened matron nodded and rocked. Lori addressed the younger Laurie. "Do you speak Czech?"

"A little."

The old woman mumbled excitedly.

"Babi wants me to tell you something. She doesn't speak English, but I'll translate." She studied her great-grandmother's lips and expressions. "My babi says you're very pretty. She thinks you have lots of secrets. I hope you don't mind her words."

"No, that's fine. She's right. Please thank her for the compliment."

"She understands thank you." The girl heeded her great-grandmother. "She says you're very sad. A sadness in your heart. You wear sadness like a cloak. Great loss. But your life will start over. Not now. But it will. Your trials are many, and they are not over."

Hanna reentered. "Have I missed anything?"

The family matriarch became silent again, having said all she intended. The foursome sat close to each other.

"Why don't we move to the dining room? The goulash is ready." Hanna reached behind the two-seat couch for a cane.

"May I help?" Lori carried the weight of the old woman's words as she rose to her feet—*your trials are many, and they are not over.*

Hanna passed the cane to the withered hand. "My grandmother is blind. Since 1955."

After dinner, Lori exchanged contact information with Laurie Petruska and her mother, Hanna, and promised to be in touch when she returned to the States. She thanked them for a delicious meal and bid her goodbyes. In the most articulate, strong voice, the blind woman said, "Visit again."

Hours later, in her hotel room, Lori stirred in her sleep and awoke startled. *Visit again.* The Czech matriarch wasn't speaking of her household, her granddaughter, or her great-granddaughter. She spoke of the Infant of Prague high above an altar.

On her last day in Prague, Lori knelt transfixed in a pew at the Church of Our Lady of Victory. She recalled sitting in the same spot more than twenty years earlier with Grandma Lottie. Oh the defiance she held on to that day!

Life had worn her down. *Was it time to surrender? Surrender to what?* She envisioned the girl of fourteen who had approached her on a summer day in 1956. Fresh in her mind, she etched out the face—thin, angular, almond-shaped eyes, and reluctant smile. She remembered the teen handing her a pamphlet before vanishing by a side door. Lori had written down the words on the pamphlet from the strange, silent girl. *Come back to me.* She'd tucked the notebook into her purse, made a slight bow and a sign of the cross with holy water.

Lori met Hanna, Laurie, and Anna before leaving Prague. She insisted on treating the trio to dinner, but Anna, the great-grandmother was not ambulatory. Hanna, with her passion for cooking, convinced Lori to dine with them again.

Hanna welcomed Lori with a warm hug. "My husband prefers a hot dog slathered in mustard, so I enjoy making these dishes." The dining table was set—roasted pork, dumplings, and a side of braised cabbage. She and Lori drank beer. Laurie and Anna sipped homemade apple cider.

"I'm not a beer drinker but this is pretty good." Lori drained a mug of pale ale.

"Thanks. Pilsner beers are from the Czech city Pilsen. We have the highest beer consumption in the world for what it's worth. Maybe you could do a story on breweries."

"I'll pass on that one, but I'm glad to be back in Prague."

"Where next, Lori? You lead such an adventurous life!" A proud and happy cook, Hanna served up dumplings, a double portion, to her guest. Anna nodded contentment to have company and homespun fare with family. Her meals were usually brought in by a kindly neighbor who looked after her, along with a hired nurse that relieved Hanna of guilt. Hanna's visits were sparse, especially during her daughter's school year. Long-distance calls to her grandmother usually ended with assurance of a one-month summer vacation and a week in the spring.

Lori regaled with photo stories, including the one about her first muse, a turtle on a teaspoon now named Sandra Dee. Tales from the four corners of the world enraptured the young Laurie. Anna spoke and her great-granddaughter translated. "My *babicka* wants to know if you're married."

"Was. It lasted six months. We got an annulment."

Hanna cleared her throat and signaled her daughter to clear away dishes. "I baked an apple and pear strudel for dessert. You have to try it."

"Dumplings and strudel? You'll have to roll me to the airport." Lori pulled a few papers out of her pocketbook, searching for her flight information. "I leave in a few hours. I hope we can keep in touch. Thanks again for a second invite."

Laurie entered, bearing apple strudel on a dessert plate.

"I'll look for your photos, Lori. *National Geographic*?" Hanna wrapped a piece of strudel in wax paper. "Breakfast."

"Yes, *National Geographic* and others." She high-fived Laurie. "Please tell your *babicka* to pray for me."

"Yes, I pray for you." Anna peered directly at Lori, the traveler, as if seeing her with unseeing eyes.

Back in New York City, Lori attended Sunday mass at St. Patrick's Cathedral. The words of the blind Czech woman echoed within. *Sadness in your heart . . . sadness like a cloak . . . great loss . . . life will start over . . . not now . . . but it will . . . your trials are many, and they are not over.*

Lori thought of the Samaritan woman at the well when Jesus asked her if she had a husband. The woman replied "Yes," and Jesus told her the entire truth. Possibly Anna, the wizened woman, already knew Lori's answer. She wondered if the grandmother would've had more to say if her granddaughter, Hanna, hadn't interrupted the awkward inquisition. Lori scoured her purse fruitlessly for the brochure with the drawing of the girl from 1956 and the words *Come back to me* printed on the front.

"Okay, I'm here," she said, a prayer on her lips. "What next?" She chuckled to herself, as if God would reveal any day beyond the present one. "Okay, I'll take the wildcards." She genuflected and lit votive candles in a row—one flame for Gerry, one for Barry, one for Giuseppe, one for Peter, and one for Adriano, who changed her life in a few hours. "For those I've hurt and who've hurt me." She prayed the Our Father and left behind a heavy heart.

Renewed in spirit, Lori avoided her old Manhattan haunts that still haunted her. She declined club-hopping invites from freelance writers and photographers, a restless lot in between paid gigs. The new craze,

Studio 54, refurbished a former television studio into the world's hottest nightclub. Celebrities and regulars pranced about in wanton revelry as strobe lights reflected off mirrored disco balls. Open drug use and discotheques, especially in the Big Apple, were synonymous. She heard the stories. Mick Jagger's wife, Bianca, saddled on a white horse for her thirtieth birthday party.

Guests were selected at the door based on appearance and style. Lori's foray into the club's kaleidoscope world was as a hired photographer to shoot the club's one-year anniversary on April 26, 1978. The job paid fantastic money. At the mobbed entrance, she held up her press ID lest she be passed over by the doorman perched on a step stool, who granted admission at his whim.

The milieu was a three-ring circus with pounding disco beats. She dodged frenzied dancers and headed for the stage to shoot models clad in "East Meets West" designs by fashion mogul Issey Miyake.

A bare-chested guest with a handlebar mustache, red velvet shorts, leather boots, and cowboy hat rubbed against her. "Get me on camera!" He bumped her hip and spilled a flute of champagne down her silk blouse of a similar color.

"Are you a model?" Lori checked her flash attachment.

"I'm your model, baby!"

"I'm here to shoot models." She moved closer to the stage, and as she turned around, she saw him.

"Peter?" The last time she'd seen him was at the annulment, though certain their paths would eventually cross again. New York wasn't big enough for two people in the world of film and photography. She barely recognized him dressed in white designer jeans and a black polyester shirt unbuttoned to his waist. Coal-black mascara rimmed his eyes, like an Egyptian pharaoh, a stark contrast to his blond waves combed back into a ponytail.

"Lori? Never thought I'd see you in here!" Peter yelled over the music booming like a loud, rhythmic heartbeat. "How are you, Lovey?" He kissed her on the cheek. The man in shorts loomed behind him.

"Do you know her? She's a photographer but won't photograph me.

How about the two of us?" He placed the hat on Peter and wrapped a glistening, muscular arm around him in a tight embrace. She felt the heat and swirl of emotions flush her cheeks, unsure if it was the pulse of the disco beat, the obnoxious dancer, or the sincerest "I'm sorry" in Peter's eyes.

"Sure, why not?" She snapped a photo and moved into a swarm of revelers.

"Hey, sweetie, how do we get a copy?"

Lori shouted above the din. "I know where to send it."

She bumped shoulders with Carrie Fisher à la Princess Leia of *Star Wars* fame at the entrance to the restroom. Lori dabbed cold water on her flushed cheeks. Bent over the sink, she heard a familiar voice.

"Lori Hopkins?"

Bette's skeleton-like frame disappeared under black satin shorts and a black sequined tube top. Bright red lipstick gave her a cartoonish appearance. Platinum bangs fringed blue eyes edged in cobalt blue liner. Lori shook loose her pity. She wanted to shake the addict back to health, if it were possible. Heroin killed the spirit before the body.

"I'm off the junk." Bette snorted a line of cocaine from a handheld mirror. "I was the walking dead."

"Bette." She had nothing more to say. Offering to help her get clean would be futile. She took the waning actress by bony shoulders. "Take care of yourself."

"I'm surprised to see you here." Bette shook her long blonde tresses with wild abandon. She gazed in the mirror, her lips curved in rapture.

"Photo shoot." Lori turned to leave.

"Watch out for the dead birds."

Two models in matching cowgirl costumes and flame-red layered wigs barged through in spurts of giggles. One model lifted a vial out of her leather holster. "Did you see Dolly Parton run up to the balcony?" She dipped a tiny spoon into the white powder and passed it to the other model.

"Yeah. Was she freaked out or what? That farm crap was for her." The other model snorted a line, like second nature.

Lori checked her camera flash. "Birds?"

The models, oblivious to Lori and Bette, laughed hysterically.

"Doves released from the balcony." Bette spread her arms like wings. "They fly to their death in a panic with the pulse of music."

Lori waved goodbye to Bette—a dove, vulnerable and confused, flying to her death.

Returning to Portugal filled her with dread and resignation. Fate had dealt her a losing hand thirteen years ago. She believed numbers had meaning. The number thirteen was no exception. The thirteenth day thirteen years later. Lori planned to meet her Egyptian confidante in Fátima on May 13, the sixty-fourth anniversary of the first apparition to the three shepherd children. She couldn't erase the events of the summer of '68. The pleated fan—light and dark, good and evil. She focused on the light and associated the name Miriam with light, not the dark moments. Her mother, Miriam, provoked her to create the Christmas dugout. Darkness. Another Miriam linked to the devastation of being violated. Further darkness.

But, on a deeper level, the bomb shelter had saved her life. The unplanned pregnancy had offered new life to another woman. Lori experienced irrepressible joy with thoughts of Francine. She loved the woman in the red coat captured through a view finder on a busy London street.

The circumstances, like kismet, defied logic. She recalled the words of her eighth grade religion teacher lecturing distracted, restless students. "The past, present, and future are all here. We separate strings wound together. We catalog days, months, and years. God gave us intelligence and an innate ability to mark time."

A week before her rendezvous with Miriam, Lori's plans changed. She received an assignment in Rome for a pictorial overview of Pope John Paul II.

Lori thumbed through her address book. "Miriam, I'll be in Vatican City on May thirteenth. I'm sorry."

"You'll be with the Holy Father. Our Lady will be happy. Shalom."

The exchange lasted thirty seconds. Brevity was the key with Miriam. She spoke at length when she had something vital to communicate.

May 13, 1981. Rome was in good form, weather-wise. Lori's affinity for the Eternal City grew with every visit. The multitude swelled in St. Peter's Square in anticipation of sighting the pope mobile. She fixed her camera's telescopic lens and scoped out faces. Perfect.

Pope John Paul II appeared to uproarious cheers, clicking cameras, and waving arms. Lori was flanked at the vehicle's front end yards away and watched him through her view finder. She closed in on his face—serene, loving, and holy. He moved slowly through the throng and grasped extended hands. She repositioned her camera to the left of the pope mobile and saw a raised hand with a slim, dark barrel of a pistol extended over heads. She shifted focus to the pope. Then a crackle or pop like a firecracker. The Holy Father pitched forward and clutched his midsection. A veiled woman held him.

"What?" She dropped her camera and let it dangle from its strap. Chaos ensued in St. Peter's Square. Photographers snapping, people running. She picked up her camera. The crowd was regrouping. Police ascended and pushed through the swarming, terrified mob. The pope was ushered away from the scene.

Lori returned to the foreign press office. Phone lines burned up. Reporters shouted. She recognized at least seven languages. A British newsman yelled over the din to his correspondent. "Lost six pints of blood! Not looking good . . ."

The world prepared for horrific news. Lori recognized an American colleague, Sam Cutrona, in the pressroom. "There was a lady helping him, right?"

"Dunno. What's in your film?" Cutrona pointed to Lori's camera.

"Nothing. I didn't snap any."

He shrugged. "No proof."

A few days later, a Vatican spokesperson claimed that after surgery, the first thing Pope John Paul II requested was a rosary. The pope confided that Mother Mary directed the four fired bullets in a path through him missing vital organs, leading to his miraculous survival.

Memorial Day, 1981. Lori glanced at the alarm clock radio, rolled over, and slept another hour. At 8:00 a.m. she picked up the phone, noting the seven-hour time difference. "Miriam, she was there. I saw her in my camera."

"Yes, I know. Our Lady saved him."

Chapter 34

At War with Peace

No one knew. Not family. Not friends. Even so, her final operation before she retired went utterly wrong. Barbara was now the most vulnerable person in the world—her world.

The destination—Japan. The mission—collect and disseminate a list of confirmed connections to the mob. A minor assignment. A breeze. Nothing like the KGB. Her Japanese was deemed passable. No one expected proficiency from an American. It would have caused suspicion. Only trained intelligence personnel would be fluent. Albeit her Japanese was excellent. No conversation escaped her, embarrassingly so when she overheard American women equated to cows and other insensitive criticisms. At least she never overheard a personal insult and spared a spontaneous reaction on her part.

Barbara's cover—interior designer. Code name—Sarah Stewart. Job—working for an American company, Designing Spaces, and hired to add Western flair to sparse corporate offices that, due to their sterility, distracted American businessmen and made them feel ill at ease.

The CIA wasn't too concerned with the Japanese mob. They didn't pose a national security threat. Like Barbara believed—a minor assignment. No sale or development of biological or chemical weapons involved. She'd hustle décor to mob members who had their own cover in legit businesses. The bonus? Exposure and access to Americans doing business with the Japanese mob. Oftentimes, she'd say, "There's always a bonus, if you pay attention." She'd collect relevant information and submit a written report for intelligence analysts to assess potential threats. Any policy recommendations were relegated to the Pentagon.

In 1980, the Intelligence Oversight Act passed and charged the Senate Select Committee on Intelligence (SSCI) and the House Permanent Select Committee on Intelligence (HPSCI) with authorizing the programs of the intelligence agencies and overseeing their activities. None of that mattered to Barbara as code name Sarah. She was on a cakewalk assignment, if there was such a thing. Unless the extraordinary happened. The in-a-blue-moon factor, like being recognized, even by a hardly known or long-ago acquaintance.

Barbara, alias Sarah, a self-professed party animal, appeared younger than her early forties. She frequented discotheques crammed with young adults writhing to techno music and middle-aged men winding back clocks to recapture their glory days. American businessmen forged deals and explored *la vida loca* away from their family routines, backyard barbecues, and ho-hum jobs.

The discotheque, Lotus Flower, was a visual contrast to the symbolic pureness of delicate petals floating atop peaceful ponds. Sarah, the interior designer persona, assimilated into the chaotic world of throbbing music and glittering bodies. In her first week, she hit pay dirt and amassed a small number of essential names of American businessmen connected to the Japanese mob. And there, at the Lotus Flower, she bumped into Lori from Texas.

At first, Barbara didn't recognize the thirty-something redhead she had met while playing chauffeur to a high school homecoming dance. Lori from Texas. Lori who broke her brother's heart or vice versa. It really didn't matter. What mattered was she knew the woman from Texas, a handful of years in age difference. Lori from Texas could blow her cover. The solution? Deflection, denial, and dismissal. Sarah, a.k.a. Barbara, a.k.a. Babs, anticipated the worst. Lori would ask her what she was doing in Japan. And the inquisition would roll out. That's how it usually happened.

On the dance floor, they rubbed shoulders, faces inches away. Barbara, dressed in a silver blouson top and designer jeans, headed to a private booth, her business clients in tow. A relentless partier as code name Sarah, she worked hard and played hard. Lori did the classic double take. "Barbara?" Oh how the years, even the decades, melted away with instant recognition.

Barbara knew the routine. If it's someone you haven't seen in a decade or more, deny it, especially if you don't plan on seeing the person again. "Name's Sarah." Denial 101. Maintain physical distance. In this case, she had a persistent pursuer, a "Chatty Cathy," she called it.

"Oh, I'm sorry. You look so much like someone I knew in Texas."

Next phase. Deflect. "Must have one of those faces." She smiled her way out of the impromptu limelight.

Lori's photographic memory stretched back to 1956 and the homecoming dance. The smile sealed it.

Sarah ordered from the waiter. "A mugi shochu."

The "boys," as she called them, had their usual round of beers.

Sam, an American businessman, caught the snooping bug. "Where are you from, Sarah?" He belched up the brew he guzzled.

"All over."

Mr. Somo lit Sarah's Virginia Slim cigarette. He was a businessman in the burgeoning pharmaceutical industry, a key member of the expanding illegal drug industry, and at the top of her list.

"Army brat?" Sam signaled the waiter for another round.

Sarah chuckled, doing her best to deflect the Barbara incident. "Dad was a professor of mathematics. A bit of an itinerant."

She guessed Sam wasn't sure what that meant and hoped it would shut him down. It didn't.

"Where'd you live?"

"Mostly New England, never anywhere long enough for tenure." She appeared nonchalant and bored. "We settled in California."

"Parents alive?"

"Dad died a few years ago."

"California?" Sam lit up a cigar.

"No funeral. His ashes were sprinkled in the Pacific. Not a cool subject." Sarah waved away the first whiff of smoke.

"Enough questions!" Mr. Somo raised his glass high. *"Kanpai!"*

Sarah raised her glass half as high in deference to her host. *"Kanpai!"* She avoided Sam's penetrating glare.

"When do you head out?" Sam asked.

"Tomorrow." Sarah downed her cocktail.

Barbara, a.k.a. Sarah, skirted round glittery bare shoulders and flashing medallions. She tailed Lori entering the ladies' room. A model-thin Japanese woman with a blunt cut of copper-colored hair snorted a line of cocaine and exited. Barbara checked all the stalls. A pair of high heels, but not Lori's. She did a head turn. No Lori.

"I'm right here, Barbara." Lori came from behind a door leading to toiletries and cleaning supplies.

The woman with stiletto heels exited the stall, washed her hands, smeared on a thick coat of magenta-colored lipstick, and headed for the door without acknowledging them.

Lori continued, "I saw you following me."

Barbara cornered Lori at the door's hinge. She drew a pistol from her purse. "Here take this."

"Why?"

"You'll be shadowed. The Japanese mob thinks you're a spook."

"What? Why?"

"Because I am."

Lori took the pistol. "I don't want any part of this . . ."

"You blew my cover."

"Your cover?" Lori tucked her purse under her arm.

"Identifying me could be part of a code. You put yourself in danger." Barbara moved away from Lori. "Take the pistol," Barbara insisted. "If you don't need it, toss it."

Lori left the disco and walked the busy streets to her midtown hotel. Music blasted from bars into even noisier streets. Duran Duran's meteoric hit "Girls on Film" echoed from another disco's open doors.

With two blocks to go, Lori, vexed by her Barbara encounter, switched attention to her morning schedule—the annual Cherry Blossom Festival with its traditional regalia and welcoming of spring. She quickened her steps. Footsteps behind grew closer. She shivered away the notion of being shadowed and pushed against a barricade of outdoor partyers. Pink and white neon lights reflected on sidewalks slicked by a slight drizzle.

She snuck into an alley shortcut leading to her hotel entrance. The corner turn was blocked by a shadowy figure and an outstretched arm holding a silent revolver. The sting of a bullet grazed her right calf. Lori reached for the pistol in her handbag and squeezed the trigger, hitting the man in his right arm. He switched the gun to his left hand. She aimed and fired again.

A man hoisted her off the gravel. "Come with me." Stunned, she didn't resist his forceful rush to leave the crime scene. A white Honda Civic drove up to the corner. Lori was pushed into the backseat.

"Let's take care of your wound, Miss Hopkins." He flipped open a leather wallet to a badge. "CIA. We got word you were being followed." He returned the wallet to his jacket pocket. A light brown comb-over gave him a nondescript appearance. Penetrating, cold gray eyes were difficult to read.

Lori pressed against her bleeding leg. "I shot him in the chest."

"Your second fire missed. I killed him." He applied a compress. "Let's get you to a hospital."

They traveled to a remote medical facility behind a fenced-in property ten miles from center city Tokyo. A sign designated the area as a research center. An American nurse tended to Lori's leg and bandaged it up. No other information was offered. No names were given, not even the agent that saved her life, or the other, Barbara Wilkins, that called for a tail when Lori left the discotheque.

Hours later, back in her hotel room, a whirl of images—dark alleys, shadows, and flashing lights—prevented sleep. Insomnia—a personal curse. Lori craved just one pill, knowing the consequences. Tossing and turning, she dozed at 4:00 a.m. with a hotel wake-up call scheduled two hours later.

The Cherry Blossom Festival rekindled a spirit of joy. Lori hopped a train to Shinjuku Gyoen, a Tokyo park, and viewed the impressive display of one thousand various species of sakura trees and their profusion of dainty pink and white blossoms against a rising sun and blue skies. Perfect weather and a perfect day for a spring picnic. She balanced photos of nature's flowering canopy against unpacked bento boxes with noodles, rice, and pickled vegetables on blankets serving as tablecloths. In the afternoon, she visited outlying areas for a rural take on the blossoms. Back to nature and its short-lived beauty.

The day before leaving Japan, Barbara took a train to Akita and waited for the mule—a Japanese college student paid generously to deliver a manila envelope in a backpack. Her instructions were to drop the envelope with *Donations for Peace* written on the outside. A college professor told her it was for the convent and their missionary work. A former spook, he shed his retirement status when called upon.

The mule, a petite female with a charcoal-colored perm, stood at the chapel's offertory box nailed to a wall. If the mule had gotten nosey and opened the envelope, she would've found a check payable to the church of her destination. Invisible ink verified names of American industry leaders tied to the Japanese mob. They included car manufacturers, investors, and stockbrokers. Corruption reigned when it involved making money. As instructed, the mule opened the lid and dropped in the envelope.

Nearly thirty years had passed since Barbara entered a confessional box. The last time was at age sixteen following a night of under-age drinking and French kissing a boy named Roger she met at a high school dance. The drinking she had confessed; the rest she'd added silently with an Act of Contrition prayer.

The kneeler carried the weight of revealed sins. She was willing, if not ready, to bear her own with precious time to prepare mentally or spiritually.

Knowing her brother was on the other side of the confessional offered little comfort. Years ago, she had planned to tell him of her secret life, but not in this way. A shaft of opaque light entered as the shutter opened, baring a profiled silhouette, head bent down awaiting the confessor.

Father Gerry murmured, "Be at peace with your Lord and Savior."

Barbara, hearing her brother's voice, fell silent.

"You may begin," Father Gerry said. Again, silence.

"I don't . . ." She faltered. "It's been thirty years since my last confession. I kill. I mean, I've killed, for my country. I work for the CIA. For many years now."

"Self-defense?"

"No. Not really. Cold-blooded murder," she confessed with no emotion.

"Are you remorseful?" Father Gerry asked.

"I'm not supposed to feel anything. I serve my country. Is that a sin?"

"It's not a sin to serve your country. You're fighting a war. I'm a servant of God. He absolves, not me."

Father Gerry's brow beaded with sweat. He was sure he recognized the voice. Not at first, but when she uttered, "cold-blooded murder," his mind reeled. He experienced a sudden pang of insecurity and called upon the Holy Spirit for renewed strength, grace, and enlightenment.

"I don't know what's in my future. But I do feel pain, incredible pain. A hit last week in Japan. An American. He almost blew my cover."

"Is there anything else?" He spoke in a muted tone, as if the world was listening in.

"Isn't that enough?"

"For your penance, say four Our Fathers and four Hail Marys. Do you know the Act of Contrition?"

"No, Father."

She sounded childlike, and a jolt of empathy entered his heart. "Please recite from the prayer card on the ledge."

She prayed. He listened and made a furtive promise to recite three rosaries for her that evening.

Father Gerry raised a hand. "God, the Father of mercies, through the death and resurrection of His Son, has reconciled the world to Himself and sent the Holy Spirit among us for the forgiveness of sins; through the ministry of the Church may God give you pardon and peace." He made the sign of the cross. "I absolve you from your sins in the name of the Father, and of the Son, and the Holy Spirit. Go in peace."

"Thank you, Father." She rose from the kneeler.

"Pray for me," he added. The sliding panel closed. The sanctifying grace endured.

After Evening Prayer, Father Gerry prepared his homily for Sunday mass. He wrote down his favorite passage from Paul's First Epistle to Timothy and reflected on the words. *"Be strong in the grace that is in Christ Jesus."* The same words, *Be Strong,* that had prompted him to write a note to a young, heartbroken Lori. He penned a note with the words from Holy Scripture and addressed an envelope to his sister, Barbara Wilkins.

Chapter 35

Horse of a Different Color

A practical man, Preston Rogers chose a burial plot for his baby sister, Norma, when she first entered the insane asylum. She outlived him, his wife, Merle, and their son, Jake, before giving up the ghost.

At the cemetery, Barbara and Father Gerry walked hand in hand, reconnecting to summer childhood days. "I confessed something years ago. Do you . . ."

Father Gerry released her hand. "I'll tell you a story."

Barbara dug deep into her raincoat pockets. "So you're not going to answer me."

"A French saint. Margaret Mary Alacoque claimed to have apparitions of Jesus. No one believed her."

Barbara picked at the lint in her pocket. "Sorry, Father, but I'm not feeling the connection here." Slowly, she walked ahead.

"A priest said to ask what his last mortal sin was when she next saw Our Savior. So she asked Jesus, and He answered, 'I don't remember.'"

Barbara, a few feet away, turned toward him. "That's your answer?"

"There's more." He bent his head in a prayerful manner.

"I'm all ears." She shuffled the dirt at her feet.

"If you, O Lord, should mark iniquities . . ."

"Who could stand? Psalm 130. I have it framed. A gift from a friend." Barbara sighted storm clouds gathering in the distance. "I once heard that sorrow washes away sins. What if there's no sorrow?"

"A woman washed the feet of our Lord with her tears and dried them with her hair. That's sorrow."

"You lost me."

"Find your sorrow and bring it to the feet of Jesus."

Struck by the message's simplicity, Barbara welled up with unforeseen remorse at Norma Wilkins's gravesite. Hatred for her mother's mental illness had tarnished her visits as she left behind hurtful words for a sad woman with a tattered brain. She had purged anger and frustration between the walls of the sanitarium. Bitterness too.

"Father? I think I found it." Cherishing his company, she added, "You're who you were meant to be. Who am I?"

"The same."

A misty rain settled upon the burial ground. The gathering, their cousins, Samuel and Mary Ellen, and a handful of mental institution staff, had dispersed fifteen minutes earlier. Father Gerry widened his sturdy umbrella, a Christmas gift from a parishioner. Its span was enough for two. Barbara buttoned up her raincoat with its tiny white dots against cocoa brown.

"Babs. You always liked polka dots."

She linked arms with him. "And you white collars."

On a Saturday afternoon, Father Gerry sat in the confessional box and called upon the Holy Spirit as the panel slid open and shut. Penitents whispered their transgressions, many convicting spouses, neighbors, co-workers, or strangers who'd invoked their wrath and led them to a sinful response. Each confession concluded with a sign of the cross and absolution.

A male youth entered the confessional, his voice cracking between manhood and adolescence. "Father, I'm sick. I have AIDS."

"Having AIDS is not a sin."

"I don't know where to start."

"God loves you and is all mercy. But you must have contrition."

"I feel like I'm being punished, Father."

Head bent low, Father Gerry prayed fervently for the penitent. "God tests us, but you need to confess your sins to receive absolution."

"I have sex with people I don't love."

Father Gerry said, "You've made a good confession. Is there anything else?"

A minute passed by. "I had sex after I found out about my disease."

The priest understood how sin affects the entire body of Christ, rippling like an undercurrent with souls drifting to their demise. If only more of the faithful believed in the sacramental power of reconciliation. Confession was not a time for counseling, and Father Gerry was confident that the Holy Spirit would guide the penitent soul into the next step of his conversion.

March of 1984 went out like a lion in mid-roar. A spring blizzard crippled most of the Northeast and buried many areas in two feet of snow. One million people experienced the biggest blackout in years. In New England, gale force currents kept travelers' advisories in effect for days. Fierce winds shattered windows in downtown Boston and other cities. Tornadoes killed at least sixty-nine people in the Carolinas.

Lori's flight to Boston Logan International Airport from her Badlands shoot was delayed by whiteout conditions. She'd arranged to attend Bernadette's retirement party, thirty plus years at the same literary publication. Her husband Bill taught music at the same academy. They lived in the same apartment Lori had visited so often in the ups and downs of life. Bernadette, her rock of refuge. Her stability.

"Bernie, I hear it's the worst blizzard since 1978. Three feet of snow." Lori studied her chipped nail polish and decided on a manicure.

"Yeah, the Boston Tea Party ship broke away from its mooring. It's frightful up here. My retirement party's canceled until mid-April. Can you make it?"

"I wouldn't miss it. I'll see you then. I have a few photo shoots lined up, but I can juggle my schedule."

Spring's arrival was eagerly awaited by winter weary Easterners. Back in Manhattan, Lori immersed herself in a ritual cleaning, clearing away old magazines, dust bunnies, and packing up clothes for donations. A phone ring interrupted her concentration. At first annoyed, she brightened up with the sound of Tally's voice. They jabbered like old times.

"Let's set a date. I'm booked solid with shoots right now. Can you meet up in Boston?" Lori asked.

"Sure! Summer, when I'm not teaching."

News traveled fast that Paragon Park was closing permanently. Lori learned of it from Bernadette, who mailed an article featuring its history and plans for dismantling and selling off amusement rides.

In April, a postcard, worn and frayed, arrived in Lori's mail. An old-fashioned illustration of Paragon Park's celebrated carousel graced the front. A tiny inscription said, *The Philadelphia Toboggan Company, 1928.* She recognized the handwriting: *Meet me at the Carousel, July 25, 2 p.m.*

The carousel was resplendent. Tally sat sidesaddle waving her arms like a flagger on an airport runway. She yelled out. "I knew you'd be here!"

Lori climbed on a horse, its nostrils splayed as if crossing the finished line. "You did say regrets only. Sorry I'm late."

"Only five minutes. I expected it."

They reached out and held hands. The years in between melted like wax with each bob of the horses.

"You've been through so much, Lori. If I could take away your pain . . ."

"You already have. Your invitation. Let's enjoy the ride."

"What's going on with you? Anyone in your life?"

Lori smirked. "That's a horse of a different color."

Tally squeezed Lori's hand with reassurance and filial love that defied words. With a sudden release, Lori gripped the pole. "I married a man I didn't love. How foolish . . ."

"Did you give it a chance? Maybe over time . . ."

"Tally, it was a mistake. I rushed into it . . ."

"Okay, I won't dig . . ."

"Tally? I'm okay . . ."

"You say that a lot . . ."

"I am. I'm okay with mistakes." She stretched her right arm and touched the brass ring on their last go round.

Tally tilted back as the carousel ride slowed to a stop. "Lori, you're the best. Always and forever."

Lori jumped down. "No, you are."

And the two were transported to a carefree, happy summer day in 1956 when pain and sorrow were ameliorated by a pact between budding friends. They were schoolgirls again, unafraid of silly antics, secret wishes revealed, or the critical eye of their peers. They quoted the best of literature from senior year in high school. A cap for life's many episodes.

"The heart was made to be broken. Who said it?" Lori asked.

Tally answered. "Easy one, Oscar Wilde. Okay. Never allow someone to be your priority while allowing yourself to be their option."

"Ah, one of my favorites. Mark Twain," Lori said. "Last one. Don't cry because it's over. Smile because it happened."

Tally curtsied. "Dr. Seuss!"

Even!" Lori exclaimed.

"Steven!"

Tally and Lori joined hands and continued their walk down memory lane.

Early Monday morning, October 7, 1984, three years after President Anwar Sadat's assassination, Lori landed in Egypt. This time, it was Rami, Miriam's son, who sent the invitation. He signaled to her at the arrival gate. Lori recognized him immediately. Neither had changed much in nearly ten years.

"How are things, Rami? How's Miriam?"

"My mom had pneumonia last winter into spring. Coughing spells kept her awake most nights. I stayed with her."

On the drive through Cairo, a mélange of old and new, rich and poor, Lori flashed back to her touring with Peter and Rami, far removed from the present.

"Lots happening here in Egypt."

Rami grinned. He grew more handsome with age, like fine wine. "President Mubarak promises changes. So much poverty here in Cairo. I was at the parade three years ago when Anwar was shot. A celebration of the Yom Kippur War in 1973. Men dressed like soldiers opened fire from a truck. Total chaos. The fundamentalist Muslims are growing, Lori."

When they entered the apartment, Miriam sat like an empress awaiting her royal subjects. She wore an emerald-green dressing gown embroidered in gold. Lori guessed the color was her favorite, calling back to their first meeting in Portugal. A Bible sat in her lap, its leather covering worn and its pages yellowed and creased. Her former beauty unmarred, smooth cheeks of light olive skin. Her hair, pulled back, had a few gray strands.

"It's been too long, dear one." Miriam, now eighty-seven, was less vibrant but her lambent eyes glimmered like a candle burning brightly.

"Yes, Miriam. Too long. Rami tells me you've been ill since last winter."

Before the fifth and final call to Islamic prayer, Lori became privy to the whole story. They talked of faith, failures, forgiveness, and fortitude in their private lives. Miriam contracted a disease destroying her liver after being hospitalized outside of Cairo while visiting friends. The resident doctor insisted that her dizzy spells were caused by dehydration, and she drank tainted water carrying a virus.

"How ironic, isn't it, that water which gives life is now destroying me."

"I'm so sorry, Miriam. It seems so unfair . . ." She wanted to rail against the doctors or staff who gave her friend infectious water. Such an injustice!

"Rami takes good care of me."

"I'll stay with you, Miriam. As long as you want."

Lori rearranged her work schedule. She ran errands, took Miriam for walks, prayed with her, and comforted her while Rami traveled for three weeks on a film shoot.

On his return, Miriam rested all day. Rami fixed Lori a casual meal of homemade hummus, grilled pita bread, and mahshi—roasted red peppers stuffed with rice. While Miriam slept, he broached an unavoidable topic, the elephant in the room.

"I should have warned you, Lori . . ."

"That my husband's gay?"

"He's no longer your husband."

She spread hummus over the grilled bread. "Eat while it's hot."

Rami didn't dish out anything for himself. "His parents were accepting, but his grandmother held a trust for him, and I can't believe I'm telling you this, but—"

"Then don't." Lori talked between bites, the first she'd eaten all day.

"Lori, I have to tell you because it's only fair."

"Fair?" Lori tossed a gold linen napkin in the middle of her plate and chuckled. "I gave up on that one a long time ago." She picked up the discarded cloth and dabbed her lips. "We make choices, good and bad. But you know, Rami, it all works out."

"Peter's trust money kicked in when he got married. He told his grandmother, on her death bed, that you annulled the marriage."

"Well, he didn't lie about that one."

"Lori, he's a good person. I think he did love you, but he should never have married you."

"You've got it wrong, Rami, I should not have married him. I could have said no. I actually did at first. It was my choice. A reckless decision."

"Lori, don't judge us or yourself."

"I'm not! Are you two together?"

"No, I don't have a partner. I'm single. I have many friends and a good life."

Lori esteemed the man who only sought peace for loved ones and comfort for his mother in her final days. His eyes, dark and luminous, glistened with tears. He opened his arms for an embrace, hurting for her, hurting for Miriam, and anyone shunned by society.

"You're a good soul, Rami. Let me stay here with Miriam."

"She's in caring hands with you, Lori. Your timing is God's timing."

Lori held vigil until the last beat of Miriam's strong heart. For once, she watched the stages of dying, the human body shutting down, the unceasing vigil of prayers, the sacramental anointing of the sick, and all the phases of awaiting death. And she experienced an overwhelming peace. This Miriam was not taken from her in a violent tunnel of wind. This Miriam did not leave the world suddenly like Grandma Lottie while Lori shopped for the holiday season. This Miriam died a happy death surrounded by loved ones and Lori, a friend from across the world.

Rami drove Lori to the airport. "Your time with my mom was a grace, yes, a grace." He stopped at the departure gates terminal. "Probably won't see you again."

She kissed him on both cheeks. "Never doubt, Rami. Maybe God's got something else up His sleeves."

"Yes, and He's got very long sleeves!"

He unloaded her luggage from his trunk. They embraced like kindred spirits from mother to son to friend to destiny.

Chapter 36

A Lone Star

Goodbyes filled the ensuing years. In 1986, Grandma Penny died of old age, a diagnosis met with skepticism by the Hopkins family.

Ben criticized the brash neophyte doctor for his lack of bedside manner and accuracy. "No one dies of old age," he said. "Glad he's not a surgeon."

"Mom was ninety-six, Ben. It's possible." Portia Rose resigned to her given name. She bore the most children, six girls, of the Hopkins siblings. Most likely none would carry the family surname with their own progeny. A minor triumph for Portia.

At the funeral viewing, Lori greeted kinfolk, many unfamiliar to her, especially Portia's daughters, referred to as "the garden" by a handful of cousins.

"Hi, Lori! You remember my girls? Lily, Daisy, Iris, Marigold, Violet, and Zinnia," said Portia. Lori nodded a greeting and took a seat in a corner until Bernadette caught up with her.

"You okay?" Bernadette, petite and spry as the first day Lori met her, was becoming more like her mother Penny. Grandma Lottie would say with a trace of her Virginia drawl, "the apple doesn't fall far from the tree."

"Yes, I'm fine, Bernie. I'm glad I spent time with Gran this summer, and I'm glad you didn't put her in a nursing home. I can't imagine . . ."

"It was rough, but we pulled through. The old Yankee spirit."

"Remember you're talkin' to a Texan. Although it seems a million miles away."

"Do you think you'll ever go back?"

"Why? I have nothing there."

On November 9, 1989, East Berlin's Communist Party allowed its citizens to cross the country's borders, the first crumble of the Wall built on August 13, 1961 that cordoned off West Berlin.

With the Cold War essentially over, Barbara Wilkins retired from the CIA in January 1991. She accepted a faculty appointment at Texas A&M University, the first public institution of higher education in the Lone Star state. Now a former agent in her midfifties and strong enough to compete in a triathlon, she taught political science and spoke freely of past missions minus names, faces, and details.

On a mild October morning, Lori sorted the usual pile of monthly bills, ad circulars, and a few trade magazines. She checked her mailbox twice a week, Tuesdays and Fridays, more than enough for someone who disliked opening envelopes. She read the *New York Post* and *Wall Street Journal* to stay current. Lori picked up a small envelope. An invitation. A clown held a bouquet of blue, yellow, and red balloons. A party for a grandniece or grandnephew in Boston? The RSVP phone number was Texas.

"How'd you find me?" Lori read the card again.

"Old habits die hard." Barbara studied her lesson plan for the following day's lecture and propped the phone receiver under her neck.

"Am I really invited to a birthday party?"

"If you want. We'll talk when I see you. Take care, Lori."

Lubbock. Once home. The arranged meeting's location, inconvenient for both of them, intrigued Lori. With a New York home base, she missed the Texas heat every now and then, especially at Christmas during bitterly cold winters.

On a fall day, when leaves showcased their brilliance, Lori strolled through Central Park, an urban sanctuary in the midst of teeming traffic, honking horns, and sirens. Mid-October was Lori's reflective time before the holiday sweep—Halloween, Thanksgiving, and Christmas.

The plane hit ground like landing on a pillow. Lori didn't stir until passengers wrestled with overhead bins. Lubbock, Texas, a reminder of total loss, a ghost town in her mind, filled her with dread and wonder of her own perseverance. On her journey, she reconciled with God that her strength was in recognizing her weaknesses. A paradox. Each return to Texas was a different experience. This time it was cloaked in mystery. Why would Barbara invite her for a visit? What would she confide that couldn't be communicated by phone?

She had a pang of foreboding while exiting the airport in her rental car. Could it be news about Father Gerry? Usually, bad news was shared in personal meetings if and when possible. Good news traveled joyfully over phone wires and mailed announcements. How bad could it be? She steeled herself for a dose of sadness. Life's bitter pills made her more resilient.

They met at the ranch Barbara and Gerry called home. Uncle Preston and Aunt Merle were dead and buried. The grown children and grandchildren wanted nothing to do with the inherited piece of land, a prime slice of real estate. No doubt it would sell in a heartbeat with the influx of transplants from every which way into Texas.

Lori drove up in a white Honda Accord. If she counted her rental cars over the years and the added expenses of gas and mileage, she could make a down payment on the ranch herself. Her thoughts turned to Gerry, the boy brave enough to approach giggly, self-conscious teenage girls at a cafeteria table. The boy who passed her a note the first day at school after the storm. The boy destined to serve God and shepherd His flock.

Barbara waved from the porch. "How was your flight?"

"I wouldn't know. I slept." Lori noticed the *For Sale* sign. "Any buyers?"

"Yeah, a few. I'll miss the old place." She extended both hands in welcome. "Thanks for coming."

"So why all the mystery?"

Barbara gestured after a brief hug. "Let's go inside so I can breathe in some stale memories."

A tiny, secret part of Lori hoped for a surprise with Gerry sitting at a table to greet them. Although sparsely furnished, the space, empty of life, awaited a new family story.

"Thanks again for coming. You could've said no."

Lori took a seat. "And then what?"

Barbara opened a dusty shade for early afternoon light. "Not sure. Guess it doesn't matter."

Lori observed the former CIA agent so accustomed to spying as everyday life that she lured everyone into her web of intrigue. Today, she was all business and pragmatic.

"There are two things I want to share." Barbara marched to and fro, addressing her points as if lecturing to her students. "First, Gerry, Father Gerry, only has a few months. Full-blown AIDS from Vietnam."

"Vietnam?" The shocking news struck her. "But that was so long ago."

"A blood transfusion when he was released from the prison camp. It contained the virus." She continued, "There's a stigma . . ."

"I'm so sorry. What's he afraid of? It's not anything he's done."

"The bishop asked him to keep quiet about his illness."

"Where is he?"

"Africa right now."

"Isn't that where the virus started?"

"First detected in 1920 in the Congo. It's been around longer than people know. He's helping other AIDS patients live out their last days."

Lori thought of Damien, the Belgian priest who contracted leprosy from the diseased he served and lived amongst in Molokai, Hawaii.

"I'm sorry, Barbara." She paused. "You said there were two reasons you wanted to meet."

Barbara reached in her hip pocket. "Remember the locket you gave back to him?"

"You mean threw at him?"

"Here." She extended her palm. "He wants you to have it. And a note."

Lori grasped the locket in one hand and opened the folded paper, which read, *Whom should I fear? No one!*

Barbara wiped away a tear. "Okay, my job is done. Let's eat. I'm famished." She brushed fine dirt off her gray slacks. "Where to?"

"I'm new in town."

"Yeah, me too."

They hugged like long lost comrades, or even sisters.

"Your car or mine?"

"Mine. I like these rentals close by." Lori clasped the locket around her neck. She read the note once more and stuffed it in her purse.

Later in the evening, Lori drove by Grandma Lottie's house. A retired café owner and his wife rented the property arranged by a real estate management firm.

The ghosts were never too far away. Lottie, her guardian, her foundation, the beginning of a new life—London, Paris, Rome, and Prague, and then back to Texas. Home. Now home was a New York apartment or a rental car with Sandra Dee. Someday, she'd settle down. Maybe New York. Maybe Texas. Maybe somewhere in between.

After Barbara's retirement, CIA agent Tom Phillips informed her of an ongoing assignment wrap-up. The message was in his code name from their Vietnam mission. "You want this one, Babs. You were on his trail for years."

They met at a park bench in Washington, DC, three days later. Phillips drank coffee from a thermos. Barbara read a newspaper. "Who'd you bait?"

"Dressmaker in Lisbon. Her daughter was his mistress. Mom agreed to have the daughter's apartment wired. Finds out he's married. He's all yours."

In a barren room, the double agent slumped in his chair. Barbara observed him via a two-way mirror. *"As parades tem ouvidos."*

"Who's that?" His tone was commanding and belligerent.

"Your cover's blown, Adriano. We have enough to execute. No country wants a traitor."

"Who are you?"

"You'll be tried for treason. You're a spy without a home."

At Washington, DC headquarters, Barbara opened the top-secret file listing Adriano Peres, a.k.a. Antonio Lanzetti. Aside from his work with the KGB, he had a substantiated list of crime victims. She traced her finger to *Miss Lori Hopkins, American citizen, 1968* and said a prayer of thanksgiving. The first in a very long time.

Chapter 37

Eye Witness

In rapid sequence, the inevitable arrived. Digitalized images replaced film and negatives with mixed reviews. Some photographers believed the darkroom spelled the Dark Ages of the film world.

Ben Hopkins was eighty years old when he "hung up his boots." He couldn't utter "retirement" and "photography" in the same breath. He counted on his now middle-aged protégé to adopt his kids—cameras that made every day worth waking up to with surprises, disappointments, and manifold joys behind their lenses.

His wife, Kathleen, retired from professional golf, wanted to clear away clutter, including unused photography equipment. Her notion of photography was capturing Kodak moments with an instant camera for developing at any convenient drugstore.

On a Saturday morning, April 29, 1995, Lori hesitantly agreed to meet Ben at his Boston studio, a corner building. Word got to her that Ben planned to unload his extensive camera collection. She hoped her reluctance wouldn't be obvious, as she mentioned to Bernadette the previous night in her apartment.

"Fair warning. He can't part with his stuff and Kathy won't even let him store it in their basement."

"Well, I can understand both sides," Lori said.

"And they have no kids to pawn it off on."

Lori chewed on a piece of day-old Boston brown bread. "That's pretty blunt."

"You know what I mean." Bernadette cleared away dishes. *Still like a bird*, thought Lori. No wonder she's rail thin. Busy like her mom. They were more like sisters than aunt and niece. "Oh, did you hear Giuseppe is in town? He went to Italy to visit *la famiglia* and returned with a wife half his age. She's a runway model from Milan."

"So happy for him." After wiping off the counter, Lori stood in the archway facing Bernadette's living room, her sanctuary when she returned from London, emptied of life with a resolve to begin again. So many beginnings. Now, she was vexed by any Boston news. She loved the Hopkins family for seeing her through the worst of times but always felt on the periphery raised apart from the clan of cousins. Even so, Boston was her touchstone for family ties.

Lori evaluated her uncle's studio. "What are you going to do with this stuff, Ben?"

"You'll think of something." Ben exuded the same sureness in his eighties as he did at forty. What he didn't realize was that Lori tired of her days behind the lens as well.

"I have more equipment than I need."

"So does every photographer."

"What about this studio?" She wandered amongst shelves of equipment, a veritable museum. "Wow, a Kodak Brownie Starflash!" She examined the red and white camera. "Coca-Cola model!"

"Yup, manufactured from October 1959 to December 1960."

"Ben, you have a museum here."

"Why don't you open one?"

"Wait, now you want me to open up a museum?"

"Sure. Why not? Rent free!" Ben's eyes twinkled like a leprechaun extending his pot of gold. "You could live upstairs. No one can explain all of my kids like you."

"Boston?" A long silence. "The winters?"

Ben gave his best nothing-is-impossible shrug. "Make it seasonal."

Boston. Texas. New York. A three-sided coin toss. "Hmm . . . I'll think it over."

Ben clasped his hands as he worked his magic. "Wonderful! Now I have one more request. Not to spring the spring ball on you, but Kathy has a bad sinus infection. Would you attend with me tonight? It's at the Boston Ballet and begins at eight o'clock. Plenty of time."

"Uh, I don't have a gown."

"You can wear Kathy's. You're the same size."

Lori staggered and leaned against a shelf. She detested gowns and ballrooms that ripped open wounds she thought healed. "Sorry, Ben. I'm feeling a little dizzy."

"Here, sit. Probably all of this dust. It needs a spring cleaning."

Without knowing why, she heard her answer, as if from an unfamiliar voice. "Yes, I'll go."

"Great! I'll pick you up at seven from Bernie's."

"I'll need the gown."

The wry leprechaun wore an impish grin. "I dropped it off at Bernie's. You're all set! We can dance the night away to the music by Four Guys in Tuxes."

Lori stopped and bought silver shoes to match the dress as described by Ben. The gown, an A-Line off-the-shoulder of navy chiffon, hung on Bernadette's bedroom door.

"You look totally rad, Lori." Bernadette fastened a metal hook.

Lori swung around. "Rad? That's so eighties!"

"So's the dress." Bernadette cackled.

"You're a pip, Bernie!" Lori slipped on her shoes and brushed cheeks with her favorite aunt.

After two dances, Ben introduced Lori to South End Historical Society members who talked passionately about preserving old factory buildings targeted for demolition. A man in his late fifties and an exotic female half his age approached her from across the room, obviously spotting her first.

"Ah, Princess Lorena. You look wonderful!" Giuseppe raised her hand and kissed it. The woman by his side resembled a feline—green eyes, large dilated pupils, stalking her prey, and raven hair brushed away from prominent features. "Darling, this is a friend of mine from thirty years ago."

"My goodness, I wasn't alive when you two met. Are you really a princess?"

Lori guessed she knew the answer and inquired purely to add weight to a leaden situation. Her Italian accent was thick, but her message was clear. She didn't welcome the introduction.

"Oh, I believe Giuseppe calls everyone Princess. I'm Lori."

"Giselda. Pleased to meet you. Giuseppe, shall we dance?"

Giuseppe winked at Lori and moved to the dance floor. Ben approached her with a glass of champagne. "Isn't that . . . ?"

"Yes, one and the same. Are we staying much longer?" She recalled the candid photos she snapped of Giuseppe in her college days. He was a natural. The camera caressed him, and his magnetic quality hadn't diminished. Yet, she felt empathy for Gio. He seemed lost and easily carried away by his beguiling effect on everyone in his path. What was the word? *Ungrounded.*

Ben reached into his tuxedo's inside pocket. "Lori, I know you have more equipment than you need. But, please, consider the museum. Oh, and here's something you don't have." He handed her the wrapped package.

"You found it!"

"You know?"

"I thought it was gone forever." She placed the champagne glass on a high table and hastily opened the surprise.

The silver teaspoon defined innocent and simpler days before covering a war and fighting personal demons. "Uncle Ben, it's still my best work. Turtle on a Teaspoon." She hugged him like a child at Christmas who got her first wish from Santa.

"I found it while cleaning out my shop."

"I'm considering the museum."

"And?"

"Boston winters are a deal breaker. I'll run the shop from May to September, but you'll need to find someone else . . ."

"Deal!" said Ben. They shook hands, as business partners.

"Where will you live the rest of the year?"

Lori watched the Italian lovebirds perform a perfect foxtrot. She assumed Gio and his model wife enrolled in ballroom lessons. "Not sure."

"Keeping secrets?" Ben noticed her distracted gaze.

Lori grinned. "I come by it honestly."

"Welcome back."

Ben suggested Museum Pieces. Lori countered with Eye Witness and insisted on supplying the latest digital camera equipment. "We can't only run a museum. We need inventory."

Ben conceded. "I won't fight you. So tell me. Where are you headed in October?"

She confided that Peter and she had dined recently in New York. His longtime partner and he split up. Peter traveled most of the month on multiple film projects and had persuaded Lori to apartment-sit while he was away . . .

"We won't even be ships that pass in the night," Peter had said.

"It's temporary, Peter."

"So's my apartment. I'm moving to Hawaii in three years."

Lori had recognized the restless spirit she witnessed in their short-lived marriage. "That's pretty far off."

"Not really. I bought property, and I'm building a house. I'll be out of Manhattan before the new millennium. If we all live that long."

Eternal youthfulness had emanated from a suntanned face and golden curls. The sun god. Yes, Hawaii would suit Prince Charming. "Peter. Be strong."

He raised his eyebrows.

"I always wanted to use that on someone," Lori said.

"Anyone?"

She echoed his words. "Not really."

A smile in his eyes that reflected her own. A new trust sealed with faith, hope, and charity. All from God.

The Eye Witness Camera Shop and Museum kept Lori in Beantown, close to familial life and death events—holy communions, confirmations, wedding showers, baby showers, baptisms, and funerals for generations of Hopkins. Ben scheduled Tuesdays at noon to check in. They spent time over lunch discussing family matters and the apex of their careers.

Settled into their usual booth, Lori ordered the same sandwich week after week—corned beef on rye and a side of slaw. Ben cajoled their regular waitress. "What's the special, Wendy? I'll kick the bucket soon, so give me the best sandwich money can buy. But no onions."

The waitress drummed him lightly with the menu. "You say that every week, Ben."

"What was your best?" Lori unrolled utensils from her paper napkin.

"What? Sandwich?"

Lori groaned. "Photo shoot! Your best."

Ben allotted Wendy a thumbs-up to his heaping plate of lobster salad. "Had to be Easter Island. Not sure it was my best, but nothing like it in the world. There are nine hundred statues on an island in the middle of nowhere. It's a five-hour flight over the Pacific. How 'bout you?"

"Hoping my best is yet to come."

"I have to ask you, Lori. The name Eye Witness. Anything to do with what you've seen? Where you've been?"

"Like Forrest Gump in the movie?"

Ben chuckled. "Well, I'm not saying that, but you've seen history through the lens."

"Yup. Like St. Augustine wrote. 'The world is a book . . .'"

Ben lifted his Sam Adams Boston Lager. "'. . . and those who do not travel read only one page.'"

In 1999, Peter moved to Hawaii with intentions of a blowout millennial party at his plantation-sized mansion with pineapple fields. He urged Lori to fly out and join the celebration as they packed up the apartment and marveled how they had only encountered each other a handful of times during her six-month stays. "C'mon, Lori, it'll be much bigger than the bicentennial!"

"You had to mention that one? I'll pass, thanks."

In September 1999, Lori bid goodbye to Boston and Eye Witness Camera Shop and Museum and returned full-time to Manhattan's Upper East Side. Urban life had agreed with her. The wide expanse of Texas evoked memories of loss.

The twenty-first century reeled with technological transformation and "planned obsolescence" drilled into the social psyche. Emails usurped the intimacy of handwritten letters and postcards. Buzz words included "wireless." Mobile phones substituted as cameras and video recorders. Digital photography's full impact didn't occur until the first decade of the new century.

Ben Hopkins joined the ranks of eyewitnesses to his own milestone event. At the age of eighty-five, he stayed with Lori and attended a lifetime achievement award ceremony in New York City. The dinner celebration occurred on Sunday, September 9, 2001. He arrived on Saturday and planned to leave on September 11. Early in the morning, he phoned for a taxi to JFK airport, insisting that Lori rest up. The heavens, brilliant and blue, greeted commuters. On the FDR Drive, along Manhattan's East Side, he witnessed the first plane hit the North Tower of the World Trade Center. Nothing in his eight decades of experience behind a lens had prepared him for terrorism.

In Lori's apartment, they watched the shocking replays. American Airlines Flight 11 departed Logan airport in Boston at 7:59 a.m. The Boeing 767 plane, en route to Los Angeles, had a crew of eleven and seventy-six passengers, not including five hijackers. Film cameras captured the grim episodes, bedlam, and bravery, even though digital images were prolific in news stories and magazines. Ben phoned Bernadette in Boston to inform her that he and Lori were fine. Lori got a call from Tally, now living in Oklahoma. They promised, once she retired, to reconnect via a road trip.

"Well, Lori, I'm now an eyewitness to a single moment. I've joined your ranks," Ben said.

"You saw so much in war."

"Nothing like what I saw today."

At eighty-seven, Ben died after a year-long battle with lung cancer. All the Hopkins brood, those in Boston, including children, grandchildren, and great-grandchildren, gathered outside his hospital room. Bernadette and Lori were there at the final moments. On September 14, 2003, hours before Lori's sixty-second birthday, Ben Hopkins gave up the ghost.

The next ten years, Lori traveled the world five times over and built a legacy her Uncle Ben would be proud of before she hung up her own boots. She never declared her favorite photo shoot to anyone and was quoted in a trade magazine upon her retirement: "They're all my favorite."

Chapter 38

Moore Troubles

April was Lori's favorite month in Manhattan with walks in Central Park as trees sprouted their greenery.

Tally pulled up in front of the Rockefeller Center, their planned rendezvous, at the wheel of a 1966 Thunderbird.

Lori stood in wonder and shook her head. She wheeled a compact traveling suitcase at her side and Sandra Dee in tow. "Are you serious?"

"Hop in, you two, before a taxi hits me!"

"What on earth? Do you really think you'll get us all the way to Oklahoma?"

"Sure as shootin'! It's in tip-top condition, like the one in the movie, *Thelma & Louise.*"

Lori tucked Sandra Dee's cage in the backseat and hopped in the front. "You're not planning the same ending are you?"

Tally threw back her head and laughed. "No thanks. I like happy endings."

"Well, some folks might think the car-over-the-cliff ending is happy!"

"That's my Lori!" Tally winked at her friend. "Let's blow this popsicle stand."

And so the adventure wound its way south on I-95 into New Jersey and Delaware.

"Do you have a plan?" The sky was darkening to a blood-orange horizon.

"No, I thought you did. I'm just the driver."

"Are you serious?"

"Of course not. We're stopping for dinner in Maryland and then overnight in Virginia."

"Okay. So what's our route?"

"We're heading to Arkansas and over to Oklahoma, like Thelma and Louise."

"You know it's a movie, and those locations were near Los Angeles and Utah."

"Okay, so we'll pretend."

"You're a piece of work. You know that, right?" She paused and sucked in the chilled night air. "But I'll say this much, Tally, no matter what happens, I'm glad I came with you."

"Spot on from the movie!"

Lori couldn't resist, "Even the chickens under the porch know that."

The challenge was on.

Tally: "Crazy."

Lori: "One brick shy of a load."

Tally: "Two sandwiches short of a picnic."

Lori: "Finish this one. Porch light's on but . . .

Tally: "No one's home! A few pickles . . .

Lori: "Short of the barrel . . . Missing a few . . .

Tally stopped short. "I don't know that one."

Lori turned sour. "Don't lie. You know it."

Tally took the defense. "Okay, fine. Missing a few buttons off his shirt."

Lori settled in with her uneasy triumph. "Tally? Do you think she was crazy?"

Tally watched for her turnpike exit. "I didn't know your, Mom, Lori. I can't say."

Lori checked on Sandra Dee. Certain days, she wished she had a shell to slide into and escape the world. A road trip with Tally was a satisfying alternative. Dinner in a Maryland seafood restaurant was delectable. Lori was blissfully satiated and in good humor after a platter of sweet, delicately flavored crab cakes, creamy coleslaw, and a slice of deep-dish cherry pie. By nightfall, they headed into Virginia with a sky full of stars sparkling like gems hanging on a black curtain. For the first time in years, a weightless Lori—no regrets, no haunting memories, the proverbial clean slate.

On the fifth day, they crossed the state line into Arkansas. Throughout the trek, they laughed until they cried and soaked up sunrays with the convertible top down. While stopping for fuel outside of Little Rock, the gas station owner sauntered up whistling. "That's a beaut you got there, ladies. Fill 'er up?"

"Yes, sir." Tally stretched her brawny arms to the sky. Lori got out of the car and made a few waist bends.

"Yup, that sure is the Thelma and Louise Thunderbird. But you two ain't no Thelma and Louise." He put the gas hose back. "That'll be thirty-nine dollars and forty-eight cents.

Tally passed him two twenty-dollar bills. "And you ain't Brad Pitt. Keep the change." The traveling duo fist-pumped and peeled off with a final wave at the gas station owner.

On Saturday morning, May 18, they arrived at Tally's rancher in Moore, Oklahoma. Lori whistled in appreciation. "All to yourself, huh? It's pretty big."

"Well, I'm not ready for retirement living. I like seeing kids, dogs, grandmas, young couples, when I go for my walks."

"We're not old, are we, Tally?"

"Depends on who you ask."

"Well, it wouldn't be that gas station owner in Arkansas."

They giggled like schoolgirls and unpacked the car. Lori slid Sandra Dee's cage across the backseat. "She could live for another forty or fifty years. Makes me feel young."

They settled into a den crammed with board games, books, and jig-saw puzzles and talked of old times in Lubbock and the Paragon Park rendezvous.

"Can you believe it's been fifteen years?" Lori said.

"What took us so long?"

"Life. Why'd you move from Oklahoma City?" Lori perused the collection of hardback books and pulled out a classic, *Robinson Crusoe.*

"When Marty died two years ago, I wanted to start over. I like it here in Moore."

"Sorry I didn't make it to the funeral."

"Lori, it's okay. You never met the right one."

"Thanks for the reminder. There were a few . . ."

"What about the soldier?"

Lori placed the book on a rustic wooden coffee table. She opened up Sandra Dee's cage and added a garden-fresh pile of shredded cabbage and carrots. "He saved my life. Not in Vietnam, but he saved me from myself." She pointed to her head. "I'll always be grateful."

"Whatever happened?"

"Went our separate ways. Then I met Peter. He was a friend, comrade with a camera. My failed marriage."

"But that wasn't your fault."

"It's no one's fault, Tally."

"He should never have asked you to marry him." Tally saw matters as black and white.

"No, he wanted it to work. We deceive ourselves more than anyone."

Tally didn't bring up the G names—Gerald or Giuseppe.

On Saturday morning at the kitchen table, Tally scrolled through her laptop for a listing of matinees. "Let's see . . . We've got *Pain & Gain, Oblivion,* and *Iron Man 3.* Oh, and *Evil Dead, G.I. Joe: Retaliation,* and *The Croods.*"

Lori washed ceramic coffee cups at the kitchen sink.

"You know I have a dishwasher, right?" Tally glanced up from her screen.

With hands immersed in warm, sudsy water, Lori stared wistfully out the large picture window. "That's quite a field out there. Reminds me of Kansas. Why don't we stay here and read?"

Tally sagged a bit. Her favorite pastime was spending a few hours in a pitch-black theatre and digging into buttery popcorn. "My treat!"

"Okay, okay. Either *Evil Dead* or *Oblivion*."

"*Oblivion* stars Tom Cruise."

"*Evil Dead*."

"Wait!" Tally said. "How 'bout *42*?"

"Jackie Robinson bio pic. Let's do it!"

At a local diner, they hit the early bird special—spaghetti and meatballs at half price. On the way home, Lori bought a novel, *The House We Grew Up In,* at a bookstore. She curled up on a wingback chair and finished up half the book in one sitting. Tally snored lightly on the adjacent sofa. Lori covered her dear friend with a throw embroidered with *Talia & Martin.*

Turning on the hallway light, Lori returned to the kitchen window. A vast expanse of stars dotted an inky sky obscuring the simple, unadorned landscape. She stood transfixed and spotted the Big Dipper alignment. A shiver shot up her arms with no warning, and dread flooded her senses. She pulled down the white vinyl shade and walked away.

They had a late start Monday morning. Lori woke up at ten o'clock and lolled in bed. So far, the day was calm and peaceful. She was relaxed, refreshed, and ready for a stop off with Ruth Lieberman in Texas. She booked a flight for early Tuesday on Tally's insistence she spend an extra day.

Lori unfolded the newspaper on the kitchen table. "Well, you know what Benjamin Franklin said about fish and guests."

"Yeah, they both stink after three days. It's day three. You're good."

"What're you making?"

"Monkey bread."

"Oh, you didn't." Lori rubbed her eyes.

"Indulge! When did you last eat anything like monkey bread?"

"Like never."

"You stayed thin. Not like me. But I never really was . . ."

"I'm like my gran." Lori held up the tabloid. "Dr. Joyce Brothers died a week ago."

"Who's she?"

"You're kidding."

Tally shoved the monkey bread in the oven. She grinned and perused the article. "Who of a certain age doesn't know Dr. Joyce Brothers? She was mainstream. Talk shows, games shows. Remember *The $64,000 Question*? She memorized twenty volumes of encyclopedias."

"And?" Lori breathed in the intoxicating aroma of caramelized brown sugar, nuts, cinnamon, and melted butter buried in the crevices of biscuit dough.

Tally peeked inside the oven door. "Twenty more minutes." The oven door creaked shut. "Oh, she was the only woman to win the top prize. Biggest winner of television quiz shows."

"There was a big scandal with cheating . . ."

"She was cleared. But can you imagine memorizing twenty books?"

"I can barely remember what I had for dinner yesterday."

"So what else is new?" Tally watched the clock. She'd forgotten to set a timer. "I meant in the news . . ."

"Yeah, yeah." Lori cherished her friend's spark of humor and uncanny way of balancing the world.

Into the early afternoon, they pulled apart chunks of monkey bread and gulped hot, freshly brewed coffee. They debated on global warming, the state of the environment, and the country. Lori pontificated. "Tally, for every coal mine we close, three more start up in China."

Tally propped her elbows. "I can't control the world, Lori, but I can make a difference right here."

Framed by the kitchen window, the sky turned olive green. Lori noticed the change before hearing the rumble like a train speeding toward them. "It's here."

"What?" Tally bolted up. "I've never seen . . . We've got to get out of here." She pulled frantically on her friend's white cotton sweater. "Lori! The shelter under my garage. Let's go!"

"I can't . . . Leave me here, please!" She watched the deadly cone come in view.

"Are you freakin' crazy? Stop it now. Get on your feet and follow me, or by God, I'll pull you out of here by your hair." Adrenaline surges bolstered her physical strength. "I swear I'll kick your ass to get you down those stairs," she cried. No response from Lori. The roar grew louder, and the storm cast a shadow over the house. "Dear God, this is a level five. If you stay here, it's suicide, you idiot!"

Overcome by Tally's strength, Lori was swept out of the house and into the storm shelter beneath a two-car garage. The safe place was a major selling point, even though she didn't need the double garage. But living in Tornado Alley was a liability, and Tally heard news of previous tornadoes that devastated Moore at least twice in recent years.

Afterward, Tally's ranch house was a pile of sticks and rubbish. Her sense of total loss subsided as she observed her dear friend sift through the debris, like a child in search of a cherished toy. Tally bit her lip and choked back her own tears as she wiped the grime and tears from Lori's face. She embraced her tenderly. "I'm sorry I was mean and nasty. You scared me so much, Lori."

Lori stared straight ahead, as if seeing a mirage far off on the horizon. Screaming sirens pierced the resounding quiet—the aftermath. She blinked twice as slow as a normal person, and Tally acted with haste and covered Lori with a blanket before calling 911.

Chapter 39

Buttonholes

Pine Meadow Manor, an assisted living complex, annoyed Lori with its sterile, antiseptic environment and bile-colored walls. A nurse's aide, robust and plucky, greeted her. "Hi, my name's Mike. I started here last month, Ms. Hopkins."

Lori studied her playing cards. "What's that horrible smell?"

"I don't smell anything."

"Exactly. Odorless. Can't you spray a floral scent in here?"

"How 'bout we bring you fresh flowers every morning?"

Lori rearranged her solitaire deck into a winning row.

"You have a visitor. Maybe he's got flowers," Mike continued.

"Who is it?" Lori moved a line of cards.

"A priest."

"Really?"

Father Joe O'Malley, a retired clergyman, waited outside. Mike approached him. "I'm sorry, Father Joe. Ms. Hopkins isn't up for visitors today."

Father Joe was a humble wizened man of God embodying the patience of a saint. "That's okay, Mike. Another time. Thanks for asking." He checked the list of patients awaiting him and headed down the corridor whistling "White Christmas."

Two weeks later, Father Joe met fourteen-year-old Peggy Mitchell by happenstance, through Father Tim Norton, who urged him to have a meeting with her. Peggy and her accomplices, Fran and Larry, had stumbled across a bomb shelter while hiding stolen tech gadgetry until they resold the hot items.

Peggy claimed the Christmas bunker was a time capsule with a television broadcasting shows from 1955! She confided to the two priests that a girl her age appeared out of thin air in the unlit shelter and vanished at will. Peggy sought answers from the priests on the advice of her friend Fran, a lanky teenage boy with a clever mind and slothful spirit. "Her name's Lori Hopkins, and she's not a ghost," Peggy said. "She's convinced it's still 1955 and doesn't know anything about now." Peggy admitted that she and her friends, Fran and Larry, discovered the fallout shelter while hiding stolen goods. As a priest, Father O'Malley would concern himself with their criminal activity later but focused now on the description of a fourteen-year-old Lori that haunted the malcontent and sullen Peggy.

Father Joe puzzled out the case in point. "I know Lori Hopkins from Lubbock High." He collected the evidence. "Your Lori, by description, is very similar to the Lori Hopkins of sixty years ago. The only solution is to arrange a meeting."

In her first few weeks at Pine Meadow Manor, Lori dreamt of her shelter. Several nights, in her deep sleep, she descended the steep underground steps. Radiant light brightened up the bunker. Family and personal treasures materialized the way she remembered them sixty years ago. She conjured ornaments in detail, but they became nebulous an hour or so upon waking. Many mornings, after vivid dreams, Lori lay in bed for at least fifteen minutes allowing all the shelves and boxes of Christmas memories to sift through her semi-awake state. When she tried to recall the room hours later, it returned to a murky and dark space.

On an early December morning, Nurse Clara approved Father Joe's rounds. When he arrived at Lori's room, she was asleep. He turned to leave and heard a voice, faint and distant. "Yes?"

"Hello, you're the new kid on the block. I'm Father O'Malley or Father Joe, and I've come to give you communion, if you like."

Within minutes, he recalled the lively, energetic teen—a lower class-mate in high school with a starry-eyed gaze and a sprinkle of freckles on the bridge of her nose that matched strawberry blonde hair tucked neatly behind well-shaped ears. Now she appeared slack and depressed, possibly with dementia. He wasn't sure what circumstances had led her to Pine Meadow Manor.

"You're the priest who stopped by a week or so ago." Lori propped herself up and grabbed a robe draped across her comforter.

"Mind if I come in?"

"You already are, so have a seat."

Father Joe eased himself into the visitor's chair. His stiff knees were achy, a plaguing injury from a motorcycle accident in his youth.

"We went to high school together. You were a few years behind, but I remember you in the homecoming court. You wore a red dress."

Lori nodded her head. "That's right, and my date became a priest."

"Yes, Father Gerry Wilkins. We met in seminary. I heard he went to Africa."

"I'd rather leave the past alone, Father Joe. Too many memories and no place to hide from them."

"Can't hide from the past no matter where you are."

"I've made a lot of mistakes." Lori felt comforted by the gentle man.

"Without mistakes, we wouldn't know what to do or where to go next."

And the floodgates opened. All the sins Lori had confessed over a lifetime resurfaced. She repeated them methodically, offenses forgiven so many years ago in a confessional box in Prague or other instances of her spiritual journey. Stories poured out—the buttons secreted away in a bomb shelter awaiting Christmas Day with a note of apology; a mas-querade ball leaving her deeply wounded and hating a man she didn't know; prison time with the death of a man at her own hands. Now, after retelling it to Father Joe, Lori doubted her self-defense argument.

Her would-be assailant represented every man who would physically, mentally, or emotionally assault or abuse any woman.

"But you said he had a knife?" Father Joe interrupted believing there was an issue further to explore.

"Yes, and part of me wanted him to use it. I wanted him to kill me, and I've never told anyone. And I wanted to die in that storm in Moore, Oklahoma."

Father Joe uncrossed his legs to ease the pain of arthritic knees. He placed both hands on his lap.

"Your scars run deep, Lori. Why'd you want to die in Oklahoma?"

"Because I survived, and they didn't." She dropped a weighty mind on her pillow, unsure of relief or inciting further pain. Re-released memories exposed and opened up scar tissue once again.

Father Joe allowed the fresh wound of words to linger. The ensuing silence could heal, especially when the heart spoke out. Her words penetrated his own heart, and he contemplated how human suffering was a mystery. Unfounded guilt could be as destructive as real guilt, and unraveling the two was complicated. Guilty—she stole her mother's fallen buttons and hid them. Guilty—anger led her to build a defense by decorating a Christmas room in a bomb shelter, partly to punish her mother. Not Guilty—she had nothing to do with her parents' deaths, yet was inextricably entwined with the trauma itself. Loss, pain, and guilt.

"Is there anything else?" He knew better than attempting to convince her that December 18, 1955, wasn't her fault. Lori stared at a water stain on the ceiling. Father Joe made his pitch. "Lori, there's someone I'd like you to meet. Her name is Peggy Mitchell. She's fourteen." No response. "She found your bomb shelter. No one's been in there for sixty years."

"Why should I meet her?"

"She has a story to tell you. Can we set up a meeting?"

On a Sunday afternoon, Father Joe O'Malley and Peggy Mitchell walked through the doors of Pine Meadow Manor. Nurse Clara was doing a double shift and appeared spent and tired. Mike, the nurse's aide, anticipated an unpleasant exchange. The fourteen-year-old visitor exuded a stubborn, defiant nature.

Lori sat in a high-back chair with flat, wooden armrests and faded orange upholstery. Peggy sat across from her, the box of buttons in her hands. After introductions and the exchange of a few pleasantries, the defiant teen blurted out her reason for the visit. "Yes, we met when you were fourteen. You fixed up a bomb shelter for Christmas and spent hours in it. You even had a working television."

Lori mused on the improbable circumstances. "How old are you?"

"Fourteen."

"You found the shelter. I was fourteen."

"And you haven't been back."

"Only in my dreams. I'll wake up in my Christmas room, wondering why the world seemed so alarming and quiet." She refocused on the reed-thin teen. "And who are you?"

"I'm Peggy. As I said, I met you—the former you—in your shelter."

Lori reacted, her suspicion growing. "But that's impossible. Who sent you?"

In a tug of war, they pulled on opposite ends of the same story, trying to find a meeting ground other than a bomb shelter. Nothing made sense, but all the pieces fit together. Peggy knew Lori's life up to age fourteen and December 18, 1955, and about Joy Lieberman's death through research at the local library.

"I'll go if you want, but here, these are yours." Peggy extended the round container.

"My buttons. Her buttons." Sixty years gone in a blink of an eye with each round object of plastic or cloth-covered metal, fourteen in all. In Lori's mind, there was one treasured item that begged further exploration. "Are you familiar with this prayer?" Lori held out a piece of tattered paper.

Peggy's puckered lips spelled impatience. "Probably not."

"It's called St. Andrew's Prayer. We pray it fifteen times a day from November thirtieth through Christmas Eve. Would you like to read it?"

A reluctant Peggy read aloud. "Hail and blessed be the hour and moment in which the Son of God was born of the most pure Virgin Mary, at midnight, in Bethlehem, in piercing cold. In that hour, vouchsafe, O my God! To hear my prayer and grant my desires, through the merits of Our Savior Jesus Christ, and of His Blessed Mother. Amen."

"I had one special treasure," Lori added. "A statue. Do you have it with you?"

Peggy yielded. "I gave your infant statue to my little sister, Miriam. Actually, she took it, and I never, in a million years, expected to meet you in the flesh."

"Miriam. My mother's name."

"My mother's aunt's name, by marriage."

Peggy's rush of words spilled out like water from a spigot. "We're actually related by marriage. Your mother was an only child, but she married into a large family from Boston. One of the brothers, Tom Hopkins, was my mother's uncle. My sister, Miriam, was named after your mother. I checked it all out, did the ancestry thing. Tied all the strings together. Even so, it doesn't explain why in the world I would meet you in a bomb shelter. Unless it's not really you."

Lori studied the youth, barely in her teens. Angry, hurting in ways inexplicable, yet strong, determined, and unwilling to show vulnerability. She considered herself at fourteen, and the same description came to mind. She recalled the mysterious girl who appeared out of nowhere in a church in Prague. "Maybe I met you first."

The two, Lori and Peggy, bonded without knowing it. Their time together went from a tug of war to a peaceful truce and back to a tug of war, the bumpy road of trust, breakthroughs, and ultimately, friendship.

On Christmas Eve, 2015, Miriam Mitchell, a precocious five-year-old, presented a crudely wrapped package to Lori and wiped a runny nose against her free arm. "Here."

Lori held the package to her chest and let the tears flow.

On March 16, 2016, Laurie Petruska-Kovac, a middle-aged woman of fifty-four, scheduled an appointment to see Lori Hopkins at Pine Meadow

Manor. She'd buried both parents, Hanna and Joseph Petruska, the year before. Two months earlier, in mid-January, she devoted a long weekend to sorting through piles of "stuff," including childhood memorabilia, papers, and clothes. She'd discovered her Hungarian *prababicka's* guardian angel holy card in a desk drawer from high school years. Forty years ago, she promised to mail the card to Lori.

Lori and Peggy waited in the third-floor lounge lined with sun-bleached orange chairs and two coffee tables with mug ring stains and scattered magazines. Open shades heralded the late morning, giving ivory-colored walls a blinding glow. Lori told Peggy about her second trip to Prague in 1977. "I heard someone whisper my name," Lori said. "I thought God was talking to me."

Peggy covered her mouth, her practiced reaction to break a bad habit of snide remarks and hurtful barbs. When really challenged, she'd pretend to zip her lips shut with a thumb and finger. This occasion called for a taped mouth.

Laurie Petruska-Kovac burst into the room like a teacher on the first day of school. Her short blonde hair tapered off at the neck. Her pudgy cheeks reminded Peggy of a chipmunk storing walnuts in its mouth. A speculative Lori beckoned her to have a seat. Laurie Petruska-Kovac glanced at a threadbare cushion, hesitated, and finally settled in, hands in the deep pockets of her black cardigan jacket.

"My great-grandmother, Anna, asked me to give this to you, Lori. I'm sorry it's taken me forty years. Actually, I forgot until cleaning out my parent's house here in Texas. I found it in a desk drawer."

Lori adjusted the pillow behind her lower lumbar. She grimaced from the ache that settled in her lower back when sitting too long. "How in the world did you find me?"

"Soon after I discovered the card, I googled your name. Anyway, I read about your bomb shelter . . ."

"The whole story. I know."

Peggy's dangling foot swung impatiently from her crossed legs. "They're serving lunch soon, if you'd like to join us. The food's crap, but you're invited."

Laurie Petruska-Kovac got the hint. "No thanks. I'm leaving Texas tomorrow and have a few things to do." Her demeanor eased. "Lori, I'm sorry it took me a donkey's years to get this to you."

"A what?" Peggy pinched herself for getting cross. The two women ignored her.

"I should've mailed it when we exchanged addresses." She gave the card a longing look. A guardian angel watched over a boy and girl crossing a wooden bridge heedless of its broken slats. "It probably has no meaning for you, but, well, here it is." She read the words in Czech.

"Translation, please?" Peggy's patience wore thin. She zipped up her mouth with thumb and index finger.

"My little angel, my little guardian, look after my little soul."

"That's it? You came all this way to read eleven words? Why didn't you just mail the card?" Peggy's sudden outburst surprised the two women.

Miriam skipped into the room escorted by Mike. She added a happy note to the somber trio.

"Mr. Mike gave me gold coins." Miriam showed off the foil-covered chocolates. She noticed the card. "A guardian angel!"

"There's another reason I'm here." Laurie Petruska-Kovac searched her black leather handbag. Peggy likened her to a former spy fessing up to a life of espionage and intrigue in her black ensemble.

"When you visited us so many years ago, you forgot your notebook and a pamphlet. My grandmother didn't throw it away. She said it had great meaning."

"But how could she know? She was blind if I remember."

Laurie Petruska-Kovac, with a sheepish grin, held on to the notebook. "Yes, but she could see in a spiritual way. It's hard to explain. A sixth sense. She saw many things that we don't. Her blindness was late in life, and it was like a gift."

Little Miriam drew closer. "May I see it?"

"It belongs to Miss Hopkins." Peggy kicked out her foot in Miriam's direction.

"Let her have it." Lori waved her hand, giving permission.

Miriam opened the pamphlet. "It says, 'Come back to me.'"

"You're very young to be reading . . ."

"I have lots of brothers and sisters. They taught me." Miriam turned a notebook page. "Peggy, it's you!" She studied the penciled portrait of a teen with almond-shaped eyes, high cheekbones, and shoulder-length hair that framed her face.

"Let me see," said Lori.

"When my great-grandmother gave me the guardian angel card, I tucked it inside this pamphlet," Laurie said. "I thought I'd lost it."

Peggy chimed in. "Well, let me see."

Lori hesitated to confide her story as deep emotions surfaced. The time in Prague may have saved her a lifetime in prison. Who would understand? Was it all coincidence? Meeting an actor who testified on her behalf years later. And the girl who handed her the pamphlet and disappeared as quickly as she appeared out of nowhere. But, most importantly, the words on the pamphlet, *Come back to me.* And the time with Grandma Lottie that led up to the Prague destination.

Peggy was startled by the resemblance. "When . . ."

"I was in Prague with my grandmother at the church. A girl handed me a pamphlet. I drew her picture from memory."

"My teacher said that the past, present, and future are all the same." Miriam waited for a reaction. "I asked mom, and she said it's true."

"Okay, so now I'm a space traveler too?" Peggy noticed Mike standing near the entranceway. "You're still here?"

"Not for long. Lunch in a few. I'll let you folks come down to earth." He backed out of the doorway.

"Maybe it was Miss Lori's guardian angel," Miriam said.

"But I wasn't born yet, punky girl." Peggy sighed. Her vow to kindness vaporized like steam from a tea kettle.

"Space traveler?" Laurie Petruska-Kovac asked.

"Private joke," Peggy answered.

Laurie Petruska-Kovac shut her purse. "I better get going. Lori, I know my great-grandmother prayed for you. She was special. After she went blind, she said she saw her guardian angel."

"What did it look like?" Miriam asked.

"Not sure, but a feather . . ."

"I have a feather!" Miriam jumped up.

Old wounds attached to memories surfaced from deep inside Lori. Her European escapade with Grandma Lottie filled her mind with static images like slides clicking through a film projector. "It was nice hearing from you, Laurie, and I appreciate your visit."

"Have you seen the feather? Do you have it?" Miriam insisted.

A bell chimed for lunch.

"Enough with the Spanish Inquisition, squeaker!"

"I'm not sure. I do remember my *prababicka* mentioning it."

"I hope you find it!" Miriam joined her palms in a wishful prayer.

"I'll walk you out." Peggy regained her composure. "Miriam, would you escort our Lori to the dining room?"

Miriam took Lori's hand. "Can I show Mr. Mike your drawing?"

Peggy shot back. "No!"

"Well, the boss has spoken," Lori muttered.

"She's not the boss, and it's not her picture!" Miriam's willfulness was a match for her older sibling.

Peggy gave Miriam a stern look and escorted Laurie Petruska-Kovac into the hallway, passing the nurses' station, and addressed Mike. "Keep an eye on the munchkin. She's making up stories again."

"You're disturbed by the drawing. I don't blame you. It's uncanny," Laurie said to Peggy.

"You don't know the half of it, sister."

They passed by several residents filing into the dining room. Peggy recognized a few—Hatty O'Donnell, who wore a hat at every meal, and Mark Raniere, who sported bow ties. She nodded a greeting.

Peggy and Laurie Petruska-Kovac shook hands in the lobby. "Thanks again. You're right. It's spooky. But in certain ways, it makes sense."

"Peggy, I have the feather. Do you want it?"

"No thanks. You keep it."

"Okay. Fair enough." Laurie Petruska-Kovac, her mission completed, made quick strides to the exit. "Your sister's right, you know. The past, present, and future?" She lifted her hands like scales on a balance. "All here right now!" The exit doors flew open. "Like the sixty-year-old drawing. It's you." She vanished down the walkway.

Peggy stood in the lobby's center, hands dug deep in her pockets.

The remainder of 2016 became an election year battleground. "Ugliest campaign I've ever seen," Lori said.

Peggy showed little interest as they watched a debate on a flat screen mounted in the lounge. She observed Sandra Dee nibbling on a radish and opened the cage to let her explore the room.

"Peggy, thanks for taking care of Sandra Dee. I've had her since I was fifteen."

"Wow, she's sixty years old?

"And could live another forty years."

"So what happens when you kick the bucket?"

"That's where you come in."

"Sorry, I'm not a pet owner. What about that friend of yours or all your peeps in Boston?"

"Sandra Dee likes Texas, and you."

"Yeah, right, and how would you know? Anyway, I don't plan on staying in Texas."

"Fine, she likes to travel."

"So you're saddling me with a turtle?"

"Not just any turtle. Sandra Dee."

Peggy stretched out her gangly limbs. "Let's go, Sandra Dee." She placed the turtle in the cage. "I have to work at the Five and Dime tomorrow. I'll see you next week. Don't get too wrapped up in the political crap."

Tally met Father Joe O'Malley on Friday, May 27, before Memorial Day weekend. She planned to remain in Texas for the holidays. Her monthly visits were a means to connect with old school friends, and time with Lori made it worth the long-distance drive.

On Friday, June 3, her mobile phone lit up while she dug up dirt for tomato plants, already weeks late for getting into the ground. A call from Father Joe. She readied herself for bad news about Lori.

"Hi, Tally. When are you planning to come for a visit?"

Tally appreciated Father Joe's straight-shooter approach. He got right to the point in every conversation.

"Well, I was there last weekend." She listened to the surprising if not shocking news. "It's best she find out firsthand."

In the early morning hours of June 12, 2016, the world awoke to news of a mass shooting at a nightclub in Orlando, Florida, killing forty-nine people and wounding fifty-three others. Lori ate her breakfast of oatmeal, raisin toast, and a soft-boiled egg, and listened to the news of the devastating massacre. Peggy, with Miriam in tow, stopped in the dining room as Lori finished her meal. "My sister, Matilda, is crazier than all ten of us. She swears she's got the Zika virus after spending a few days in Peru last year."

Lori patted her mouth with a beige linen napkin. "And good morning to you."

"Good? Nothing but bad news." Peggy paged through a magazine, the *Atlantic*, next to Lori. "You read this Yankee rag?" The cover, emblazoned with a photo of Donald Trump, read *The Mind of Donald Trump*.

"My Aunt Bernie mails it to me."

Peggy flipped through the magazine. "You have living aunts and uncles?"

"Surprisingly, yes. Where's your sister?"

"Tilda? Asleep in the car she rented. She doesn't plan on staying long. The Boomerang. She leaves home but always returns."

Miriam visited Hatty O'Donnell, who treated her to a full stack of uneaten pancakes.

The nightclub incident added a pall to the beauty and bliss of a late spring morning.

Mike bounced in the dining area with a song in his voice, "Then sings my soul, my Savior God to thee / How great thou art . . ."

"That is my favorite hymn, Mike. It was a Swedish poem. My husband—"

"Wait! You're married?" Peggy shook her head in disbelief.

"Was."

"You have visitors, Miss Hopkins. Father Joe and another priest."

"Yeah, it's probably Father Norton, who thinks you were bilocating, which still doesn't make sense." Peggy put her hands on her hips. "I mean, how can you bilocate at ages like fourteen and seventy-four?"

Miriam, maple syrup smeared on her cheeks, yelled out. "The past, present, and future are all here! Right now!"

"Pipe down, pipsqueak. You'll wake the dead, or the near dead." Peggy scowled in full teen angst. "I prefer not to hear further of the past or present."

Father Joe greeted Lori, Peggy, and Miriam with a bounce in his step. "I brought a visitor."

"At least we got a heads-up this time." Lori readjusted her lumbar pillow. "The priest who thinks I bilocate?"

Father Joe stroked his chin. "Hmm, no, but he says you'll remember . . ."

The priest crossed the dining area. "A note I passed to you."

"Gerry? Father Gerry?" Lori squinted as if spotting a desert oasis. "I thought you were dead!"

Peggy murmured to Father Joe. "Beats any of my tactless remarks."

"So did I." He greeted and shook hands with Peggy and Miriam. "Hi, I'm Father Gerry Wilkins." He clasped Lori's hands. "Lori. How are you?"

"Old and cranky. You're a sight for sore eyes. Your sister told me you were dying in South Africa."

"Lesotho. I signed up for experimental drugs, the first antiretroviral treatments. So far they're working."

"And your sister knew?" Lori pushed away her plate and shifted focus.

"Yes, but not at first. It was pretty rough. I wasn't sure they'd work."

"Well, that was over fifteen years ago."

Miriam chimed in. "You should be happy Father Gerry's alive."

"Okay, munchkin. Why don't we let them visit? Welcome home, Father Gerry. I'm Peggy Mitchell. This is Miriam."

"Yes, I've heard about you, Peggy, from Father Joe."

"Great. I'm sure it's all good. Okay, then." She shook hands again with Father Gerry and ushered Miriam out of the dining room with Father Joe. Out of earshot, Peggy turned to him. "Did you tell him about, you know, my Lori?"

"No, ma'am. That's your story." Father Joe whistled a happy tune and greeted a resident with an encouraging hug. They were fast becoming friends, Peggy and Father Joe. She enjoyed spending time with the humble man dedicated to serving the Lord.

Lori and Father Gerry talked of their days in Texas, mutual friends, his sister, Barbara, but little of the war and their time as prisoners, he in Vietnam and she in Texas. "So Barry was there for you? I'm not surprised."

"Why not?"

"God has a plan."

Lori sucked in her breath. "That was part of God's plan, that I go to prison? And then meet Barry there? Here we go again, Gerry. It's all choices and consequences."

"You're right. But His grace is there, and He knows our destiny without interrupting our free will."

"But that doesn't explain how Barry and I met again while I was in prison."

"It was part of your journey, and his. Why does it need an explanation?"

Lori adjusted a lumbar pillow. "Gerry? I'm so glad to see you. I have lots of family in Boston, but I'm losing touch with them. My friends are few."

"Tally?"

"Tally saved my life in Moore."

She told him about how she'd become traumatized when looking out at the dark storm, the descending funnel, and heard the rushing sound of wind like a speeding train.

"Lori, I'm returning to Lesotho in six months. But I'll be here in Texas until then."

"Not to pry, but aren't you retired?"

Father Gerry replied, "Not with work to do. Every day is a gift with this disease."

"Gerry, thanks for stopping by. I do have one question." She opened her nightstand drawer and took out a locket tucked in a jewelry box.

"Why did you give this back?" She held up the locket, the present before she went to college in 1959.

"Peace offering. You were so angry when you threw it at me."

"Yes, and I'm sorry."

They clasped hands, old friends on divergent paths. Lori was grateful for the Holy Spirit's gift of understanding, one that she struggled with and prayed for daily. God's plan for Gerry, Father Gerry, sealed early on with grace along the way, and she had been privileged to be a crossroad on his journey. As if reading her thoughts, he parted with similar sentiments.

"All is grace, Lori." He made a slight bow and promised to visit again.

Social media news spread of the preserved bomb shelter. Most of underground sanctuaries—built in the 1950s through 1970s—were damp, empty, and unadorned. If anything, a few dusty canned goods lined shelves long forgotten. Lori's hideaway was a treasure trove of Christmas ornaments from sixty years ago. But no mention was made of Peggy's ghostly companion—Lori at fourteen.

Father Gerry and Peggy broached the topic of Lori returning to the shelter. His time was getting short and plans to return to Lesotho were underway.

"Why on God's green earth would I ever return to that place?" Lori said.

"It might be healing." Father Gerry wasn't sure either, but Peggy was insistent. Maybe it was for her own healing for reasons inexplicable.

After three discussions, Lori agreed to visit the shelter following her seventy-fifth birthday on September 15, 2016.

Peggy unwrapped an ice cream sandwich from the Pine Meadow's vending machine. "Used to be you couldn't say the word *tornado* without her getting all weird."

"I don't think the shock ever goes away totally," Father Gerry said. "I remember her first day back at school. My heart broke. She's been through a lot."

"Yeah, and I'm hearing parts of it. I'll never understand her appearing as a . . ."

"A yealing."

"What? Is that a word?" Peggy threw the wrapper in a nearby wastebasket.

"Yealing. It means someone the same age as you. Angels appeared throughout Holy Scripture."

"Yeah, yeah, I know. Father Joe hammered that one in my head. I'm okay with mysteries, Father Gerry. I don't need answers to everything."

"Wise of you, Peggy. Because many things remain a mystery."

Father Gerry drove the two of them to the spot on a Friday morning in September, the day after Lori's seventy-fifth birthday. Peggy opened the bulkhead door leading to the Christmas room forged by a fourteen-year-old Lori. A frightened field mouse jumped out and scurried away.

Peggy registered her surprise. "Well, that's a first. I don't remember seeing any little critters. Bet he was glad to see us!"

Halfway down the stairs, she heard Lori's breathy voice behind her. "I want to remember it like it was with Joy, the last person I saw there."

Peggy nodded, shrugged, and descended on her own. She swung her flashlight wildly from corner to corner. The bomb shelter was stark and empty, only cinderblock walls and cement floor, the glaring reminder of its true purpose.

"What happened? How?" Peggy paced frantically.

Lori descended and let out a deep sigh. "It's okay."

Peggy tearfully succumbed to her misery. "It's not okay." She flared up. "You're my ghost!" No proof remained of a fourteen-year-old Lori that materialized from an invisible curtain of time. And no proof of a shelter preserved from 1955—all she had to hold on to. She retraced her steps. "Larry! I bet he did it!"

"You're going to wear out the cement floor."

Peggy stopped in mid-rant. "Seriously? This is no joke, Lori!"

"Can't do anything now."

Father Gerry drove away with the angst-ridden Peggy furiously texting Larry. *ISWYDT.*

Lori peeked at the message. "Why don't you call him?"

Peggy brooded. "What? And give him the satisfaction of not picking up?" She stared at the phone. No reply.

At Pine Meadow, Miriam and Fran greeted them in the foyer. Miriam sprung off a blue velvet wingback chair. "Where were you, Peggy? We've been waiting for you."

A few feet away, Peggy yelled out. "It's all gone. Everything!"

Fran shook his head as the six-year-old flopped again on the cushioned seat. "Miriam, didn't you tell Peggy?"

"Tell me what?" Peggy reversed a ferocious glance from Miriam to Fran.

"We cleaned out the shelter last night. Miriam said she told you."

"Miriam's a liar!"

Miriam's feet swayed. "I meant to tell you, Peggy. Honest."

"You're lying, you little hoodlum!"

"Leave her alone, Peggy." Lori's commanding voice cut through the growing conflict. "It wasn't meant to be. I didn't want to relive the past."

"But she's lying!"

"I'm sorry, Peggy." Miriam, visibly upset, whimpered. "I saw kids checking it out. I was afraid they'd steal Lori's stuff. I'm sorry."

Peggy's heart melted instantly, and she lowered her shrill pitch. "You lied to Fran, munchkin."

"But I wrote you a note. In your room. I did tell you in the note."

Father Gerry interjected. "Miriam, where is everything?"

Miriam sulked. "Fran and Larry stored the stuff in a locked shed."

"Aha, so Larry was a part of it!" Peggy checked her phone.

"Calm down, Peggy. It's over. No harm done," Lori said.

Peggy seethed. She wasn't ready to let go of what she'd witnessed in the preserved underground shelter. The television tuned to a live show on December 25, 1955, of Sonja Henie, the Olympic figure skater from Norway. The chalkboard with *Merry Christmas, 1955* written by a fourteen-year-old Lori. The record player spinning Eartha Kitt's "Santa Baby." The tree, green, after sixty years. "The tree?" She heard the plea in her voice.

Fran rubbed his neck. "Uh, the only casualty."

"Casualty?" Peggy laughed hysterically. "I'm the only casualty!" Her reaction, like a firecracker, sparked and died away.

Her phone lit up. *What's up?*

She texted Larry. *Just saying hi.*

Early on July 16, 2019, Mike dropped off Lori's mail and a breakfast tray with a bowl of oatmeal and a carton of grapefruit juice. "Thanks, Mike. I'm a bit under the weather." Atop circulars and a photography magazine, Lori spotted an envelope with a United States Government seal. "What's this? Probably cutting my Social Security."

Mike poured half a glass of water into a cactus plant. "We need to sweeten you up, Miss Hopkins."

Lori smirked and ripped the seal. She read intently and teared up.

Mike set down the glass. "That bad?"

Lori trembled and met Mike's compassionate eyes. "That good. Eleven Korean War POWs were identified." She rubbed away tears from heavy lids. "My grandfather's coming home."

John Mitchell's remains landed at Boston Logan International Airport one week later. Peggy Mitchell, her mother, Mary, Bernadette, and Uncle Farley's son, Brian Hopkins, accompanied Lori to greet the plane. Soldiers saluted as John Mitchell's bones, dog tags, and teeth were transported by hearse to the Cathedral of the Holy Cross, New England's largest Roman Catholic Church. Every generation of the Hopkinses and Mitchells attended the memorial mass. Following the liturgy, John Mitchell, American surgeon and medic, would be interred next to Charlotte Mitchell.

Lori Hopkins's words, as a fifteen-year-old, echoed within. "Boston. Where a young nurse named Charlotte met a handsome, tall doctor named John, and the rest is . . ." And then Grandma Lottie's loving response: "Our family history!" And there, in a private vision, Charlotte Mitchell, a ruby-red strawberry to her lips on a summer morning.

Chapter 40

Museum Pieces

Fran stopped by now and then to check on Peggy, his lifelong friend and confidante. He was heading to Texas A&M in two weeks to study oceanography. "So how's the secret project coming?"

"It's done. All's in place."

"Does she know?" Fran raked through a black swath of hair on his forehead.

"No, she doesn't know."

"Do you think that's wise?"

"Yes."

"But it's like another shock."

"A good one though, right? Like the dose of the right medicine for an ailing body."

"You're the boss."

"Figured you'd see it my way." Peggy smirked.

"Is there any other?"

"The highway?"

He chuckled. "You're so endearing."

Peggy worked doubly hard to gather surprise guests for Lori's seventy-eighth birthday. She opted for September 21, the Saturday after Lori's birthday, to keep the big surprise a secret. On the actual day, she and Miriam stopped by the nursing facility to wish Lori a happy birthday.

Mike stopped in with her mail, mainly birthday cards from the Boston cousins, nieces, and nephews.

"No surprises, right?" Lori ripped open envelopes and read sentiments. "These are like get well cards. Lots of prayers."

Peggy showed mock concern. "Would I surprise you?"

At the evening dinner of lasagna, green beans, and salad, residents sang "Happy Birthday." Mike wheeled in a buttercream frosted chocolate cake bearing seventy-eight candles. Miriam insisted on helping blow out the mass of flames. "I'll take one side; you take the other!"

Lori and Peggy moved to a corner as happy diners ate dessert and homemade strawberry ice cream, hand churned by Mike. Lori reminisced over life behind a camera, documenting nature in its beauty and disasters in their disregard for creation. "It wasn't what I captured that haunts me. It's what I saw through the lens and didn't record. Those images are still with me."

"Memories?" Peggy inquired with searching eyes.

Over the years, Lori retained the unforgettable, positioning her camera like a weapon in a private war of seeing. "More than memories. They're part of me. It depends on how deep they go."

On Saturday evening, September 21, Father Gerry, Peggy, and Miriam stood up as Lori entered Pine Meadow's lounge. She wore a knee-length black chiffon dress with see-through sleeves gathered at her wrists. Her hair was center-parted and pulled into a chignon.

"You look like a model." Miriam clapped with childlike enthusiasm.

"Thanks, Miriam, dear." Lori heard Lottie's voice in her own. "So who's this new artist?"

Peggy cleared her throat. "Ah, not actually new. Just a new showing of her work."

Father Gerry winked at Peggy and jangled his keys.

The art museum, in the heart of Lubbock, appeared quiet and empty. "Are you sure you've got the right night?" Lori focused on the darkened building.

"Regular hours are over. A gallery's opened for the artist," Peggy said.

"Who's the artist again?" Lori asked.

Miriam, the first out of the car, flashed a smile. "You'll see."

Lori's antenna went up. Father Gerry helped her out of the Honda Civic he'd borrowed from his cousin Samuel. "Okay, so this isn't a new artist?" She dug in her heels with an all-knowing stance.

Peggy whispered into Lori's ear before they entered the museum's doors. "More like an old photographer. So don't have a cow."

Prized photos spanning Lori's career were mounted in the main gallery, a wall of fame spanning the decades. Sandra Dee in Cape Cod. Francine in a London phone booth. Barry in Vietnam. Lori marveled at the treasured collection of images—friends greeting her after a long absence.

With painstaking efforts, Peggy contacted the subjects memorialized throughout Lori's prolific photography. On inspiration, she unveiled her secret. "And before you fall and break a hip, I invited Louis Brittingham Williams."

Lori inhaled. Her pulse quickened with the name Brittingham. "My son?"

"Figured I should warn you in case you keel over." Peggy opened a door to a separate gallery wing. The vestibule led to a set of double doors.

Lori hesitated. "Okay, fine, but you should know by now how I feel about surprises."

Beams of light streamed from the adjoining gallery. Peggy preset the stage for emotional surges. She'd arrayed an old wingback chair, confiscated from the bomb shelter, with streamers. Lori's party guests held candles and walked in procession. First came Sandra Dee in her cage ornamented with balloons and crepe paper, compliments of Miriam, who barely contained her glee as she presented the turtle. With the first sighting of Sandra Dee, Lori held out her arms. Miriam placed the sixty-three-year-old turtle's cage into the awaiting lap. "My first love." Her eyes glowed with her expression of gratitude. Next came Tally, a respectful distance behind Miriam and Sandra Dee, her quick gait slowed down.

Tally embraced her dear friend and whispered, "You're still lovely, like the day we tried on dresses in Filene's Basement." Lori's eyes watered with memories stretching back to virtuous days.

Next in the procession was Bernadette, a spry ninety-one-year-old, now a replica of her mother, Penny. "Don't say it, Lori. I know. I'm Mom minus the cuckoo bird, right?"

Lori laughed. "Well, if you insist, Bernie!"

"Portia broke her hip, so she couldn't make it."

The cafeteria klatch, Abigail and Jane, filed in next with trays of hot dogs, Texas chili, and grilled sandwiches. "All your cafeteria faves, Lori. Even the rubbery cheese."

Lori inspected the tray. "Sure 'nuff!" A group hug included Tally.

As the team stood by, Paulette Briggs, formerly Mason, walked up with a crown on a midnight blue velvet pillow, the crown she wore as queen for the homecoming dance in 1956. "Lori, you're the queen today. I got word of the party and, well . . ."

"Thanks, Paulette. I'm glad you could make it."

Paulette placed the crown on Lori's head and bowed before moving aside.

Connie, from college days, waltzed into the gallery wearing the black silk bowling jacket she'd offered Lori for a date with Giuseppe. She carried a six-pack of diet soda. At first, Lori didn't recognize the slimmer version of her roommate, minus at least fifty pounds. Connie slung her jacket over one shoulder and modeled the red tulip dress Grandma Lottie bought in Filene's Basement. "Connie? Is that my . . . ?"

"Sure 'nuff! I tracked it down!" Connie's catwalk drew applause from the high school cafeteria friends. "I let out a bit, or a lot, but it fits pretty well!" She plunked the soft drinks at Lori's feet and leaned over. "You were always my idol. Style and strength."

Lori cocked her head. "Don't tell me you still drink that carbonated poison."

"I'm pickled in it! Happy birthday, roomie!"

"That's right; we built a fort out of pink cans! You look marvelous, dear Connie." Yet again, Grandma Lottie's voice echoed inside Lori. On occasion, she saw the world through Lottie's eyes, or so it seemed.

The curator, Joan Corbett, leafed through the guest list and counted champagne glasses. She approached Peggy. "Most of the guests are here."

"Who's missing?"

"Me." Ruth pulled a black poncho over her head and brushed her short silvery hair in place.

"Miss Lieberman!" Joan, the curator, shook hands with Ruth. "We're honored to show you next month. Congratulations on your National Geographic award."

"I owe it all to Lori." Ruth rushed to greet Lori. They held hands like old friends, the memory of Joy between them.

Peggy rang a triangle dinner bell, a borrowed piece of antiquity from the museum's collection. "Before we do our toast, we want to introduce another guest." She turned to Joan. "Is he here?" Joan nodded.

A tall man, six feet three, with thick, wavy medium brown hair and large, dark eyes entered in a gray silk suit, blue tie with white polka dots, and white oxford shirt. He carefully wheeled in a frail woman. Lori's lips trembled. "Francine."

Peggy raised her shoulders in a gesture of surprise in Lori's direction.

Louis put a reassuring hand on Francine's shoulder. "Mom insisted on coming. She wanted you to see what a good job she's done." His kind demeanor and physique reminded Lori of her grandfather, John Mitchell. A hush overwhelmed the gallery space. All eyes were on Francine, Louis, and Lori. Even the framed portraits seemed to pay deference.

Lori, shaking with emotion, regained composure as she stood to welcome mother and son. A watery-eyed Francine adjusted the red velvet throw in her lap. "Meet Louis."

Lori extended her hand. "Louis, I've thought of you so many times."

Louis took Lori's hand and kissed it. "Me too."

"Lori." Francine drew their attention. "This blanket is from my cape. It's my gift to you. Thank you for giving me a family." Lori held the blanket to her cheek.

Peggy grabbed a champagne flute from the tray. Joan busily handed champagne to all of her guests. "Okay, everyone, before we get washed away with tears of joy, I propose a toast." She lifted her glass. "To Lori Hopkins, my hero. I won't go into all the details 'cause you wouldn't believe it anyway, but she saved my life."

Joan discreetly pulled Peggy aside. "There's a woman who'd like to join you. She heard about the party from a friend of a friend and has a message for Miss Hopkins." Joan twiddled her thumbs, anxious in her role as messenger.

Peggy sighed. "Well, why not? Bring her in. The more the merrier."

Miriam added two candles—one 7 and one 8—to a birthday cake shaped like a camera and lens in a corner of the gallery wing. Matilda instructed the caterers regarding the food setup.

Lori noticed Joan Corbett and the unidentified woman hold back as guests sang "Happy Birthday." She narrowed her gaze. The face was familiar. Yes! A school picture of a five-year-old girl with a semi-toothless smile and sprinkle of freckles across her nose. "You're Bonnie!"

"How did you know?" Bonnie nodded and put on a decent disguise of looking comfortable in an awkward situation. The assembly was more than curious.

Matilda murmured to Peggy. "Another kid? Didn't you do your home-work?" Her sardonic remark elicited a swift shin kick from the accused.

"I never forget a face, darlin'. Isn't that what Barry would say?" Lori's eyes shone brighter than the two candles she blew out. "I want y'all to meet Barry's sister, Bonnie. Barry, the soldier who saved me from my-self." She gestured to the adjoining wing. "There's half a wall in there dedicated to him."

Lori took a deep breath and paused at the hospital room threshold. "Sure beats a jail cell."

"Sure feels like one. What took you so long?"

"Well, it's not like you went out of your way to find me."

Barry pushed up on his elbows. A smile reached his eyes, and the years in between melted away. "I sure as shootin' did go out of my way. I got a hand-delivered birthday card to you."

"Relax. I'm just kidding."

Barry held out a hand, steady even in his feeble condition. "You still clean up real nice, Bluebonnet."

They held hands and felt each other's warmth and vital pulse. "Why do you call me Bluebonnet, anyway?"

"You're my Texas flower. C'mon and sit a spell. How was your party?"

"Filled with surprises."

"Good ones?"

"All good, Barry. I've had quite a life."

"Had? The best is yet to come."

Lori chuckled and lugged over a chair. "You're a dreamer, Barry."

"Every day's a miracle, darlin' and that's the best. You are a sight for sore eyes, Lori."

"Well, it was worth hearing you say my name, for once."

They didn't need words. They held hands again. With labored breathing, lungs nearly spent, Barry had days left. They both knew it. Lori, the one with secrets, sensed her own time was near. Dreams of Grandma Lottie, the beloved Charlotte Mitchell, had filled her nights in the last week. So real she heard Lottie call out her name.

"Read to me, Lori." Barry, eyes closed, waited.

She pulled out the Good Book from a large, worn canvas tote bag. She wanted to comfort him as he had when she passed a small eternity in prison.

With conviction, Lori proclaimed from the Song of Songs: "*See! The winter is past; the rains are over and gone; Flowers appear on the earth; the season of singing has come; the cooing of doves is heard in our land; the fig tree forms its early fruit; the blossoming vines spread their fragrance.*"

The beauty of the words pressed against Lori's heart, mind, and soul, leaving her breathless. Barry opened his pain-filled, tired eyes, the windows to the soul, and recited the next verse: "Arise, come, my darling; my beautiful one, come with me."

Epilogue

In 2015, Peggy had shot the first photo with the Canon AE-1, given to her by Lori, on a dreary Saturday afternoon. Peggy had set aside her homework, a series of algebra equations, for a bowl of mint chocolate chip ice cream. She'd propped an instruction pamphlet against the bowl on her desk.

"What are you reading?" Miriam, the precocious five-year-old had jumped on her sister's bed.

"This camera's worthless. They stopped making it in 1984."

"Take my picture, Peggy!" Miriam had perched on a faded sunflower print bedspread. She hugged her spindly legs and rested her chin on raised knees. "I'm ready!"

"Okay, munchkin, just one."

Peggy had recalled Lori's words. "Film is finite. Only so many images per roll. Be judicious in what you shoot. Practice and discipline. You don't get the immediate results. It's not a guessing game, but close enough. And there's the miracle of the darkroom."

In 2019, Peggy read in a blog that, "Film shooting is like a natural stimulant to creative growth in photography." The camera, a Canon AE-1 given to her a few years back, sat on a shelf in her room. She most recently had snapped photos at Lori's seventy-eighth birthday party, the one with surprises galore.

With the dawn of the digital age, Fran's father, Bruce Dalton, a former hobby photographer, retained his darkroom. For Peggy, the darkroom was new territory, although she had learned how to develop film, a skill foreign to many photographers finessing images on a computer.

Two weeks before Christmas, Fran and Peggy awaited images to emerge. Awash in red light, they gently bathed the exposed paper in a solution-filled tray. "Lori told me to leave the paper alone, don't poke, it leaves marks." Once the process was finished, they dried the prints. "Wow, these are really bad. Oh, here's the worst of all."

"Be patient, Peggy. They're not that bad."

Fran tended to the film processing while Peggy and Miriam sorted through the remains of Lori's Christmas collection in Larry's shed.

Miriam handled a glass ornament painted sky blue with white clouds bearing the words *Merry Christmas Miriam*. "My name! Can I keep it?"

"Sure why not?" Peggy boxed up the last ornaments.

Miriam pocketed the ornament.

"Let's go, munchkin. I'm feeling a chill." Peggy shook dust and dirt from an angora wool blanket and swaddled herself.

When they got home, Fran was waiting for Peggy. "Your mom said I could stay. She's out shopping with your brother." He handed her a packet.

Peggy shuffled through photos like a deck of cards. "Seems like yesterday." One caught her attention. "What happened here? There's a cloud behind Miriam."

"That's no cloud."

Peggy examined the photo under a floor lamp. "White feathers?"

Miriam entered the living room juggling a peanut butter and jelly sandwich and glass of chocolate milk. "You have my picture? Lemme see!"

"Looks like we had a visitor for this one."

Miriam placed her dish on an end table. "One of the angels."

"Angels?" Peggy traded glances with Fran.

"They're preparing the way." Miriam gulped half a glass of chocolate milk.

"For what, munchkin?" Peggy examined the photo and its fringe of pearly white feathers, like the edge of a wing.

"Don't know yet." Miriam settled into a rocker and bit into her sandwich. "But I'm sure it's soon."

Reading Group Questions and Discussion Topics

1. In hindsight, Lori's mishaps may have prevented her further demise. What is one of those instances? What example in your own life would you consider a blessing in disguise?

2. A priest tells Barbara to lay an unforgiven hurt at the feet of Jesus Christ. How would you reconcile something or someone you haven't forgiven?

3. Lori mentions the Holy Spirit's gifts, especially Understanding. How would you describe the spiritual gift of Understanding?

4. It's been said that people come into our lives for a reason, even if briefly. Do you recall a person(s) who made a significant impact in your life? Why?

5. Society changes dramatically in the span of Lori's lifetime. What changes in the first half of the 21st century do you believe will leave the greatest impact?

About the Author

Anthea graduated from the University of Delaware in Film Studies and Theatre and honed acting at the American Academy of Dramatic Arts in New York City and screenwriting at Act One: Writing for Hollywood. Her first novel, UNEARTHING CHRISTMAS, began with a dream. Anthea is an identical twin—a club she was born into!

www.ingramcontent.com/pod-product-compliance
Lightning Source LLC
Chambersburg PA
CBHW030101310726
48970CB00004B/1102